A MENAGERIE OF Eclectic SOULS

Raven F. Grillo

 FriesenPress

Suite 300 - 990 Fort St
Victoria, BC, V8V 3K2
Canada

www.friesenpress.com

ISBN
978-1-5255-7254-8 (Hardcover)
978-1-5255-7255-5 (Paperback)
978-1-5255-7256-2 (eBook)

1. FICTION, ROMANCE, PARANORMAL, VAMPIRES

Distributed to the trade by The Ingram Book Company

BE EMPOWERED BY YOUR BEAUTIFUL SOUL,
LET IT SHINE ITS BRILLIANCE INTO THE UNIVERSE.

By Francesca Grillo

To my amazing sons, Luc-Michael and Matteo:

Be not afraid to lift your feet off the ground
and allow your spirit to soar as high as it can
as it reaches for your dreams unbound.

Love your biggest believer, Mom.

PART 1

Love

CHAPTER 1

Appearances

Adriano slowly bends down and puts his hand on Rebecca's shoulder, whispering into her ear. "My beautiful Rebecca, ma *Belle âme*." Rebecca tilts her head upwards, towards the gentle voice speaking in his natural French. Her long hair falls in front of her face. "You're my beautiful soul, Rebecca."

Rebecca faces him, and Adriano is struck with shock. Rebecca appears much older. His eyes move down her body, examining the drastic physical changes: her petite, feminine, youthful hands now look very different. *These are the hands of an older woman*, he thinks. Her luscious long dark brown hair is now thinned out and dry. Then he looks back to Rebecca's eyes. He is troubled to see the faded and dim hue of her irises. They had been beautiful hazel eyes, a mixture of khaki green and gold. Now the colors are fighting to return, blocked by discoloration and made slightly opaque. Adriano can't process any of this. He is struggling not to stare, but how can he not? Adriano is aware that his reaction is making Rebecca uncomfortable, so he presents one of his charming smiles to reassure her,

"It's okay Rebecca, I'm here now, and it's going to be okay." Adriano's spirit sinks. Rebecca shows no recognition of her name or him, and this concerns him deeply. He takes a few minutes to compose himself. *She is still my beautiful Rebecca. Thank you, God, for bringing her back to me.* Even though she has been gone two months without a trace, for Adriano, it felt like an eternity. Night after night he walked the streets of Paris near the accident, coming back to the apartment mentally exhausted and thirsty because he spent more time searching than finding his own nourishment.

The last few weeks were especially difficult, with the phone calls from Rebecca's distraught parents trying to understand why he was not in the taxi with her that day, the request for updates by her brothers Joseph and Marcus, but most of all, the sadness in the voices of Rebecca's young sons Adam and Ethan. They were begging for him to find their mommy.

Adriano felt so helpless and guilty for not accompanying Rebecca in the taxi on December twentieth. Rebecca insisted that she would take the taxi alone; she was determined to fight through the anxiety of going places on her own. And what better place than in Paris, where she barely spoke the language? But she knew she could trust Adriano; she told him that he gave her the courage and belief in herself to do this. She knew Adriano was on the other side waiting for her. Adriano had reservations booked at the restaurant just outside of Paris, and he was supposed to arrive earlier. He had purchased a bouquet of black and red roses, Rebecca's favorite. He wanted to show her how proud he was of her courage. He knew how difficult and scary it was for her. It was just an hour's ride, and they were talking on their cell phones on the way. Then, about forty-dive minutes into the ride, Adriano heard Rebecca scream, and the phone went dead.

Adriano looks at Rebecca. He feels so elated. Earlier this evening, something inside of him pulled him towards the Eiffel Tower. It was Rebecca's favorite place to stop and admire. Even though he had come here many days and nights after she disappeared, hoping to find her, something inside told him to come back here tonight. His instincts were right, and he saw a woman in the distance near the tower before she disappeared into the woods. He followed to discover what he never thought in his mind.

Adriano's thoughts return back to the present and he smiles reassuringly at Rebecca; her glazed eyes just stare through him. Adriano notices her confusion. With each moment passing, Adriano begins to feel more disheartened, and the painful disturbing truth begins to sear deep into his mind. He forces himself to suppress the anger and disappointment building inside. He has no choice but to accept the awful truth; he isn't the one who has given Rebecca this new life as a vampire!

He is troubled by the growing puzzling questions stirring inside. *When did she become a vampire? Was it the night she disappeared? Why does she look older now as a vampire than when she was human? She just drank, her body should be rejuvenating!* Adriano struggles not to stare, but Rebecca appears different, even as a vampire. He doesn't want to make Rebecca feel uncomfortable, but finding her in this state is deeply upsetting. Rebecca still doesn't speak, or even move from her kneeling position in the snow. Adriano is relieved that she is not moving away from him in fear, but he can't help the cloud of anxiety passing through him. *What happened to her?*

Adriano reaches down to pick up the dead rabbit lying beside Rebecca, doing his best not to react emotionally. Rebecca just watches this stranger as he carries the animal away, into the bushes. Rebecca's spirit feels gratitude towards the animal for its sacrifice for her needs.

Adriano turns back to Rebecca, but suddenly stops a few feet away, staying hidden from her sight. An overwhelming feeling of dread passes through him. His mind is fighting through reality. He leans his tense and stressed body against a tree and just watches Rebecca from a distance. His thoughts are scrambling and his mind is lost in confusion. He is torn between the elation that he found her and devastation that she is now a vampire.

Rebecca stands up quickly and looks around. Adriano realizes that she has not mastered her movements. She starts walking quickly out of the woods, and Adriano rushes to her. He can't lose her again, but he is also concerned that a human might notice her peculiar quick movements. It would definitely raise alarms and unneeded attention. Adriano gently reaches for her hand, still puzzled by how much older it looks. She just drank, she should physically be back to normal. Her hair is still dull, too, but he can see her eyes are regaining their beautiful hue.

They walk slowly out of the woods, and seconds later something extraordinary occurs. Adriano can feel the transformation of Rebecca's hands occurring, in real time. He carefully bends his head down to see and he is excited, witnessing her skin rejuvenate. This is too spectacular for him to not witness. He tenderly removes a strand of hair from Rebecca's face. It seems softer, and is regaining strength and shine. Her eyes are still in between transforming back to her beautiful hazel hue. Rebecca stops and pulls her head away slightly, and Adriano feels hurt by her reaction. He gives a friendly smile and speaks softly.

"Please, don't be afraid, I just want to see your beautiful eyes."

Rebecca continues to show little recognition of him, but something in his voice brings her back in slowly. She stops pulling away. Adriano feels reassured, but the feeling doesn't last long. His mind continues to poke sharp little pins of reality in his relief. He has to tell her family and her little boys that she is alive, and he has no clue how to deal with the difficult circumstances that now present to all of them. He needs to get Rebecca back to their apartment without drawing any attention. He looks around, and from a great distance he notices a man sitting on a bench at the entrance to the park. He needs to make sure that Rebecca moves at a normal pace. Adriano takes her hand again, thinking, *how do I make her feel at ease in my company?* A thought comes to mind, of when he first introduced himself to her.

He extends his hand slowly and smiles. "Hi, I don't think we introduced ourselves—my name is Adriano—may I please escort you out of the park? It can get quite cold when the wind blows through."

Rebecca looks at this stranger, caution in her eyes, but she isn't feeling threatened. She finds herself falling gently into his kind ocean-blue eyes, and she extends her hand. "Hi Adriano, my name is Hazel Eyes."

Adriano looks at her with confusion. "Your name is—Hazel Eyes?"

Rebecca tilts her head slightly, not sure what to make of his reaction. "Yes—Hazel Eyes."

"Hi...Hazel eyes? ...Nice to meet you." Adriano smiles charmingly. Casually, he reaches into the pocket of his jeans, pulls out one a tissue, and shows it to Rebecca. With a nervous tone in his voice, he asks, "May I—?" And he gently wipes the blood drops off of her lips.

Suddenly his eyes are locked on to hers, and he's bewitched. He can't stop gazing deeper, as if they are luring him into a warm and private space. He thinks, *they are changing! How extraordinary!* His eyes remain cemented to hers as he watches their incredible transformation in disbelief and awe. He is amazed to see the new specks of deep amber and cinnamon appearing in her irises. Adriano is entranced by this stunning occurrence, which causes an unexpected rush of heat through his body. Rebecca has the most beautiful eyes as a vampire—his vampire!

He cannot help but smile warmly, and he takes her arm gently. She shows no resistance, and they walk carefully out of the woods. Rebecca stops to stare at the Eiffel Tower. Adriano waits patiently, looking around, and cannot help but pick up some of what the man at the bench is saying on his cell phone. He turns his head slightly as if he is looking towards the tower, but he uses his vampire ears to listen in,

"I'm fine, stop worrying, I just needed to get out of the hotel room. It's not like you can't reach me, Nathan—I know, but you worry too much—I know, I'm sorry, I should have left a note—No, really— I'm not being sarcastic! I'm agreeing with you. I realize this—Yes, I do appreciate all that you do— But—okay, but—yes, I understand your position, but nothing will happen—"

Rebecca starts walking again, and Adriano carefully takes her by the arm to keep her pace normal. They walk leisurely towards the man sitting on the bench, who is still on the phone. Suddenly, the musty odor from minutes ago seems stronger to Adriano. He looks around but doesn't see anything to cause it. He redirects his attention to the gentleman sitting on the bench, growing more curious for some reason. The man is dressed in a long black winter coat, a grey- and burgundy-striped scarf wrapped tightly a few times around his neck. He is wearing a black fedora, but thin strands of his hair showing at the sides of his head reveal chestnut brown hair with hints of grey streaks running through. He has a grey streaked goatee with reminiscence of dark brown coming through. His free gloved hand is occupied twirling a black cane around and around by the pewter emblem on top, which looks like it is the shape of some kind of animal.

Suddenly, they are both aware of each other. The gentleman smiles as Adriano and Rebecca pass in front of him. Their eyes meet. Adriano slows Rebecca down, and the man continues talking on the phone.

"Okay, okay, you're right, I should have been more careful—Anyway, were you able to find those specific chains?—Uh huh—Oh, and they had the rope too?—Excellent, then—what's wrong?—Uh huh, okay—I know it's stressful, but we have no choice, I won't risk carrying these things in our luggage— I know, don't worry, all of this is only as a precaution—I'm fine! Strong as an ox! —Funny—Yes, I'm heading back now, see you soon. Okay, sounds good, cheers." The man closes his phone and puts it in his pocket. Adriano and Rebecca are just passing him as he stands up, needing a little push up from his cane. He straightens his winter coat, brushes off some of the falling snowflakes. Carrying himself with an air of traditional class, he smiles and greets Adriano and Rebecca,

"*Bonsoir Monsieur et Mademoiselle.*" He tips his hat in a friendly respectful greeting, an accent colouring his French.

"*Bonsoir, ca va?*" Adriano smiles,

"*Oui. C'est tres fraud ce soir, non?*"

"Yes, it is cold."

"Oh, you speak English? Good, because my French only takes me so far." The gentleman smirks. Adriano can detect an English accent. The gentleman walks towards Adriano and Rebecca with a slight lean on his cane on his left side. He extends his hand to Adriano and they shake. "My name is Lucan Forrester." He smiles, his wintery grey eyes looking directly into Adriano's, then they move to Rebecca's.

Adriano pauses; he senses something very peculiar and unsettling about this older gentleman. Alarm and concern rise inside Adriano, his predator instincts pricking up. But he can't figure out what it is that is making him feel uneasy.

"Adriano Rossi, and this is—" he pauses again. There is something off about Lucan's demeanor, but it is not threatening. In fact, Lucan carries an air of gentlemanly elegance. Adriano is confused by his own reaction and thinks perhaps he is just emotionally overextended from finding Rebecca. Nonetheless, he wants to move Rebecca and himself away from this man. Adriano is surprised when he sees Rebecca extend her hand to this gentleman without any hesitation,

"Hi, I'm Hazel Eyes, nice to meet you."

"Hazel Eyes? What an…*interesting* name? Your eyes are beautiful, mademoiselle, the name suits you well." His voice is deep and soft, and he bends slightly as he gently reaches out and lifts Rebecca's hand to his mouth to kiss it. Lucan's eyes meet Adriano's again. Adriano is now on alert.

"Thank you, how kind, what a gentleman you are." Rebecca smiles, but a hint of shyness escapes.

They all walk out of the Champ-de-Mars. Adriano is still dealing with the unpleasant odor in the air; it's like it's following him, itching his nose. He looks at Rebecca and Lucan, but neither seem to notice. They arrive at the beginning of the street, which is filled with rapidly cars passing. Rebecca suddenly stops walking, her eyes are scanning the area, and she looks nervous and lost. Adriano and Lucan both notice. Lucan is intrigued but stays quiet, just observing these two individuals. Adriano is growing more irritated; he can feel this older man studying them both with his inquisitive eyes. If Adriano were alone with him, he would be more direct with his concerns, but now he just wants to get Rebecca back to their apartment. Adriano needs to close off this encounter,

"Well it was nice to meet you sir."

"Lucan, please, I like to be called Lucan."

"Yes, well, we have to go now, Lucan."

Lucan's phone rings, and he politely excuses himself to answer the call. Adriano uses this opportunity and quickly takes Rebecca's arm, moving out onto the busy street. He looks back. Lucan is still on the phone, but his eyes follow them both.

Once Adriano and Rebecca are further down the street, Adriano slows his pace and Rebecca looks back, confused as to why she has been rushed away suddenly. Adriano looks at her, smiles, and reaches gently for her hand, and again she allows him to take it. Adriano is relieved by this, but that relief turns to concern when he feels how cold it is considering, she just drank. Nonetheless, he swiftly guides her carefully, at a slow human-like pace, through the crowd of pedestrians.

A few minutes go by, until Adriano is distracted by a strange tingling from Rebecca's hand. He looks down and witnesses an extraordinary event. Rebecca's hands are changing, becoming younger again. Adriano can feel the warmth rising from her skin as the cells slowly rejuvenate. Her hands feel softer to the touch, and look healthier. Even her age spots are fading away completely.

Adriano and Rebecca continue walking hand in hand. He has a firm but gentle hold on Rebecca's arm to keep her from moving at vampire pace through the busy crowd. No words are spoken by either of them. Adriano has so much he wants to say and to ask, but he knows this is not the right time. But he feels a ray of hope, and is grateful that they are at least holding hands as they walk in awkward silence back to their apartment in St. Honoré.

Adriano uses the quiet space between them to internally process all that has happened since the car accident back in December and her disappearance. His mind struggles to remove the image of the rabbit's blood dripping from Rebecca's mouth, a rabbit she killed! He is so profoundly affected by her turning, his mind desperately trying to grasp this reality and the difficult consequences that await her. His thoughts provoke him with the many different unkind and disturbing labels given to their kind over the centuries. Rebecca is now part of this kind; she is undead, a blood sucking demon, a predator. *Rebecca is a vampire!*

The crisp evening air is becoming colder on this dark February evening. Adriano and Rebecca have already passed through crowds of people on the main street. The many restaurants are already buzzing with patrons. There is a rich aroma of coffee and espresso brewing, and ovens are on, busy baking or cooking various French cuisines and delicacies. The line of street artists and vendors that braved the winter weather are packing up after a long day.

Adriano is very mindful that Rebecca continues to be unable to control her movements. He has been observing her since they left the woods. *Has she been walking the streets and through crowds with this vampire pace all this time? Has anyone noticed?* Then he crosses these thoughts out of his mind. *If they noticed there would have been major panic. Calm down, all is fine!* But then logic knocks at his mind's door. *She must have been seen, but these humans must be too occupied in their own thoughts, distracted by their cell phones. Unless she only walks the streets at night, that makes sense, less noticeable.*

Adriano's mind is starting to play havoc with his energy, but he has to keep them walking at a pace that won't attract any attention. He knows through his own experiences as a vampire that no matter how hard he tries to not stand out, the charismatic energy, attractive aura, and physical appearance that he possesses is irresistible. It's impossible to veil amongst humans. And this is precisely what is taking place. Adriano hears whispers and notices human eyes directed their way. He is mindful now that Rebecca's vampire nervous system may not be fully developed. *It has been two months, at least I think it has? Do I really know when she became a vampire? But maybe each individual is different, all vampires can't be the same?*

Adriano is aware that Rebecca might be overly stimulated by all the sights, sounds, and smells, possibly causing extreme sharp pain in her head. Trying to focus on details, bright colours, sounds, and movements could make her dizzy. Adriano is trying to walk quicker but still keeping within a human's pace. He just wants to get her back to their apartment. He needs to talk to Jonathan, he isn't sure how to handle the police.

Suddenly, there is a distinct fragrant aroma in the air that flares Adriano's nostrils. He stops a few feet away from one of the street artists. *A female vampire? After all these years, other vampires!* He feels at ease to come across his kind; this woman appears to be friendly, she is smiling warmly at the pedestrians passing by her table. Then his thoughts darken. *What if there are more like the one who turned me, Signore Domenico?* A glimpse of those cold, ruthless black eyes come into his mind; he remembers the dangerous vampire who killed his mother Elizabetha and then turned him.

Then his mind propels his thoughts forward, to the night he himself changed over a woman when he was just a few months old as a vampire. He never knew the woman's name. She disappeared while he was asleep sometime later that evening, after she went through the painful change to become a vampire. Adriano felt hurt and confused; he never got a chance to teach her anything. There are many moments like this that creep into Adriano's mind, and he struggles with dark disturbing memories from his life. The human family life on the farm he grew up in Sicily as a young boy was filled with cruelty. His two young siblings and their mother worked long hot days on the farm experiencing emotional, mental, and even physical abuse from their alcoholic father Massimo. Adriano doesn't want to ignore these memories; they are his history, they are what helped mold him, as a human and as a vampire. But he has to protect himself, too, or he risks becoming angry or bitter. He keeps parts of his past troubles to himself. Not even his human friends, Jonathan and Sandra, know all the details about Adriano's long and disturbing past.

Adriano continues observing the female vampire. Adriano doesn't want to let go of Rebecca, who is still holding his arm, but he also doesn't want to lose sight of the vampire. Her bright blonde hair is tied up in a loose ponytail. He is struck by her resemblance to his little sister, *Maria*. His heart suddenly feels sadness. Although Maria was barely a teenager when she died, this woman has a remarkable likeness to Maria. It could be her kind and sweet demeanor, or maybe her endearing smile. Adriano is not sure which it is, but he can almost picture what his little sister would have looked like if she had reached her twenties. He continues to admire this young vampire, but he can only guess her age; after all, a vampire is ageless in many ways. She is wearing a short red winter coat and black scarf that bears traces of snowflakes that fell a few minutes ago. Adriano's instinct is compelling him to approach the girl, but then suddenly his nostrils flare again and a new scent emerges, stronger but not unpleasant, like the one earlier near the Eiffel Tower. He sees a male vampire walking towards the female one. Their conversation takes place in low whispers that only vampires can hear. He tries to listen in, aware that Rebecca is becoming nervous just standing in the noisy area.

"Hi Jules, I didn't realize I am this late? Sorry—Monsieur Coultier and I were just finalizing your pieces for the exhibit next Wednesday."

"Oh, you're not late. I'm just packing up early, not too many sales today. Too cold for *them*, I guess." Her head gestures to the human pedestrians in the street. "So—we're all set for the exhibit?"

"Yes, he really likes your Mystery Man collection. I left it with him so he can work out the display area. He's interested to exhibit both the collection and some of the sketches you provided him. Isn't this great! Who knows where this can lead for you!"

Jules chuckles. "Don't get too excited—after all, I'm an amateur compared to some of his other artists. I'm grateful he's even allowing my pieces in this exhibit."

Adriano can sense from Rebecca's fidgeting that the city noises and human crowds are becoming too much stimulation for her, and he gently moves Rebecca away from the busy street. Adriano isn't too concerned; he has gained important information about these two vampires, and hopes he can visit this exhibit next Wednesday. But he knows this means somehow they have to prolong their stay in Paris. *Can I really do that to Rebecca? Extend our time in Paris?* Both Adriano and Rebecca walk on.

Meanwhile, the two vampires begin packing up the two small display tables. Veneur notices that Juliette is distracted, looking to one side further down the street.

"What is it?"

"I'm not sure, but I thought I sensed the presence of *our kind* nearby a few minutes ago. ...I guess I'm still just a bit sensitive to distinguishing our kind from the others. I'm trying to adapt and get used to what I am now, but when I feel the presence of our kind it startles me a little. Silly huh?"

Veneur lowers his voice to a deep whisper only a vampire can hear. "No, I understand. I know what you mean, it was like that for me when I was first *turned*. It's like you're looking in a mirror casually and then you have to take a second glance because you can't believe you're seeing what you're seeing. It's disturbing in some ways, and yet is a reflection of you too. It takes time." Veneur continues delicately placing Juliette's homemade jewelry pieces into a small pink velvet-bottomed box. "The last few years I've noticed more and more of our kind settling in Paris. Even Gabriel said he's getting calls from many of the wealthy ones planning to move to Paris, asking him to find high end homes and property resales. It's important for these vampires to outshine each other, appearances matter. There is such a competitive nature, between these older generations especially. I've observed it with Enzo's interactions with his associates. Evil competing with evil." Veneur places the unopened boxes of jewelry into the large suitcase. "Anyways, my real worry is that the increases in human disappearances will bring more investigators and police to our city. It will become harder to do what *I do* for Enzo without being detected. It may mean me travelling further out of Paris, which creates more complexity transporting *food* back to him. Look at all the new cameras being installed. Based on what I hear on the local news reports, police suspect there are a few human trafficking rings rising through Europe. I've heard Enzo and his associates talking. They're worried too, about the rising of vamps."

Juliette opens another empty small square velvet box. "Oh, that is not good, but Paris has a large population of nationals and tourists, do you really think vamps would risk been detected?"

Veneur, mindful of his surroundings and the pedestrians nearby, keeps to a whisper. "We can't assume otherwise. These are not like the roamers and stragglers; those are annoying tricksters and pickpockets, harmless to our kind. The ones we need to be more concerned about are the vamps, as they like to call themselves. They are like terrorists to vampires. They're recruiting vulnerable, lonely vampires and brainwashing them to believe in their corrupt cause. For some, it is about revenge for the severe cruelty they experienced from their traditional Masters. For others, they are jealous of our kind who have managed to find a way to exist and work among humans without detection all these years, and enjoy the benefits of social and technological advancements. They can't handle that many of us have also continued to educate ourselves and become financially success-ful without corruption and violence to humans." Suddenly a worrisome thought crosses Veneur's mind, and he stops packing. "I hope it wasn't vamps that you sensed?" Veneur nervously scans around the streets, both sides feeling on edge.

Juliette feels his anxious tension invade her tranquil state. "No—no, I wouldn't be as calm. What I sensed was very different. I got a warm and friendly energy from his presence; actually, I think there were two of them."

"Warm and friendly? It can't be vampires then," he chuckles. "Be careful—it's not easy to spot vamps. Remember, if they think you have something they want, they will do what suits them to get it. It's very unpleasant, or even fatal for their unsuspecting victims."

"I know, you told me over and over."

"Well, it's important you understand this. They don't always stay hidden in dark alleys just waiting for an opportunity. They're getting clever in their attack strategy; they will either swarm you or follow you home. Either way, if they have you in their sights there is very little you can do on your own. It will be a matter of time, I suspect, that they might even form alliances with some human terrorist groups, make deals with them so both sides are protected. They are hypocrites and use their belief systems to suit their own selfish needs."

"That's scary to think—I don't feel safe sometimes even with the human attacks by humans on their own kind. I can't believe any of this is real."

"I know it's crazy, even after all these years I still sometimes wonder if I'm in some kind of nightmare, or maybe a coma—I almost would prefer that. I would never have believed any of this years ago; that our kind actually exists, and has for centuries."

"It's not at all like the monster stories."

"What do you mean?" chuckles Veneur.

Juliette seals a jewelry box and places it in the trolley. "It sounds silly, but there was this girl at the orphanage, and she had these old monster comic books. Many of the older girls would huddle in the corner in our room and she would read to them. Of course, I wasn't allowed to be around, they hated me so much, but I found a way to stay close enough but hidden so I could listen." Juliette leans in closer to Veneur, whispering in a vampire voice so only he can possibly hear. "It's ironic, it's like life or the universe was preparing me during those horrible years for the road that would lie ahead. But life as *our kind* is very different from the stories in books. Thank God for that. I can't imagine not being able to walk in the sun or see a sunset. I enjoy visiting churches if I have a few minutes before we have to leave." She sighs heavily. "If only I could wear a cross or crucifix, I have seen one in the shop window, but of course the Master would rip it off me."

Veneur's spirit droops and his body wilts. "I'm sorry, Jules, you should be able to dress and be who you are, not what you are assigned to be."

"Hey, at least we don't look grotesque, in fact I think we look beautiful. Our hair is not wild, we don't sleep in coffins! Juliette chuckles.

Veneur sees her eyes light up, and it makes him feel good to see her laugh. "Oh Jules, you're crazy," he laughs. "I'm trying to picture you liking monster stories. That I wouldn't have ever guessed."

"Like? That's a strong word. I wouldn't have chosen them if I were given a book to read. But that was what was available to me, and over time I adapted and tolerated the gruesome stories and characters. I think it was meant to be."

"What was?"

"Think about it, there were no other books around except this monster comic book belonging to another orphan."

"You don't really believe that?"

"You don't think fate is playing a part in our lives?"

"Nope. I want to believe that I do have some agency in my life."

"I wish that were true for me."

Suddenly there is an awkward silence between them. They continue delicately packing up the remaining jewelry, and place the boxes into the larger suitcases and into the trolley. Veneur feels the weight of his role in Juliette's circumstance. He needs her to find hope for her future; he doesn't want her to fall into despair.

"So are you excited for the exhibit? Did you ever imagine showcasing your art in a gallery? This may be a real chance for you!"

"Well—my mystery muse is the reason for the collection I built up. If only I knew why I see his image in my mind. Did he come to the orphanage one day and I saw him? Did I see him in a crowd and he just stayed in my mind? He feels like a ghost—he continues to haunt me, but it doesn't frighten me. Even in my dreams, I see him, but I can't get close enough to talk to him." Juliette suddenly stops packing and gasps. "Ven—what if my muse disappears from my mind? Then what? What else can I draw or paint that will be just as good or interesting! Maybe this is a mistake! Maybe I'm fooling myself thinking—!"

"What? No—calm down, you're getting yourself worked up for no reason. It's just your nerves. It will all be fine. It doesn't matter if your muse is real or in your mind. You're a creative soul—an artist." Veneur picks up Juliette's sketchbook and opens it, carefully turning each page. "Look at these, see how you capture the city so realistically, the details of the different buildings, their unique architecture." He turns the page again and admires the next one that follows. "And look at this one! You bring your mystery muse to life, capture the spirit of this figure. His eyes express so much emotion. You capture when he is happy, or when he is thinking deeply, and when he is sad. I think when people see this collection of paintings, they're going to want to buy one just so they feel close to him. They will imagine who he is and create their own narrative! You are giving them this story to tell."

"I guess so."

Veneur looks more closely at Juliette, and picks up more boxes of unsold jewelry and places them in the larger suitcase. "Okay, I've gotten to know you quite well this year, I can tell that something else is bothering you, so spill it, sis."

Juliette places her sketchbook and charcoal pencils in the knapsack on the chair behind her. "It's nothing."

"Don't say that. If something is bothering you tell me." Veneur stops packing up, waiting,

Juliette turns to face him, and her voice dips very low. "It's just that, even if for some miracle pieces of mine are sold—then what? I won't be allowed to take this further." She continues packing. "Master won't allow it. I can't travel anywhere. So how can I truly be excited about a dream career I can never pursue?" Her sadness is rising and a heavy sigh escapes her; then she realizes Veneur is just standing lost in his own thoughts, and she feels bad for burdening him. "Don't get me wrong, Ven, I'm grateful you got me this exhibit, and you're a dear for believing in me. Trust me, it's amazing to have someone look out for you. That has never happened to me until you came along." She distracts her emotions by looking busy and concentrating on the table items trying to decide what to pack next.

Veneur doesn't respond right away; he returns to his tasks wondering if he should share how he is feeling. "I do believe in you. I understand what you're saying. I'm working on it, trust me. These circumstances we're living in are taking their toll on me, too. I might not show it but there are nights when the years of guilt eats at me. Frankly you're the only one I can actually share this much with. This is why we need to get out of that toxic environment."

Juliette's eyes widen in concern. "Shhh...someone might hear you." She nervously turns her head and looks around, then she turns back to Veneur, who is busy closing boxes. She whispers so only he could hear. "If you mean running away—forget it! Look what almost happened to Pietro. I can't—"

"Pietro! Don't get me started with that fool! Oh God—what a night that was!" hollers Veneur, catching the attention of some humans nearby.

"Shh…keep your voice down."

"I know, I know. Sorry," he sighs in frustration.

"Anyways, we better hurry up, we don't want any reason for Father to get angry with me."

Veneur slams shut the suitcase and startles Juliette, who jumps. "Juliette! He is not our father! I told you to stop saying that in my presence! We're alone, you can be you!" Veneur places the last piece of jewelry into the box with little delicacy.

"Veneur—please, be careful!"

"Sorry! It just gets to me!"

"And you think it's easy for me! At least you can be you all the time!" Juliette throws the knapsack over her shoulders and finishes packing up one of the suitcases. Veneur grabs it from her and places it in the small trolley cart. Juliette then folds both white oblong tablecloths and places them in a bag and into the trolley. The air between them feels uncomfortably crisp. The small tables are folded in and Veneur carries them by their handles.

They start walking, keeping a human pace, neither saying a word. They pass cafés and office buildings. Humans cannot help but stop and stare. It's these two vampires' eyes that are the attraction. Juliette's are light grey, with a delicate fine hint of violet encircling them as if a tiny detailed brush was slightly dipped into magenta and blue paint. Veneur's eyes are a distinct green, with hints of cool blue and honey yellow that make his eyes into sparkling emeralds.

Finally, the silence is broken by Veneur. "Jules, before, about those vampires you sensed."

"What about them?"

"Did you say—two of them?"

"Yes."

Veneur is aware and uncomfortable with the distance airing between them. "Sorry Jules, I just feel a bit stressed lately, out of sorts. My worry is Enzo is having us spied on, especially with this new vampire who has joined us, I don't trust her." Veneur suddenly feels uneasy; he looks around again nervously, but he only notices some humans walking around on the street. A sigh of relief escapes him.

"Why would he? He knows we wouldn't dare cross him."

"For now at least! Just buying time Jules, just buying time."

Juliette stops walking, followed by Veneur. "I hope you aren't planning anything dangerous?"

"I'm just thinking, working things out."

"Am I supposed to understand this?"

"No—Jules don't worry, let's keep moving."

Juliette is feeling exasperated; she can sense Veneur is up to something but she can't deal with anything else tonight. They both resume walking.

"I hope I will see them again!"

Veneur looks at Juliette. "Who?"

"The vampires, from earlier. If only I had a better look at their faces, I only saw a glimpse of them from behind. There was something familiar about the man. Too bad. We don't know too many others, other than when those business associates come by the house—and those I stay away from. But these ones, I would have loved to talk to them, you know, maybe find a way to connect with them. And they would trust me, allows me to see into their past, share special memories with them."

"Juliette!" whispers Veneur harshly. "I told you, you have to be careful. You can't just tell people about your gift! It's bad enough you use this for Louisa."

"Veneur! She doesn't know!"

"For now! If any of them find out your ability, Enzo could force you to use it for wicked reasons. Your ability could be used as a weapon to find out other's weaknesses too, imagine what Enzo could do with that information. I can't allow him to stain your soul as he has mine!"

"For God's sake, what has gotten into you tonight? Do you see anyone listening to us? I am just sharing with you. You don't think I know the risk? I only use my gift to help me play this role the best I can. It's frustrating for me to hear her go on and on about this Paula, but I let her talk and tell me all she can, just to appease her. My gift helps me be the best Paula! Louisa just thinks her daily teachings and lessons of her past memories of Paula are molding me to be like her. That's what she thinks. Give me some credit!

You need to calm down, your emotions are too strong right now, it's affecting me! I don't need this. I can't take yours on. Not tonight," cries Juliette, and without thinking she runs ahead in vampire speed. Immediately she realizes and slows down, then stops entirely, her head bent down, waiting for Veneur. He briskly reaches her at a human pace, his eyes and expression showing disapproval.

"Juliette! What are you doing?" he whispers.

"Sorry! I didn't mean to do that. That was careless of me—my nerves are frazzled. It doesn't help that you and I are getting upset at the littlest things!"

Veneur sighs. Pushing his own frustration and anxiety down, he puts his arms tenderly around Juliette with brotherly concern, and they continue walking heading towards the woods.

"It's okay Jules, you caught yourself in time, and no one was looking. We're okay. Relax, you're safe. Come on, let's get to the woods so we can relax a little. Nature always calms us. We have a bit of time."

They enter the woods and take a few minutes to enjoy the crisp winter air. Within minutes Veneur is feeling more relaxed and walking more leisurely. Juliette is still troubled the more she thinks about the evening ahead at the house. She stops walking and sits on a snowy rock, her body wilted.

"Veneur—I don't think I can do this evil dinner tonight. I feel like sometimes I'm going crazy. I still have nightmares from when Pietro came into the family. It's wrong, it's just cruel! …Why can't we welcome new members into our family with a nice animal hunt? That I can handle. This, this psychological and physical torture *he* puts them through, and makes us participate in, is just unspeakable! Especially for me, I can physically feel the fear and terror in them, the begging, pleading, and the screams! And there is nothing I can do. I have to pretend I'm fine. If I don't drink *it*, Master will be angry and disgusted in me. But drinking it, I am participating in the murder of a human! Why can't he just allow us to freely choose to feed from animal blood instead of human blood whenever we want? I'm trying extremely hard to stay on his good side. But this is destroying me! I never realized the horror of being a vampire!" Juliette begins to sob.

Veneur, feeling responsible, bends down and takes Juliette into his arms. "Shhh…it's okay, I know, Jules. It will take time to adjust. You're doing quite well considering you only joined us less than a year ago. You're adjusting much better than Pietro. You have a head on your shoulders." He delicately lifts her chin upward, her sad grey eyes looking at him. He leans against a tree. "You have to understand the complexity of this household. The rules were put into place a long time ago. Enzo needs to be in control of all of us! That's who he is. It's a power tactic he uses to keep us in line. He's a master manipulator, and he hates humans. He sees drinking animal blood as a weakness. After all, according to him, we are the hierarchy of the food chain, and he enjoys feeding from humans at every opportunity—humans who *I* find him! This is a heavy burden to me too, and Gabriel as well."

His voice rises. "All of us have blood on our hands, not just you! I'm ashamed to admit this, but after I taste human blood it's hard to resist the next time." He takes Juliette's face into his hands firmly but with care. "But I do resist, and so do you. We have some power, but we just have to hide it from him. This is important for you to believe. You are not bad, you are forced to do bad things! That is what separates you and me and even Gabriel from the others. They have no remorse, they see it as their vampiric right to feed from humans." Veneur releases Juliette's face. He stops talking, leans back against the tree. "It breaks my heart to see you suffer. I had hoped after a few months this would subside. Things could have been so different, if only my uncle Theo didn't invite this monster into our home. Now our home is taken over by these ingrates!" Veneur slams the ground with his vampire strength, making such a noise that birds and animals flee the area immediately. He sighs heavily.

Juliette moves to the ground beside him. "It's okay, and you're right, none of this is our fault." Juliette places her petite hands around her brother's face, looking into his sad emerald eyes. She sees such remorse and guilt invading them.

"How can you forgive me Jules, for what I did!? I don't understand how you can be near me, be as kind as you are to me! I led you falsely to this monster. I will never forgive myself for lying to you." Veneur bends his head down.

Juliette takes a deep breath. "It's in the past, Veneur—I'm sorry for saying all of that earlier. I'm grateful I'm a vampire, you saved me."

"Saved you? What do you mean? Tell me, please, help me understand how you are still able to be sincerely kind and caring towards me?"

"Because I love you, my dear brother." Juliette nudges her shoulder into his, and they both stand up. "As far back as I can remember, as a human, I knew I was *different*. I knew I had this ability to sense emotions in others, good and bad. That is why it was so hard for me in that place. I could sense the loathing and the hate from all the other girls. I wanted to die! You can't imagine what it feels like to live and breathe every moment in a space of pure negative energy and hate towards you, when the only thing you did wrong was to breathe the same air, to exist." Juliette pauses, then takes a seat on the rock once again. Veneur sits beside her, listening. "I never understood and still don't know what was so horrible about me that I was instantly hated?"

"There is nothing wrong with you. You are amazing and loving! But— why didn't you run away?"

"I thought of it, trust me, but where would I go? At least I knew my enemies in that place. The Director could have kicked me out once I turned eighteen, but I pleaded with her to let me stay. I begged them—and I got my wish. But it came at a price. I cooked, cleaned, did their laundry, I did all the tasks that were usually distributed between the older orphans. But I learned something very valuable about myself."

"What was that?"

"I learned to have pride and self-worth—they can't take that away from me! If I'm given a job, I put my heart and soul into it." Juliette bends her head toward the ground, feeling a bit overwhelmed and exposed, sharing so deeply with Veneur about her past. "I'm looking forward to spring. I have plans to have my own flower garden; the beautiful aroma of roses and lavender will fill my bedroom. You'll see. It will be okay. I just need time, like you said, to adjust to everything and everyone." She sees an odd expression on Veneur's face. "Why are you looking at me like that?"

"You always see the good where there is not much good to see. It frankly surprises me that after how cruelly you've been treated. You manage not to be jaded. Then you come into this disastrous clan and you still manage to find positives in spite of the hell we endure in that house of horrors."

"I have to believe a tiny glimpse of light can make its way even in the darkest of our lives. ...Look at me. Who would have thought I would have servants! Martha is so kind and caring. She secretly finds ways to surprise me with tiny mice that Guy captured, just so I can snack throughout the day."

Veneur stands up abruptly. "Be careful with those two! Listen—I love you for your heart, sis, but you need to open your eyes. I say that with care. You don't know this world we live in like I do."

"My eyes are open—I try to weigh both the good and the bad. Martha is kind to me. She really cares about me. It isn't an act she puts on, or out of fear that she treats me so well. I truly believe I *affect* her."

"Of course, you do. I'm not taking that away from you. But you have to look deeper. You're blinded by the desperate need for affection. I understand why, we can thank that orphanage for that. But see through the layers. Think about it, Guy and Martha, you don't know them like I do. They have been with us for a few years. They see the evil that takes place in that house and yet they manage to show up every day on time acting as if nothing horrific ever occurred. Doesn't that strike you as odd?"

"Well, yes I guess—"

"It's money. Guy's gambling has caused a lot of trouble for him. He was lucky Gabriel and I got involved. Once again, we're called upon to do the dirty work, and who benefits? Enzo! It was a bloody feast for him that night. I'm glad you weren't in the family yet. But Gabriel and I had to stay and participate, as usual, Enzo needs to spread his evil to others. ...And now he uses this as leverage against Guy and Martha." Veneur brushes the snow from his pants; he walks back and forth from one tree to another, feeling restless, then takes a seat back on the rock next to Juliette. She can feel that he's slipping further away into guilt and unhappiness. "All it takes sometimes, most of the time, is lack of money and fear. People will turn a blind eye if it keeps them alive. Never forget that, Jules." Veneur pushes the snow on the ground around with his boots.

Juliette sits quiet at first, just taking in the important message coming through, and at first, she tries to resist the negative perspective, but then it truly starts to sink in. Perhaps she should be a bit more cautious, but she is afraid she may become jaded.

"Yes, you're right. I hate to admit it. You raise an important point. How can they show up with a smile on their face, and just roll up their sleeves and wipe and mop up the floors and walls knowing what transpired—then help dispose of—" she pauses, she doesn't want to say it. "And yet they can be so kind and attentive to me? Oh, what was I thinking?" Juliette, disturbed, pushes hard against her temples. "Oh, we are monsters! All of us. I can't escape them. The gruesome images!"

"It's okay, Jules, calm down! We're not monsters. You are not evil. Never compare yourself to Enzo. We are safe, here in the woods. Look at the beautiful trees, the birds are chirping. ...It's getting late, we should get going."

Veneur puts his arm around Juliette. She lowers her head toward the snow-covered ground, her eyes filling with tears. She then wipes her eyes, and looks up at her brother. He can see there is something Juliette needs to ask. "What?"

"Why did you choose *me*?" Even as Juliette asks the question she has wanted to know since she first met him, she had already discovered the real truth. But she wants to hear the delicate lie that this vampire who has become her brother will tell her. She knows it will only be to protect her, a lie surrounded with tenderness and care.

Veneur stands up, followed by Juliette. They continue walking through the bushes and trees. Veneur bends his head toward the ground, collecting his thoughts. "I told you why? I saw you and well, I just knew you were the one. I never had a sister and I just thought—I liked you, you were sweet—okay? Can we move on?"

There it is, the lie wrapped up with tenderness and care, and it is more than Juliette can ask for. She knows Veneur is meant to be part of her life; he is her brother and her protector. Juliette realizes that Veneur can't tell her the truth; it is already disturbing enough that she learned bits and pieces of the reason through Louisa one day. How Veneur was ordered to search out the right human female to play a part in a real-life stage drama.

But for Veneur it is another heavy burden to add to his tormented soul. Louisa had given him a picture of her daughter Paula, who had died a few years ago. "Find her, Veneur! Find my Paula!"

Veneur went around town, hunting for a picture-perfect victim to play the role of a dead girl named Paula. An orphanage was a good place to start, and he got lucky. He found Juliette. She was a close resemblance to the picture of Paula he carried, except for her black hair. Veneur pulled her aside and, using his charm and endearing manner, convinced Juliette that she could have a better life if she went with him. There was an instant sibling connection between them that pulled them together.

Juliette thought she was finally free. Then she was greeted by Louisa, who was overtaken with joy that this human resembled her daughter Paula. She was already planning to make few alterations to the young woman: dye her hair blonde, dress her in flashy clothes, and teach her the mannerisms her daughter possessed. The night Veneur brought her home, Juliette was swiftly moved to another room hidden away near the back of the house, accompanied by Louisa, Gabriel, and Veneur. She was confronted by this older unfriendly man who immediately announced himself as the Master. Juliette looked at Veneur, confused and nervous. Veneur just lowered his head in shame. Juliette became frightened, taking a step back, but then she was harshly pushed forward by Louisa towards the Master. He grabbed her and she screamed, but it was futile. The vampire smiled and enjoyed showing his protruding sharp teeth. She heard Louisa plead to the vampire, "Please, Enzo, bring my Paula back to me!" Juliette fainted at the sight of the vulgar protruding teeth coming in closer. The vampire quickly turned her, and she was then taken to her new bedroom. Veneur stayed with her, waiting for her to regain consciousness, then he spent the next few hours with her as she changed to a vampire.

Juliette believes with all her heart that Veneur feels deep remorse for his role in this insane command given to him from the Master.

Juliette takes a deep breath, consoles her-self privately as she tries to push that horrible night far away. She has forgiven Veneur already, and she needs him to know. "I understand, Veneur, really I do! Sometimes we have to make difficult choices that affect many lives. I never knew what love or belonging really meant until you came along. We might not be surrounded by love and affection in that house, but really, are we worse off than other vampires out there or humans?"

"Jules, you're too kind."

"It's not too bad, really. I accept my place, my role in this *family* as daughter to Louisa. I accept I am to live and breathe this role to please her, to please *Master*." Her voice rises. "I accept that I will never be good enough and will be under his command *always!*" Her heart suddenly begins to beat faster. A surge of panic jolts her body and she finds it difficult to swallow, repeating over and over, *Breathe Jules, breathe, I accept my role, I accept my role.*

Veneur puts his hands to his head in total frustration and disbelief. "But that is wrong! Do you hear yourself? My God! We are not in the middle ages. You and I have a right to be free to choose what we want for ourselves. I promise you one day we will be free."

"I told you, I didn't run away back then—I can't run away now that I'm a vampire. I can't be looking over my shoulder. Not with *him* as my hunter. Look how quickly the Master found Pietro." Her voice is cracking from stress, and her hands begin to shake.

Veneur stands up, struggling to keep his temper at bay, whispering, his mouth barely moving, "Listen. Pietro was a fool thinking he could go off and make his own family. Enzo was looking for an excuse to get rid of him. After all, Louisa turned him, not Enzo. Thank God you were asleep that night. It was chaos. Gabriel, Louisa, and I followed after Enzo. He was in such a rage. If Louisa hadn't stepped in and calmed Enzo down, or should I say begged to spare Pietro's life, he would be dead."

Juliette reaches in and gives Veneur a tender hug, but he is so uptight and tense that he breaks out of it. "It's all about appearances. Enzo wants other vampires to think he has wealth—he keeps ordering us to buy all these expensive things for Louisa to keep her happy, and keeps asking us to upgrade his car—he doesn't even drive! Appearances, all about appearances. Gabriel is a smart real estate agent and has had some good luck, but even he worries the money will run out, and then what? It's bad enough we live with him in riches, imagine if we had to live with this insane vampire with no money. You have to accept we are not dealing with level minded beings. Don't forget that!"

"I know, I know Ven! But there's nothing we can do."

"Yes, there is! I can't do this anymore. I can't be that horrible *man* that he is forcing me to be, how many more lives ruined, or worse? How much longer must I endure his commands? It isn't normal for us to be this afraid! Gabriel and I do the dirty work, and that vampire gets to enjoy the benefits.

Imagine—Gabriel, this strong muscular vampire, is afraid to disobey or overstep. We are all dealing with a bully, not a great and respectful leader. Gabriel has confided in me, he has his own dreams of finding a mate."

"Oh, wouldn't that be nice." Juliette stares deep into the woods, dreaming of her own fantasy to be in love and have her own family one day. But the dream becomes scary, and Juliette feels trapped in a small cage, the space around her closing in. She feels lightheaded, her body suddenly weightless like she is falling.

"Oh Jules! I got you, you're okay! Breathe! …Jules?" Veneur gently lays Juliette down. "Jules? Can you hear me?" Veneur delicately taps Juliette's face repeatedly, trying to revive her. "Jules!"

"I'm okay, I'm okay— sorry, not sure what happened." She quickly stands up, brushes herself off, and as if nothing happened shapes her mouth into what was supposed to be a smile but fails. "We better hurry, we can't be late for—"

"Yeah, I know. It's got to change. We have to make this change!"

"You have to come to terms with this. Stop fighting what is. You are worrying me Ven! I try to be grateful to Louisa for allowing me two days to come into the city weekly. The jewelry I make and sell gives me something to look forward too, something to feel proud about. I finally have something that is special about me, and not Paula. And now I have a chance to show my paintings, too. Don't do anything to make Master angry, or he will take this luxury away from me! Please, Ven, these outings are so important to me. These outings keep me sane."

They continue walking through the woods which will bring them to the edge of their property. Veneur can't hold back his frustration much longer. "Do you hear yourself? *I am grateful that Louisa allows me to come into the city!* I just don't know how you can continue like this. It's insane!"

Juliette doesn't respond. She sighs, shakes her head side to side, and keeps walking.

"I see a rabbit up ahead; these woods are making me hungry! Do we have time to stop?" Veneur asks.

"And risk Master finding out? No—we'd better pick up speed."

"He hasn't found out yet! But—alright Jules."

Juliette is relieved that finally Veneur is calming down, then a curious thought enters her mind. "By the way, I meant to ask: where did you find her?"

"Who?"

"Bianca."

Veneur doesn't respond right away. "It doesn't matter. Let's pick up speed." They move quicker through the woods.

"It matters to me. After all, she has been with us a day now and she barely says a word to me."

"Jules—please, leave it alone!"

"I will not! Tell me, please, I have a right to know."

Veneur abruptly stops, followed by Juliette, his frustration rising. "I found her in some abandoned warehouse! I was out looking for another human as demanded by *him to* bring home and join us, but to my surprise I was confronted by a foul stench. I heard hissing and all I could see were many sets of glaring eyes. There was barely any light coming in and even with my vampire eyes it took a minute to adjust. I pulled out my cell for some light. It was a horrible sight. I could see all kinds, different ages, male and female gathered in small groups."

"Oh—you mean vamps?"

"No, these weren't vamps, these were too pathetic. I think maybe some of them had dealings with vamps and that is why they are there. Homeless. They were more frightened of me than I was of them. It was very sad and unnerving; we both know how quickly life can change. Suddenly this woman vampire approaches me and tells the others to stop hissing, and she kept them back in the corner. Right there I knew she had a power over them, and in my stupidity and pride, I thought, *she is the one. Enzo will like this one.* That is my gift, my talent, I can seek out those who would not be missed and make them feel safe and wanted. That is my role. Just like I found you." Juliette feels a sting from his words.

Veneur sighs, quickly returning to her side, and takes her hand in his. "Oh Jules! I'm sorry! I don't mean it! You would be missed—honest!"

"I know you don't. I sense your remorse—and I would miss you too!" Juliette squeezes his hand. "What's her role? I'm trying to make her feel welcomed but she just—"

"I don't want you to get attached to her. And don't trust her so easily, either! Frankly, I was surprised that Enzo has taken to her; after all she was someone else's reborn, not his. There is something so baffling about this. It has me and Gabriel worried. It's weird, as soon as he met her, he was drawn to her. He asked her how far she would go for him, and she said, "As far as needed." I didn't get a good vibe from her after that comment, but it was too late. Enzo was impressed by her loyalty."

"Veneur—we better hurry."

The two vampires begin running at vampire speed through the woods. Veneur is carrying the trolley and tables, and Juliette is carrying her knapsack, but the heaviest weight they are carrying between the two of them is anxiety, disappointment, and fear. The woods lead them to their backyard, which is located in a more secluded part of the 16th Arrondissement, in one of the rich neighborhoods of Paris. In the summer, the back of the house features a beautiful rock garden that Louisa is proud of, and a wooden gazebo surrounded with a variety of flowers and plants. The tennis court sits unused, but the servant Guy is instructed to maintain the outside to pristine appearance. Even the swing set and monkey bars that once belonged to Veneur, when he was a little boy living with his Uncle Theo, are still maintained. Enzo is very particular about appearances, even though the closest neighbor is a mile away. They pass the multi-car garages and walk through the snow to the front of the house, and unlock one of the large black wooden doors. The two vampires walk onto a large ceramic foyer with a round wooden table placed in the center on top of a large area-carpet. Displayed is a glass vase is fresh lavender, delivered an hour ago. A beautiful inviting scene veiling the darkness and dysfunction breeding deeper within its walls. Juliette removes her winter coat.

"Hello, anyone here—we're *home*!"

"Is that you, Paula?"

Both Juliette and Veneur can hear the clanging of gold bracelets and click, click, click of high heels as Louisa struts down the marble hall, wearing black leather Prada shoes.

CHAPTER 2

Her Vampire, Adriano

Adriano is still thinking about the two vampires he saw. They seemed so normal, kind—very different from Domenico.

Their walk back to the apartment took longer than usual, since Adriano redirected them through more wooded areas. He could see that Rebecca was uneasy with the city traffic, which sounded much louder to her new sensitive vampire ears.

After a long route, Adriano and Rebecca finally arrive back to the apartment at eight p.m. Adriano unlocks the gate, and they enter into a small private court. Rebecca allows this stranger to guide her; she feels reassured, and she doesn't feel any danger. Adriano cautiously measures her every move, studying her from head to toe. Adriano was worried earlier that Rebecca would not want to enter. Rebecca looks around, and from the expression on her face she seems comfortable and calm. Adriano unlocks the front door and welcomes Rebecca inside. She glances at Adriano and, trusting this man, she steps into the apartment. Adriano follows behind her and closes the door quietly. He gently guides her through the front entrance.

"Welcome, please come in, it's okay." He steps in carefully, hoping that the familiar surroundings will trigger something in Rebecca. As Rebecca slowly moves away from Adriano, she looks up and around, but her eyes show no recognition.

The emotional strain of finding Rebecca and then seeing two other vampires is beginning to set in for Adriano. Adriano is feeling fatigue, anxiety, and panic creeping in. The panic is becoming stronger and anger is building. He feels his heart racing, his body temperature rising, and his hands are shaking. *Does she have amnesia from a car accident? Was she consequently traumatized by the turning that she blocked out everything up to the accident? Is it possible that one of those vampires turned Rebecca? Or maybe she felt abandoned by me and that is why she is acting so distant!*

Adriano takes in a very deep breath, hoping to calm his troubled mind. *Is this a panic attack?* He is unsettled by this sudden feeling of fear and losing control. He takes a few deep breaths, and manages to slow down his breathing. His anger slowly subsides, his mind becoming clear and calm again. Adriano focuses on Rebecca. She is here, with him.

Rebecca walks into the living room and observes the room and her surroundings. There are three large windows to the right that look out to the private court. The blinds are halfway down. Rebecca steps onto the dark brown wooden floor; in the middle there is a large cream area rug, with abstract blocks of red and black running through it. Rebecca is careful not to touch anything but just walks around, noticing the art deco pieces, books, and candles displayed on shelves and on top of the wooden coffee table.

She notices a small silver picture frame on the side table near the black leather couch. She picks it up, confused to see her own image. She looked very happy in the photo, and she's pointing at the Eiffel Tower. Her black peacoat is dusted in snowflakes, captured and frozen in time in this photograph. She's wearing silver buckled platform leather boots, and looks youthful and vibrant, her hair shiny and long. Rebecca looks down at her own boots; they too have silver buckles, but still she doesn't speak a word. Adriano is just watching carefully. Rebecca then looks at the black coat that she is wearing, and a strange feeling passes through her. For a split second she has a small recollection of when this photo was taken. She smiles, but then it's like the memory is swept away. Rebecca is unaware that this photo of her, which Adriano took, was taken a few hours before the car accident.

The room is filled with uneasiness, and Adriano feels strained. He turns on the CD player, the sound of Bono's voice playing at a low volume. Rebecca stops to listen. Adriano notices she is moving her head side to side still, holding the picture frame.

"Oh! You like U2 too! Does anything look familiar to you, Rebec— Hazel Eyes?" Adriano struggles to use this name for his Rebecca. It just adds to his questions. *Who called her this?*

The question puzzles Rebecca. "Familiar to me?"

"Never mind, please sit down." Adriano gestures to her to sit on the couch. Rebecca puts the frame down. Adriano can see it is significant to her, but the reason is trapped inside her mind. Adriano asks for her coat, and she suddenly backs away from him and wraps her arms tightly around herself, as if the coat is part of her somehow. Adriano is taken aback; it pains him to see her not trust him suddenly.

"Hey, it's okay, I'm not going to hurt you." Adriano's voice is soft and reassuring, but inside he is ruminating about this disengagement between them. Rebecca, hearing his voice, slowly looks up at him. This time she really pauses and looks into his blue eyes. Their warmth is unmistakable. A sudden sense of friendliness and familiarity arises within her, and she is drawn in by these eyes. She feels an inexplicable solace. The music playing is soothing and familiar. To Adriano's pleasant surprise Rebecca slowly begins to unfold her arms, and she comes in closer to him, she puts her hand on his warm face. Adriano closes his eyes, smiling with pleasure and taking in the touch of her warm hand. He reaches out to touch the hand that is still on his face. Rebecca accepts his touch, and Adriano stays in that moment, not moving.

Then Rebecca unbuttons her coat. Adriano opens his eyes, and helps her off with the coat. He breathes in the pleasant scent of Rebecca, but it is slightly different. "Thank you, I will just place it on the couch here so if you need it at any time it is right here for you."

Adriano suddenly has a flashback of a nice memory of when they passed by a French boutique, and Rebecca admired the leather boots and black winter coat that were modelled by the mannequin in the window. They went inside, and a few minutes later she stepped out wearing these items that Adriano purchased. "Thank you, Adriano, I love it! My first Parisian coat! And these boots are so amazing!" Rebecca was twirling around in the coat, just laughing and smiling like a young woman in love.

She thanked him with exuberance, expressed with a big warm hug and kissing him on the lips over and over. Their kisses created such wondrous energy and romantic lust, and he nestled his face into her beautiful long hair. His warm lips delicately kissed her neck. He was always in control and very aware of the vein that teased him from the forbidden blood he desired to taste. His lips on her body made Rebecca purr, imitating the sound of a cat, which turned Adriano on immensely. He was careful not to let Rebecca see the instant change of his light blue eyes to the midnight blue, almost black hue they took on when his senses were overstimulated.

The aroma of her own scent mixed with her perfume triggered such an erotic ache inside of him that his blood felt like it was on fire as he held her tightly in his embrace, speaking French to her. "*Tu donnes envie à mon sang d'éclater dans mon coeur*," translating to her so she would understand, "You make my blood want to burst out of my heart." He had to control the urge to growl in pure delight like a wolf, not just because they were in public but because the vampire in him couldn't resist the undeniable scent that she carried and wore. He just wanted to rub his body into it, capturing her sensual essence. He moaned quietly in pure pleasure, that only Rebecca could hear, teasing her as she heard the sound of his deep sexy voice speaking French. She snuggled her face into his chest listening.

"*Dieu, j'ai tellement envie de toi, Qu'est ce que tu es entrain de me faire?*" Again, translating for her he said, "I want you so badly, what are you doing to me?" Rebecca just melted when he spoke French in that voice she found so sexy and alluring. And he knew this made her weak at the knees, and he laughed mischievously.

There were so many treasured moments like that, and Adriano thought of them as he lay in bed alone during her disappearance. Now, seeing the torn coat triggers so many unanswered questions. Rebecca's expression is still ambiguous; she seems lost, and Adriano's heart and mind are racing for the right to help Rebecca feel safe in his company once again.

Then suddenly an idea comes to him. *Her perfume!* Adriano remembers those agonizing nights during Rebecca's disappearance. For comfort, when he was painfully missing her, he sometimes sprayed her perfume around the apartment, so he felt her close to him. Adriano dashes into the bedroom and within seconds he is back carrying a small bottle of perfume. He sprays some into the air, hoping this will instigate a memory. The fragrant mist travels to Rebecca, who puts her nose up into the air, taking in the pleasant fragrance.

"This is Allure Sensuelle, it is your favorite perfume." Adriano watches with great hope to see if she reacts at all. Rebecca reaches out and Adriano gives her the bottle; their hands touch ever so slightly and she smells the lid. "Do you like it?" Adriano is hopeful, anticipating that she will finally say something.

"Yes, but why do you say—*my* perfume? "

Adriano's hopes suddenly take a dive, and he doesn't know how to respond. He can see she is struggling desperately to remember something. "Everything okay?" Adriano is so anxious.

"I don't know, I just feel tired—why am I here?"

Adriano is worried, and without thinking he blurts out, "Are you hungry, thirsty, how about I make you your favorite green t—" He stops himself from finishing the word tea. A flood of questions races through his mind. *Will she even remember what her favorite tea is? How can she even enjoy it now, it will taste and smell different very different, perhaps disgusting to her, like burnt ash or sulfur! Think, Adriano, think! What should I say? You found her—just be grateful!* And then another disconcerting thought entered his mind. *How will I tell her family? They don't know yet that she is alive. Do I keep this quiet for now? I still don't know myself what to do or say to Rebecca.*

Rebecca's voice is polite but detached. "May I please use your bathroom?"

"Yes of course, let me show you where it is." Adriano leads Rebecca to the hallway and into their master bedroom en suite, enjoying the fragrance of her perfume immensely as it travels down the hallway.

Adriano then returns to the living room. He is exhausted both mentally and physically, and he slumps onto the black leather sofa. He pulls the silver crucifix pendant from his jean pocket and holds it in his hand tightly expressing gratitude to the universe. *"Thank you, God, thank you for bringing Rebecca back to me."*

Adriano makes the sign of the cross and lets out a heavy sigh. His mind can't help but travel back a few months to a conversation between him and Rebecca. Adriano tried without success to convince Rebecca to free herself from the brain tumor which she had been diagnosed with two years ago. Adriano wanted to change her over. He knew in his heart that he could do this carefully, and with gentleness and love. But he also completely understood how difficult it would be for Rebecca both physically and mentally if she became a vampire; she had her sons to think about.

But now, as he reflects back, he realizes that a part of him was being selfish to ask her to make such an impossible choice. How can he have expected this woman and mother to choose this option, just to survive, knowing that she would experience such horrible emotional pain, watching her loved ones dies while she lived on? How challenging and painful it would be to exist and interact with her sons, family, friends and colleagues without the constant desire to drain their blood. And now this is exactly what she faces.

Adriano knows the depth of acceptance needed to endure such an existence, and the required skills and strict discipline to be able to compartmentalize his strong craving for blood and his undeniable desire for friendship and lasting connection. A vampire's journey is filled with emotional and physical pain, and in some ways, he can empathize why many vampires behave in a horrifying manner. They allow their anger, depression, and bitterness to lead them down such a dark path of isolation and destruction.

At first, his own insecurities and mistrust also led him to an isolated life, and he didn't put much effort in seeking out more vampires. He couldn't risk more hurt, or finding more like Domenico. Adriano knew better than to see himself as a romantic character. He always tried to stay true to himself, even when the monster that was inside showed its shadow. He believed that he did have a soul, despite what folklore and literature dictated as truth. He knew the powerful physical strength and supernatural gifts he possessed and the capacity of indescribable destruction he could inflict on anyone if he ever abandoned his soul or hope of a better existence.

The path he walks involves basic survival, a need for atonement, and protection of the only two humans who entered his world, Jonathan and Sandra. That protective instinct expanded once he met Rebecca, to include other humans: her young sons and her family. Adriano is feeling even more protective now that Rebecca is a vampire. He feels like a male wolf protecting his pack, but this is an unknown landscape.

Adriano has to accept that he wasn't the one that turned her. His body is resting, absorbing into the couch as his mind tries to settle down. He is finally allowing himself to release from all of these long months of not knowing where Rebecca was and despairing. Tomorrow he will have a better perspective on what to do. Then it hits him like a car slamming into a brick wall. *Mon Dieu! What can I possibly tell her family?*

Panic once again rising, his mind races to come up with believable scenarios. Rebecca is alive, safe and with him, even though mentally and especially physically she has changed. *Hope now has a chance, and everything else will follow as it should*, he thinks. For now, he feels it best to not let her family know anything. He still needs to understand so many things about Rebecca and her transformation, and he realizes after all these years of being alone as a vampire, that not all vampires are alike. And this intrigues him to know more about his Rebecca, this beautiful creature taking a bubble bath in his washroom.

Adriano closes his eyes, but his protective instinct is still on high alert. Meanwhile, he's suppressing the pain of his own thirst rising from his abdomen and trying to travel to his raw throat. Again, without warning, anxious thoughts creep in. *Is she in shock from becoming a vampire? Mon dieu, did the vampire who made her hurt her or abandon her during the death of her human body?*

Without warning Adriano shouts out, "It should have been me to change her over!" He can feel the tension and anger that he suppressed all these months releasing in that outburst. He realizes Rebecca might have heard him, and puts his head in his palms trying to calm himself down, quietly taking deep breaths. He feels frustrated and doesn't know what to do. Normally you would call a doctor or go to hospital to be checked out after such an ordeal, but how can he possibly bring Rebecca to the hospital now that she is a vampire? Reality pounds at him. *She is a vampire!*

He pulls out his phone and texts his friend Jonathan.

Hi J, I found her! She is ok, but I need help! Keep this to yourself for now.

Can you handle the police?

Will call you later

In the meantime, Rebecca is freshening up, and too preoccupied to hear the burst of anger seconds ago. She is unaware of the torment Adriano is feeling in the living room. She looks in the mirror. It has been a while since she had looked at herself properly in a well-lit bathroom and mirror that is not broken. Suddenly, she feels the symptoms rising, she knows she needs to drink again, the rabbit was just not enough with all the walking they did to get here. Her mind is now realizing that the man in the other room is not a man, he is a vampire! Her instincts reassure her that he is a friend, that she can trust him with her thirst needs.

She rinses out her mouth and washes her hands and quickly glances back to the mirror. She gasps in horror. A few minutes ago, her reflection seemed fine. She puts her hands to her face, feeling her thin white skin and tired eyes. She has prominent wrinkles, and her hair seems thin. Without warning, a flood of images crosses her mind, snapshots of familiar people and places, and she sees an image of herself in a different place. But what catches her attention the most is images of two little boys holding her hands, smiling and laughing as they come out of a movie theatre. *"Mommy, that was the best Spiderman movie ever!"* The image is broken like a slit is cut through it, and she sees a small dead animal with blood on its fur laying at her feet beside these two boys. The shocking image pricks Rebecca's mind and she yells out, "NO! No!" and smashes the mirror.

The crash sends Adriano, who was drifting off, running at lightning speed to the bathroom door. He pounds hard on the door yelling out, "Rebecca—Rebecca, are you okay!? Unlock the door!" Rebecca doesn't answer, but Adriano can hear her breathing. He uses his vampire strength, and turning the knob he pushes open the door forcefully but with control, not wanting to break it down in case it hits Rebecca.

Rebecca is standing there with her hands full of blood, and she looks at them and turns her head away. "Don't look at me, please."

Adriano sees the broken pieces of mirror scattered in the sink and on the floor and thinks, *Mon dieu! She must have seen the reflection of herself as a vampire in the mirror and it scared her!* "Rebecca, it's okay, what you saw in the mirror is not real, that is not how you look, you are beautiful, your eyes are perfect, your face is perfection, your lips are amazing, do not believe what you see in the mirror! It takes time to adjust to the distorted image you see of yourself. Don't be frightened, the elongated face is not real!" Adriano prays that his words reach Rebecca. But she is still facing away from him, her face covered with her bloody hands. Rebecca, hearing this man's kind sensitive voice, turns around and looks up at him. Now he looks shocked, and takes a step back.

Rebecca sees his reaction, and feeling very stressed and fatigued she collapses. But Adriano catches her and, taking a towel hanging on the bar, he wraps her hands in them. He is surprised that her exposed blood doesn't entice his thirst, but then he realizes that he doesn't crave vampire blood. When Rebecca was human, Adriano's strong urge and desire to taste her blood at times was relentless, especially with the romantic connection they shared. Controlling his animalistic thirst for her had been very difficult.

Adriano picks Rebecca up, brings her to their bedroom, and gently tries to revive her. A few seconds later, she opens her eyes. Adriano runs quickly to get a warm wet cloth to gently clean the small cut on her hand, even though he is expecting it to heal quickly. He soon becomes alarmed; her body is not healing this cut?

Rebecca becomes emotional. It seems that all that has occurred today and these last two months is coming out in waves of hysterical tears. Adriano brings her into his warm and loving arms and her face snuggles into his chest. She hears the pattern of his slow heartbeat and it soothes her: babump, bump, bump, babump. Babump, bump, bump, babump.

Kissing the top of her head, speaking endearing comforting words to her, the French just naturally comes out. She listens to his soft deep voice, and he becomes more familiar. She can't understand it, but she adores hearing his voice. "Rebecca, belle âme, je suis là pour toi." He raises her chin so he can look deep into her eyes as he translates his words for her. "My beautiful soul, I am here for you."

Her crying subsides until she finally stops, and Adriano wipes away her tears. He realizes at this moment she is trusting his touch again, and recognizing her own name. A growing realization stirs in her mind, a memory is coming forth albeit fragmented but clearer, she knows this man holding her, this is her vampire—Adriano.

CHAPTER 3

Hunters

The thick darkness of midnight tries to shield the unsuspecting prey
But the relentless thirst of the predator sees it from a great distance away.

I t was almost midnight. The events of earlier that Thursday evening exhausted both Adriano and Rebecca physically and mentally, and without warning they had both fallen into a deep sleep. Adriano wakes up but doesn't want to disturb Rebecca. She is lying in bed, her body turned away from Adriano. He can hear the steady rhythm of Rebecca's breathing and quietly leaves the bedroom and goes to clean up the shattered glass in the bathroom. Then Adriano lays back down beside Rebecca on the bed, over the covers, and just closes his eye. His body is still exhausted and he knows it is telling him that it needs rest. He doesn't sleep much, being a vampire, but occasionally his body sends off warnings to him that he is overexerting himself and that is usually when the thirst increases. He is lying there and suddenly he is aware of a strange unfamiliar troubling noise coming from Rebecca. Adriano quickly leaps out of bed and turns the light on. Moving to the other side of the bed, he is taken aback in shock. Rebecca's hair is thinned out, and he can barely see any of her dark brown color, the greys and white overpowering. Her face has aged tremendously, she looks like someone in her late seventies or more. The prominent wrinkles, deep lines, and age spots invade her face and hands. Her eyes are now open, and they too have lost their youthful glint and brilliance.

Adriano is bewildered to see this extreme transformation take place.

"We need to feed!" Just hearing himself say *we* sounds outrageous to him, but it is reality now. He has no clue if Rebecca has only fed from the blood of animals or if she has experienced the blood of a human. Both are very different in taste and fulfillment. Adriano needs real nourishment that he knows only a human can provide, animals were just not enough for him. He needs to keep up his strength and agility. But he had no time to look through any of the criminal files that Jonathan risked sending through password-protected email from the police station in Toronto. Pedophiles, rapists, and drug dealers were safe from Adriano, at least for tonight.

"Rebecca, we need to go out, I know your thirst is very painful, I can see it in your eyes and your body, you are trembling—I am here for you, you do not have to hide from me, I understand."

Rebecca reaches out her hands as if she was talking with someone, calling out the names of her sons Adam and Ethan, and then she another name. "I am coming Sebastien!" Adriano realizes that she is hallucinating; he fears that Rebecca is in more danger than he first thought.

Adriano holds onto her gently; she seems so fragile and delicate, like glass that could break into pieces. He quickly dashes out of the apartment with her, and with accelerated vampire speed and with the cover of this moonless night, he runs as fast as he can into the nearest wooded area, praying for any animal or even a wandering adult human. At this point his consciousness isn't stabbing him, this is a matter of survival for Rebecca! A low fierce growl rises from him, partly due to hunger but mostly fear for the state Rebecca is in. They travel many miles in a short time, Adriano still carrying Rebecca in his arms. She is too weak to run, and Adriano realizes the danger she is in. The hunter instinct in Adriano leads them back into the isolated woods where he found her. His vampire sensory powers are on extra alert now that there were other vampires that could be lurking in the shadows.

Adriano keeps talking to Rebecca, but she barely responds. Suddenly he stops, something catching the attention of the predator inside him. His keen vampire vision focuses on movement up ahead and to the left, between some trees. Gently, he puts Rebecca down to rest against a rock, and takes off his winter coat to cover her. With increased strength that only a vampire's legs could possess, he leaps into the air as high as his adrenaline can take him. Using his acute eyesight, he scans the ground to see if he can home in on the movement. The unsuspecting fox is busy eating his own meal, a small field mouse. With controlled accuracy Adriano pounces directly on the tail of the fox; shrieks and cries are heard. He grabs it and within seconds he is back at Rebecca's side.

"Rebecca, Rebecca, open your eyes, look!" Rebecca hears a voice but it seems so far away; she opens her exhausted eyes and hears the fox squealing from the excruciating pain of its broken tail. Rebecca's sharp teeth grow with the smell of the animal, she pierces her razor-sharp teeth into its neck and drinks and drinks in the warm nourishing blood. "Drink my love, all of it, you will feel so much better." Rebecca's eyes are open wider now as the warm blood flows deep into her very raw, sore throat. Adriano sees her hazel eyes beginning to show life again, the unique color of her irises turning back to deep amber and cinnamon. Adriano notices her hands; the cut is healing, and her skin is firming up, the age spots fading. Wrinkles and lines are no longer visible on her face. Life is returning to Rebecca as death is greeting the fox. Rebecca releases her mouth, and Adriano quickly sinks his teeth into the fox to make sure Rebecca drained it completely. She needs this nourishment even more than him. Adriano's head pounds as if someone just took a brick to it, fighting a migraine trying to surface. There is barely a trickle of blood remaining in the animal and Adriano releases his hold on it. The corpse falls to the ground.

Rebecca just lays on the ground, taking in deep breaths, and within moments she stands up with regained strength. She looks at Adriano. "Thank you—thank you! What about you? Do you need to drink too?"

"Don't worry, I will be right back." Adriano gives her a charming wink and smile and dashes back into the woods, searching for any moving creature. He sees a rabbit and grabs it instantly by its long brown ears, and moves his other hand swiftly to grabs its neck. This might not be enough substance for him with all the excitement and stress of today, but he drains the blood of the animal on the spot and quickly runs back to Rebecca. She's standing up with more strength, showing increasing ease and warmth.

They travel deeper into the woods, hand in hand, still covered by darkness and both with their red-stained lips. The familiar images of people and moments that had moved through her thoughts earlier are now set further back in Rebecca's mind, like a cloud moving through the sky and shadowing her memory. At one point, Rebecca stops and Adriano instantly follows, but he isn't aware at first why they've made the sudden halt. He scans the surroundings with acute awareness, then he looks at Rebecca; she quickly tilts her head upward and smells the air with her powerful nose. Her head straightens, her eyes wide and focused, and she detects movement in the thick bush a distance away. Adriano stands very still, amazed and curious at this new predator standing by his side.

Adriano wants to see how Rebecca behaves and hunts as a vampire. Swiftly Rebecca leaps as high as one of the tallest trees nearby, an incredible sight to behold. He looks upward to watch her as if she is reaching out to touch the stars in the night sky, shocked and mesmerized by the height and distance of her leap into the air. Not even he can leap that high with such a controlled form. *Mon dieu! Mon panthère! Belle panthère!* Rebecca lands gracefully, like a majestic cat, a few feet away from an unsuspecting deer. Adriano creeps slowly a few feet away from her, careful not to disturb her in her hunt but observing her every move. The deer freezes as it anticipates the danger. Rebecca approaches the animal very slowly and cautiously, and still the deer doesn't move. They both hear its frantic heartbeat, and smell the fear rising. The scent travels through Adriano, teasing him, but this is Rebecca's kill, not his, and Adriano forces himself to stay back even though his throat is aching for the warm liquid. Adriano is shocked at what he sees next: the deer lowers its head and body to the ground as if it knows it is in the presence of a greater being. Adriano is bewildered by this behavior and wonders if this is a miracle or is this some kind of supernatural power that Rebecca now possesses as an apex predator.

Adriano has never had such a submissive reaction like this from any animal he was about to kill. His ability to engage with animals in a deeper way doesn't reach this capability. Rebecca bends down to pet the deer's head. "Thank you for your sacrifice." Rebecca and the deer seem to be communicating somehow, and the deer seems to be in a trance. Seconds later, Rebecca leans in and bites into the neck of the deer. The jolt from Rebecca's teeth piercing its skin awakens the deer from its trance, but her vampire saliva numbs the wound and the instinct to struggle lessens, and suddenly it's as if the animal accepts its fate and purpose. Rebecca keeps a firm hold on its neck as she drinks in the nourishing blood. She then stops drinking and calls out to Adriano to join her. Adriano is by her side within seconds, astounded that he just witnessed another one of Rebecca's gifts as a vampire. He is entranced himself in some ways, discovering that she can subdue prey and engage in an honest integral moment with it, knowing it is going to die.

Adriano is thrilled and curious to learn more about his Rebecca, this new creature of the undead, his *belle panthère*. They both feed with zest, almost like they are sharing in a romantic dinner together, minus the music, wine, and candles. Rebecca admires Adriano as he drinks and she sees his beautiful ocean blue eyes becoming exceptionally deeper, midnight blue. She can see tiny specks of white, silver, green, and crimson in the irises, and it reminds her of an image of a galaxy. It is spectacular. Adriano enjoys Rebecca watching him as he feeds, and he is transfixed by her eyes and her body. She appears to be younger again, and her warm amber cinnamon eyes gleam with life.

For Adriano, this is a profound moment. He feels a great sense of satisfaction for the first time as a vampire. He is feeding in the presence of the one he loves. There is no more shame in what he does to survive, he is free to drink blood in the company of this woman. He feels he just woke up from a lengthy dream. They both continue to drink in this life sacrificed by the deer, and feel such elation. They drink to completion, and now Adriano so desperately wants to steal a kiss from Rebecca and taste her lips now quenched with blood, but he's still not sure if she will welcome this intimacy. He takes a tissue from his pocket and wipes Rebecca's lips and then his.

Under the cover of night and at vampire speed, they travel and explore other woods and forests around Paris. With each new successful hunt their speed increases and leaves them feeling more nourished and satisfied.

Their personal connection is intensifying more and more, their spirits are entwined once again, rekindling their bond. They spend the remaining early morning hours before dawn frolicking like teenagers, leaping through trees, showing off their individual speeds and strength by racing to see who can climb a tree the fastest. Of course, this game disrupts the sleep of many birds and squirrels. Then they test their strength by breaking thick tree branches like they were twigs, but Adriano is still the winner in this category. Laughing and playing like two teenagers after dark, they hunt a few more animals and feed from them. They are in a different world, a safe space where their thoughts are free of shame and guilt, and their souls untouched by the reality of who they really are. With each new kill that Rebecca nourishes her body with, Adriano witnesses the powerful connection between animals and this vampire. Adriano isn't sure how long Rebecca's nourishment will last. They drank quite a lot the last few hours, so he hopes she is nourished enough to last until the next day at least. He really is not sure. Curiosity strikes him, and he wonders if Rebecca has tasted the blood of a human. But he struggles to find the right moment to bring this question up, and sets it back in his mind for now.

Adriano looks at his watch; it is four twenty a.m. He sees a text message from Jonathan, but he can't read it now. He is concerned that in a few hours it will be dawn and the sun will be rising, and even though it is winter, he is not sure if exposure to sunlight affects Rebecca physically. He can tolerate only short bursts of sun, and prefers to find shade where possible. Adriano can also tolerate very low temperatures without a jacket, but he doesn't know what Rebecca can endure physically. Right now, she is only wearing gloves and the Peacoat Adriano found her with hours ago. Adriano knows that his knowledge of vampires as a species is limited. He only has his own life experiences to draw upon and depend on for guidance, safety, and well-being. Adriano had to discover his own powerful strengths and weaknesses. He discovered that direct exposure to sun triggers migraines and sometimes skin rashes, but doesn't prevent him from being outside. He just takes precautions to avoid direct exposure for too long. He wonders if Rebecca shares these traits or others that he needs to know about. He already discovered in these last few hours hunting with her that Rebecca has different gifts, but is there fragility in her as a vampire to be aware of?

Adriano knows she needs to feed often but is there more? He turns toward her. "Rebecca, we need to get going now, the sun will be up shortly and it looks like the weather is getting colder."

"Oh! Why? Are you cold—my sexy vampire?" Rebecca gives Adriano an alluring glance, then slowly runs her fingers through his soft black wavy hair. Adriano weakens inside.

"Not at all, my sexy *panthère*—are you?" He brings her closer, into his arms. Rebecca can hear a low growl coming from Adriano, a sign of affection, and it triggers a reaction. She feels her knees weaken, and there is a tingling sensation between her legs.

"No, this air is so fresh." Rebecca holds Adriano's hand, smiling, and breathes in the wild crisp air of the forest.

They continue walking leisurely in the forest a few more hours, but when Adriano sees the sun creeping up, his protective instinct kicks in.

"I am concerned that the sun will be rising soon—*my* love." He reaches out gently and removes a stray hair from Rebecca's face. She is touched by his attentiveness.

"Don't worry, *I* won't burn up into ashes!" she says with a mischievous giggle.

"Haha, very funny!" He nudges her shoulder and kissed her on the lips.

"Interesting—I never really thought about the sun until you just asked me? I usually go out at night, it's just more peaceful and quieter."

They reach the entrance to the forest, and Adriano as usual scans his surroundings to make sure they are not detected or noticed by humans. Feeling secure enough since it is still early morning, he taps Rebecca on the shoulder.

"Tag-you're it!" He runs out of the forest into the open park.

"OH! I don't think so!" Rebecca playfully shouts, and she quickly gains speed and passes Adriano, laughing with all her heart. She is now further up ahead. Adriano can hardly see her in the distance and he panics and calls out frantically, then races to her and grabs her arm firmly but gently. Rebecca is surprised.

"Hey, everything okay Adriano? You're squeezing me."

Adriano releases his firm grip on Rebecca's arm and hugs her tightly. "Yes—sorry, I just—never mind, come on, let's get going, you never know if humans are observing—we don't want to attract attention."

Rebecca looks at him. She can sense that Adriano was alarmed, but she doesn't want to press him. The more time she spends with this man, the more she sees he is very protective, and it makes her feel so secure. She really wants to remember more about him, about their relationship. *Hmm, is he my boyfriend?*

Their games have brought them to the next day, six thirty a.m. on Friday, a crescent moon barely visible through the winter-clouded sky. They are already a block away from their apartment in the 1st Arrondissement. Adriano is hoping that now that they have spent the night together learning more about each other, and seeing how confident her demeanor is now, the other difficulties Rebecca experienced as a human might have disappeared. He especially wants to know if her social anxiety and the physical symptoms she experienced still happen. Does she still suffer migraines before she is about to go out for an evening gathering? Does she experience moments where she feels dizzy, loss of concentration and focus when she feels anxious? Does she have anxiety attacks? Adriano remembers Rebecca's world and social life as a human. He witnessed her migraines when they were out, he saw her shy nature affect her social network. These are questions he needs to ask.

They arrive back at their apartment, and reality comes crashing back to Adriano's mind. *Today we have to let them know.* Adriano can't keep this news from her family any longer, but he isn't sure how to approach this sensitive subject with Rebecca, or how to prepare her to tell the biggest lie they will now have to tell her family.

CHAPTER 4
Forgotten Life

Rebecca spent Friday morning familiarizing herself with the apartment and her belongings, feeling more at ease, that she belonged there with Adriano. Once in a while she would walk outside into the courtyard with Adriano, and he would open the wooden gate. Rebecca just stood at the gate, watching, listening, and absorbing the different smells, human and non-human. Her vampire eyes reached further into the distance as she scanned both sides of their street; her vampire ears listened to sounds that at times were too strong for her new vampire ears. She watched the humans as they walked, and she observed and studied their pace. Rebecca was aware that she had a lot of work to do in this regard; her body movements were still too quick and she was still not ready to walk further out onto the cobblestone sidewalk among the humans. Adriano spent the time observing her.

Now, Adriano follows Rebecca into their bedroom. She walks towards the dresser and picks up a piece of jewelry sitting in a silver tray on top of the dresser. Memories are coming back in bits and pieces. She opens drawers and looks at the different tops and sweaters and even recognizes her picture from her passport. She is aware that her memory is coming back, but in fragments. After some time goes by, Rebecca turns to Adriano and tells him that she is going to take a nice hot shower. Adriano walks back to the living room, but he can hear her rummaging through her drawers.

Adriano goes outside into the courtyard again and just breathes in the crisp afternoon air. He needs time and space to think. He feels his stomach fluttering with nervous twinges. An important question surfaces, nagging him. *Does Rebecca have any memory that she had a fatal brain tumour when she was human?* That leads to more worries; he will have to come up with a realistic reason to give to her family, to explain how the tumor disappeared, or at least convince them that it is now in remission. He goes back inside and takes out a piece of paper and pen, sitting at the coffee table. Thinking and thinking, he writes and rewrites different stories. He is concentrating so hard. This lie has to be convincing! He gets up, he needs a break. He goes to check on Rebecca, but she is still in their washroom; he hears the blow-dryer. He returns to the paper, and writes down more important points. Gradually pieces of threads are forming in his mind, sewing together a story that just might work. But first he thinks, *I need to find out what Rebecca remembers.*

Adriano turns the radio on and searches for a station playing music. He doesn't really care what song is playing, he just needs a background distraction, and his nerves are jumpy. He lowers the volume so he can still hear Rebecca in case she calls him. He sits on the couch taking in a few deep breaths, practicing his meditation. He hasn't done his yoga in a while. He is feeling more anxious ever since Rebecca's disappearance in December. But now his anxiety is stemming from his need to delicately bring up the subject of Rebecca's children and family. He is just not sure if Rebecca is ready for this. He needs to explain to her that they just cannot go back immediately, he will have to spend some time preparing her to be back among her human family. His worry festers. *Will she have a setback?*

He realizes he doesn't hear the blow dryer anymore. Panic rises again, and then he hears the bedroom door open, then in a steady voice he whispers to himself, "It is time."

Rebecca walks out of the bedroom, feeling relaxed and carefree; she comments how nourished she feels from all the hunting earlier. A fresh aroma travels through the air, teasing Adriano's nostrils as the scent of sweet roses lingers. Rebecca's long, dark brown hair is shiny and falling over her shoulders and down her back. Adriano notices that she straightened it, so it is very smooth. Her new enhanced hazel eyes have a twinkle, and her lips look luscious in a warm dark burgundy lipstick. She is wearing a cream turtleneck and black jeans. Adriano's sexual urges are awakening and he wants to take her right there, but he controls himself and fondly calls her over to the couch. "Hey beautiful, please—come sit beside me, we need to talk."

Rebecca is quickly at his side, her vampire movements still not under control. "Everything okay?"

Adriano takes her hand; it is still very warm and soft, and he caresses her hair, feeling the smoothness and softness. He is working up his courage. He smiles at Rebecca, then finally begins. "Rebecca, *mon amour*—how much of your memory has come back?"

Rebecca looks into his eyes, and then around the room. "I don't know, I have small flickers of memories popping up. I remember you more and more." She smiles. "This apartment is feeling more familiar—Adriano, why are you asking?"

Adriano still holding Rebecca's hand gently in his. "There is no easy way to tell you this, *mon amour*, but what you are not remembering is…that you are a mother of two young—"

Before he can finish the sentence, Rebecca's eyes widen. An image crosses her mind and she gasps, covering her mouth with her hand. "Adam and Ethan! Oh my God—my babies! What will I do? What will I tell them?" Rebecca covers her face with her hands and begins to tremble.

"One step at a time, my love, I have been thinking about this all morning. There is so much more I need you to remember."

Rebecca grabs Adriano's arm. "Just tell me! Tell me—I need to know everything." Rebecca is desperate for information, her eyes searching Adriano's for reassurance.

"I know, but I don't want to overwhelm you with too much. I just feel this was important for me to mention, you need to know."

"Yes—yes! Tell me everything!"

Adriano sighs, cautious how much he needs to reveal. He holds her hand more tightly, giving her support, and he begins. "Two years ago, you were very sick. You were diagnosed with a brain tumor." He pauses, allowing her mind to absorb this shock before he continues.

"Brain tumor? Go on."

The next hour is spent with Adriano telling Rebecca about the brain tumor she had, and how he surprised her with this trip to Paris in December. He talks about her sons, and the fact that she is divorced; where she lives, and her life up to the accident. He ends with his idea for the story they would tell when they return.

Rebecca sits there quietly, taking in all this information about herself. She feels like she is learning about some stranger, and yet it is about her life, her family. She is desperate to remember more about every part of her life. As he speaks, flashes of images and memories cross each other, confusing Rebecca. Feeling overwhelmed, she fights tears. She insists on hearing more. Adriano continues to tell her whatever he knows about her.

"I know I have told you a lot now, and maybe I shouldn't have gone this far, but your family, your sons are suffering, not knowing where you are or if you are alive, and in my conscious I cannot let this go on. Do you understand? We need to contact them." Rebecca leans back on the couch, wrapped up and tangled in many confusing thoughts and memories. "Rebecca? Are you okay?"

Rebecca opens her mouth to speak, and the sound of her voice seems so far away. "I have to lie to my sons? My family? That's what you are telling me? No! I am not okay—is this going to be my life now? Lies?" She abruptly gets up and before Adriano can stop her, she opens the front door and walks out into the private courtyard, leaving the door open. She sits down on the cement bench, her head and torso bent over into her knees. Adriano comes out and quietly sits beside her, his body o heavy. The weight of this extraordinary complexity in Rebecca's life pulls them both down. "I had no choice, I had to tell you—you needed to know. I am sorry, Rebecca."

Rebecca remains crouched.

Adriano gently lifts her head. "Rebecca, I know how difficult this is, I understand what it means to have to lie to the ones you love. But they're suffering, and I know once you talk to your boys you will realize you are doing the best thing for them." Adriano brushes a piece of her hair from her teary eye, holding her hand and kissing her delicate fingers, and she doesn't resist his touch. "I'm sorry, I hate to see you so stressed and worried, but we can't wait any longer, or there will be even more questions and upset from your family." Rebecca looks up, her lips trembling; she is struggling to hold back from crying.

"I remember my sons. It's all flooding in, I see my cute little boys. How could I have stayed away from them, forgotten them?"

"Shh…it's okay, belle âme." Adriano gently takes her face into his hands, kissing her trembling lips. He whispers soothingly, "Shhh…it's ok beautiful, trust me, we will figure this out together. For now, let's keep to our plan and I will contact your brother Joseph just as we discussed, I know he can help." Rebecca's eyes fill with trust. The name Joseph sounds familiar. But her mind is still giving her gaps in images, and she can't see him clearly. Adriano puts his arm around her and leads her back inside to rest.

CHAPTER 5
Adam and Ethan

Catarina parks her car in one of the parking spots in front of the school and looks at her watch. *They didn't even make it to lunch.* A heavy sigh escapes her. She grabs her purse and locks the door behind her, walks into the elementary school towards the office. She is immediately greeted by Jeanine, the staff administrator, who sees Mrs. Dimondo quite regularly now.

"Good morning Mrs. Dimondo. Everything okay? You're here quite early?"

"Hi Jeanine, yes, I know. Can you please call them down for me?" Caterina stands patiently at the front reception desk, going over in her mind the list of errands she still needs to do.

"Sure, just a second. Rough morning, I take it?"

"Rough week—for the boys. I got a call from Adam's teacher, he couldn't concentrate, he was too tired and just wanted to be picked up." Catarina then shared a little more. "They were up a few times last night."

"Poor things— it must be very difficult for all of you. I'm hoping you will get good news soon. Well, at least you have the weekend—too bad, it's pizza day! You sure they won't stay?"

"I'm afraid not."

Jeanine understands. She picks up the telephone, dials Adam's teacher, and informs him that Adam's grandmother is here to pick him up. She then dials Ethan's teacher and has him sent down, too.

Although Catarina in the past engaged in small chats with Jeanine, lately, she just doesn't have the strength to stay longer than needed. A student walks in and approaches the desk. Catarina steps aside, feeling relieved that she no longer has to force a smile. Catarina needs to stay positive but she sees the calendar posted on the wall, it's like it is screaming out to her. *"It is now February fifteenth, two months and five days have passed since Rebecca's disappearance."*

Catarina sees her grandsons walking down the hall, and pastes her smile back on. They walk toward the glass door, waving. Adam is carrying his black and red Spider-Man knapsack over his shoulders. His mother bought both boys these knapsacks in September; they were so excited that they each got to choose. They were so proud to show these off to their friends at the beginning of the semester.

Adam is wearing a blue winter jacket already zipped up, with his black Batman woolen hat placed securely on his head, hiding his thick wavy dark brown hair. His matching scarf is stuffed inside his jacket and his jeans are tucked into his black winter boots that are already tied up. Trailing just a little further back is Ethan. His thick curly dark brown hair has a mind of its own today, some of it slightly in front of his eyes. He is wearing a red Spider-Man sweater over a pair of black jeans that are just a few inches too short. He is going through another growing spurt. He insisted this morning that he didn't need to match his socks and preferred his Spider-Man running shoes today. Catarina just watches him, his unmatched socks exposed, his shoes lighting up in red and white as he walks. Ethan's arms struggle to carry his red winter coat, his black Batman hat, and his black and green Green Goblin knapsack, which is dragging slightly on the floor along with the coat. The knapsack is partially unzipped and his hat and red scarf are almost falling out of the bag, which is already stuffed with his homework and agenda booklet to be signed by his Nonna Catarina or Nonno Vince. She can also see the edges of two small binders, his Batman pencil case, and of course a half-eaten salami sandwich.

Catarina's heart melts as she watches her little grandsons coming closer to the door; their smiles are there for their grandmother, but she can see in their big innocent eyes, it just isn't a good day for either of them. They miss their mom.

Catarina waves goodbye to Jeanine, quickly leaves the office, and greets the boys with a warm and loving embrace. She takes each of their hands in hers, and already as they are walking out into the winter air little Ethan is sharing with her about the homework he has for the weekend, and how he and his friend Kevin traded M&Ms for Ethan's chips at recess, and most importantly, he asks, "Nonna, can we go to McDonald's then to the Dollar Store? We can pick up Nonno at home then go?"

Adam is older, he is more of the quiet reserved type. But he barely has a chance to speak now, between Ethan's continued talking. He too encourages the outing and says he feels like a hamburger and fries and would like to pick up the newest pack of Pokémon cards if they go to the Dollar store.

Catarina can't say no to these little guys, and off they go. First stop, home to pick up their Nonno Vince, and then next stop the Dollar Store. Catarina is hopeful that this little hour or two of joy will give them something to enjoy, or at least distract them, for today.

It is now noon, and they arrive back at their grandparent's home. Ethan is anxious to get to his room, he's excited to unpack the Bionicle package and start building his new robot to add to his robot army. In the meantime, Adam brings his bag from the Dollar Store into the kitchen and places it on the wooden table, unpacking his Pokémon cards.

Catarina stays in the kitchen with him enjoying his company while listening to her CBC radio, and starts peeling potatoes for their dinner. Vincent goes into the family room to watch a movie on TV.

Adam suddenly becomes agitated. His logical mind nudges him to speak. "Nonna, why can't we go to Paris to help Adriano find Mommy!?"

Catarina stops peeling the potatoes, takes a deep breath, and walks over to the table. She pulls out a kitchen chair to sit beside Adam. She looks into his big hazel eyes; he has so many similar features like his mom, but his eyes are hers—no mistaking them. Catarina takes Adam into her lap, hugging him. "Oh honey—Adriano said it was best for us that we stayed here, just in case your mom called. Besides, your mom wouldn't want you to miss any more school. Adriano's friend Jonathan said he would go to Paris as soon as he can, and help Adriano keep looking with the French police."

"But it's been so long! What if something happened to her and she's alone! I want to go! I want to go find her!" He pushes himself away from his grandmother's embrace, grabs his Pokémon cards, and angrily throws them into the air. The cards scatter on the floor; he bangs his hands on the table and begins to cry.

Catarina embraces him tightly, holding back her own tears. "It's okay Adam, let it out, let it out." Catarina is relieved that Adam has finally poured out his emotions, it has been very concerning to both Catarina and Vince that he held back so much after they learned Rebecca had vanished.

Catarina's husband Vince runs into the kitchen when he hears the commotion, but Catarina privately waves him away so as not to disturb Adam, who just needs to let out his emotions privately.

Vince mouths to Catarina, "Is he okay?"

Catarina nods yes and Vince understands and goes to checks on Ethan. He opens the bedroom door and he can hear sounds of play and imagination. Ethan is building his Bionicle and is getting ready for a big battle between several different Bionicles that he collected already. They are organized by their fictional ranks. Ethan doesn't even notice his nonno standing there quietly just watching him play in his own world and then the door closes again.

CHAPTER 6

And So it begins

Adriano pulls out his cell, shocked at how quickly this day is going. "Are you ready?"

Rebecca slowly nods, privately saying to herself, *and so it begins.* She takes a deep breath, strength rising within. "It has to be done, there is no choice."

"Do you want me to keep it on speaker?"

Rebecca nods, and Adriano kisses her gently on the lips.

"It's going to be okay—if it gets too much for you, I will take over, I promise." Rebecca swallows suddenly. Adriano scrolls down the list to Joseph and makes the call; the phone rings a couple of times. He puts it on speaker.

"Hello?" comes Joseph's busy voice. Rebecca quietly gasps, her eyes showing immediate recognition hearing his voice.

"Hi Joseph, it's Adriano. Hope I—"

Joseph interrupts. "Adriano—did you find her?"

"Yes, she's—"

A burst of excitement can be heard from Joseph's voice. "Oh, thank God! Is she there, can I speak with her? Hang on, I'm going to conference call with Marcus, just a second." Joseph links Marcus to the conversation.

"Hello? Marcus?"

"Yeah, I'm here."

"I've got Adriano on the line. He found Rebecca."

"Adriano, hi!"

"Hi, Listen, Rebecca is here with me, we just got back from the hospital—"

Joseph's voice turns to panic. "Hospital?"

"Is she okay?" simultaneously spoken by Joseph and Marcus.

"Guys, it's okay, she's fine—really—but she is very tired. I will explain more to you later, for now I just thought you would want to speak with her."

"Yes of course!"

Adriano put's his cell on speaker.

"Hi guys."

"My God, Rebecca. How amazing to hear your voice!" shouts Marcus.

"How are you? Are you hurt? What happened?" said Joseph.

"I know you have a lot of questions, but I can't answer all right now, you see I have a bit of amnesia." Rebecca doesn't elaborate.

"Amnesia, you're kidding—is it serious?" queries Marcus.

"No, at least not anymore. Don't worry. In fact, I've started having glimpses of memories returning. I'm remembering a lot more now. Please understand, this is why I haven't been in touch. I'm sorry for all the worry. I didn't remember anything about myself, but once I remembered I had the hospital contact Adriano immediately." Rebecca is nervous, she hates lying like this.

"Of course, don't worry—thank God you're okay." The words are simultaneously spoken by Joseph and Marcus.

"I am, but I need to rest a lot." Rebecca looks at Adriano, needing reassurance that this tale they are telling is convincing. Adriano nods, giving her a confident smile.

"Of course. When is your flight? Marcus and I can meet you at—"

"Flight? Oh, um, the doctor doesn't think I should travel yet—it's complicated."

"Complicated? How?" There is an awkward pause. "Is everything else really okay? Is there something you're not telling us?"

The phone becomes silent again.

"Yeah sis, Marcus and I are worried."

Rebecca panics, not sure how to respond. She looks to Adriano who quickly responds, "Hi guys, listen, Rebecca is really tired, I appreciate you're worried, but she is fine, just needs to rest. She is still recovering and it takes a lot out of her. I promise we will call you again in a while."

"Okay, but Rebecca, are you still there?"

"Yes Joseph."

"Will you be coming home at least by the end of week?"

"Guys, the doctor said that she needs a few more days before she can travel. I realize this is very difficult for all of you. But we just need to trust the doctor. Trust me, we are anxious to get back, but I can't risk a setback for Rebecca. I hope you understand." Adriano's eyes stay on Rebecca, he can see how this is upsetting her.

"Yes of course. The main thing is Rebecca is safe and with you."

"Absolutely, no pressure Rebecca, Marcus and I will get in touch with mom and dad and explain."

"Thank you for understanding guys. I will call Mom later. But I need one huge favour."

"Yes, of course."

"Please tell my boys I love them and will talk to them later too."

"We will, they miss you so much."

Adriano takes the phone again "Okay, guys, we will talk later."

"Okay, bye for now then, I'm hanging up, talk later Joseph. Bye Sis!"

"See ya Marcus."

Marcus hangs up his connection.

"Okay, sis, if you need anything, just call, okay? You take your time and get better. You can't forget your favorite brother, after all." Joseph laughs.

"Oh Joseph, you're too much. It is Joseph I'm talking to, right?" The phone goes silent. "Kidding!" chuckles Rebecca, followed by Adriano and Joseph.

"Take care sis. And thanks Adriano for looking after our little sister. Bye."

"Bye," Rebecca and Adriano say in unison.

Rebecca can barely contain her emotion. Her hands are still shaking, but Adriano just holds her tightly as she tears up. "I don't know if I can do this! I don't know how I can lie to them for the rest of my life."

"We will figure this out. At least your family will have you back, we will manage it. I promise you, I will teach you how to live—both lives." Adriano kisses Rebecca's lips, caressing her face, and embraces her. "My beautiful Rebecca, you are home with me and soon you will be back with your sons, that is all that matters—*mon amour.*"

After a few seconds in Adriano's embrace, Rebecca releases herself. She feels restless and emotionally pulled down, and needs time to herself. She goes to their bedroom to lie down, needing space to process her life; the truths that need to be protected, the lies that need to be told. Her mind takes her back to that moment over a year ago when Adriano sat her down and told her that he was a vampire. Her memory begins to unwrap in detail that eventful day. Finding out he drinks blood to survive. Realizing she unknowingly brought a vampire into her family circle, around her precious sons. She remembers the anger, the feeling of betrayal. But also, how deeply she searched her soul, finding a way to accept Adriano's truth. She loved him. She trusted him with her life, with the lives of both her sons. And Adriano never failed her.

Small memories surface. At the oncologist, Adriano holding her hand. This trip to Paris, was a dream come true. He found her, he never gave up searching. Love accepts all. She found a way to rise above the secrets then, so she should be able to overcome this devastating challenge now. Rebecca thinks, *will my truth will be accepted too? My secrets and lies forgiven? These are powerful truths. Can I expect my sons to accept, one day, hat I'm a vampire?* Her thoughts prevent her from resting. She can feel the thirst rising, stress and anxiety weakening her resistance. She took very deep breaths.

In the meantime, Adriano is thinking of Jonathan's text. He takes out his phone and makes a call.

Rebecca isn't registering the fact that another gift she possesses as a vampire is the ability to hear at great distances. Up to now, this gift hasn't presented to her, but now she becomes aware that she is hearing the conversation that Adriano is having on the phone in the living room. The absence of other sounds and voices in the apartment make it easier for her to hear. She wants to listen in but then feels it is wrong. Besides, she is tired and wants to rest her eyes. As she drifts in and out of sleep, parts of the conversation weave into her ears but don't stay.

"I know I can trust you, thank you Jonathan for making this trip so suddenly. Okay, call me when you are at the airport. Salut." Adriano's mind is compartmentalizing, tracking lies and stories told, lies and stories still to tell. A thought suddenly panics Adriano. *Rebecca will be going home as a vampire, as a mom. She thinks she can just resume her daily life, her motherly role, tucking in her boys at night, going out to hunt? What if she craves their blood, what if she can't hunt and loses control!* His mind takes a quick detour; he feels something is unsettled and unfinished. Then it hits him, he realizes what it is-the important item that he pushed away and boxed up in his mind hour ago. He steps into their bedroom. Rebecca is up and standing in the closet just familiarizing herself with her clothes. "Rebecca, love—um—who is Sebastien?"

Suddenly as if all the blood just dropped to her feet, Rebecca stares at Adriano, her eyes wide and panicked. "Sebastien! Oh my God! I have to go back, he may be in trouble. Oh God—I have to leave now!" She runs past Adriano at vampire speed, barely able to control herself, and knocks down a vase on a small three-legged hall table as she races out the front door, not even taking her coat with her. Adriano is right behind her; he too is coatless, and he catches her arm before she opens the gate. Adriano is panicking; if she moves this quickly down the street, she could be detected.

"Rebecca—wait! I'm coming—I'm not letting you leave again. We can't just dash out, we have to make sure we are unseen."

"I don't care! We need to go—he's alone."

"Hang on. Tell me where we are going?"

"Saint Denis!"

Shock crosses Adriano's face as he registers the name of the town. This is where the car accident took place! He has no clue if she realizes this and he is too alarmed and worried to mention it.

"Let me go rent a car."

"No time—Sebastien could be in trouble. We must hurry!"

CHAPTER 7

Sebastien

Adriano and Rebecca pass cautiously through several unique Arrondissements. Restaurants and cafes are filled with an array of human activity. Adriano manages Rebecca's speed as she struggles to control her vampiric determination to run at lightning speed to St. Denis. Adriano isn't sure if a taxi would have been faster. They travel on foot great distances and as soon as they reach wooded areas or forests they propel through the woods with their proficient vampire legs. Adriano continues to keep a watchful eye for possible humans, but it's highly unlikely in the deep forest route they are taking. The sky is already turning dark. They pass several long and winding country roads running through different dense forestry areas, neither of them breaking a sweat. Adriano makes a mental note to himself—*Rent a car.*

They practically fly through the woods, leaving dust winds behind. Even the birds are startled by the strong breeze, and they flee their nests, squawking in annoyance at this evening disturbance. The vampires arrive at a long stretch of deserted country road, with many trees lined up on both sides. Using his vampire eyes, Adriano is relieved that no cars are travelling in either direction. This area is secluded. He is surprised that Rebecca seems to know her way, even though there are no street signs. Her direction-sense as a human was not good. Now she is leading the way confidently through these winding isolated roads. Adriano continues to stay alert and survey the area; there are no other houses around. The landscape is covered with mature trees, thick bushes, and some plants. *Ideal hunting ground*, he thinks.

They continue on another mile. Adriano catches sight of an architectural peak in the distance, not too far from them, but he can't distinguish yet if this is part of a building or a house; it is hidden by very tall, thick, mature trees.

Then Rebecca suddenly turns to the right, and they are now running on a long curving hidden driveway. Adriano sees the peak in full view, which he realizes is part of a large brown brick house with two large bay windows visible at the front. The exterior looks old and abandoned, although if one looks closely it gave the impression that at one time it was quite a spectacular home. It has large windows, a wrap-around porch, wood front double doors, and an attached two car garage. There stands a large statue a few feet from the home, but it is covered with snow and ice.

Rebecca stops abruptly. She hears a faint voice calling out for help, and then Adriano hears it too. In a panic, Rebecca runs to the front door, but it is locked. She realizes she left without her coat, and the keys were inside. She bangs on the door, pushing it with all her weight, but it doesn't help. Adriano is quickly at her side and pushes with all his strength. He busts the door open and his nostrils immediately flare, confronted by the distinct smell in the air. *Another vampire?*

Rebecca runs past him and Adriano follows. As she is about to leap up a flight of stairs Adriano grabs her arm. "Wait here!" His protective instinct in full force. He lets out a low guttural growl; his ocean blue eyes become almost black and his canines protrude. He is on alert, ready to attack.

Adriano leaps to the top of the stairs and he realizes Rebecca is right beside him. He looks back at her with a stern look, which she returns. Adriano is learning quickly that Rebecca is not going to passively sit behind the sidelines of her life anymore, she is not going to be afraid of the unknown. They both hear the faint moans coming from the room in front of them and Adriano quickly opens the door. He finds an elderly man lying on the wooden floor in a puddle of spilled jars of paint; there is a canvas and easel, also on the floor. Rebecca immediately enters but Adriano holds her back with his strong arm, blocking her from moving any further. All he knows is a male vampire is here, he has no idea if he poses a threat.

Rebecca is annoyed. "Let me through!"

"Rebecca, wait!" shouts Adriano in panic.

"Sebastien—it's me!" cries Rebecca.

Adriano moves in to inspect the vampire. "He is injured and weak but he's awake."

Rebecca quickly kneels by Sebastien's side. Adriano's protective instinct remains active and alert, but Rebecca ignores him. Her focus is on Sebastien. Adriano is about to move Sebastien from the floor, but Rebecca stops him. "Careful Adriano! Don't move him too suddenly, his bones are delicate—fragile."

Adriano picks Sebastien up very carefully, and Rebecca leads him to Sebastien's bedroom. Adriano notices an X painted in white on the door; he finds that odd, but he redirects his attention and lays Sebastien on the bed.

Rebecca is quickly at Sebastien's bedside. "Sebastien, I'm sorry—can you forgive me?"

Sebastien's eyes slowly open; they're opaque with a beige tint, as if they are tea-stained or like slushy muddy snow. Sebastien looks at Rebecca and he struggles to lift his weak thin arm. He touches Rebecca's face and speaks in a very frail and cracked voice. "You're ba-ck! Thank G-od—I was worried—Haz-el—Eyes. Where—were—you?"

Rebecca kisses his bony, gaunt cheek. Immediately Adriano steps in closer, observing the situation, as Rebecca gently pushes back the thin strains of silver and black hair on Sebastien's forehead.

"I am so sorry Sebastien. So much has happened, but you need to eat first!"

Sebastien just lays still, looking up at the strange male vampire who is glaring at him with intense midnight blue eyes standing inches from Rebecca. "Who—is—this?" Sebastien squeaks out weakly.

"This is Adriano—but never mind that." Rebecca quickly turns to Adrian. "Adriano please. We need to get him downstairs, he needs to eat." Adriano nods in understanding and carefully picks up the vampire, who is starting to lose consciousness. He moves swiftly down the stairs and Rebecca follows right behind him.

"Here—lay him on this couch. Sebastien, Sebastien can you hear me?"

Sebastien opens his eyes. His shaking arms extend into the air, and he looks past Rebecca and Adriano. His mouth opens. "Come to me James, please. Come."

Rebecca gasps. "He is hallucinating—this hasn't happened before—oh God, we have to hurry! Sebastien, stay with me."

Sebastien moans from the sharp and intensifying pain travelling up his body. His throat is very dry and tender.

"Adriano he's suffering, in pain—please! You need to hunt down an animal, he needs to drink quickly or he could die. I will stay here with him. Please go quickly—at the back of the house." Rebecca points with her finger towards the kitchen.

Adriano is torn between leaving Rebecca alone with this male vampire and hunting for him. He sees the fear and worry in Rebecca's eyes, then he looks at the vampire and realizes he is in physical danger. He races to the kitchen and out the back door, and at accelerated speed he runs into the woods.

"Sebastien, stay with me, you are going to be fine." Rebecca grabs a blanket from the La-Z-Boy near the fireplace and places it over him; he's shivering uncontrollably. His mouth opens again and in a cracked frail voice, "Jaammmes—Jammmes! Donnnn't leeeeave."

Rebecca is frantic as she sees his body is aging rapidly, she gently wipes the blood from the cut on his forehead and cheek that hasn't healed.

"Sebastien, please stay with me, listen to my voice, it's going to be ok, Adriano will be back soon."

Rebecca delicately holds his hand, mindful that any wrong move could fracture a bone. The minutes go by, but it feels like hours. Sebastien is in and out of consciousness. Rebecca is terrified that his heart may give up. Suddenly, Rebecca hears fast steps approaching from the back of the house. "He's back—stay with me Sebastien. Please."

Adriano hears Rebecca's panicked voice calling, "Hurry, Adriano, hurry!" He moves expeditiously into the room, holding a struggling rabbit by its hind legs and ears.

"Sebastien is too weak to sit up yet, please—bring the rabbit to him and hold it while I raise his head." Rebecca gently lifts Sebastien; he moans from the pain in his bones and throat, and the rabbit struggles with all its might. The scene is so chaotic that Rebecca doesn't think to use her powers to subdue it.

Adriano brings the rabbit to Sebastien's mouth. Sebastien smells the aroma of fear and life; his canines protrude and grow longer. Sebastien grabs the neck of the struggling rabbit while Adriano keeps a firm hold on the ears, then Sebastien quickly penetrates the jugular vein. The warm oozing blood flows freely into his wanting mouth. He moans, elated, and drinks in this nourishing liquid. Adriano observes as this vampire feeds. His own thirst tickles his throat, but no cravings rise. How very different it is to watch this vampire feed. When Adriano watched Rebecca, it was spectacular. Watching and listening to Sebastien's small moans of delight doesn't appeal to Adriano. However, for Rebecca, her own thirst awakens, the aroma of life and fresh blood teasing her own cravings. But she focuses on Sebastien, making sure he is getting enough.

All three vampires can hear the rapid beating of the dying rabbit's heart and smell the fear in its glands. The rabbit isn't squirming as much now, its life energy fading away. Sebastien completely drains the animal until the heart beats no more, then he releases the corpse and it falls to the wooden floor with a thud. Sebastien reaches over to the box of tissues and wipes his mouth. He lays there quietly, allowing the nourishment to settle into his body and do its magic. He is still struggling to breathe. His lungs reopen more with every breath. Seconds go by but it feels like eternity as Rebecca waits for a sign that his body is rejuvenating. Then suddenly, his breathing is steady, and his lungs feel stronger. His eyesight and hearing become sharper. His skin tingles as the cells rejuvenate. His heart is beating regularly and he feels more energized.

He sits up and smiles. His eyes are returning to their deep warm chestnut brown. Thin fine grains of ochre and tiny dark specks of crimson are sprinkled inside his irises. Adriano is amazed to see this incredible transformation. Minutes ago, Sebastien was an elderly man on his last breath. Now he looks like a man in his late thirties. The stunning realization sinks in for Adriano. *They both experience the same symptoms, transforming from elderly to youthful.* His eyes remain dark blue, and anger builds as he concludes, *- Tis must be the vampire that turned my Rebecca!*

"Thank you both," manages Sebastien softly.

Rebecca picks up the dead rabbit and both Adriano and Sebastien look at her. "Rebecca, leave it, I will go to dispose of it," Adriano says.

Sebastien turns towards Rebecca, hearing her name for the first time.

"Actually, Adriano, I don't want to just dispose of this rabbit. It deserves more respect, it saved Sebastien. I want to bury it. I just feel it is the right thing to do."

Adriano and Sebastien look at each other, confused. Rebecca picks it up and heads towards the back door, and Adriano and Sebastien follow her.

"So your name is Rebecca? I'm so used to calling you Hazel Eyes, it just seems more natural to me, I hope you don't mind?"

"Of course not, I like it when you call me that."

Adriano twitches. *So this is who started the Hazel Eyes nickname!*

The vampires leave the house. Adriano scans the area, he sees many thick trees and bushes all around the property. "Excellent feeding ground you have here."

"Yes, it suits well."

Rebecca looks around for the right spot. "Here" She lays the rabbit down gently under a large mature tree.

Sebastien walks towards the shed to find a shovel. Adriano just stands beside Rebecca, admiring her. At times, he still can't believe she is back with him. Sebastien returns with the shovel and begins to dig. He looks at Rebecca, smiling. Adriano catches this; he is becoming very curious about this connection shared between his Rebecca and this other vampire.

"I know we consume a lot of animals and they too sacrifice their lives for us, but this animal today truly saved Sebastien. He was really in danger—minutes away possibly from—from the unthinkable."

Adriano puts his arm around Rebecca "You never stop amazing me, *belle âme.*"

Rebecca leans in and kisses Adriano on the lips, lingering there for a few seconds. Adriano brings her closer to his chest and closes his eyes, absorbing the pleasant feeling stirring inside, losing himself for the moment in this perfect moment of connection with Rebecca.

Sebastien coughs purposely to politely disrupt this moment. His strength enabled him to dig the hole fast. "This should be deep enough."

"Thanks Sebastien." Rebecca places the rabbit into the hole. "Thank you little one, for your sacrifice today." Rebecca nods to Sebastien and he fills the hole with snowy dirt.

Adriano's phone rings and he signals to Rebecca to go on ahead, he needs to take this business call. Sebastien and Rebecca return the shovel to the shed and walk back towards the back door, and Adriano can hear Rebecca giggling with Sebastien. He suddenly feels uncomfortably warmer than usual.

"Do you need to drink Hazel Eyes?"

"I already did earlier, with Adriano. I feel pretty good."

"Yes, but you know our energy diminishes at an unusual speed, without warning at times."

Sebastien opens the door for Rebecca and they walk in. Seconds later, Adriano enters. Sebastien is still unclear who Adriano actually is to Rebecca; he extends his hand out to Adriano to shake. "I don't think we were properly introduced."

Adriano obliges, but he is still not sure how he feels about this male vampire. Sebastien leads them all back to the living room. The room is drafty, so he places some logs and paper in the fireplace and starts a fire. Within a few minutes the room feels toasty warm again. Adriano just looks around, so Sebastien gestures to him to take a seat on the couch.

Suddenly Adriano's phone rings again. He takes a deep breath, and after checking the screen he turns to Rebecca. "It's Joseph—I guess he has spoken with your parents." Adriano calmly answers the phone while Sebastien looks over at Rebecca with a confused and curious expression.

"Hi Joseph—fine thanks—no problem, yes she is here. Sure, hang on."

Adriano gives Rebecca the phone. Their eyes meet and he smiles with encouragement. This moment feels so surreal for Rebecca; it marks the beginning of the new unfamiliar road she is about to travel full speed. In this space she is her truth as a vampire among these two other vampires; one is her lover and the other her friend. On the phone she is another truth, a sister, a mother, and a daughter.

"Hi Joseph—yes I am fine. I hope they weren't too shocked? I know, thanks for taking care of that. Yes, I agree, thank you. Yes, I will call them right now. I will be in touch—okay, yes, you too, bye for now." Rebecca disconnects, deep in thought. Sebastien still doesn't understand what is happening, but he is becoming aware that she isn't abandoned as he thought weeks ago when he found her and took her in.

"You ready for this? This call may be the most difficult one yet for you," Adriano says.

"I know, honestly, I'm not sure I'm ready. But I can't put it off, they've suffered enough."

Rebecca touches Sebastien shoulder tenderly on her way to the room she was sleeping in. "I will explain later Sebastien, I just need to do this first."

"Of course, I understand, well actually, I don't really, but from both of your expressions it is quite serious, important, *family* stuff always is." As she left, he turned to the other vampire. "Adriano, can I get you some wine? Oh—do you drink wine? Or something else?" Sebastien is nervous alone with Adriano.

"I am fine thanks."

Sebastien slightly frowns, then excuses himself and walks to the kitchen. Adriano is more concerned about how Rebecca is managing on the phone. He can clearly hear her voice but struggles to hear the voice on the other end.

"Mom, I know it's not my fault but still, I'm sorry that I put you through all of this. Yes, I am fine really, I know, but trust me. Yes—tired mostly and still foggy with my memory, but it's getting better—I am grateful for that. Yes, I'm remembering more about him too— I know that. Oh, he knows that you appreciate everything he's done. It's okay, I understand. Poor little guys, it was a tough day for them today. Mom—put the boys on for me. We can talk again after, but I just need to hear their voices." Rebecca's heart begins to beat faster.

Adriano is worried, he doesn't want Rebecca overly stressed now that he is learning more about her condition. But she sounds so excited.

"Hi Adam, Ethan, so good to hear your voices! Yes, mommy is fine, just a bit tired, but I missed you both so much—I know but you just have to be a little more patient. I will be home very soon—I don't know the exact date yet—yes Adriano too, I promise. In the meantime, tell me what you have been up to? — It's okay Adam, let Ethan talk first and then you have my attention. I love you too, you can stay on the line Adam. So Ethan, explain to me again, you said you got a new Bionicle and you're preparing them for battle with Batman and Spider-Man ...?" Rebecca feels at peace, listening to her son Ethan share all his different stories and events. She can hear Adam once in a while trying to interrupt and get a word in. Rebecca laughs, she is so happy to hear their sweet voices again. But she feels this large lump in her throat as she fights back the tears, she doesn't want them to hear her becoming emotional.

Meanwhile, an awkward silence remains in the living room between Adriano and Sebastien, both doing their best not to listen to Rebecca's phone conversation. It's harder for Sebastien, who can hear both sides of the conversation. He turns the record player on to muffle the sounds. He's heard enough to put things together. Adriano recognizes the song playing: Heroes by David Bowie. He comments what a great song it is, and asks Sebastien what other types of music he has in his collection. Sebastien starts naming off some other bands.

Adriano notices pictures and art pieces hanging in the room. There's a large black and white photo on the fireplace mantel. He recognizes Sebastien at the entrance of the Louvre, but is curious about the older man snuggling into Sebastien with his arm around him. *Was he also a vampire? Or human?* Adriano is still adjusting to meeting another vampire after all these years, and now as he is looking at Sebastien, he just seems so normal. Not at all like the image that haunts him of the monster Signor Domenico.

Sebastien is still busy reviewing his albums. He seems a lot healthier now, muscle tone completely back. He stands a few inches taller than Adriano, with a thin, attractive stature. His hair is sandy dark brown, no longer grey and thinning.

Adriano continues to observe the room. There's very little seating available or even furniture, other than the large charcoal grey sectional he is sitting on and the black leather chair that Sebastien is now sitting on.

Adriano spots another La-Z-Boy in the far corner of the room. It almost seems as if it is hiding. He finds that odd; why wouldn't it be placed near the fireplace opposite the other chair? Then he sees a large long sheet covering something, possibly a piano, but the lighting in that corner of the room is so dim he barely noticed it. The coffee table too is very dusty; it appears to be missing something because there are several indents that would suggest a top layer was once placed inside the grooves. There are some tea lights and votive candles in holders. Adriano returns his eyes to the main area and admires the large wall-to-wall chocolate brown bookshelf behind Sebastien. It's full of both medical and fictional books. He notices there is no TV.

"You read all of these, they look like medical books?"

"Yes." A moment of silence returns, and they are both grateful to have the music playing in the background. Sebastien remains quiet, then he gets up with his empty wine glass. "You sure I can't get you anything Adriano?"

"Okay, I will try some of that wine—thanks."

"Sure, be right back."

Adriano occasionally tolerates wine, mostly red, but still can't acquire a taste for beer. He has noticed over the years that his tolerance for human drinks and even some food is getting better. In his first few outings with Rebecca, Adriano had no choice but to find a way to train his taste buds to accept human food again. The textures and spices were a challenge, especially with Italian cooking. At times he ended up spending a difficult night with stomach issues. He tried his best to hide this from Rebecca, and if the opportunity allowed he would sneak out to hunt. He knew the blood would soothe him.

Rebecca returns back to the family room, and Adriano can see that she is struggling to keep tears from escaping her reflective eyes. She sits beside Adriano and he kisses her, lingering a bit. "The hard part is always the first step, you did it."

Rebecca stays quiet. Sebastien returns to the room and hands Adriano a glass of red wine.

"Hazel Eyes—sorry, habit—Rebecca, some wine? I think you need it!"

"Sure, thanks."

A twinge of annoyance crosses over Adriano. He doesn't let it show, but knowing that Sebastien has this pet name for his Rebecca irritates him. He has questions and needs answers. Adriano observes Rebecca; she is drinking the wine and seems to be enjoying it. He is pleased. At least they can still enjoy a nice glass of wine together, just like a normal couple. He is curious to know what other human foods she can tolerate, but shelves this question for now; these stored thoughts are becoming quite cluttered in his mind.

"Is everything okay on the call Haze—Rebecca?" Sebastien seems annoyed at himself for not keeping her real name straight, correcting himself again. He can see Adriano looking annoyed, shifting in his seat.

"It was the strangest experience. I can't put it into words properly. I was listening to my mom's voice, but a part of me was trying to remember everything I knew about her, and there were blanks—the worst was with my sons. I could see their faces in my mind and their voices were familiar, but images mixed up, memories trying to come through, it was confusing." Rebecca takes a sip of wine.

"How old are your sons?" Sebastien's curiosity fails to register the important revelation, until a light turns on his mind. He swallows loudly, horrified, as he realizes he changed over a mother.

"Adam is—"

"Oh God—you're a mom!"

"Yes, I am."

"Yes, she is, Sebastien!"

Sebastien demeanor droops, hearing Adriano's anger. Rebecca is concerned as Sebastien's face turns pasty, as if whatever blood remained in his body from the feeding a few moments ago was being absorbed rapidly. The remorse and guilt wash over Sebastien's face. "I'm So so sorry. If I had known, I—"

Rebecca quickly kneels beside him. "Hey, Sebastien, you didn't know. Besides, would it really have made a difference? Your instincts were to save me! I know that."

"It should have been me!" Rebecca and Sebastien immediately turned to face Adriano. His eyes are fixed on Sebastien. "I need to know what happened and how, exactly."

"What would you like to know, Adriano? After all, you saved my life today—±did I thank you? My mind is a bit scatt—"

"Adriano, maybe we can talk about this another time." Rebecca sees how this tension is affecting Sebastien and she also feels stressed. She doesn't want to remember that moment she became a vampire. For now, it is a blank in her mind, she can create her own story around it. She's already starting to have flashbacks of seconds before the accident, she can't go there not now, it's too much. "I know you have lots of questions and I will—that is, *Sebastien and I* will try to answer as best as we can. But for now, can—"

"Rebecca, you have to know how much this is affecting me."

"It's affecting me too! I learned from you just hours ago that I have two small boys in Canada waiting for me! I'm a vampire. I'm a mom. Does that register with you? Can you imagine what I'm feeling right now?"

"It's my fault! I'm so sorry Rebecca! I just wanted to save you." Sebastien can feel the guilt growing roots inside. He feels lightheaded.

"I know Sebastien. It's no one's fault. We can't go back, so let's not focus on this. I'm alive, and I will be back with my sons."

"Christ! Rebecca—I need to understand, damnit!" Adriano stops, shocked at himself for his sharp outburst. Rebecca stands, but she still remains beside Sebastien. "Sorry, I didn't mean to yell." Adriano sees Rebecca's anger and disappointment. He puts his wine glass down on the coffee table, stands up and starts to reach for Rebecca's arm but then he stops. He excuses himself and storms out of the room, feeling embarrassed. The next sound is the front door opening and closing with a thunderous bang.

An uncomfortable silence takes over the living room, Bowie's *Ashes to Ashes* the only sound. There is a heaviness in the air. Rebecca takes a seat on the couch, agitated and overwhelmed. Sebastien fidgets nervously in his chair. He takes a sip of wine, but it tastes sour. He can't stand the silence.

"Rebecca, maybe you should go and talk to him?"

Rebecca stands up stiffly. "I am so damn exhausted! Sorry, but this is too much for me all in one day. Do you realize I just spoke with my family, my poor little sons? They were crying and asking when I was coming home and I couldn't tell them! What kind of mother doesn't rush to the airport grab a ticket and head back home immediately?" Rebecca places her head in her hands.

Sebastien stands up and takes a seat next to her, putting his arms around Rebecca. "A loving and caring mother who is processing the return of her memories and wants to make sure she does the best thing for her sons." Sebastien gently lifts Rebecca's chin. "Tell me honestly Hazel Eyes, do you think you can go home and just pretend you're not a vampire? Do you think you can just go on, hours at a time, ignoring the craving for human blood? Don't be mistaken, it will happen, you are still just a new vampire. This can be dangerous to your sons, your family." Sebastien is remorseful.

Rebecca gasps, her eyes become very large. "I wouldn't harm my children or my family! How can you even—" Before she can finish her sentence Adriano interrupts, his voice is steady and calm. Both vampires had been unaware that he had returned.

"Rebecca, Sebastien is right, you're not ready yet to engage with any human, you need to be able to control—"

"Do you think I can't control my thirst? I haven't killed a human! I haven't!"

Adriano sits down on the other side of Rebecca and takes her hand. "But you haven't interacted with them in such close proximity that their scent travels through your body, teasing you. Your ability to control your emotions is also affected when becoming a vampire. We can go from zero to one hundred without warning and it can be dangerous. It takes time to manage. When the thirst comes it can threaten your ability to gage your emotions accurately. You haven't been exposed enough to humans as a vampire."

"Adriano is right—I haven't been able to take you into the city among the humans. As a new vampire, even when you know it is wrong, the craving for human blood is there, deep down. It can destroy—" Sebastien pauses, deep in thought. "It can destroy you if you—"

Suddenly all three vampires turn toward the front door, hearing footsteps on the porch. Someone knocks. Sebastien gets up, relieved for the distraction. "Oh—Jacques must be here. Excuse me, I will be right back."

"Who is Jacques?"

Rebecca is too upset to respond. The front door opens and the scent of a human floats through the air.

"A human?" Adriano is curious.

"Yes, a human! Are you afraid I'm going to attack him?"

Adriano's hurt, and Rebecca realizes and feels bad. She adjusts her tone, whispering, "Sorry, Adriano."

"It's okay."

"I haven't met him yet. He's a friend of Sebastien. He comes every Friday to deliver snacks and stuff. This is his only human friend."

Adriano looks at her and a blank expression covers his face, whispering back, "Snacks?"

Rebecca continues whispering, ignoring the confusion on Adriano's face. "Apparently they met at a market when Sebastien was *human*. They've been friends ever since. I haven't met Jacques yet. Sebastien obviously agrees with you, he doesn't think I'm ready to be trusted with a human." Rebecca knows her tone is curt; her kinder side is losing its battle.

Adriano tries to ignore her tone, "Why would a vampire need snacks delivered? Am I missing something here? And I agree. You are not ready."

"I know my movements are too quick, but Jacques would understand, he is used to Sebastien. I am sure I can control my blood craving." Rebecca takes a sip of her wine, feeling agitated.

Adriano is still processing that a human is delivering snacks to a vampire. It takes little effort for Adriano to listen in.

"I hope this scented shaving cream will be okay for your skin, it's a new brand, if you don't like it or if the scent is too overwhelming—"

"Thank you, Jacques, it smells nice. Oh, come in, I want you to meet some friends." Sebastien walks back in the room with a young man wearing a white winter coat with a blue toque and scarf. Rebecca stands up too quickly. Jacques is startled momentarily, and Adriano quickly reaches for Rebecca's hand.

"Jacques, these are my friends—Adriano and Rebecca. They are from Canada."

Jacques is immediately aware he is standing in a room with only vampires. A shadow of anxiety crosses over him.

"Hi There—nic-c-ce to meet both of you." He looks at Rebecca "So-o-o…you're the mystery woman."

Adriano doesn't let go of Rebecca's hand.

"Yes—nice to meet you too Jack—I mean Jacques. Thank you for the groceries."

"No problem, you can call me Jack."

Rebecca smiles. Adriano can sense her uneasiness.

Jacques can't help the sudden embarrassing crackling in his voice. "Sorry, I haven't come across other—well you know. Oh! Not that I am worried or anything, I don't think you are dangerous—that is not what I mean, that is—"

A wicked smile creeps into Sebastien. "Jacques, relax, you are fine—we just *ate*." Jacques quickly turns to Sebastien pale and confused. Adriano and Rebecca are shocked at Sebastien, who bursts into laughter, smacking Jacques' shoulder. "Kidding!" Jacques laughs nervously, almost hysterical, and Adriano and Rebecca chuckle.

"Good one Sebastien—sir, you ha-a-ad-d-d me for a s-seccond there. W-w-well I'd b-better g-get going, bye!" Jacques quickly makes his way to the front door with Sebastien.

"Hang on." Sebastien reaches into his pocket and pulls out two hundred dollars and gives it to Jacques. It's from the secret stash that he and James had saved up. They were saving to either renovate and furnish their home, or create a proper lab in the basement. He sighs heavily to himself.

"That is too much sir—for berries, wine, soaps, and deodorant"

"No, you do a lot for me."

Jacques whispers, not realizing he can be heard by all the vampires, "Sebastien, are you sure you don't want me to get you one? It's no problem—you know it would make your life easier, you could text me too, in case you need anything."

"Thank you, but no—I don't need it. I don't have a reason for it, anymore."

"Sure you do. I'm worried, it's been two years since you've isolated yourself. Trust me." His voice becomes withdrawn. "The grief can eat at you. I see it all over you."

Sebastien, holding back emotion, bends down to the box of groceries and begins to rummage through it.

Jacques's voice dips to a very sad level. "It's hard to believe my brother has been gone all these years. I've seen what our loss has done to my parents. I know it was difficult because we never found the body—at least those two are reunited. I can tell he loves her, I see it in his eyes. Please, I don't want to see you become so void of life."

Adriano and Rebecca can hear everything, and Rebecca turns up the volume on the stereo, not wanting to eavesdrop.

Sebastien stops combing through the items and looks up towards Jacques. "Don't worry about me. I'm so sorry Jacques, the pain you must feel." Sebastien can't take too much more. He can feel the heaviness dwelling in his heart. He stands up, reaches into his pocket and pulls out another hundred dollars and gives it to Jacques.

"What's this?"

"I want you to take out the girl you mentioned last time."

"Denise?"

"Right, Denise—please, life is too short. Trust me. Enjoy the connection."

"Thanks, sir. You sure you are alright?"

"I'm fine."

Then Jacques sees Adriano walking towards them. It makes him very nervous and he quickly moves out of the house. "Bye!" He runs quickly down the long snowy driveway, calling over his shoulder. "Same time next week, sir?"

Sebastien waves back, hollering, "Yes, see you next Friday Jacques, and—it's Sebastien. Please, we have known each other too long for sir."

Sebastien closes the front door and picks up the box of groceries. "Where's Rebecca?"

"Oh, she just went into the washroom."

"Need anything?"

"No, thanks." Adriano looks around. "This is a really big place you have here."

"Thanks, well go sit down, I will bring in more wine." Sebastien picks up the box of groceries and brings it to the kitchen and begins to unpack the items. He tries to ease his mind, but wishes he was alone to allow his emotions to be.

CHAPTER 8
Marbles and Pet Rocks

Juliette is sitting outside under the gazebo. She is wearing a thick pink cashmere turtleneck over dark grey corduroy pants that were ordered for her as instructed by Louisa. She has her sketch-book out. Brief moments of last night try to invade her mind, and a tear rolls down her cold cheek. Suddenly she hears footsteps in the snow and quickly wipes away the tears. She looks up and Veneur is coming briskly towards her. He enters the gazebo, his tone soft and endearing.

"There you are, I was looking for you."

"Oh? Are Martha and Guy finished cleaning or am I needed inside by Louisa?" Juliette's voice is heavy and sad.

"No—they are still at it. Never mind that, I just wanted to see how you are?"

"I'm still here. I just needed to get away from all of it…them."

Veneur looks her over, he is worried Juliette is slipping into a melancholy. "I heard you crying last night."

"Oh no, I'm sorry, I tried to—did *he* hear me? That would explain Bianca's cruel words to me this morning. You're right, she is mean and hurtful."

"No, he was occupied with Louisa, she was nagging about something. And don't feel you have to apologize for your true feelings, this is what makes you more remarkable, human in some ways."

"Human? That is stretching it."

"You have more humanity than many." He continues to observe her. "What are you doing?"

"Nothing, just trying to sketch a bit."

"That's good, I'm glad you are using your creative outlet." Veneur can feel her distance and it worries him. "Jules, be honest, how are you-—really?"

"What am I to say?"

"Jules, talk to me. I know last night was—"

"See those trees over there? I can't seem to capture their essence. I've been sitting here sketching and sketching out the details of each of the lines on their bark and the exact number of branches and yet it just seems so hard to get their exact image on this paper. I mean, they deserve to be admired, they suffered cruelty this winter. I want to let them know they matter."

"Jules, look at me."

Juliette slowly turns to face him. Her eyes are so distant, sad and troubled. "You should really call me Paula, that's what I am meant to be. I find Juliette and Jules too confusing."

Veneur is very concerned now, he can see Juliette is shutting down. "Let's take a walk. We both need a change of space."

"I can't Ven. I already went out yesterday. I can't be asking to go out again."

"I mean just around the property, that is allowed."

"Sure, okay."

Veneur takes Juliette's cool hand and they walk slowly around the property. They both take a seat at Veneur's childhood swing, still standing strong, and they just rock back and forth.

"Did I ever tell you what my dream is?" Veneur asks.

"No."

"I told you my uncle Theo was a publisher. Well, he was really devoted to helping writers, especially ones just starting out. He actually developed a reputation of accepting some unsolicited manuscripts at our door, and many times he would do just that. He figured if someone was brave enough to meet him face to face with their manuscript, then they deserved to at least hand over their pride and joy to him directly. He was very kind and respectful. Sometimes he even let them in, so he could learn more about their writing journey."

Veneur stops talking, his mind brings him back to the dark event that sealed his fate. A haunting image surfaces, a knock at their front door. His uncle Theo opens it and sees this older gentleman with dark dull eyes, dressed in an old-fashioned shabby suit, carrying a vanilla envelope tightly to his chest. His Uncle Theo mistook this stranger as a fragile elderly man desperate for someone to read his manuscript. Veneur remembers his Uncle Theo inviting the man into their home. His mind keeps injuring him with the memories of what happened. He entered the library, saw scattered blank pages on the floor. The open empty envelope beside it. His uncle lying dead on the floor, the warm fire, the elderly man hovering over his uncle's body. Veneur remembers the blood drops coming down his uncle's neck and falling onto their shiny hardwood floor. Then he sees the stranger turn around and stand up, snarling, with his red-stained protruding teeth. The next thing Veneur remembers is after he turned, the physical pain, the incredible craving for blood, the emotional agony. The threats from Enzo. The commands to dispose of his uncle's body into the woods. Suddenly Veneur clasps his hands against the side of his head.

"Veneur, are you okay? What's wrong?"

Veneur wipes his eyes. "Sorry, just gathering my thoughts, where was I?"

"You said your uncle invited some writers into his home sometimes."

"Yes. Anyways, I would watch him pour over these unsolicited manuscripts for hours and hours. Some were pretty good for first drafts, others we just felt so bad for the writer. I learned a lot from him. He always encouraged me to journal and that is where I developed my love of writing and seeking out the best words to present on paper.

"Did you ever write anything? A story?"

"Yes, short stories mostly. He thought I had the potential, I felt it too. —I was going to take creative writing at university, at least that was my plan until ---Enzo" Veneur stops talking.

Juliette sees Veneur's expression changing, she realizes that Enzo destroyed his dream, and then she sinks back into her own rising despair.

"I'm going to write one day, Jules. I have a lot of experience to write about, and no one will stop me."

"What would you write about?"

Veneur takes a deep breath. "Us."

"Us—I don't follow."

"Our lives as vampires."

Juliette stands up abruptly. "What? Are you crazy!" Juliette screeches, her eyes filled with fear.

"Ssh…Jules, calm down." Veneur lowers his voice to a deep whisper. "I've thought a lot about this and something is compelling me to do this."

"But it's dangerous, we would be exposed," whispers Juliette, mindful of their surroundings.

Veneur can help but grin. "You assume that humans will actually believe my story? This is the beauty of it. All of it will be considered fictional when I present it to a publisher. They will eat it up. At least I hope so. My uncle Theo always said to me, the best writers are those who write about what they know. Well hell—I know a lot about this subject. I have to do this. I hope you will support me."

"I don't know what to say, of course I want to support your dream. At least one of us will have a chance at their dream—but it is risky."

"I haven't forgotten about your dream, Jules. I'm working on it."

"You said that before. I need you to explain."

Veneur moves in closer and whispers directly into Juliette's ear. "Our passports have arrived, they are sitting in a P.O. Box that I am renting."

"Our passports? I forgot all about them—but wait, you said Master asked for us to get these prepared in case we need to move, because of the vamps. Was that a lie?"

Veneur feels really warm suddenly, flushed. "Yes."

"Ven—how could you lie to me? You're the only one I trust and you lie to me?" Juliette rises abruptly, angry and betrayed.

"Jules, I had to. I knew if you knew my reason, you wouldn't complete the forms. I told you I don't plan on living like this much longer. It is destroying both of us!"

"You are putting both of us in danger!"

"You think I would do that to you? I know what I'm doing. Enzo will never find us. He barely leaves the house anymore, even to hunt, his paranoia is getting worse. I really think there is something mentally wrong with him. Odd, since he is a vampire."

" I don't care! You can't expect me to do this. He will hunt us down."

"Calm down, I've thought this through carefully. When the time comes, we will grab a taxi and head directly to the airport—and board a flight to the U.S."

"U.S.?"

"Yes, we can't move anywhere else in Europe or the U.K. I've read a lot about places in the U.S. and I think we would disappear easily in a small town. I personally like living near the mountains of Colorado or Montana even. I've even checked out parts of Canada. Jules, we can do this. We just have to be smart and careful."

"I don't believe this. When are you planning this?" Juliette's voice is cracking and sounds frail, and her hands tremble.

Veneur doesn't respond. He can't tell her because he is worried that her emotions will reveal something and make Enzo and Bianca suspicious. He only shared his plan with Gabriel, who is helping to make this happen and hoping that he too can escape, and join them later.

Veneur looks at Juliette; she is so frightened. He is regretting sharing this with her, risking his plan.

"Ven? Did you hear me? When is this happening?"

"Still many things to work out, so you will have to be Paula for a while still." He hates lying to her again but he has no choice, this is too dangerous and he has to keep a lot of this close to his chest.

"How would we live? We have no money."

"Yes, we do."

"What—how? That's not possible."

Veneur feels it is time to share a secret he has kept for over a week now. It was his birthday recently and he turned twenty-five years old. But birthdays don't matter anymore. He finds it difficult at times to process that he will forever be in an eternal state of twenty-four years old. He leans in very close to Juliette and whispers, "I received a call from my uncle's lawyer.

He not only left me his house and any money he had, he also was wise enough to set up a trust fund for when he was gone. It's a lot of money, more money than his own savings. I found a way to sneak out the other night and I signed the papers, and instructed that these funds be moved to an offshore account until I am ready to transfer them safely to a bank. Why do you think I am so confident that we can do this? Let's drop it now, I don't trust us talking about this here."

Veneur stands up. "I'm trusting you with this information."

"Do you think I would tell anyone?"

"No, of course not, but your emotions could. Please, we have to be careful. I need you to act normally, well, you know what I mean. This is our lives." Veneur has an expression of hope, and it touches Juliette. For a moment she can almost imagine a beautiful life elsewhere, oceans away. But then fear creeps in and Juliette begins to feel strained.

"I can't think of this anymore."

Veneur feels he needs to distract Juliette, he knows this information is a lot for her to handle. "Can I show you something personal to me?"

"What? Sorry, I'm so tired, I think I just want to go lay down. You have shared so much and it is all so overwhelming."

"Okay, but just this one last thing, then I promise I will give you space, if this is what you need."

"I don't know what I need."

"Come on, I think you will like this, if it's still there."

"If what's still there? Ven—I can't handle more secrets from you right now."

"Come on, humour me, this one will give you a nice memory if you want to see into my childhood."

Veneur takes Juliette's cold hand and leads her out of the gazebo. They walk towards the other side of the property. He hasn't thought about his old childhood tree house in years. He hopes the elements didn't completely destroy it over time or that Enzo didn't order their handyman Guy to dismantle it. As they get closer, he is relieved to see it is still in the tree. He smiles as he climbs the tree effortlessly, in two brisk movements, without needing the wooden ladder his uncle installed for him years ago. He breathes in the crisp winter air and looks around the outside of house to see if it is sturdy enough. He opens the door, and it is filled with spider-webs and dust. He calls down to Juliette, "Hey, come up, it's great up here. Trust me."

"I'm not up to it."

"If you don't come up I will have to come and get you. Come on, please?"

Juliette sighs, but she sees how happy Veneur is and she clings desperately to this beautiful moment. She takes hold of the branch and begins to climb effortlessly. Veneur clears the cobwebs from inside and enters, and Juliette can hear him rummaging through his stuff,

"I can't believe it, I completely forgot about this. Man, the things I used to collect." He comes out carrying a little red toolbox and sits on the thick branch beside Juliette. He places the box on his knee and opens it. He pulls out a spotted grey and white rock, then he reaches back in and picks up two googly eyes that once were glued to its flat surface. He carefully places the dried googly eyes on the flat surface of the rock and presents it flat in his hand.

"What is it, you got—rocks?"

"Not just any rocks, these were my pet rocks."

"Pet rocks?" Juliette can't help but chuckle.

"Yeah, what—you never heard of pet rocks?"

"No." A slight smirk leaves Juliette

"Well, this is Henri."

"Henri? You named your rock?"

"It's a *pet rock*, of course. Here, hold him."

Juliette grins and takes the rock.

"Gently now, he's old." Veneur is privately smiling, happy to see Juliette is still here with him. He reaches back in and pulls out a white rock, dusts it off, and finds two more googly eyes inside the box. He places them on the rock's flattest surface. "This one is Marcel. The conversations we would have, you would not believe."

Juliette can't help but laugh. "Were you that lonely as a child?"

"No, not at all, I just had a great imagination. I didn't have pets, my uncle was allergic, so I found my way around it."

"If you say so—did you share these friends of yours with others?"

"Nope. This was my secret."

"Good. What else is in that box of yours—you nut."

Veneur feels joy, it's as if his heart is relaxing and smiling. And it's working, she is laughing. "Here, hold Marcel." Veneur reaches back into the box and pulls out a yoyo, a rusted yellow toy sport car, and some marbles.

"Marbles, oh I always wanted marbles. I saw some girls at the orphanage playing with them, they used to trade them. Oh, let me see these. Here, take back Marcel and Henri for a second. Ooops, be careful, watch their little eyes, don't lose them."

"Ha ha! See, you're already becoming attached to my rocks. They grow on you, as soon as you see their eyes you are hooked."

Juliette smiles, shaking her head side to side. She dusts the marbles off and wipes them on her corduroys. "Oh gosh, they are so beautiful, once you wash them off."

"Keep them—I want you to have them, they're yours."

"Really?"

"Absolutely."

"Thanks Ven." Juliette continues to admire them; her troubled mind slowly being released from the grip of horror that was washing over her minutes ago.

"What's wrong, you're tearing up?"

"Because of you—you are so sweet and yes, I admit, I like your pet rocks too."

"Shall we get down now?"

"Yes, I want to clean these up."

"Okay, sounds good."

"Oh, bring Marcel and Henri. We'll glue their eyes back on."

Veneur feels satisfied, he did good, at least for Juliette, at least for now. Somewhere in his mind he knows that these childhood trinkets he is sharing with Juliette are working a miracle. They are giving her a gift to take with her in her life as she sits in her very first tree house holding marbles and pet rocks with her brother Veneur. Even Veneur's mind is absorbing the beautiful winter landscape spread across their property. Veneur has given Juliette a small precious piece of her own childlike experience that she can enjoy anytime as an adult. But Veneur needs to continue to work on her fear of leaving this house, for soon his plan will be in action.

CHAPTER 9

Vamprogeria

"What's this?" Adriano politely asks as Sebastien returns to the living room, places a bowl of mixed nuts and another bowl of mixed berries on the coffee table, and sits in his La-Z-Boy.

"I thought maybe a snack would be nice. This was a special thing we used—" Sebastien suddenly pauses and readjusts himself on his chair, speaking in a more subdued voice with a forced a smile. "Please --help yourself."

"Thank you, Sebastien, we haven't done this too much recently. This is a nice way to spend the evening. Too bad the wine has no effect on us." Rebecca smiles, taking a strawberry and some nuts in her hand.

"Yes, I do miss that truly relaxed state that wine had on me. But some human pleasurable routines are just difficult to let go or dismiss entirely. I think it is important to hold onto the ones that can still hold some kind of value, personally. I'm sorry that I haven't been my best host these past few weeks. I do enjoy these moments of normalcy and connection. I have to thank you for reminding me of this, Hazel Eyes. Ever since you came into my life, I have noticed a difference in myself. It feels good to talk and share. I do enjoy your company."

"Aww, it's okay, we were strangers and yet you took me in. You know, I don't think you and I really have gotten to know each other until now. The amnesia didn't help. I didn't even know about my own life these past two months. I am learning more today about you, your life and my own life. Actually, we owe it to you, Adriano. If you didn't find me, who knows if any memories would have returned?"

"Yes, thank you Adriano. You helped me discover more about this wonderful woman."

"Sebastien, I hope you know how much I appreciate all you have done for me. You have been so kind and generous to me. You are very special to me."

"Aw, stop it—you bring it out of me."

Adriano is growing irritated. *I begged her months ago to let me turn her and she refused, and now she is just fine with Sebastien, who turned her. How can Rebecca feel so relaxed at being a vampire? She has no clue what complexity awaits her.* He feels a sudden burst of uncomfortable heat in his body as he is sitting on the couch, and his jaws clench so tight he feels a pain in his temples. He takes in a deep breath. *I need to focus on the positive.*

"Adriano? You are so quiet, just sitting there. Don't be shy, try some of these strawberries, they are still quite tasty. I wasn't sure at first if I could still enjoy these."

"Sorry, it's been a while since I've sat down like this drinking wine and snacking." Adriano observes Rebecca; she seems more relaxed and calmer. He can't figure out why Sebastien just gets under his skin sometimes. Adriano decides to let the irritation he has with Sebastien go. He wants to feel calm and just enjoy this little bit of peace. He puts the wine glass down, takes a handful of nuts and raspberries, and smirks quietly to himself. *Groceries.* He takes a strawberry and offers it to Rebecca, who takes it. Adriano feels better; the air between them is warmer now. Adriano crosses his legs and sits back on the couch. "Rebecca, what other foods have you noticed you can tolerate?"

Rebecca swallows the last bite of the strawberry. "Oh—I haven't tried too many other foods. Sebastien just orders nuts and berries."

Sebastien looks over to the chair in the dark corner. How he misses those little romantic gestures. "These are just fillers. There is no nourishment here. Please, remember this—it is important."

"Yes, of course—hey, are you okay? You seem—"

"Hm? Oh. No, I am fine— so please tell us Haz—Rebecca—how was it meeting Jacques?"

Rebecca is not sure what to make of Sebastien's hot and cold behavior. She takes a sip of her wine. "It was odd. I mean I was so nervous. Strange, just because I'm a vampire, I'm suddenly feeling weird around a human. He seems nice. I didn't know if I should attempt to get up to shake his hand, but see—I didn't crave him. I can control myself. He seemed extremely nervous around us. I hope I didn't make him uncomfortable?"

"Oh no, not at all—he is shy that way. I'm sorry, I didn't give you much warning. I thought it was time to test the waters. I wanted it to be as natural as possible."

"Maybe we should expand a little more and go out for a walk around the city tomorrow?"

"Adriano has a good idea, Hazel Eyes. You should get out there, mix with the crowd. The noises and smells will be challenging enough. You need to practice your body movements. Jacques almost fell over when you stood up so quickly. Don't forget, to a human, seeing that kind of speed is hard for their brains to process. It can make some dizzy if not prepared."

A thought suddenly beckons loudly for Rebecca. "I want to go home. Back to Toronto."

Adriano sets his wine glass down on the coffee table "Rebecca, we discussed this. We—"

"I don't care. You don't know what it feels like. You're not a mom."

"You're not ready!" shouts Adriano. Sebastien is suddenly uneasy.

"Don't say that! You saw me with Jacques, I was fine. My sons need me!" Her tone expresses her frustration, her worry. "You didn't hear them on the phone." Rebecca stands up and moves at vampire speed to the guest room, slamming the door.

There is an obvious unease and awkward silence left for Adriano and Sebastien to navigate, but Adriano doesn't wait long. He gets up, harshly places the wine glass down, and goes to knock at Rebecca's bedroom door.

Sebastien remains in his chair, just staring at the wine in his glass, not sure what to do.

"Rebecca, please let me in, let's talk."

Both vampires can hear Rebecca sniffling. Sebastien can't stand it, and he comes up behind Adriano, gestures to let him have a try. Adriano reluctantly moves aside. Sebastien scratches the door lightly, like a small animal hoping to be heard. "Hazel Eyes, it's me—can you open the door, please? You know this stress isn't good for you, and if you are stressed, I will be too." The door remains closed. "Please, I'm sure we can talk about this. Stress is not good for either of us—please?"

A few seconds later the door opens, and Rebecca steps out. Both male vampires just watch her.

Adriano stands to the side of Sebastien. "Rebecca, *mon amour*, please let's talk."

Rebecca moves back into the living room followed by Sebastien and Adriano. She takes a seat on the couch. Sebastien grabs a tissue and hands it to Rebecca. Adriano sits beside Rebecca, but her body language is reserved, she is not inviting him too close.

"I know you want to go home, it hurts me to see you like this. But *mon amour*, there are still things we need to work out, organize, prepare you for."

Rebecca looks at him, her eyes holding back tears, her body stiff. "Once I am home, I can figure everything out—I need to be with my sons."

"Rebecca, *mon dieu*! You're not thinking this through. How will you hunt? You work full-time downtown, you live in an apartment, you are not near woods. You can't live by yourself anymore."

"What?! What do you mean?"

"I think Adriano meant to say, you shouldn't be on your own. Of course, you can be, but it is really not recommended."

"Sebastien, I *did* mean that she can't be on her own. Please don't assume that I mean something else. Thank you."

Sebastien is losing his patience. He sits back in his La-Z-Boy, suddenly feeling scolded. The air in the room feels stuffy and unwelcoming.

"Sebastien is right. I am very capable of living on my own in my condo. I've done so for several years now."

"Not as a vampire. A very big difference. And not as one with a condition as yours. *Mon amour*, be reasonable. It will be a challenge already living in a condo. Very little privacy. Trust me, I know."

"Hey Hazel Eyes, I just noticed, you said you live in a condo—you remembered that—that's good."

"You're right—my memory is returning. Slowly, but it's happening." Her eyes light up with hope. "I remember my condo. In Brampton."

"That's great, *mon amour!*" cries Adriano in delight. The room seems to be feeling light and fresh again. Adriano delicately continues. "But it's a small unit. You can't add any more space or storage to it. You may need to purchase a small fridge for an extra emergency supply."

"Supply? Of what?"

"Blood," is simultaneously spoken by Sebastien and Adriano.

Rebecca is growing anxious.

"Don't worry, *mon amour,* we will figure this all out. I will teach you." Adriano's eyes become bright suddenly, it's almost as if he is excited knowing Rebecca needs him. He misses being her hero. "But all in good time. We have to find you a new place where you can hunt easily, like this set-up here that Sebastien has."

Rebecca's whole body feels as if she is suddenly slipping into a dark cave. Her world, her life, is crashing in on her like a heavy boulder falling off a steep cliff. As the reality sinks in deeper, the complexity overwhelming. "Move? Oh God, how will I do this?"

Adriano tenderly takes her hand. "Don't worry, *mon amour*. I have been thinking about all of these things. I want you back with your sons as soon as possible. Believe me-I want our lives back to normal."

Rebecca stands up too quickly. "Normal? Nothing is normal for me anymore. Too many changes. I'm feeling overwhelmed." Rebecca's energy is slowly draining from her body, her spirit wilting as her thoughts circle in a loop of confusion. Her hands shelter her head and fatigued mind.

"Where do you live, Adriano? Can she stay with you for now?"

Rebecca releases her head from her hands. "No, my sons need to stay where they are. Their father and I agreed we would stay in close proximity while our sons were young and in school. I can't change that—I won't!"

Adriano takes her hand gently, holding it. "It's okay, Rebecca, don't get upset, come sit down, you need to remain calm. I know you have that parenting arrangement. We will find a place close. I have been in touch with Richard, my real estate agent. He is looking for a house that is close to a wooded area or backs onto a ravine."

"But even with the money I make once I sell my condo, I won't be able to afford a house. Never mind behind a ravine—the mortgage will be too high!"

"I know, I will help you."

"No. Adriano, I can't let you do that!"

Sebastien squints and squirms in his seat. He is not used to this yelling. He can't remember a time that he and James ever raised voices to one another. Their disagreements were conducted in a civil and medium tone, with the mutual understanding that yelling gets you nowhere.

"Rebecca! For God's sake—I can afford it! We need to be rational!" Adriano feels this day wearing him down. "I'm sorry, I didn't mean to yell, and it's been a long and eventful day for both of us. We are both emotionally worn out—let's talk about this *privately*, later, with fresh clear minds." Adriano puts his arm around Rebecca, bringing her gently into his chest. She is too mentally fatigued to respond.

Sebastien takes the hint, and suddenly he feels like the third wheel in his own home. He is craving alone time.

Rebecca's mind is racing with ideas; she's determined to figure this out. *I can do this. My sons need me.* Out of nowhere, Rebecca gains a surge of positive fortitude and will. "Okay, I will give it a few days so we can figure out the details. But I plan to be back in Toronto no later than next Friday. That gives us a week to prepare me, whatever that means." Rebecca sits back down on the couch, followed by Adriano.

Adriano kisses her on the cheek. "Thank you, I promise you we will sort this out. I have got your back, *mon amour.*" Adriano runs her hair affectionately through his fingers. The energy in the room seems to be returning to a natural calm.

Sebastien falls into his own moment of sadness; he misses the warm affection touch and comfort from his James. Sebastien takes a sip of his wine. "So Adriano, are you staying in this part of St. Denis while you are in Paris? This area is quite secluded."

"No, I have an apartment in St. Honoré."

"St. Honoré—that's curious."

"What do you mean?"

"What brought you out here? It's quite a distance? I mean, how did you find Rebecca out here? Did you plan on hunting this far out?"

Adriano sips his wine casually. "Oh, actually it wasn't around here, I found Rebecca just behind the Eiffel Tower, she was—"

Sebastien chokes on his wine; in shock he turns his eyes towards Rebecca. "*Mon dieu*! Eiffel Tower. Rebecca! You travelled that far?! What were you thinking? Are you crazy?!"

Adriano suddenly stands. His eyes darken, a threatening growl emerges, and he points his finger harshly at Sebastien. "Do not speak to Rebecca that way! Lower your voice, vampire!"

Sebastien is shocked at this sudden rude outburst from Adriano, but he adjusts his tone immediately, and in an apologetic voice turns to face Rebecca. "I am sorry. I meant no disrespect to you, Hazel Eyes." He is aware of his deliberate use of the name. He is standing his ground with this male vampire who is showing disrespect to him in his home. "Sorry—it is just very dangerous to travel that far—I mean by yourself. You are still a new vampire. I dread to think what could have happened. But it is partly my fault, I just haven't been up to travelling outside of this area. I was worried about our energy travelling long distances until you were ready to be around humans without anxiety or cravings. This disease can be so unpredictable and dangerous if not prepared."

"Disease? What disease are you talking about Sebastien, vampires are not diseases!"

"That is not what I meant, Adriano!" Sebastien is growing more annoyed, irritated, and determined to stand his ground. It's like watching two male wolves demonstrate their dominance over each other. His tone aloof and curt. "It is complicated to explain."

"Enlighten me." Adriano's glaring eyes fix on Sebastien.

Sebastien places his wine glass down with a bit of aggression. Annoyed and flustered, he takes both hands and brushes his hair to the back of his head aggressively, trying to steady his tone. "I was waiting for the right moment to tell you this, Hazel Eyes." His eyes shift sternly towards Adriano, and he sighs. "It is not going to be easy to hear. But I can see delicacy and timing are not Adriano's forte." Sebastien suddenly is propelled back in time to a teachable moment he learned from James. He realizes this is one of those moments. He has to be mindful that vampires have an extraordinarily heightened emotional response, and this can affect their ability to reason rationally when presented with obstacles or in this case a challenger. Sebastien is suddenly aware of his own tendency to overreact or become easily offended by others. He must find his calm space inside and approach this situation with Adriano with calm and ease. He takes a deep breath, but it is interrupted immediately,

Adriano is steaming. "Just tell us, for God's sake."

Sebastien can't contain his temper. "Fine. We have vamprogeria!" He waits, and the room is paused momentarily. He is not surprised. Adriano and Rebecca both look at each other, confused.

Rebecca politely speaks up. "Sorry, what did you say?"

Sebastien feels his confidence returning. "We have vamprogeria. The disease I was referring to."

Adriano looks confused, and Rebecca's eyes show concern. Sebastien feels for her. She is about to learn another shocking fact about her life. "You probably didn't think that vampires can have diseases, well neither did I— until I met this amazing brilliant man, Dr. Huntington." He glances over to the chair in the corner but it is empty. He clears his throat and continues in a more matter-of-fact voice, looking at both Adriano and Rebecca. "Have you heard of the human disease called progeria, by chance?"

Adriano shakes his head side to side. "No."

"I didn't think so." He can see he is irritating Adriano and he feels empowered again in his home. It is up to him now to lead, and as a scientist he feels intellectually superior to this male vampire who is obviously physically stronger than him.

"What is progeria and vamprogeria?" asks Rebecca, her instincts warning her that this is something dramatic, but she doesn't know what.

"I will explain. Progeria comes from the Greek word *pro,* meaning "before" and "geras" meaning old—it is a human disease, but is not common like cancer, diabetes, Alzheimer's, and so on. It can occur at an early age or later on in life in very rare cases." Sebastien pauses, giving them a chance to digest this information. He is feeling more at ease speaking in his scientific tone. It has been a long time since he could feel and speak like this. "The main symptom is premature aging. Well, Dr. Huntington discovered that he inherited the vampire's version of this disease, through his blood-linked benefactor, and we eventually gave it the scientific medical term vamprogeria."

Adriano interrupts. "Wait? What? Blood-linked benefactor?"

"Yes, that's what I said. It is the scientific term we developed to explain and identify the genetic and cellular connection between the vampire's blood and the blood of the human they turned—I will get into that part in more detail later, but for now, I need you to both understand vamprogeria and how dangerous it can be."

Rebecca interrupts. "Sorry, but trying to follow, Dr. Huntington is a vampire too?"

Sebastien continues keeping his tone professional, holding back the emotions as he gets up and takes the photo from the fireplace mantel; he noticed Adriano was looking at it earlier. "Yes, that is—*James*."

"Sebastien—that's the name that you were calling out earlier. You were hallucinating."

Sebastien runs his fingers through his messy hair, privately asks himself, *Was I hallucinating or were you with me, James?* His tone becomes sober. "I don't remember, Hazel Eyes, but it is possible—the disease plays cruel tricks with the mind when the thirst is not *satisfied*. Anyways, *James* specialized in progeria. However, once he became a vampire he finished his medical degree as a scientist in biology and dedicated a large portion of his time to researching the condition shared now by myself and Rebecca. He gave it the scientific name vamprogeria. I have the greatest respect and admiration for Jame—Dr. Huntington."

"How did you meet?"

"Rebecca, never mind that—Sebastien, tell us more about this vamprogeria."

Rebecca feels a bit hurt that her question is being dismissed. She is just trying to ease Sebastien into sharing. She can see the emotion on his face, how affected he was when he touched the photo of James. A sudden flashback returns to Rebecca, but she cannot understand the context of it. She sees herself sitting at her family kitchen table when she was a young girl, and feeling invisible, her voice unheard, as conversations happened between her siblings and her parents.

Rebecca feels annoyed suddenly.

Sebastien notices; he too is not pleased that Rebecca's question is being dismissed. He turns directly to speak to Rebecca. "We met one day when he was dropping off some blood samples to my lab. I am a clinical pathologist."

"A clinical pathologist? Sorry, but you will have to explain."

"No apologies necessary, Hazel Eyes. Basically, I study diseases through examining body tissues, liquids, blood, etcetera. Anyway, I am sure you can imagine how difficult and frankly impossible it was for us to find any reliable and authentic research on the existence of living vampires. There were no medical journals, books, or archives that we could find and we searched thoroughly. We had nothing to rely on relating to vampires' anatomy and physiology, disease history, or health and wellbeing. There was no previous medical data to compare and analyze DNA or blood cells of a vampire with vamprogeria, nor were there any markers to indicate a precondition existed in the human who became a vampire, nor in the vampire with vamprogeria who turned them; what we call in a more scientific term the blood link donor, though benefactor is fine too.

"We could not find documented medical data to explain this vampire disease or anything specific to vampire's genealogy at all. The scientist in us knew not to expect to find any data or medical journals about vampires, but we didn't want to lose hope. Unfortunately, though our scientific minds prevailed, there was nothing about real vampires. This angered and frustrated both of us so much and at times jaded my—uh, Dr. Huntington. We knew vampires existed, so we knew there was an origin of the vampire species going back centuries! But the reality is we would have been shocked if we did find anything officially written in medical textbooks because how can we exist in medical books if, according to humans, we don't even exist as a different species."

Sebastien's voice is becoming louder; he stands up, his demeanor stiff with frustration, waving his wine glass in the air. Almost spilling drops, he begins pacing the room. "Humans refuse to accept the fact that vampires have existed since possibly the beginning of mankind. They see all of us as these soulless predators like fictional characters and in movies. It's simply not true. Just like humans, there are good and evil among us. Vampires are no different. Yet our kind are all cast under this one ugly umbrella that we are just killers. The various misconceptions and myths about us are astounding."

"Well I know the one about us burning up in the sun is false—we won't disintegrate," grins Rebecca.

"Although some vampires have been known to develop an allergic reaction if exposed to the rays," Sebastien says.

"There is one aspect of the vampire that frightens me."

Adriano looks concerned. "What, *mon amour*?"

"Immortality. Don't get me wrong, I appreciate that I will be around for a very long time, but once my sons live out their long lives I can't imagine just going on and on once they are gone. No offense Adriano, but it's different when you're a parent. It's hard to describe. No parent wants to see their child go before them. It frightens me to know this is part of our journey as vampires, we see our loved ones leave us in the future."

The room becomes awkwardly silent. Sebastien is shifting uneasily in his chair. "Actually, Hazel Eyes, it's a misconception that we are immortal."

All eyes are on Sebastien.

"What do you mean?" interrupts Adriano. "I've lived past a human's life expectancy already. I'm healthy as can be. Good luck trying to kill me—us."

"I realize this is difficult for a vampire to comprehend, but your beliefs have misguided you. From the beginning of time organisms have lived and died. It is the natural cycle of existence to all living creatures. The planet could not sustain itself otherwise. Anything that lives will die eventually, by nature or *other*. Immortality of the physical body for vampires is a myth; we are just as vulnerable to death's coming. It is to our own psychological detriment to believe otherwise. Our life expectancy reaches far greater than that of humans, of course, but *we will* eventually come to our end. It is just a longer journey until that end arrives, at least that is what we expect. And where this myth came from that we cannot be killed is beyond me." He pauses, careful not to reveal too much in his expression and tone. "Mind you, it is extremely difficult, almost impossible, for a human to kill us. They can't sneak up on a vampire and attack him, only a vampire can sneak up on a vampire."

Sebastien is beginning to feel the strain of this difficult conversation, but Adriano is curious to learn more. "So how would a vampire kill a vampire? Not to sound morbid, but it is interesting—and difficult to imagine."

Sebastien offers more wine and both Adriano and Rebecca extend their glasses and he fills them, then fills his own glass and sits back down on his La-Z-Boy. He looks over to James' chair, which remains empty. He is relieved; death is not a subject he wishes to discuss in front of James.

"Well, actually, a vampire can kill his own kind a few ways. Of course, the most obvious way to kill a vampire is the stake through the heart." He laughs loudly. "My God—of course this will kill him. Anything piercing our hearts will kill us, it doesn't have to be a wooden stake. I mean really, how ridiculous, right?" He taps his goatee, his mind combing through the various demises of a vampire by a vampire. "Hmmm...let's see, ways to kill a vampire—oh, here's one, a powerful vampire, I mean one gifted with extreme physical strength—" He pauses, aware that Adriano has this gift of strength; he witnessed it earlier while they were hunting, comparing the unique set of gifts they inherited. Showing off between each other. Adriano lifted a medium-size boulder with little effort and moved it beside another tree. When Sebastien tried, he only managed to lift it a few inches off the ground. Sebastien knows he is stronger than humans but not stronger or as strong as Adriano.

He clears his throat. "A strong vampire can drown another vampire if they become weakened or subdued. You might not know this, but a vampire will become almost powerless if they are bleeding out severely. Then there is hanging them, but it's very difficult to restrain the hands. They would need to be chained up in thick unbreakable chains." Sebastien continues on with such methodical processing in his mind.

Adriano and Rebecca are listening intently. Sebastien continues, "Necks can be snapped or broken, as the neck bone does not automatically reconnect or re-align. The myth or misconception that our necks just snap back into place kills me." Sebastien stops pacing and picks up the photo of James from the mantel; holding it, he returns to his chair.

Rebecca turns to Adriano, whispering (though Sebastien hears perfectly), "I have to say, I'm guilty of believing that some of these myths were true. I feel silly now."

"You mean you believed in real vampires?" Sebastien looks shocked.

"No—I mean, not until I met Adriano, of course. But I was fascinated with the myth growing up, the legend of the creature. I was kind of a goth enthusiast for a long time—especially the legend of vampires. I'm sure neither of you believed vampires existed?"

"I didn't even watch those monster movies. I was more into science fiction myself."

"Why am I not surprised?" smirks Adriano as he takes a sip of wine.

Sebastien's eyebrows cross, and his smile turns into a frown. *Go to your calm space,* he thinks.

Rebecca gently slaps Adriano's shoulder. "Adriano, be nice."

"You see, this is what I mean. Even we vampires didn't believe in our own kind until we became one ourselves! We are all guilty of this. Our ancient ancestors are to blame for a lot of this."

Adriano takes a sip of wine. "I don't follow?"

"We shouldn't have to wait until someone becomes a vampire to realize we exist! But that is how this is for us. This is why James and I were so frustrated. Precious time was wasted with every dead end we came to when trying to research factual medical vampire history. We appreciated why some vampires felt abandoned, even by their own kind, when it came to hunting and staying well nourished. Not all vampires make great stealth hunters. And with the condition we have, the frequency needed to drink can be relentless. James and I were struggling to manage our own condition with this disease and also be scientists."

"I have a question—if you worked in a lab, wasn't blood supply at your fingertips? That is—I assume you and Dr. Huntington would have brought blood home for your own use?"

Sebastien stands up, not responding yet, collecting his thoughts. He places the frame back in place and sits back down. He is feeling restless. "Unfortunately, you assume incorrectly—but I can understand your thought process and how that seems like a logical strategy for us—however, the blood supply from the animals that were kept at James's university lab was never brought home for us to consume. This was test tube stored blood that had been poked at; the plasma was divided, moved around, and mixed with other chemicals. Not very appetizing. It was our work ethic to not cross boundaries between the life substances we needed from blood and the blood samples we collected for experiments. Both James and I made that ethical agreement as scientists. As James used to say, 'The real nourishment comes from the blood kept hidden in the veins beneath the skin.'" Sebastien maintains his scientific tone, avoiding bringing in too many personal emotions to the information he is talking about. He is not sure if he is ready to share more personal aspects of his relationship with James, but it has been a very long time since Sebastien felt a small glimpse of social normalcy returning just with this action of sitting around the fire, drinking wine, and enjoying the company of others.

During the first few days and weeks with Rebecca, his time was spent adjusting her to being a vampire both physically and mentally. The hardest was getting her used to the taste of blood; it was still foreign to her, but her body craved it even though her mind wanted to refuse it. Sebastien taught her how to hunt and discover her unique gifts. He didn't know her real name because of the amnesia, and he wasn't in any hurry for her to remember anything. He wasn't aware himself that deep down, he was afraid she would leave and he would be alone again.

Sebastien sips his wine, sits back in his chair, and lets out a calming sigh. "Aww, this is nice—just sitting here talking and sharing in my home." His voice drops lower, his body wilting as thoughts darken his mood. How he misses this with James; their quiet evenings alone, listening to James's selection of Bach or Beethoven, or Sebastien's array of singers including Kate Bush, Sarah MacLauchlan, and Bowie, and soundtrack pieces like Kiss from A Rose.

Rebecca notices the tears building in Sebastien's eyes. "Sebastien— everything okay?"

Sebastien waves his hand politely, indicating he is fine and not to mind him. "I'm fine—thank you Hazel Eyes." Sebastien shifts in his recliner, wondering if James will be okay if he shares parts of their life with Rebecca and Adriano.

"James means a lot to you. The way you talk about him tells me your relationship is very special. Your eyes light up with such admiration and love—where is—" Rebecca is suddenly distracted by the flame on the candle sitting on the mantelpiece. The flame is moving rapidly as if it is in distress—or is it joy? Out of nowhere, a cold breeze travels into the living room and touches Rebecca; she reacts with a quick shiver.

This doesn't go unnoticed. "Oh! Are you cold, *mon amour*? Is there a draft somewhere? "

"It's strange, suddenly I just got this unusual chill all over my body, but I am not cold?"

Adriano takes the blanket from the back of the couch and wraps it tenderly around her. He's feeling concerned. *Maybe her symptoms are rising again?* "If you are thirsty we—"

"No, I'm fine, thanks sweetie—sorry Sebastien, please continue."

Sweetie? How long has it been since Rebecca has called me that? Too long. Adriano feels close to Rebecca once again.

Sebastien notices their connection and feels the sting of his own loss of affection and connection. He runs his fingers through his hair again, holding back a heavy tear trying to escape from his eye. He soothes his emotional injury with another sip of the wine, but the lump of sadness forming in his throat urges him to look across to the other chair. He sees the spirit of James now occupying it. He is dressed just the way Sebastien remembers him the day he died. James always groomed himself, and hygiene was very important to him; he dressed his best even if wearing his lab coat. At night when they were alone in the lab, they would find themselves desiring each other. James would tease Sebastien, whispering quietly in his ear while kissing his neck, "*You find me sexy because you are wondering what is beneath my lab coat, ahh! The mystery is the hidden treasure just for you, my Seb.*"

At this moment the ghost is wearing his favourite pair of black jeans and a grey shirt, and his beard is trimmed very short and neat, just the way Sebastien liked it. Sebastien doesn't care to be the scientist at this moment; he allows his mind to consider the possibility that he is really seeing a ghost.

"Don't get me wrong, we did have our disagreements, dark moments, secrets. James had difficulty sharing all of his experiences with me." Again, Sebastien glances back at the spirit still sitting and listening, a warm smile of encouragement showing through his ghostly transparent face. Sebastien clears his throat and continues. "And I didn't want to force him to let me in. I thought when he was ready he would let me in. Share his dark period in his life, share the pain and heal." Sebastien pauses, deep in thought, swirling the wine in his glass as if he is searching in the deep red liquid for past memories with his lover James to surface, so he can be carried away momentarily by their magical charm.

Sebastien hears the ghost whispering again. "*I am deeply sorry, Seb, for not letting you in. I know it was difficult for you to deal with my emotional walls at times, and the nightmares. But I didn't want you to have images of the horrors I saw; I couldn't bring your mind and thoughts into that darkness of my past. I wasn't ready to speak of that horrible time out loud. But now my Seb, I see how my secrets hurt you, made you feel my walls. Don't make my mistakes! These vampires could be your friends, and your road back to living. You have punished yourself too long—and for no reason, it wasn't your fault! It breaks my heart to see you carry this burden of unnecessary guilt! You couldn't have prevented the inevitable, this disease is relentless!*"

Sebastien straightens up in his chair; the room is filled with respectful silence. Sebastien's eyes stay on the other chair, but the apparition of James vanishes in a blink. The room now feels cold and dark to Sebastien. If he could only have said, "*A bien tot*" or "*A plus tard, mon amour.*" But he couldn't, so he keeps talking, temporarily pushing away the grief and memories of James's ghost, who rarely visits him anymore. "Dr. Huntington was a great man and scientist; he deserves to be known, and I haven't done well in that regard."

Rebecca leans forward, speaking gently and with care across to Sebastien. "We appreciate you sharing."

"Wait, what do you mean, he was a great man? Sorry, I don't mean to be insensitive, but from what you have shared, James is no longer here?"

"I don't want to talk about it."

"Oh Sebastien, it's okay, we don't mean to pry—do we, Adriano?" Rebecca gives Adriano a look to back off. Adriano complies, but is fuming inside.

Panic sets in for Sebastien; he can feel his body temperature rising in anxiety. He realizes he said too much. "In fact, I need to hunt. Hazel Eyes shall we go?"

"Yes, I think we should hunt—Adriano are you coming?"

"Yes, I will join shortly, go on ahead. I have to make a call." Adriano waits for Rebecca and Sebastien to leave. His curious mind compels him to call Jonathan, but he doesn't want to leave him a voicemail message. He decides to text him instead.

Hey Jonathan,

Need some help. Find out what you can about Dr. James Huntington, Medical Scientist. I don't know the University, but I assume one in Paris.

Private. My eyes only. Specifically, when/how did he die?

See you soon. Safe travel.

CHAPTER 10

The Others

Sebastien gets up to change the album and put on Les Misérables, and Rebecca recognizes the song playing.

"Oh, *Bring Him Home*, such a beautiful song—I saw Les Misérables in Toronto years ago, what a performance. Oh, I remembered! My memory is coming back more and more."

They all smile.

Meanwhile, Adriano sits quietly, his mind absorbing and processing what he has learned about vamprogeria. Suffering through a thick cloud of anxiety, he tries to keep himself present, repeating in his mind, *this too shall pass, this too shall pass.* He knows what complexity awaits Rebecca back home now that she is a vampire. And with a rare and dangerous condition. But what Adriano can't seem to shake off in his puzzled mind, is why Sebastien didn't answer his question about James. *Where is he? Did he leave? Or is he dead?* Adriano is growing suspicious. He thinks, *I need to approach this at a different angle.* A question comes to mind.

"I am starting to understand more about this complicated disease. Did James ever meet any other vampires who had vamprogeria?"

Sebastien sits back in his chair and takes a long sip of his wine, the significance of the lyrics not missed by him. *If I should die, let me die, let him live'*. He gathers his thoughts to respond to Adriano's question. Sebastien feels at odds within—how much should he reveal? "No, unfortunately not. However, as he explored different caves hoping to find more vampires to interview, he at times came across some dwellings." Sebastien's tone dips. "He found skeletal remains—of vampires."

"How could he tell—the teeth perhaps?"

"Precisely, Hazel Eyes, but also more gruesome ways. Some bodies were not fully decomposed, so there was evidence that they died of severe malnutrition. Their skin was so thin and translucent, their eyes sunken in, and they showed that particular indescribable greyish milky hue that happens to some vampires if they become dangerously malnourished."

"Oh, how awful."

"Yes, it was difficult for James to remove these images from his mind, it affected him so much. He found remains at times with broken arms or legs or necks, and he could only hypothesize that they died a horrible painful death—alone." Sebastien takes a sip of wine. "He didn't know what caused these vampires deaths—did another vampire attack them and break their bones, making it difficult for them to hunt? Possibly, but difficult unless they were overpowered somehow, injured first. Or maybe they were swarmed by a group of vampires. James sometimes found a skeleton lying outside the entrance of the cave. It disturbed James to see the conditions many vampires were forced to live in, then die alone." Sebastien pauses, his own anxiety of isolation and loneliness creeping in. "These poor souls never had a chance. Ostracized just because they had different needs. There might have been such great special gifts from each of them that were never appreciated or carried on into new vampire generations." Sebastien pauses, sips his wine, and sighs heavily.

"Sebastien, is everything okay? You seem quite troubled, if this conversation is upsetting—"

"Thank you, Hazel Eyes, your kindness and understanding are deeply appreciated." Sebastien runs his fingers through his hair, clearing the lump in his throat that has returned. "Sorry if I seem out of sorts—where was I? Oh, right. James continued on. He hoped that these were just unfortunate circumstances that happened to these vampires, and he was on a quest to find more vampires, hoping to find them in better living conditions and health. The caves were depressing. He journeyed on. He was determined not to lose hope of finding vampires who had made a better life for themselves out in the world. He was hopeful he would encounter like-minded individuals in academia or in other fields of interest, including corporate or labor sectors. James didn't believe it was healthy to isolate oneself for long periods of time. He thrived on engaging with others; he told me once that his dream was for a society with harmonic coexistence and respect between humans and vampires. He believed that with proper discipline, training, and education, vampires could evolve and overcome their weakness for hunting humans. He believed strongly in this because it was possible for him, for us. He didn't turn me right away. We started out as colleagues, then friends…from there it grew, and a couple of years later I knew I wanted to be with him as a vampire couple."

Adriano jumps in. "I have two close friends who are human, Sandra and Jonathan. Rebecca and I were together while she was human. I engaged with her family and friends. I worked among humans at different Universities in my career. I deal with humans on a regular daily basis—James's dream is possible, it has been possible for years. It is just not known. The struggle is that we don't know about our own kind, we don't have the social network to connect vampires with vampires to learn from each other."

"But I think we are all forgetting one important difference: we can only survive on blood. However, we do have a choice. We can take from animals, we don't need to take from humans." Rebecca is surprised and stunned by what she just said. The last few weeks she just did what she needed to do, it came naturally, but she never stopped to really digest the full reality that she needs blood to survive now. Not any human food or beverage source is useful to her anymore. *An image of her sons startles her, my **god** can I still cook, how will I hunt?*

"You're right, Rebecca, it is a choice, vampires do not need to kill humans for their blood. Unfortunately, there is no scientific data or evidence available to support that human blood is more nutritious and healthier for us long term, it is more speculation and who knows, maybe it's even psychological. James and I chose to drink from animals—he told me when I was just turned that I was like a wild teenager that he had to watch carefully. It's odd, I don't remember everything from the very beginning, the early days and weeks of my vampire rebirth. Just some moments, ones that stay with me, *always, I can't forget.*" Suddenly his mind grabs hold of him and propels him back forcefully to a fateful night. He sees an image of a young man in his twenties walking out from a nightclub, and then the next image he sees is himself standing over the corpse and panicking. He removed the wallet from the victim's pocket, and inside he found the man's ID; but then his heart dropped. There was a little pocket photo of the victim and someone Sebastien knew. He frantically took the wallet and ran back home to James.

Sebastien bites his lip hard; a tiny bit of blood escapes and he licks his lips, holding back the emotions of the dark secret that haunts him. "It is different between vampires, as I mentioned before; when vampires take from each other it is for other reasons. It can be quite an intimate affair."

Adriano feels very uncomfortable with the conversation about consuming human blood. He isn't sure if Rebecca remembers this secret he told her months ago, and now he has to worry that Sebastien, if he finds out, will create unnecessary drama. This is a very private part of Adriano's life, and he doesn't want to be exposed to anyone else. He knows that this could jeopardize his friends Sandra and Jonathan; they know he kills humans, and they came to terms with this difficult truth. Adriano is aware that he will have to revisit this conversation with Rebecca again, but not now, not today. He refocuses his attention, listening as Sebastien continues on.

"It is important that you both understand this: vamprogeria forces us to drink blood from its source to completion. It is very rare that we can just take a drink here and there from the source and then just let it go free. Our needs force us to drink all the blood in its body. It's a pity. But it's the only way we can sustain our thirst as much as possible between feedings." Sebastien reaches over and picks up some berries. "Adriano, do you drink animals to completion? I didn't notice while we hunted earlier."

"I never really thought about it, but yes, I guess I do. The more blood intake, the better I feel. However, I don't have the same risks as you two do—if I miss a feeding for a few days or more, it's okay."

"A few days? I can't imagine that, sometimes between hours is difficult. Vamprogeria is so unpredictable."

"I know, that must be difficult, Sebastien. And for you too, Rebecca." Adriano steers the conversation back to James. "Tell us more about James, his adventures."

Sebastien takes another sip of his wine. "My James was such a curious one. He decided to travel to parts of Eastern Europe. He believed there was some truth in those folklores. He thought it might be worth it to visit Romania and then travel towards Transylvania" Sebastien's voice becomes animated as he talks about James. "James thought it would be amusing to explore obscure shops that catered to the folklore for the amusement of tourists. He said he came across a lot of garlic strings, statues of vampires, plus posters, jewelry, and trinkets. He was amazed—centuries later and the legend of vampires was still very strong amongst the locals. There was one aspect of his travel he didn't enjoy, and yet in the older towns it kept happening."

Adriano is curious. "What was that?"

"The older townswoman and -men he passed on the streets would stop and gasp. With their hands covering their mouth, they would immediately make the sign of the cross as he passed them. He didn't know what to think of this; he couldn't believe that they knew he was a vampire. He did his best to blend in with the humans, so this really troubled him and made him feel uneasy and unwelcome. The only theory that made sense to him was that these older human generations were extremely superstitious and heavily brainwashed into believing in the legends of the vampire's character. Their customs and beliefs fed their fears and superstitions, so any stranger who seemed a bit odd was cast as something evil. James was upset and disturbed by their whispering, expressions of fear, and the speculation in their eyes. He left and moved toward the forests, out of Transylvania and toward the mountains. He felt free and uninhibited using his vampire gifts, and enjoyed scaling with ease up the jagged rocks and boulders of the Carpathian Mountains. The way he described this incredible movement, the textures of the rocks, breathing in such thin air the higher he climbed, knowing that only vampires could do perform such a feat with little danger involved—it all gave him such empowerment. At times, I admit I was a bit envious of the adventures he experienced, and hoped one day I too would experience them. But I haven't had the need to scale anything—I did climb tall trees with very little movements, and jump back down with ease. But to actually scale a mountain; that is incredible! Oh, My James, what an extraordinary soul."

Sebastien briefly falls into a state of reverie, but then he hears Rebecca's voice. "Wow, Sebastien, that sounds amazing! I can't even imagine going down a rollercoaster—well, while I was human that is, not sure now, that would be interesting, my kids would love that. But never mind—to scale a mountain is incredible." Rebecca chuckles with great enthusiasm.

Adriano jumps in eagerly. "I have scaled some buildings myself over the years, it is quite an exhilarating feeling, I have to agree! To be looking down at the ground from a vertical position, and yet having such control of your body to move with ease up or down. That is one trait as a vampire I treasure. But I agree, a mountain beats that. Maybe we should put this on a bucket list." Suddenly they all break out in laughter. Adriano takes a sip of wine and leans into the couch more relaxed, his eyes expressing interest.

"Please go on Sebastien—this is so fascinating," Rebecca says.

Sebastien chuckles. "You're too cute Hazel Eyes."

Adriano shifts uncomfortably on the couch.

Sebastien's eyes lit up and he takes a sip of his wine, feeling as if he is releasing trapped memories. He continues, his voice light and lively. " It wasn't until Slovakia that James encountered his first vampire. His name was Count Bernard the Second, Count B as James nicknamed him." He chuckles. "It was all starting to make sense to James, why there was such unfriendliness towards him in his travels. And he learned so much more about our history. Fascinating information."

"Oh, tell us."

Sebastien smiles warmly at Rebecca. "You see, this vampire, Count B, he was a Blood Master, very ancient."

"Blood Master? I've never heard of this—Adriano? Have you?"

"No, can't say I have."

"Vampires at one time were very traditional, and they had honour codes and commandments and titles within their vampire tier; this is one of the reasons Scions were established. Vampires needed to re-establish their place in aristocratic society. If they were Counts they were called Count, Master, or Blood Master. These titles were important and reinforced. Scions and titles elevated their status within vampire social tiers. Scions gave them a chance to create a new familial group. They really had no protection individually, since many of them lost their human families. Unfortunately, there were tragic cases of new reborns whose cravings were so strong, they fed on their human families."

Rebecca feels a sudden lump in her throat, disturbed and worried.

"These tragedies of course created a lot of terror in the villages. I know it is easy to blame the vampire, but you have to look deeper. Do you really think if they knew what they were really doing they would drink their own wife, child, sibling? They had no clue what was in store for them. The power of cravings cannot be explained until experienced. Many thought they were going mad."

Sebastien stops to take a sip of wine; his throat is starting to feel a little uncomfortable, but he doesn't want to lose this momentum. He can see the effect he is having, and he knows James would be satisfied to know that Sebastien is sharing unfamiliar ancestral history. "Anyway, many of these vampires were treated like monsters, and so they would act like it, and breed more monsters. They became unstoppable, stealing gold, silver, any valuables. They were clever; they bought property elsewhere where they were not known and then sold and bought and kept doing this, getting richer and richer in the process. It became a sign of power for the Master Bloods to have humans fear them, and they would feed on them to keep the fear alive. They knew they could feed from animals but it was almost beneath them to do so. It was also a cruel and severe statement they were making to humans. Unfortunately, these powerful vampires weren't insightful enough to realize this behaviour would eventually disadvantage future generations of vampires, and make us feel like we have this horrible secret about ourselves. Here we are in the twenty first century and we still have to hide our true identity, and only a few of us are lucky to have found human friends who accept us and support us." An image of Jacques comes to his mind. "Count B was shocked to hear that James was a scientist, and lived and worked among humans. He told James about the different vampires he had encountered in his life and the proper traditional titles they had, as well as the proper greetings that was to be used depending on the era they reined in. You see, the scientist in James knew this was his opportunity to research with his first willing participant—Count B."

Sebastien pauses, taking a sip of his wine, and continues. "Count B shared some fascinating accounts and personal experiences about his own life as a vampire. For instance, he explained his own theory about why many vampires avoided walking in the daylight. In his case, Count B avoided outings during the day because he was tired of enduring the harassment and harsh name calling he experienced in his village. He was a count, and still he was disrespected. You have to remember we are dealing with an era where the power of the church was undeniable and dangerous. These high priests did not like that some of these counts and warriors were powerful, charismatic, and more financially secure than the priests. They needed their parishioners to fear these males, so they brainwashed them to the point of mass hysteria. They called them demons and evil creatures of the night, the undead—you get the idea. Ignorance breeds ignorance, and unfortunately it didn't take long for humans to mistake some of these behaviours, such as avoiding sunlight, as signs these were sinners, evil incarnated, who could not be in the light. Well, fear and disharmony grew on both sides. Over time, some vampires were angry and emotionally tired of the abuse, and decided to behave in offensive ways. This included showing repulsion and aversion to crucifixes, bibles, or other religious idols. But this just reinforced the stigma that they were evil. Count B went on to tell James of vampires who actually manifested burns on their skin when they tried to touch a religious idol or crucifix. Of course, they were cast out of society, and forced to move further away. Some went towards the mountains, while others—"

Adriano cuts in. "I guess I'm lucky I don't live in those times. My favorite psalm is twenty-three, it sits at my bedside table at home. I carry a crucifix with me, I have for a long time. It hasn't yet burned my skin." He grins, pulling it out from his pocket, taking another sip of his wine.

"Oh, that is beautiful," Rebecca says. "I collect rosaries. My mother brings one back to me each religious trip she takes to visit churches. Oh—I collect rosaries—I remember this."

"Amazing! See, in no time your memory will be back." Adriano smiles.

"Sorry Sebastien, please continue, this is fascinating."

"I'm glad you are interested in our history Hazel Eyes. It is good to know about our ancestors. I was also glued to my seat as James told me more. Of course, he did it so well, so much more animation and enthusiasm."

"Oh, you are doing just fine, I'm waiting with anticipation, please go on."

Sebastien chuckles warmly, smiling. "You're so sweet Hazel Eyes—okay, okay. Where was I?"

"Some had to move up in the mountains," Adriano said, growing slightly irritated once more.

"Oh, right, so I was going to say, unfortunately some vampires had psychological issues develop after they turned. Some were convinced that their skin and eyes were burning if they touched or were exposed to religious idols, bibles, or crucifixes. The guilt and anger they felt for craving human blood and acting on this was devastating to them. What we would professionally diagnose today as PTSD."

"This really provides a new insight into what vampires lives were like back then."

"Yes Hazel Eyes—becoming a vampire is an enormous life changing experience. Unless you're willing to change your life so drastically, it can be very traumatizing for those who find themselves turned from human to our kind."

"You mean like Rebecca?" interrupts Adriano, aware that he hasn't yet resolved this peacefully inside.

"Adriano—that's not fair—I'm not traumatized. Please go on, Sebastien." Rebecca gives Adriano a stern look; she is not impressed.

Sebastien feels the lingering sting of this provoking comment, once again Adriano trying to antagonize him. "It's okay Hazel Eyes." He swiftly shifts his eyes directly to Adriano. "Your turning was beautiful and necessary for your wellbeing. I saved you. You're my blood link, a bond we carry together." His eyes move back to Rebecca. "I'm glad I was there to help you through this."

Adriano feels the sting of that fact, his agitation growing stronger.

"So anyways, many vampires were forced to move further out, abandoning their homes and families too. They couldn't talk about what was happening to them, even to their loved ones. They were afraid they would be hunted."

Rebecca picks up more berries from the bowl. "This is fascinating, don't you agree Adriano?"

"Hmm… Oh, yes, go on." His eyes at times glance at his cell phone to see if Jonathan has responded.

"Thank you. You see, Count B was described to me as a very ancient, malnourished, and lonely creature. James was surprised but glad the other vampire spoke English, and wasn't sure if and how he would be welcomed into the cave."

"Cave? I thought he was a count, wouldn't he be in some rich place, a castle?"

"You would think so Hazel Eyes, however, that was not true for Count B. He was living in misery. He was desperate for contact and he welcomed James. He was almost too trusting. James told me how difficult it was to see the horrible conditions this vampire lived in; the foul stench of bat urine was so strong that he found it hard to breathe or stay in the cave for long. But he didn't want to offend this ancient vampire who was so removed from society. James tried to encourage him out of the cave into the fresh mountain air, and it worked for a bit, they managed to find a mountain lion. James was fascinated to see how Count B, being from the much older generation; hunted. It was beyond words according to James. This is a real account from James, he wouldn't lie to me—he said that Count B actually created a mist around them and it travelled to the mountain lion, which was watching the vampire very carefully. Count B moved with such speed that James did not even realize, and all he heard was this intense growling coming from the lion and then nothing! James could not believe what he saw, the vampire just moved in the blink of an eye!" Sebastien looked across to the recliner that belonged to James to see if his ghost would return now that his adventures were being talked about, but the chair remained empty. Sebastien never knows if and when the ghost will return, and fears there will be that one last one someday.

"You mean like snap of fingers and he is out of sight?" Rebecca's eyes widened with interest.

"Yes, like that! I was stunned when James told me this. Count B wasn't too surprised when James said he didn't have this gift to create mist or transport instantly. Count B explained that most of the much older generation vampires known as the Master Bloods possessed this particular gene that allowed such instant teleportation, and the ability to create a mist from the powerful energy surrounding his body. He spoke of other gifts that some possessed, and hoped that their strength in these gifts would pass on through bloodlines generations to come. James couldn't reassure him, as he hadn't met other vampires to see what other gifts passed over. Count B mentioned gifts such as clairvoyance, powerful strength, and the ability to leap at great heights, just to name the more interesting ones." Sebastien pauses. "Leaping at great heights I enjoy, and sensory abilities come in handy, not just for hunting."

"So some of the traits like transferring to mist, that movies and literature wrote about, were really coming from some truths?"

"I know Hazel Eyes, it is kind of unnerving to think that there is some supernatural energy around." Sebastien pauses and pours himself more wine, then offers some to Adriano and Rebecca.

"Please go on, I can't wait to hear more." Rebecca grins excitedly.

Adriano remains quiet, looking at his phone occasionally, hoping for a text from Jonathan. Then a question comes to mind. "Did James mention vamprogeria to Count B?"

"Yes, he did. But Count B was shocked to learn about this type of vampire blood disease. He couldn't believe it. After all, vampires are immune to human diseases and ailments. It didn't interest him; he preferred to talk about his own life sorrows; how the villagers stormed his castle and set fire to it while he was out hunting, and how he fought so hard to restore it. Eventually he had to abandon it and move further into the forests, and then found the cave. James couldn't learn much more from Count B, but he stayed a little longer and then begged his forgiveness, out of respect to this Blood Master, that he had to leave. Count B was too proud to show disappointment in this departure and sent him off abruptly. James could hear short weeps and sniffles coming from the cave, it broke James' heart to leave this very lonely vampire. James brought Count B back a fox and called him out of his cave. The count took the squirming fox with a moan of delight, and James bowed and wished him the best and left. This was an amazing man—with a heart full of compassion. My James, such a humanitarian!"

"James sounds very kind and special," Rebecca thoughtfully comments.

Sebastien takes a deep pause, trying to be mindful of the words he is choosing. "That he—yes, so true." Clearing his throat as he collects his thoughts, he can feel his energy start to diminish and his throat becoming dry; he looks at the clock on the mantel-piece. "Oh wow, where has this day gone? I haven't talked this much and for so long in quite a while—it is time to hunt, Hazel Eyes."

"Alright. I've just been so intrigued listening I completely lost track of time—Adriano are you coming to hunt too?"

"I am still okay—but Rebecca, we should probably grab a taxi and head back."

"Head back?"

"Yes, back to the apartment, we have a busy day tomorrow before we head to the airport"

Rebecca and Sebastien both look at each other with a confused expression. "Airport? I don't understand?"

Adriano reaches for Rebecca's hands. "Well I wanted to surprise you but—Jonathan is arriving tomorrow, he is going to spend a few days with us—oh! And I made reservations for tomorrow night at *Le Miaou Du Chat*. It's a very unique restaurant." Both Rebecca and Sebastien again look bewildered, then Adriano realizes. "Oh, I'm sorry, *mon amour*, you might not remember, but Jonathan is my human friend from Toronto." Adriano can tell from Rebecca's expression that she is searching in her mind, digging back into memories; a glimpse of an image surfaces but then vanishes, and she feels frustrated.

"I don't know—I'm trying."

"It's okay, don't worry—anyway, he is arriving from Toronto, so I thought it would be nice to take him out for dinner."

"The Cat's Meow—Le Miaou Du Chat—I remember this place. It was one of James' favourite venues that he discovered. He brought me there on our first date. I was still human at the time. The chef accommodated both our tastes conveniently. I was shocked to discover one or two vampires dining there. Another example showing we do exist, but secretly. I think the chef or the owners had vampire connections. At the time, I couldn't imagine a place like this existing that accommodates vampires."

Rebecca interrupts. "Adriano, I can't leave Sebastien."

"Oh, Sebastien you are welcome to join us of course, my treat."

"Me? Thank you, Adriano, but I haven't been in that kind of setting in a very long time, but I do know—"

"Sorry for interrupting Sebastien—Adriano, you are not understanding me. I can't leave Sebastien here by himself tonight."

"No problem, we can come back tomorrow morning and pick him up."

"Adriano, you heard what Sebastien said, this disease is dangerous. I can't leave him overnight—"

"Hazel Eyes, it's okay, I will be fine, once I hunt soon I will just come home and sleep, I will see you tomorrow."

"No, I'm staying. You almost died today! Sorry, Adriano, but I can't go with you."

"Can I speak with you privately, Rebecca, please?"

Sebastien sees the growing intensity in Adriano's eyes. He stands up quickly, feeling the tension in the air, and needing to leave the room. He knows that their conversation will not stay private if he stays in the house.

"I'm heading to the back to hunt. Hazel Eyes, don't be too long. I can see it in your eyes, you need to hunt."

Adriano can also see Rebecca's eyes fading in color, and her skin beginning to change. "We will be out shortly, Sebastien, if we could please have a minute—alone."

"Yes, of course." Sebastien immediately moves to the back door.

Both Rebecca and Adriano wait for the sound of a door closing.

"Adriano, don't force me to choose, you are not in danger—he *can* be!"

"Rebecca, I understand, but listen to me, be reasonable. He is a grown man. He survived all this time without you! Once you leave he's going to be on his own."

"Me, be reasonable? You need to be reasonable! You saw what happened to him earlier. How dangerous it was!"

"I know, but—"

"You can't force me to go. God forbid something happens, I wouldn't forgive myself, you wouldn't forgive yourself—I'm tired, this tension is draining me, I need to hunt, please."

"Okay, okay, let's go hunting, we can talk about this later."

"You are stubborn."

"And so are you, *mon amour*."

They walk out the back door.

It is now midnight. They all return back to the house after a successful hour of individual hunting, but the tension from earlier does not fade.

"Rebecca, are you sure you wouldn't rather sleep in our own bed at the apartment?"

"Adriano, we discussed this. Do you understand my reason? I'm not trying to be difficult."

"Fine. We need to leave here at least by seven tomorrow morning so I can pick up the rented car, then we have errands to run. I need to buy some groceries for Jonathan."

"That's fine, I'll be ready."

Sebastien returns to the living room in his pajamas, feeling uneasy. "Sorry, don't mind me, I just have to make sure everything is locked up and the fire is completely out—oh—unless you still want the fire?"

"No, we're fine," Adriano says in a clipped tone.

"Right—okay, well, uhm I will leave you guys alone then—if you need anything—"

"We'll be fine, Sebastien." Adriano passes Sebastien and heads out of the living room toward the bathroom; Rebecca remains in the living room a few minutes.

"Good night Sebastien, see you tomorrow morning—you will be joining us at this restaurant, I hope?"

Sebastien is contemplating what the ghost of James said hours ago, and he sighs. He doesn't want to disappoint Rebecca or his James. He silently talks to James, hoping he can hear him. *I am doing this for you, my love.* "Do you really think Adriano wants me there? I mean maybe—"

"Oh, Adriano will be fine. I want you there. Okay? You need this too."

"I guess I can try, Hazel Eyes."

A loud slam is heard from the bathroom door. Adriano takes a deep breath, then another, and splashes water on his tired face.

"Goodnight Hazel Eyes," Sebastien hollers out, and moves quickly up the stairs and into his room, where he closes the door. He turns his iPod on, hoping to drown out any voices from downstairs. His thoughts organically turn to James. *James, I miss you so much, I am not used to this—this forceful vampire in our home! This Adriano, what do you think of him? He makes me nervous—I hope I'm doing the right thing. Then there's Hazel Eyes—Rebecca, I am fond of her, she really seems like a good friend, but I just want peace. I wish you would visit me now, I need you.*

Adriano returns to the living room wearing a heavy frown, whispering, "Must he call you that? You know, I think he does it on purpose to irritate me."

"Oh Adriano, he means no harm—besides, I like it. Do you need an extra blanket?"

"No—I am fine with this one—but listen, can't we talk?"

"Adriano, I'm exhausted. I have a lot to think about as we get closer to returning to Toronto. I just need to rest now—please understand."

"But that is why we should talk—I know you have a lot on your mind."

"I appreciate your concern, you're so thoughtful. But I can't do this now—I'll see you in a few hours, okay?"

"Fine."

Rebecca kisses him on the cheek and heads to her room. "Good night my sexy vampire."

"Yeah—good night." Adriano realizes his rude tone. "Sorry, *mon amour.* Forgive me. Sweet dreams."

Rebecca looks back, giving him a slight smile.

Adriano sits on the couch; his body is energized from the hunt earlier, but his mind is racing in a loop of worry. There was no way he is going to sleep. He takes the blanket from the back of the couch, stretches out his tired body, and closes his eyes. The house is very quiet, and he listens for Rebecca's breathing through the bedroom door, which is slightly ajar. Rebecca's breathing is not slow and calm at first, but then it finally steadies into a rhythm. A half hour has gone by, and when Adriano checks in on her, she is asleep.

CHAPTER 11

The invitation

On Saturday at six-thirty a.m., Adriano is already up, showered, and dressed in the same clothes. His thirst is still far away; he is satisfied from their last hunt. His mind is too occupied. He feels a bit of control coming back into his life. He is making plans and looking forward to the evening, thinking to himself *a normal outing with Rebecca once again.* Soon after he hears the door upstairs open, and seconds later Sebastien enters the living room in a flash. They greet each other civilly before Sebastien goes into the hallway, opens up a small dark grey wall cabinet hanging on the wall, and pulls out a set of keys. He walks over to Adriano and hands them to him.

"You don't need to rent a car—these keys belong to our Mercedes. It's parked in the garage and frankly it needs to be used."

"Are you sure?"

"Yes—after James—well, we didn't use it often since we didn't stop leaving this place much. You can borrow it. It would be a shame to damage the engine or warp the tires if it just sits there. I let Jacques run it around here a little these past two years, but it's been at least a few months unused."

"Thank you. Then, I am going to head back to the apartment and change. I will be back shortly, please make sure Rebecca hunts."

"Of course."

Adriano leaves and Sebastien returns to the living room and walks to the bookcase unit. He opens a drawer and pulls out a black leather-bound book tied with a thick leather ribbon. He sits down on his La-Z-Boy. The front cover of the book reads Journal. He remembers the day that he found James's journal. It was the day James' ghost first came to visit him in their home. James put the journal in their bedroom closet in a small box marked for Sebastien. Sebastien unravels the ribbon and looks to James's recliner, hoping to see him, but the chair is empty. He opens the book and turns to the page with the passage written about him. He has lost count how many times he has opened this journal, but he feels close to James whenever he does. He is worried, though, that he may have revealed too much today about James. He was trying all day yesterday to choose his words carefully but he now suspects Adriano has caught on. His anxiety builds. *How will I explain the absence of James?* He rereads the familiar script he has visited over and over.

September 6,

I am finally putting down on paper pieces of my life experiences after so many years. Unfortunately, these are mostly without dates because my memory is failing me. I fear the disease is progressing at a rapid speed. I feel I am changing; it scares me. The other day I craved a human!

I have spent many years writing this journal in my mind, organizing it as best as I could. I was just too afraid to write it down because it made what transpired more real, and my mind was not ready to face the things from my past.

So now I am trying to organize the timeline as best as my memory allows. I promised myself years ago that I would find the courage to share my story when I found a man who I can trust with my heart and soul, and who would accept who and what I am.

This was you, Sebastien, only I couldn't keep that promise, I'm sorry. I just couldn't tell you face to face some of the things you will now discover on your own in these pages. Forgive me, I know my walls have made it difficult at times for us and our relationship. But now the disease is taking parts of me away, and I need you to understand my past so you can go into the world wiser and open to the many possibilities.

Sebastien can hear movement in Rebecca's room, and he closes the journal and places it back in the drawer. He picks up a frame on the shelf and caresses it. James has this warm smile on his face as he stands a few feet away from the Mona Lisa portrait. *How vibrant and healthy you were back then, my James, such a sexy man in his forties.* Sebastien's memory takes him back to that day they spent in the Louvre. It was their museum day, other days were gallery days, and then there were the city walk days. Art and culture had their own special days for Sebastien and James. James enjoyed these cultural outings. He taught Sebastien how to be present, to quiet the mind and just enjoy each moment for what it was. Sebastien quietly whispers what James used to say, "Tomorrow can't happen today, so enjoy today until tomorrow comes." These past two years, Sebastien's whole being has felt shrouded in doubt and disappointment and grief. He believes in his heart that his life will never be that full and magical again with anyone. He places the frame back on the bookshelf.

Rebecca enters the living room, expecting to see Adriano. "Good morning Sebastien."

"Hi—Adriano went home early this morning to change. He will be back later. It's time to hunt."

Rebecca is concerned, his tone seems cold and distant. "Are you okay?"

"Yes. Sorry, I just need to drink, a little grumpy."

They return to Sebastien's home after a successful hunt. Sebastien heads upstairs to his room to shower. Rebecca's mind begins to race again with thoughts and worries of going home and reuniting with Jonathan. The words that Sebastien spoke yesterday haunt her. *Do you think you can just go on, days at a time, hours at a time, ignoring the craving for human blood? Don't be mistaken, the craving will come, you are still just a new vampire. This can be dangerous to your sons, your family. Dangerous to your sons— your sons.*

Rebecca's hands squeeze tightly against the sides of her head, trying to block out these words. She has to believe in herself, she can handle being near Jonathan now that she is a vampire. She will manage her life, raise her human children. One of her traits as a human resurfaces, she wants to clean. She quickly goes into the storage room and finds the rags and cleaning supplies that Jacques delivered a few weeks ago. Her mind just needs this therapy.

Sebastien descends the stairs, sniffs into the air. "Mmm…I smell lemons or citrus—oh? Why is the mop out?"

Rebecca stops dusting the mantelpiece over the fireplace. "Sebastien, I hope you don't mind, but I was so restless earlier and I just needed to do something. I remembered that I would clean when I was anxious and nervous. I didn't move anything. But what a nice surprise when I took off the sheet. I didn't know you had a piano! I don't play, but I believe every house should have a piano or a musical instrument. This piano sure needs a little love and care. I hope you don't mind if I wipe it down?"

At first, Sebastien seems a little annoyed, but then he switches form. "I don't mind—I guess it is a shame to cover a piano. James always kept the place so neat." Sebastien walks over to the piano, caressing the top of its black lacquer body. He moves his hand delicately over to the cover and gently opens it up. The white and black keys ache for his fingers to gently touch them and create magic like before.

"Do you play?"

Sebastien doesn't respond right away, his fingers continue to caress the waiting keys. He remembers how James loved watching Sebastien's long thin fingers stroke the keys, making them perform for him with his every touch. "I used to—for James."

"He must have enjoyed that very much."

"As the disease progressed, I discovered it was the only sound that soothed the *cre—-James* at night." Sebastien's tone appears melancholy, and Rebecca's heart carries a weightiness for her friend's grief.

Her voice is delicate and consoling. "Can you play for me?"

"Oh—I don't think I can anymore."

"Please—try—just a little."

He looks into her warm hazel eyes and can't disappoint her. He sits down at the bench, closes his eyes. There is no sheet music. Suddenly a faint sound rises from the piano, it's like the piano and its abandoned keys are awakening from a long, deep, unwanted sleep. The sound of the music grows slowly, more intense, as Sebastien plays by memory. Rebecca is captured by the most beautiful sound. She gazes at Sebastien, admiring this beautiful melancholy warm angel.

"This piece was one of James' favorites, by Chopin—Nocturne 20." He continues to play while Rebecca just stands leaning on the piano, taking in the magic. She thinks about life, Sebastien's life. A thought suddenly invites itself in, and she sits with it, getting comfortable. The music gets stronger and deeper, and so does the thought that is growing. A plan is shaping, forming, and it feels so right; she hopes Sebastien will consider this thoughtfully.

Sebastien plays on, his eyes opening with warmth and peace as the melody softens and changes when the notes are lower. His mind is transfixed, as if the piano has put a mystical spell on him. He is carried away into the depths of the music, the sounds of the notes soothing his tormented soul. The flowing sound of the music invisibly moves through the dark and stuffy room, reaching the ceiling, travelling out into the hallway, up the stairs and through the closed doors. The air and energy magically become light and fresh, transcending any dark memories that cursed the beautiful moments of joy and love experienced a long time ago, here in this house.

Sebastien finishes the piece, and the room becomes quiet. Rebecca wipes away unexpected tears. "That was absolutely magical Sebastien—my God! Thank you, my soul needed this."

Sebastien's eyes tear up too at the beautiful sentiment. "Aw—thank you. I didn't realize how much I missed playing—thank you for encouraging me." He stands up and stretches. "You ready for tonight?"

Rebecca nods her head yes but her eyes show differently.

"Don't worry, Hazel Eyes, it will be fine—maybe you should rest a bit? I don't want Adriano to see you tired or he will blame me!" He winks mischievously, with a half-smile, and heads towards the stairs.

"Sebastien—wait. Please, I'd like to discuss something with you." Rebecca fidgets with the cleaning cloth in her hand.

Sebastien can see she is nervous, he turns to face Rebecca, puzzled. "More talking? Oh Hazel Eyes, last night was a lot, Adriano is really intense—I don't think I can handle—"

"Please—I will talk, but I need you to listen with an open mind."

Sebastien moves back into the living room and sits on his chair. "Okay, what is on your mind. You seem nervous or hesitant suddenly?"

"Sorry, it's just that—well—I've been seriously thinking."

Sebastien interrupts. "Uh oh, now I think I may need a drink?" He gets up to go to the kitchen.

"Sebastien, please—I'm serious."

"So am I—Your expression is worrying me. What's going on?" Sebastien's warm chestnut coloured eyes search Rebecca's, and he sees she is troubled. "What is it?"

Rebecca takes Sebastien's warm hand in hers; Sebastien looks concerned but forces a smile. Rebecca takes a deep breath, determined now.

"I've been doing some thinking—about going back to Toronto."

"I know it must be a bit scary but—"

"Sebastien please, let me finish."

"Okay, sorry."

"You said to me many times, it's dangerous for us vampires to live alone with this disease—right?"

"Uh huh—go on." Sebastien can't help but be cautiously curious.

Rebecca takes in a silent breath. "Well—I think—it would be a great thing if you would come to stay in Toronto with me—just for a little while at least. What do you think?" Rebecca breathes calmly, she finally got it out.

A blank expression forms on Sebastien's face; it lingers, then it changes to disbelief. He just stares at her. Remaining quiet, he lets go of Rebecca's hand.

"Sebastien, please. Say something?"

"Maybe I'm wrong, and wine still affects you." He stands up to leave but Rebecca stands up and takes his arm.

"Sebastien, I'm serious."

"Where is this coming from?" Sebastien sits on his recliner, his hands running through his hair.

"It's coming from me, my worries and my concern! Please, let me finish," she interrupts as he is about to respond. "Be honest, and I mean no offense—are you really happy here?"

Sebastien can't believe her question, he stands up abruptly. "*Mon dieu*! What kind of question is that, Rebecca—there now, I got your name right, it takes anger I guess!"

"I don't mean to upset you—"

"You sure about that?"

Rebecca lowers her eyes. Sebastien realizes he hurt her, he hates himself.

"Sorry Hazel Eyes." He reaches for her hand.

"Sebastien, I would never do anything to hurt you."

"I know, I know, you just surprised me with this. I don't know what's wrong with me, lately I just feel, I don't know." He sits back down in his chair.

"Sebastien—you don't have to tell me, but I know that James is no longer with you."

Sebastien feels panic rising, and Rebecca notices his expression, "Don't worry, I don't know the details of why he left, and I'm not prying. But, I think it would be good for you to get away from here. Come to Toronto, You could live with me and my boys. I truly believe this would be a good change for you."

"Oh, I'm sure Adriano would love that—are you kidding? Live with you? Your sons?" Sebastien gets up again, leaning against the mantel; his eyes are wide with surprise. His restless spirit sits him back down on his chair, and he leans forward, his hands covering his face. He is deep in thought. "Again I ask—Rebecca—where is all of this coming from?"

"Listening to everything you shared earlier, it just hit me—I think you've lived too long on your own. You're an amazing man and staying cooped up in this house is—"

He stands up abruptly. "This house belonged to James! It's all that I have left from him." Sebastien realizes he slipped his words, but is exhausted as he is trying to hide the truth. "I feel close to him here. Besides, I'm not some kid, Rebecca. I don't need a babysitter or roommate!"

Rebecca feels the sting of his words cut to her heart. Her name shouted out in anger by her friend. The room hears and feels awkward for both of them. The air is thick and uncomfortable, and Rebecca's mind is spinning, the conversation turning sour.

"I'm sorry, I didn't mean to treat you with disrespect or insensitivity— or think you're a kid who doesn't know better." Rebecca's eyes swell, tears floating at the edges, ready to escape little by little. Her lips tremble. "I hear how you talk about James, so I know how much this house means to you and all of the wonderful memories."

Memories, he thinks to himself, *if only she knew how the memories transformed from beautiful to frightful.* But Sebastien reveals nothing. He sees the hurt in Rebecca's eyes, and feels ashamed for causing it. He knows Adriano would be angry, and feels the other vampire's intense presence even though he is not here. Sebastien feels trapped in his own gloom.

"I am sorry Hazel Eyes—I didn't mean to yell at you. You're the last person I want to hurt. You just caught me off guard—I know you wouldn't do or say anything to hurt me intentionally, but you need to understand— this is my home, and has been for many years." Sebastien hands Rebecca a tissue and sits beside her.

Rebecca composes herself, wiping her tears while quieting her sniffles. "I know, but you're alone. I can see how you drift in and out at times. You seem far away. If it's memories, these can be carried with you wherever you go—James wouldn't want you to live—"

Sebastien stands up immediately. "Don't do that, please! Don't use James as a way to get to me—you have no clue about James and I, not really."

Rebecca gently takes Sebastien's arm. "You're right. But do you just want to waste your long life here—alone? Other than Jacques coming by every week, you have no other interactions."

Sebastien's frustration is growing again; he abruptly walks toward the fireplace. His back to Rebecca, he looks at the photo of James and him, his fingers caressing over James' face. It feels like James is staring through him, and he remembers the words from his lover's ghost. *You have a chance! These vampires could be your friends, your road back to living. You have punished yourself too long—and for no reason. It wasn't your fault! It breaks my heart that you carry this burden of guilt for my death.*

Sebastien's back is still turned toward the mantel when Rebecca gently approaches and turns him to face her, kindness in her eyes. "Did you hear me? I said you're my friend, Sebastien—special friend—for life now, and that is something I take very seriously. You will not be alone! Our disease, as you have told me many times, can be very dangerous if not managed carefully. We both know how exhausting it is—we understand what we go through more than anyone else ever could."

Sebastien stands as still as a mountain. His looks wilted, his eyes facing down. "But this is James's house. I can't just leave it *abandoned*. Don't you see?"

Rebecca reaches for his hands, which are cool, and places them in hers tenderly. "We can figure that out. What is most important right now is keeping us safe, and friends help friends. You coming to Toronto is also very helpful to me. If we find a house that we can live in, we will be safe. Sebastien, I've learned over the years to only bring people into my personal life that I can trust. That is so important to me. You are now in that trust circle, my sweet friend—it is a small circle but it is a valued one. I know I'm throwing out a lot at you suddenly—trust me, this has been a whirlwind for me too."

"You think?! Geez." Sebastien gives Rebecca one of his mischievous smiles.

"Sebastien, all I ask is for you to really think about this. I know it's scary, I'm still wrapping my head around all of this too. But I have to face reality. I'm a vampire, and I'm a mother too. I need to be safe so my sons will be safe. I want you to be safe, you and I can help each other—it's really the only way. No one else will understand better than you and I what is needed when the symptoms rise. Maybe tonight this will be a good experiment for both of us." She smiles, appearing calmer. She lifts off her heels and softly kisses his cheek.

"I need to rest, you exhausted me, my kind friend." Sebastien winks, and his eyes appear friendlier again. He leaves the room and quickly moves upstairs to his bedroom.

Rebecca is feeling much lighter, so she goes to take a shower. She is relieved that Sebastien seems more open and positive to the idea after they talked. Rebecca knows time is limited, and she still has to open this conversation with Adriano. But in her mind, she already has a picture forming and settling nicely: she sees her little boys and her and Sebastien living together. Plans race in her mind, but she feels in control and normal for the first time in a long time. She is determined and hopeful; even as a vampire she can live the life she wants and deserves, and now this includes her dear friend Sebastien Woodsworth.

The day is moving quickly. Adriano drives the car into Sebastien's hidden driveway. Rebecca hears the engine turn off and excitedly goes to find Sebastien. She hears noises coming from the basement. She opens the door and descends in quick movements. "Hey Sebastien, what are you doing down here?" She observes the room more closely; she sees piles of boxes marked fragile, and some open boxes with test tubes. There are two filing cabinets placed in on one side of the wall. "Was this a lab?"

"That was our plan, yes. We had great ideas at one time—but it wasn't meant to be. Many things just weren't meant to be—for James and I." Sebastien rummages through some boxes.

Rebecca hears the sadness returning to Sebastien and approaches, laying her hand tenderly on his shoulder. "I'm sorry Sebastien. I can stay if you want, and Adriano can pick Jonathan up?"

Just at that moment, Adriano is descending the stairs. Sebastien sighs, feeling nervous again. He sees the expression of concern on Adriano's face.

Sebastien turns back to Rebecca. "You'd better go, I'm fine, really, just talking about James recently and, well, other things—just brought back so many memories. I just needed to see this space again—go on, please." Adriano takes Rebecca's hand and she gently lets go, smiles, then approaches Sebastien and reaches to kiss him tenderly on his cheek.

"Remember —you are my friend," she whispers softly.

"Thank you—go on."

Adriano's eyebrows raise, curious at the different energy between Rebecca and Sebastien. Adriano takes Rebecca's hand again. "We will see you in a bit," he says, and they walk upstairs. Adriano helps Rebecca keep a slow normal pace.

Rebecca hollers back down to Sebastien, "We will pick you up later, okay?" Rebecca waits at the top of the stairs.

"*À tout à l'heure,* Hazel Eyes."

Rebecca is satisfied. She smiles, grabs her coat, and follows Adriano out of the house.

Sebastien picks up the journal from the desk and again he opens it up to the page he left off at. He just feels a need to be once more with these last words ever written by his beloved James.

September 7,

Sorry, I had to stop yesterday. My hand was cramping.

Today, I find the courage within to write about that one significant day ingrained in my soul, the event that shook the foundation of my existence. It started on the morning of July 17, 1942. And so I begin.

Paris was occupied by Nazis. I was coming back from the market; the food rations were increasing, and there was tension and fear in the streets. I wasn't sure how safe it was for me to continue to venture out with the Nazi soldiers circling. Suddenly I saw a few large army trucks and vans coming down the road, stopping near my apartment building. A few armed Nazis soldiers came out from the vehicles and began to surround the building and grab civilians who were just riding their bikes, and they were knocked off their bikes and dragged into the back of one of the trucks, which were guarded by more Nazis soldiers. I suddenly felt dread upon me and my instinct told me to hide quickly. I ran to the back of the bakery that was a few doors down. I ran through the alleyway and crouched as small as I could behind the back wall of 2 large garbage bins. Some of the windows were open due to the summer heat and I could hear loud intrusive banging on doors followed by yelling, screaming of women and children, and pleading coming from my building.

I knew something was very wrong, and I dropped my groceries and just began to run in the opposite direction and didn't say a word of warning to anyone I passed (this is one of my greatest regrets as a human— why didn't I warn them?!) I didn't stop running, all I could think of was I had to get to the nearest woods outside of town and hide. I kept running until dark and finally I reached a wooded area and searched for a place to hide. I felt a shooting intense pain coming from my feet and shins and all I kept thinking was I had to stay alive. In the pitch dark I crawled on my belly in dirt and squeezed my body into a hollow log (to this day I don't know how I managed that small space). I scraped both sides of my abdomen as I pushed myself on my belly, desperately wedging in the log's narrow space. My feet were sticking out. My mind was racing with horrible images of what might be taking place in my town, the screams heard over and over in my mind of my friends and what they must have suffered.

My body was so tightly wedged against the sides of the log, my arms barely able to move.

Sebastien stops reading; his heart cries out for his James. His incredible bravery and brilliance bewilders Sebastien. He wishes he had known all of this through James's voice himself. Sebastien is mesmerized every time he reads this passage again. It never loses its profound hold on him.

I had a hard time breathing properly, and my stomach was crushing against the bottom of the log. I had no choice but to face down, I could barely turn my neck to one side since that part of the log was narrower. Exhaustion took over my body but the pain and cramps in my legs and feet kept me from falling into a deep sleep. To this day I think that was all meant to be. I spent hours experiencing spasms in my legs and feet and trying to stifle my whimpering at times by pushing my face into the bottom of log to stop my mouth from opening. At some point I fell asleep but woke up to the sound of birds chirping and knew it was morning. I carefully squeezed myself legs first out of the log and tried to stretch out my stiff aching muscles. I found all kinds of dry blood from scrapes on my bare arms and stomach. All I had on was the pants and short-sleeved top I had from the hot morning from the day before. I knew I needed to find water quickly. I found a tall stick and used it to stand up. I was very weak and extremely dehydrated from yesterday's harrowing frantic running out of the town. As I stood with my new improvised cane, I tried to listen for a miracle of running water, but I only heard the sounds of the woods. I limped painfully around in different directions, trying to establish a direction, but the tall surrounding trees and bushes were hindering my sense of direction. It all looked the same whichever direction I turned.

Sebastien, uncomfortable, stops reading. He takes the book, goes upstairs, shuts the basement door, and moves to the kitchen. There he pours himself a glass of wine, moves to the living room, sits at his La-Z-Boy, and opens up the book to the page he just left off at.

Suddenly I heard a strange sound coming from behind me, and I quickly turned around. I stopped to listen. The sounds became louder, and I determined that it was the sound of moaning, like someone was in pain. I cautiously followed the sounds, doing my best not to make too much noise and attract attention. My fears of encountering Nazis soldiers tried to paralyze me from moving, but I knew either way I had to get out of this area. I continued to follow the sounds as they grew louder. I was reaching the source. Then I spotted movement behind a tree a few feet away. I was ready with the improvised cane; it was now a weapon, ready to attack if necessary. When I got closer to the moans, I could see a body lying on the ground near a tree. I limped over with my cane, but I was completely shocked when I arrived at the body. It was a frail elderly man, perhaps in his early 70s or 80s. He was dressed in torn civilian clothes. I was very relieved he was not in the dreaded uniform with skulls and bones that I was expecting. My heart went out to this poor soul, alone and looking quite malnourished, curled in a fetal position. I carefully laid down my weapon and slowly eased myself down on one knee beside the whimpering man. I leaned over him. His eyes were closed, his mouth open just slightly. A foul odor came from his breath but I put that aside; he was in dangerous physical circumstances. I thought this was a chance for me to redeem myself from my cowardness of not warning my friends in the building. His mouth and lips began to move, but his whispers were too low and faint to make out. I leaned in closer and again he whispered something. I moved in even closer, my ear almost touching his mouth, and then suddenly!!

Sebastien turns the page, takes a deep breath, and takes a sip of wine, feeling such awe and amazement at the experiences his James lived. He aches to hear James's voice, with all his wonderful expressions. Sebastien reads on, taking in each word, over and over, as a gift from James.

I am continuing from the other day's entry. I lost my nerve, so I am trying again to write down the events of July 18, 1942 for my own sanity and my own truth.

And so I continue with courage and strength, to write about July 18, 1942.

I was leaning in quite close to the elderly man, and suddenly I felt this sharp instant stabbing pain penetrate into my neck. To my horror, the man was sucking the blood from my neck fiercely. I must have had an out of body experience at that moment, for all I remember is seeing myself lying on the ground and feeling trapped, my arms pinned down at my sides by the man. I know I must have struggled and screamed, horrified, but the hold on me was too powerful. I could hear sucking noises and moans of pleasure coming from the man as I could feel my own blood being pulled out from my throbbing neck; there was a strong rhythmic sucking.

I must have stopped resisting at some point, some of it is still a blur, probably my mind blocked it out to protect me. My body and mind went numb for what seemed like an eternity. Then either through mercy or something more wicked, the man stopped sucking, and his black glowing eyes looked directly into mine. I shut mine hoping he would disappear, but then I heard him say what I cannot ever forget. "Accept my blood, drink and you will be free." My eyes were still shut tightly. The next thing I felt was a warm liquid dropping onto my lips, and I opened my eyes and realized with horror that his wrist was slit and blood was trickling down. I moved my head away but he forced his bloody wrist into my mouth! I suddenly tasted this metallic foreign substance and, unaware of my own actions, something in me shifted. And my God! I accepted this blood into my mouth, and oh God I started sucking the blood from his wrist. I could feel this disgusting liquid creep down my throat, into my stomach, and as much as my mind was screaming for me to stop, my body craved more!!!

I don't know how long I was drinking from him but suddenly the man pulled his wrist away and stood up. I was stunned still lying on the ground, and then I must have passed out!!! The next thing I remember was opening my eyes. I found myself lying near a stream on some rocks, and I was looking at the blue sky.

I rolled over and fell into the cool water and that refreshed my body. Surprisingly I felt no aches or pains from my feet or legs. I searched my whole body and there were no scratches from when I was lying in the log. I rinsed off and suddenly stopped; the noises of the forest became so loud all of a sudden. I looked around and could sense something was very different in my perception; my senses of sight, sound and smell were so strong, making me dizzy. Without thinking about it my body just took a giant leap and landed on the grassy area at the edge of the stream in one quick movement, and this startled me! It was like I flew across from the rock to the ground???

Sebastien is becoming troubled. He closes the journal and ascends upstairs. He closes the basement door and moves to his room, placing the journal beside him. He sets his alarm so he can be up in time to shower for this evening. He feels emotionally drained, and just needs to stop his thoughts from racing, so he closes his eyes. His powerful vampire ears take in the creaks of the walls settling and different sounds outside from birds, and for a moment he is relieved to just have his house to himself. Soon all he hears is the sound of silence, and it soothes and rocks him into a needed sleep.

Adriano and Rebecca are still driving. It feels strange for Rebecca to be back in a vehicle again. She has already adapted to just stepping out of the house and moving through the woods on foot. The feel of soft, warm leather seats makes her relax.

"Nice jeans—they look new?"

"Oh thanks, compliments of Jacques—well Sebastien, really, but Jacques picked them out for me. He guessed close enough to my size."

"Jacques?"

"Yes, remember him? From—"

"Yes, I do—but why was he picking out jeans for you?"

"Oh—well, I had no other clothes with me, so Sebastien was gracious to have Jacques buy me some tops, jeans, sweaters, and underwear and stuff."

"Underwear too?"

"Adriano, I had nothing. I had no choice, trust me, it was awkward to say the least. But—but I needed some! I wasn't ready to go out myself—you do realize this?"

"Sorry, of course. It didn't dawn on me, but yes, makes sense! Oh, *mon amour*, I am so glad to have you back with me, alone! We will get our lives back on track. Trust me, it will all be okay."

Rebecca thinks, *this might be the right moment, but need to ease into this.* She attempts a bit of humor, just to keep the mood light and calm. "Hmmm...You sure you can drive?"

"What?" Adriano's eyebrows rise. "What do you mean?"

"You had quite a few glasses of wine earlier?" Rebecca tries to keep a straight face but a burst of laughter comes from Adriano.

"Vampires don't get drunk from wine." Suddenly the car explodes with laughter from both of them. Adriano purposefully omits one revelation. He does feel a slight buzz or high, if he drinks from someone who has consumed a large quantity of alcohol or drugs. But this is not the right time to bring this up; he is not ready to remind Rebecca that he consumes human blood. This is too sensitive of a subject in this early stage of their reunion, reconnection. Adriano leans over carefully and kisses Rebecca on the lips. "You're funny! I hope you and Sebastien will enjoy this evening. Is Sebastien okay? He seemed a bit off when I came back."

Rebecca mentally organizes the thoughts in her mind, she is ready. "Umm...Adriano—we need to talk."

Adriano keeps one of his hands on the steering wheel, the other holding Rebecca's hand. They are driving on the main country road now. "Hmm... sounds serious—but I know you're nervous about tonight."

"No, it isn't about tonight, actually—I'm looking forward to this evening, this test. I have to do this. I want to go home to my sons, I want to be back in my apartment with my things."

"I'm so glad to hear that Rebecca. I can't wait either, just to get our life back on track, together."

Before Rebecca loses her nerve, she blurts out, "Adriano—I asked Sebastien to come back to Toronto with us, to live with me."

Adriano immediately turns his head to Rebecca, releasing his hand from hers. "What?!" His eyes focus back on the road, but his head still facing towards Rebecca.

"I know it sounds sudden but—"

"Sudden is not the word that comes to my mind Rebecca, more like crazy?!"

Rebecca's eyebrows pull down. "It's not crazy! I'm offended by that, but I'll let it go. I realize this is a shock to you, but I cannot leave him alone like this, you see what we go through!"

"Rebecca! *Mon dieu*! He managed fine for two years after James left!"

"He managed, but I don't think as fine as you think! Besides, he didn't have friends, now he has me and you!"

"Christ! Did you mention this to him?"

"Yes!"

Adriano slams the steering wheel harshly, his anger building. Rebecca jumps in surprise at his abrupt reaction but is determined. "He was resistant to my idea, but he knows I'm right about this, he's just scared to leave the memories and James' house!"

"*Mon dieu*! Rebecca, he's a vampire, not a kid! And what about your kids? You have to think of them. You're not even ready yet to be around them, how do you expect Sebastien to—"

"Stop saying I'm not ready, dammit! These are my kids—do you think I would put them in danger?!" Her face is hot and red, and she pushes a tear away from her eye.

The air in the car becomes so thick. The sound of complete silence, so unbearable, stays with them until they are almost home. Adriano can't believe how Rebecca's eyes changed to such a dark hue. It upsets him to see her so angry, he is worried that this stress and upset could affect her energy, causing the symptoms to rise too soon. He parks the car on the street, near their apartment, and turns it off. Rebecca is about to open the car door but he stops her.

"Rebecca, sweetie, I am sorry. I didn't mean to upset you so much! You are the kindest, sweetest soul I have come across, and you have a boundless heart for those you care for—or love. I see this, but I just don't think it is a good idea for Sebastien to live with you and your sons —you hardly know him."

"I know him enough to know he needs me."

"I need you, dammit! Doesn't that matter? All I hear from you is Sebastien, Sebastien!"

Rebecca is stunned, she is speechless, and silence invades the car again. It seems to last only a few brief seconds, Rebecca is not going to just stay silent. "Don't get the wrong idea. Sebastien and I are just friends. I just want to do the right thing. I see my friend, who is alone, and I just want to help. Of course, I need you too. But I can't just abandon him? I can't."

Rebecca turns her head away from Adriano to face the window. Adriano calms himself down, then reaches for her hands, hoping she won't resist. He tries to use his charismatic charm; he needs to ease this uninvited hostility between them.

"Please show me those beautiful hazel eyes, I need to see them."

Rebecca is still agitated, but she can't stand feeling this tension. She slowly turns to face Adriano, her eyes sad and worried. Adriano's eyes begin to work their charm. It's always hard for Rebecca to stay mad at Adriano for long. His eyes and smile always seem to find their way back into her, soothing her. She understands his concerns and realizes the challenges ahead, but she is torn; she can't bear to leave Sebastien alone. She knows he can fall into a deep depression. She recognizes the signs, it is familiar to her, somehow.

"I'm torn, Adriano. I can't leave Sebastien like this. I really believe he would thrive in the company of good caring friends. Please help me." She rests her tired mind and body in Adriano's chest.

"Why hasn't he let us know what happened to James? Don't you find that odd?"

"No—it's not our business, maybe they separated for some reason, we don't know."

"I think it's more than that, I think he is dead."

"What? If that is so my heart goes out to him even more. Oh, I hope you are wrong, poor Sebastien."

"Anyway, asking Sebastien to move in is too much. I'm just trying to figure all this out. I'm overwhelmed right now, and I am sure you are too.

This is not an easy situation and your condition is complex; it worries me so much, *mon amour*. Can we please just put this conversation aside for now, at least for tonight? Please? I promise we can talk about it again—but tonight is a big step for you, and that is all that matters for the moment." Adriano reaches in closer, bringing his lips to Rebecca's, gently kissing hers. She welcomes the kiss, her tension slowly easing away from her.

"Mmm…this is nice, this is what I needed right now, thank you *belle âme*." He smiles warmly, rubbing his nose to hers affectionately and asks in a soft whisper, "Did you hunt enough? Rest at all today?"

Rebecca nods. "I feel fine, let's go inside, people are starting to stare."

"Of course, they are staring. They see me with a beautiful sexy woman—hang on, I will come and open your door, my lady. Just let me grab the groceries from the trunk."

Rebecca smiles, enjoying this gentlemanly manner from him. He grabs the groceries from the trunk, walks over to her side, and opens the door. He holds her hand to steady her pace and she steps out slowly. He leads her into their courtyard and into the apartment.

It is now three thirty, and Jonathan is due to arrive at the airport at around nine p.m. Adriano unpacks the groceries and Rebecca notices a few boxes of assorted berries and a couple of bags of assorted nuts in the box with the baguette and cheese and a few bottles of red wine. Rebecca helps by washing the berries, feeling more comfortable and at ease in the kitchen. It feels good to be preparing to entertain again, even if the menu selection is quite different from her usual three course meals, salads, and desserts.

"Oh, do you think we need more food, in case Jonathan gets hungry later on?"

"Not for tonight, don't worry *mon amour*. Besides tonight he will eat at the restaurant and probably go straight to sleep after."

Adriano's phone rings, he looks at the display and looks at Rebecca and gives her the phone. "It's your parents."

Rebecca answers the call. "Hello?"

She hears the faint little voice, "Hi mommy," and her heart swells.

"Adam? Are you okay?"

She hears Ethan in the background saying that he wants to talk to Mommy too.

Adriano signals that he will be right back and leaves her in privacy. He goes back to the car and takes the large bag from the trunk and sneaks it back into their apartment, into the closet in their bedroom. Adriano comes back to the kitchen, smiling and very quietly singing lyrics from a song that just popped into his mind by George Michael.

"Oh, wouldn't it be nice, if I could touch your body…"

Rebecca hears him singing, but pays attention to Adam. "Are you okay now? Feeling better now that we talked?"

Rebecca's heart feels like it is dropping from her chest when Adam asks her when she is coming home. Rebecca doesn't respond yet so Adam again asks her, hearing him call her Mommy just tugs at her heart so deeply, forming a lump in her throat, and she finally answers her son.

"I will be home very soon, I miss you both terribly!"

Adam replies that he misses her too and then Ethan who is standing beside Adam says he misses her too. And then another voice comes on the line, it is Catarina.

"Hi Mom, is Adam okay? Yes, it's me. Adam called me, is everything okay?"

Catarina didn't realize that Adam took her cell phone.

"It's okay Mom, he just wanted to call me." Rebecca sighs heavily. "Let me talk to him again." Catarina gives the phone back to Adam but tells him it is time to say goodbye, and that they can call again tomorrow. Adam takes the phone, his voice sounding teary eyed, but he still listens to his mom.

"Okay Adam, you have to be brave for me, I know you will. Okay, I better go, I love you too, bye my sweet Adam and Ethan." Rebecca waits to hear them say goodbye and then the phone goes dead. She puts the phone down and stands still, deep in thought. Adriano is busy dusting the furniture, just getting ready for Jonathan.

Rebecca returns to the living room, her voice a bit strained. "I think I'm going to take a nice long warm bath."

Adriano looks concerned. "Are you okay, are the kids?"

"They're fine. I'm just a bit overwhelmed. This day has been quite intense. A nice relaxing bath is what I need." She takes Adriano's hand and puts it around her waist, raising her head to meet his lips. "You must be exhausted too, it has been a very eventful long twenty-hour hours." Their kiss lingers, and Adriano is relieved to see affection from Rebecca again, despite the tension still lingering from earlier. "Have I told you how grateful I am for your patience and understanding with me and Sebastien?"

"I will do anything for you *belle âme*."

Rebecca kisses him again, her lips and tongue teasing his mouth. "Why don't you join me in the bath?"

Adriano is becoming aroused just thinking of that wonderful image in his mind, and he kisses her neck and down her shoulder. "Start the water, I will be right there—lots of bubbles!" A sudden low sensual growl from Adriano teases her. "My beautiful *panthère!*"

She returns with a deep purring sound.

They linger in the warm bubbly bath just enjoying reexploring each other's bodies. Adriano's hands tenderly caress her soft warm back, kissing her lips eagerly. He gently moves his hands around to her ribcage and then cups each breast with his hands, squeezing her hard nipples gently, delicately playing with them, teasing them. Rebecca leans her head back, sounds of pleasure coming from her throat. They rinse off, taking their time. As Rebecca reaches down to grab Adriano and stroke him gently, he lets out a moan of pleasure.

They leave the washroom and move to their bedroom. Adriano lays her down on the bed and pulls the covers back. He lays on top of her, and she feels him pressing between her legs. He is touching between her thighs, and Rebecca spreads her legs apart, inviting every touch of his hands to explore all of her. Rebecca moans with erotic emotion as Adriano gently and softly makes his way just inside her, and now he feels so alive as he feels her wetness. He slowly moves in deeper with his finger, leaving her in such a state of ecstasy. He then moves his other hand upward, passing her stomach and feeling her breasts, her hard nipples aching for his lips to suck them.

Rebecca continues moaning and calling his name out in an erotic whisper and wanting him to make love to her.

"Your wish is my command, my beauty."

Rebecca loves hearing his sexy whisper. Adriano looks deep into Rebecca's eyes, and he moves himself inside of her, he is so hard. He moans with rapture and elation, his body heat mixing, bonding with hers, a pleasurable frenzy. Rebecca is falling into a deep and blissful trance as her vampire continues to thrust in and out of her, leaving her wanting more and more as she stays wet for him. They explore with a new intimacy, and are both curious to try drinking from each other. Adriano first takes her hand and turns it so her wrist is exposed. His lips ever so delicately kiss her wrist, and he blows his warm breath on it. Rebecca's skin tingles, and this feeling arouses her. Adriano then moves his lips to her neck, and he gently starts sucking the skin, just teasing her, knowing his vampire saliva numbs the skin in preparation for the bite. He releases a sensual growl and gently bites into her neck and into the vein. He sucks in her blood gently, and they both moan with erotic ecstasy. He then stops and invites Rebecca to bite him, saliva and blood mixing together creating such incredible sexual delight for each of them.

They continue to make love a few more times, their bodies letting them both know how much they missed each other's caresses and kisses, and they just can't get enough until they finally begin to feel exhausted. Rebecca is again beginning to lose her energy, she is not used to this pleasurable activity now and Adriano is a bit concerned that all this activity and exchanging blood was just too much for her. But he can't help smiling. His body is so relaxed, the lingering feeling of their sexual intimacy teasing his mind over and over. Sebastien was right, exchanging blood between lovers is such an erotic and powerful feeling.

CHAPTER 12

Disconnect and Desire

At four thirty, Adriano takes a mental note that it has been a few hours since Rebecca last hunted, but Rebecca reassures him that she is not thirsty. There doesn't appear to be any symptoms rising, she just feels delightfully satisfied and wants to rest an hour before she gets ready for the evening. Adriano lays beside her.

"Close those beautiful eyes, rest, I will call you in an hour." He gets up and puts on a pair of jeans and closes their bedroom door. He decides to pour himself a glass of wine. It feels good, and he's surprised he didn't think to keep this human part of him alive before. He turns the radio on low and sits on the couch. He thinks about the day, it is a good day. But the idea of Sebastien coming to Toronto still sits with him.

Adriano sets his cell alarm for an hour and takes a piece of paper and pen from the kitchen. He has a list piling up in his mind about home; sending email to his dean, letting colleagues know Rebecca has been found, and now adding to this list, finding a place for Sebastien in Toronto if he decides to leave Paris for good. He thinks, *He can't stay with Rebecca.*

By the time Adriano stops to review his lengthy list, which includes visiting the art gallery next Wednesday, it is now almost five thirty. He quietly enters into their bedroom and hears eerie sounds coming from Rebecca. Her breathing seems shallow. He quickly turns the light on and to his fright, he sees she is aging again.

"Rebecca! Rebecca! Wake up!" He gently shakes her and her eyes open slowly; he can tell she is not well. "Come on, I will help you get dressed. We have to get you food." He helps her dress, puts her coat on, and dashes her out to the car. He races to the nearest wooded area. She manages to walk but her movements are slow. He brings her deeper into the forest and scans for any movement. "Rebecca, we need to eat—use your senses, your gift. I know you can do this."

Rebecca responds in a frail voice, "I'm okay, I'm okay." She lifts her nose into the air, taking in all the scents around her, and her head turns immediately as she spots movement. As quickly as her energy allows, she runs towards a fox. She stands a few feet away and the fox doesn't move; his heart beating fast, he senses danger upon him. Rebecca slowly approaches him but isn't sure that she had the ability to subdue her prey in the weakened condition she is in at present.

Adriano stays back so as not to startle the fox, and prays that Rebecca can still lure the animal into her grasp through mind communication. Rebecca approaches, speaking softly as is her technique, but in a weaker voice. The fox detects her frail state and doesn't bow to this predator. Instead he takes a few steps slowly back, growling. His tail is straight up. Rebecca concentrates more deeply, aligning her body to appear more predatorial, releasing sounds of assertive growling that frightens the fox. It finally bows his head down. Rebecca quickly moves in and grabs its neck. She bites hard and quick, taking in the warm soothing blood, and she drinks and drinks until she drains the fox. Adriano is relieved; he moves in closer and enjoys the moment watching his beloved. She gently places the limp corpse down.

"Thank you little one," she says, and she reaches out her hand for Adriano to help her stand back up. "I need another one, I can feel it."

"Of course! Let's go!" They walk at a brisk vampire speed, because it is soon time to pick up Sebastien and drive to the airport. Holding hands, they run deeper into the woods. Adriano spots a rabbit hopping fiercely towards its burrow, its nervously twitching nose alerting it to the vampires coming. With all his speed and adrenaline Adriano moves in like a monster predator and grabs the rabbit's ears tightly before it reaches the entrance of its burrow. He holds it and Rebecca moves in and feeds on this animal too. Suddenly Adriano feels a brief moment of fatigue setting in, accompanied by a sharp pain in his head. The stress and worry of finding food for Rebecca took a toll on him. He is very grateful to the universe for these animals, and brushes aside his own physical discomfort.

They quickly run out of the woods and back to the car. Adriano puts his hand into his pocket and pulls out a tissue, and Rebecca laughs.

"What's so funny?"

"Nothing—I just think it's cute that you're always prepared with a tissue."

Adriano smiles. "You have to be! Can you imagine if you are walking down the street with blood dripping down your lips and dressed for an evening out? Try explaining that!" They both laugh. He takes the tissue and wipes Rebecca's mouth and lips. "Come on, let's get back *mon panthère*. We need to change." He kisses her hand.

Rebecca smiles slightly, her mind focused elsewhere. "That was too close—see what I mean? I had you to help me before it got too dangerous for me. You can go a few days without drinking, but we can't. I can't let Sebastien continue living on his own. I know we will talk about this later, but—the first thing we are going to do tomorrow is to get him a cell phone!"

"I am starting to realize this more clearly. Why doesn't he have a phone?"

"He's stubborn! He told me that he did have one for a long time, but after James was gone he threw it away, deciding that he didn't need it anymore. But now I am here, and so help me he is getting a phone!

"Hmm... I see." He leans in and kisses her on the lips while his eyes are still focused on the road, keeping one hand on the steering wheel.

"I'm serious, Adriano!"

"I know, but you need to calm down." He places his free hand between her inner thighs.

"I see... And this is how I should calm down? Hmmm... Somebody's ready to play again."

Adriano growls playfully, but then Rebecca suddenly realizes something and in a concerned tone, she says, "Oh, you didn't feed yourself, back there."

"Not to worry—I'm good, the snack we had earlier and all that wine curbed my appetite for now. I never thought of snacking on berries or nuts before, I just didn't really look at human food the same way anymore. But maybe I need to explore again—anyways, don't forget, I can go longer between feedings, and lately I feel a bit different, like my body is adapting differently again."

"Really? Does that happen?"

"I don't know, I find changes in myself at times, I guess as I get older...or should I say wiser." He chuckles.

"How old are you really?"

"Where did that come from?"

"I don't know, I can't seem to place your age. You're not older than me, but I'm not sure if you told me once before that you were made at a young age, so I'm curious—am I dating a much younger man?"

"Would it bother you if so?"

"I never really thought about it, but I am in my late thirties, so how young can I go without being viewed as cradle robber as they say."

Adriano doesn't respond; he keeps driving, and the air between them suddenly seems to change drastically.

"You didn't answer. Everything okay?"

Adriano lets out a heavy sigh. He isn't prepared for such a conversation, and they just had too many of these important ones in the last day. "Yeah, I'm fine, just a bit tired."

Rebecca notices he didn't answer her question and just leaves it for now, but she wants to revisit this again. The rest of the ride is quiet and a bit uncomfortable. She turns on the radio for some noise, anything, she doesn't care. Her mind begins to drift back to her kids and going back home. Just as they are a few minutes from the apartment, Adriano glances over to Rebecca.

"Hey you—you're quiet, I can see you are deep in thought?"

"Just wondering how everyone in my family is doing now that they know I'm alive."

"Don't worry, you will be back with them soon." He kisses her fingers.

"Do you think by the end of the week?"

Adriano hesitates to respond too quickly. He hasn't forgotten that he wants to visit that gallery hoping to meet the vampires Juliette and Veneur. For some reason he just wants to know more about them. "Let's do our best but don't pressure yourself, this may take a week or so."

"A week? Why?"

"Possibly, I think we can practice more outings among humans, it is very important to keep doing this—how about the art gallery?"

"Art gallery?"

"Yes, we didn't get to do this much when we first arrived in Paris, before the accident. We can talk about it later—but the first thing we need to work on is your movements."

Rebecca can't deny that he is right about this, she knows she still moves too abnormally quickly. She nods in agreement. "I know, I realize it myself when I'm about to do anything, walk or turn."

"It's okay, it takes practice. It took me a long time to master this and I only got better once I was around humans more frequently. I had no choice for work, and then hanging around Jonathan and Sandra constantly just reprogrammed my mind."

"It's still hard to comprehend how much I have changed, and so drastically."

"I know—it's an adjustment all around, but don't put pressure on yourself. I am going to teach you meditation and yoga movements."

"What?"

"Seriously, it really helped me slow my pace, trust me."

Rebecca takes his hand, which is still holding hers, and kisses his fingers. They are already a street away from their apartment.

It is six thirty p.m. They quickly go in, freshen up, and dress. Adriano thinks this is the best time to present her with his surprise. He is hoping to regain their connection; the car ride home was quite intense and awkward near the end. He thought she knew how young he had been when he was turned over. He brushes the concern away and goes back to the bedroom closet. Carrying out a large boutique bag, he presents it to Rebecca as she is putting her earrings on.

"Rebecca, just a little something I picked up. Hope you like it." He smiles anxiously, like a child waiting to see the reaction of the gift they bought for someone.

"Really? Oh wow!" Her eyes sparkle as she pulls out the red and black tissue paper from the bag, and then she lets out a pleasant gasp of excitement and joy as she pulls out a knee-length heavy black winter coat with leather sleeves and a high leather collar, rimmed in deep red and deep purple silk ribbon. The pockets have the same ribbing stitched at the top edge. The buttons are a silver round vintage style and the inside lining is a deep eggplant purple silk with black vintage roses traced in silver throughout the lining.

Rebecca is stunned at its beauty, and then she turns the jacket to the back and sees a large black rose embroidered into the jacket reaching the middle of the back. Tears form in her eyes, her heart melting with warmth and awe for this generous gift.

"Oh wait, look inside the bag."

"More?" She pulls out a deep red see-through neck scarf that has one thumb-sized black rose embroidered in one of the corners. Adriano takes the scarf and ties it around Rebecca's neck and kisses her gently on the lips. It matches perfectly with the black long sleeve dress she has on. "Oh my God! Adriano these are the most incredible gifts I have ever received."

"Well, I thought that a new coat is needed, the other one is worn out."

"Oh, but I loved that coat too!"

"I know, but—new beginning. Your first coat now as a vampire should be even more spectacular!" His smile is so warm and loving. He puts the coat on her and buttons her up. "Ready?"

"I think so."

Adriano looks at her admiringly. "Absolutely stunning!"

They arrive at Sebastien's house around seven thirty. Rebecca is so anxious, hoping Sebastien wouldn't change his mind to come out with them for dinner. "Let me go in, wait here."

Rebecca moves quickly to the door and knocks; a few seconds later she hears Sebastien call out, "Coming, just a minute." A few seconds later the door opens and Rebecca sees Sebastien all dressed up in a dark blue suit and pink tie. His hair is combed out and his beard is trimmed short and neat.

"Impressive! You look amazing Sebastien!"

"Thank you Hazel Eyes, you are so beautiful." He smells her perfume, it is so pleasant. "Mmm, nice perfume." He bends his head down feeling a bit shy, and locks the door before taking her arm. "Shall we?"

"Let's do this!"

Sebastien guides Rebecca with her movements, keeping her steady and slow by holding on to her. They enter the car, and Sebastien greets Adriano. Then they are off to pick up Jonathan at the airport.

Adriano takes Rebecca's hand and leads her into the very busy airport. She suddenly gasps, feeling completely overwhelmed by the intense stimulation to her sense of sight, smell, and hearing. She whispers into Adriano's ear, "I can't do this!"

Adriano squeezes her hand gently to reassure her. "Yes, you can, just hold onto me."

"I am here too Rebecca, Adriano and I got you. Don't think I am not nervous too, it has been a long time since I've been in an airport."

"It shouldn't be long, his plane should be arriving, here let's take a seat over there." Adriano leads Rebecca to a seat near the window, and she keeps her head down. The movements of the humans are making her dizzy. Adriano notices and whispers softly into her ear, kissing her cheek. "You're okay, just breathe in deeply, you're doing fine."

"Don't let go of me."

"I wouldn't dare—by the way, that coat looks beautiful on you."

The three vampires sit quietly near the window, trying to seem normal, blend in. Rebecca is doing her best to manage her anxiety.

"Are they staring at me? I feel like they're staring at me. Do I look like our kind?"

"Relax, *mon amour*, you look beautiful, you are a beautiful woman, it's hard not to admire you in this coat too."

"You're sweet, but tell me the truth. Can they tell?"

"If they could, they would be running for their lives. Everything is fine. Oh look, there he is." Jonathan is coming from out of customs. "Jonathan, over here!" Adriano waves and Jonathan sees him quickly and makes his way towards them. He gives Adriano a hug.

"*Salut mon amie.*"

Then Jonathan turns to Rebecca for a hug, but she steps back, holding onto Adriano again. Adriano looks at Jonathan. "Give her a bit of time, last time you saw her she was *different.*"

Jonathan picks up the hint and realizes and just stands closer to Adriano. "Oh God, it is so nice to see you Rebecca, you look amazing."

"Thank you, Jonathan."

Adriano continues holding Rebecca's hand, and he introduces Sebastien. "Jonathan, this is our friend Sebastien."

Their eyes meet. Suddenly there is an energy of intrigue between them. Jonathan extends his warm hand and he feels as if he is being pulled in by Sebastien's warm chestnut eyes, who is awkwardly and slowly extending his warm, soft hand. Sebastien is already used to human contact from his weekly deliveries from Jacques, but this is different. It makes him nervous but excited, for the first time in a long time. They return to the car and drive off towards the restaurant.

By the time they finish dinner it's approaching midnight. They arrive back at Sebastien's place first to drop off Sebastien, but Rebecca is becoming very anxious and concerned about leaving Sebastien by himself. He invites them in for a drink. He brings out red wine, more berries, and nuts, and apologizes to Jonathan for not having more variety.

"This is plenty Sebastien, that meal was incredibly filling. I love steak-frites, and the onion soup was amazing."

"I forgot how nicely they can prepare a raw version of venison bourguignon. Please take a seat, I will light a fire." He turns on the radio and *La Vie En Rose* is playing on the French station. "Was the taste pleasing to you Rebecca, the texture?"

"It was delicious Sebastien, at first I had to adjust a little to the texture of the deer meat. I'm not used to eating the actual meat. Just drinking the blood. I can't believe they served it raw."

"I told you this restaurant is unique, and very open minded and inclusive. I just never realized that vampires are part of the inclusion. I was fascinated to see some of our kind there," Adriano says.

"Oh, James introduced me to this place, we felt very comfortable there. James said that the owner had ties to a vampire scion."

"Scion? Are you for real Sebastien? You mean some vampires truly organize like this?"

"Yes. It is an older custom, but I guess there are still some traditions carried on. Well—I am curious to see if this sustains both of you for a longer period of time." Sebastien pours his guests wine and passes the bowls of the nuts and berries around.

The energy in the room is friendly and relaxing. Sebastien thinks, *James my love, I am among friends again. I wish you could stop by just for a moment to see, they would have enjoyed your company tremendously if they knew you before!*

Adriano gets up and extends his hand to Rebecca.

"Are you asking me to dance, sir?"

Adriano bows and in a gallant tone, says, "My lady."

Rebecca giggles. "What a charmer you are!" As she rises too quickly from the couch, moving at vampire pace, she realizes and sighs in frustration.

"It's okay Rebecca, what better way to practice moving, let's dance!"

Sebastien and Jonathan just watch them dance together arm and arm. Another French song comes on and they dance once more.

Then Jonathan gets up. "May I cut in?" They all look at him in shock.

"What?" Rebecca asks.

"I trust you, Rebecca— trust yourself."

"I don't know if I can—"

"Yes, you can, *mon amour*, Jonathan will guide you." Adriano gives Rebecca's hand to Jonathan. The energy is tense suddenly, and Jonathan puts his arm around Rebecca's waist and slowly takes a step, leading Rebecca. Rebecca smells the cologne he is wearing, and her eyes travel to a vein in his neck. She looks at it, but surprisingly she seems fine. She is relieved that there are no weird sensations or cravings stirring inside her. She is mindful that she just finished a very filling dinner of high protein; still, a feeling of hope passes into her, and she smiles. *I can hug my children and kiss them good night at bedtime, I can be around my family. I can do this. I have control.*

It is now quarter to four in the morning, as Adriano discovers as he looks at his watch. All of them are still in the living room. The bowl of nuts is empty, the berries gone, and the third bottle of wine is empty too. Jonathan fell asleep a while ago. Adriano thinks it best they head back home, and moves to get up.

"Well, I think we should call it a night, it has been an exciting evening!" He looks at Rebecca, waiting for her to get up, but she hesitates.

"Adriano, I can't leave Sebastien, we talked about this."

Sebastien picks up immediately. "It's okay Rebecca, go with Adriano, I'm fine. I ate so much I should be okay until tomorrow, if not I will go in the back and find something."

"No! It's dangerous, I will stay here at least tonight so we can figure out something."

Adriano is not pleased at all with this idea, and Sebastien again picks up this tense energy. "Rebecca, please, I managed the last two years on my own, and I am fine. It is sweet that you care so much but it is not necessary."

Rebecca feels hurt hearing him say this, but respects his wish very reluctantly. She doesn't want to come across as overbearing. "Then tomorrow we are getting you a phone!"

A heavy sigh escapes Sebastien. "I have to confess—I already have one."

Rebecca and Adriano look at him in shock and say, simultaneously, "What did you say?"

Sebastien feels embarrassed. "I have a phone, but I disconnected it after James..."

If eyes could kill, Adriano's would have murdered Sebastien in that moment. Keeping down his anger, he leads with control. "You mean to tell me-—you had the opportunity to call the police and tell them that you found Rebecca and you did nothing?!" Sebastien suddenly feels very uncomfortable, and Adriano continues. "How dare you! Do you know the pain and emotional agony her family, her sons and I went through?!"

"I am sorry, I realize that was very selfish of me."

Adriano loses his temper and control. "Selfish?!" He grabs Sebastien by the throat. His eyes are glaring, his mouth showing his teeth, and he lets out a low but intimidating growl. Sebastien's eyes turn dark, and a very low growl is released from him. But then he stops; he knows he is partly in the wrong, but also believes he spared the unfolding of a complicated situation involving police and investigations.

Rebecca immediately tries to intervene. "Adriano, stop, stop! Let go!"

Adriano doesn't let go. The commotion startles the sleeping jetlagged Jonathan. "Hey, what's going on?" he says in a sleepy voice, rubbing his eyes. Then he sees Sebastien in a choke hold. "Adriano, what the hell are you—!"

"This bastard didn't alert the police that he had found Rebecca!"

"Adriano Rossi, you let go of him or I swear I will leave immediately!" Suddenly, all eyes are on Rebecca, her eyes went very dark and lost their gleam. Adriano was stunned. He has never seen such anger in her face, and he releases his grip on Sebastien.

Rebecca walks forward, standing between Adriano and Sebastien, and turns to Sebastien. "Sebastien, I am not sure why you didn't call the police—but my instincts tell me you were doing the right thing. Tell me this is true—I will forgive you."

Adriano is steaming inside, his jaws clenched, but he is keeping his temper in check with the help of Jonathan, who is now holding Adriano's arm firmly. Of course, Adriano knows he can release the hold with no effort, but he realizes he needs to calm down; getting into a fist fight with Sebastien would not go over well with Rebecca. He already feels he is losing some connection and understanding now with her, and he can't stand it. His piercing eyes are on Sebastien, and Sebastien can feel their invisible laser going through him.

"Hazel Eyes —please understand, I was shocked when I found you laying on the ground. You were so badly injured, and I knew you were dying—I just wanted to help you. I just wanted you to be okay. I acted quickly, no time to think about the future, who you were. I spoke to you—I don't know if you remember?"

They all just listen, and Rebecca shakes her head in disbelief, indicating that she doesn't remember. Sebastien's eyes tear up, and he speaks in a soft and thoughtful tone. "I said, I can't ask you for your blessing, but you are too young to die. I can't watch another person die in front of me, when I can give you—life. Forgive me if I am making the wrong choice." He pauses, and no one speaks yet. "You see, Hazel Eyes, I remember those words so clearly, they are engraved into my memory forever. I knew what I had to do in that moment. I knew I was going to be *your* blood link donor, you were my first to turn."

Rebecca breaks down suddenly, becoming emotional, but then she stops and composes herself. Adriano puts his arms around her, and when she doesn't resist he feels relief.

"There was little time. So I—I bit into your neck right there in the leaves. I really wasn't sure how effective my saliva was to numb you so you wouldn't feel much pain or discomfort. I had no clue if my vampire saliva could cause a reaction in you. I barely drank from you, then I stopped and quickly I slit my wrist—that was a very odd moment for me. But I did it because I had to. You resisted drinking at first, but I knew my saliva and cells would soon work in your body. But time was not on our side. I begged you to take it, I needed you to survive—I finally just forced my bloody wrist into your mouth and finally I could feel you sucking."

Adriano is taking this in with difficulty, feeling numb.

"I knew then my blood was already mixing in with yours. I quickly picked you up in my arms and carried your limp broken body. You were barely conscious, moaning."

Adriano keeps his anger down as he listens as Sebastien finally shares about the night Rebecca became a vampire.

"I knew you were still in a lot of pain. I just wanted to get you home and make you as comfortable as I could. I knew you had a difficult few hours ahead, as your human body began to die and the vampire blood cells took over. I remembered parts of my own rebirth, and James was the gentlest loving man with me, but even he could not prevent what I had to endure as part of the transformation. I just wanted you to have the best care possible during that transition, too. Then in the hours and days that followed, I wanted to help you adjust as a vampire, and I wanted to be there for you, to teach you how to hunt, to look after yourself. And yes! I shamefully admit I didn't want to be alone anymore." Sebastien's eyes lower to the ground, his voice following.

"You were like a miracle! I spent two difficult years in silence, on my own. I'm sorry—I'm sorry. Forgive me." He slumps back in his La-Z-Boy, his hands hiding the expression of his shame on his face.

The room is completely silent. Adriano and Rebecca are sitting on the couch, Jonathan beside Adriano on the other side. Everyone is in their own dazed thoughts, but the awkward silence doesn't last long.

"Don't you see?" Sebastien continues, looking at all three faces just staring through him, "I knew it was wrong to not call the police, but I was also afraid of them finding out who we were. Hazel Eyes—they would have taken you to the hospital, runs tests! I was afraid they might then discover anomalies with your blood, DNA, and state of your injuries. They might have shipped you away to some shady undercover government facility and performed horrific experiments on you! I am a scientist, I know this is what they would do!" he cries out. He looks at Adriano, his voice full of so much remorse. "I am sorry, I don't know what more to say—Adriano, you must agree that Rebecca couldn't go to a hospital and be examined by human doctors. Please try to see it from the logical side?" No one speaks further. Sebastien stands up, feeling ashamed, hurt, and frustrated, and starts walking away.

"Sebastien—wait, don't go, you have said a lot and we just need to process this."

"How can you be so calm, Rebecca? All these months—his friend Jacque could have helped him. I don't believe it had to be like this!"

"Adriano—please. I know Sebastien meant no harm keeping me secret."

"Adriano is right, I could have asked Jacques to try and find out more about you. But I didn't. I don't know why. Maybe I just didn't want to lose you. You were my blood link. That means something to me!" shouts Sebastien emotionally.

"Sebastien, it's okay."

"But Rebe—"

"Adriano! Please! Enough! It's my life. I don't want to hear anymore negativity about Sebastien. He is not the monster you're trying to paint of him. He feels bad enough! Stop—I need peace. It's done, we can't go back. I'm alive! Can't you just be happy about that?"

"Of course, I'm happy! I'm sorry, I just—forget it, it's been a very long day. I think it best we just all get some rest."

"I agree. Sebastien, I will stay here, I don't think you should be alone." She looks back at Adriano, her eyes warning him not to interfere or make Sebastien feel worse. Adriano rolls his eyes, shaking his head in frustration, but he is mentally tired too, he can't deal with more tension than what already exists. Adriano gets up with Jonathan, but Sebastien steps in.

"Hazel Eyes, you are the kindest person I have ever met besides my James. I can't ask you to do this for me. Please, go with Adriano, I will be fine."

"Sebastien, I won't sleep tonight knowing you're here alone and feeling all of this guilt. So please do me a favor, all of you! I need sleep. It must be four a.m. I'm going to my room. I'm tired. Some vampires can handle little to no sleep, but I can't." She moves in and lifts her feet and head and kisses Adriano on the lips. He is not sure what to think, but he smiles. Rebecca then turns to Jonathan and lifts herself and kisses him on the cheek, which surprises everyone.

"Oh! Sorry Jonathan! But —see—no craving for you!"

"Thanks, I'm relieved... I think?"

Then Rebecca turns to Sebastien and lifts her head up and her stands on her tippy toes, giving him a kiss on the cheek. "Good night everyone, I will see you all tomorrow!"

In seconds she is at her guest room and quietly enters and shuts the door. Her uncanny lighting speed departure makes Jonathan briefly dizzy. All three men seemed touched in their own way by this woman who just left the room.

Adriano interrupts this moment. "I am not leaving, so Sebastien you have two overnight guests besides Rebecca."

Sebastien understands and doesn't dare argue or disagree. "I will get you some blankets, sorry, the couch doesn't unfold into a bed, and the other spare rooms upstairs do not have beds."

"Not necessary, Johnathan, you take the couch, I am fine with one of these La-Z-Boys." His eyes move between the chair in the dark corner and the one Sebastien uses. "Besides—I don't think I will be sleeping much,

Rebecca looked exhausted and I want to be alert in case we need to go hunting very soon."

On that note, Sebastien leaves to find blankets, but secretly hopes that Adriano chooses his own recliner to sleep on and not James' in the corner. He returns and is relieved to find Adriano sitting on his own chair. "Peaceful night to you both, call me if you need me," he says, his eyes directly focused towards Jonathan. Sebastien too suddenly moves quickly upstairs, leaving Jonathan feeling a bit unbalanced. He sits abruptly on the couch, but Adriano doesn't notice.

Jonathan isn't used to such unnatural movements like this. Adriano is so careful and used to moving at a normal pace around humans, so this is very unusual for Jonathan to see, and will need some getting used to.

Upstairs, Sebastien slumps on his bed, his body feeling drained, his emotions raw. Thankfully the dinner is still holding up strong, keeping the thirst symptoms at bay. He pulls the warm blankets on top of him, and he whispers out into the air, "Oh James, what have I done?"

CHAPTER 13
Breakfast with Vampires

Adriano is already awake. He looks at his cell, and the display shows nine a.m., Sunday February 17. Jonathan is still fast asleep. He quietly peeks into Rebecca's room and hears steady breathing, but he needs to make sure and turns on the light. Rebecca is asleep, and her appearance seems okay. Adriano wants her to rest longer. In the meantime, he feels responsible to go and check on Sebastien too, and he quietly moves up the stairs quickly. Suddenly he remembers when he first met Sebastien, there was an X painted on his bedroom door. But now he is struck with curiosity when he sees another door that is painted in a deep red. He knocks at Sebastien's door.

"Who is it?"

"It's Adriano—sorry if I woke you, just thought you should be ready to hunt soon."

The door remained closed. "You didn't wake me, I was up already. Yes, will be ready soon. Is Rebecca okay?"

"Yes, I will wake her soon."

"Fine, thanks. I will be down shortly." Sebastien's bedroom door remains closed.

Adriano is still curious as to why his door has a large X painted on it in white. He takes the opportunity to look around, and he notices how dark the hallway is. He looks up to the ceiling and there is a light fixture, but no bulb. His eyes work around the hall and he notices two other doors on the opposite side of Sebastien's, slightly ajar. His curious mind wants to open the doors but he restrains himself. He feels bad to snoop into any of these rooms. Then his eye catches another door further down, but the absence of light almost hides its existence. Adriano's vampire eyes see through the darkness. He walks toward it quietly and is suddenly confronted by a strong unpleasant odor in the air, but just in this spot. He then focuses on the dark patch in the center of the closed door, which is not on the other doors. He is becoming very curious and puzzled. Then he turns and sees the torn curtains covering the window at the front of the hall. He is about to open them to see some light come in, but then he hears Sebastien's door begin to open. Sebastien is startled to see Adriano still standing at the stairs. "Adriano, I thought you were downstairs?"

"Sorry, I umm...just didn't realize how large this house really is. There are quite a few bedrooms up here, and I am admiring this wrap-around hallway."

"Yes, well, you should go check on Rebecca, she should be waking up soon. I will be right there." Sebastien can feel his anxiety rising and Adriano senses some irritation in Sebastien's tone.

"Right, see you downstairs." Adriano descends the stairs quickly, feeling a bit embarrassed, but he is mostly curious. He enters the spare washroom and notices the lighting is scarce and the mirror is cracked, making it more difficult for him to see past the distorted reflection he is accustomed to ignoring. He looks very tired, even as a vampire; the stress of the hours earlier could not disappear. He hates looking so worn out. He knows that more blood would help, even though he isn't thirsty. He decides to leave Jonathan sleeping. Adriano enters Rebecca's room and gently wakes her up. She drowsily opens her eyes. She tries to smile but it seems a bit forced, the argument from hours ago still lingering in the air. She gets out of bed and goes to wash up. Soon after, all three vampires quietly leave for the woods, each in their own hunting space, little words spoken between them.

Jonathan is just waking up and finds a note on the coffee table, he opens it and reads.

Dear Jonathan,

I just wanted to let you know that we are out of the house for a little while. We will be back soon. Hope you had a restful sleep.

Sincerely
Sebastien Woodsworth. ;)

As he finishes reading it, he hears the back door open and three vampires enter, but no talking between them is evident. The three vampires walk back into the living room.

"Good hunt, everyone?" Jonathan hopes the tension is gone, but by the cool expressions on Adriano and Sebastien's face, the chill is still in the air from last night's episode. Sebastien is shocked to hear Jonathan acknowledge their hunt, he is not used to sharing this private aspect of his life with a human.

"Oh—umm, it was fine. Hope you weren't waiting long?"

"No, just woke up myself. Thanks for the note, Sebastien. Do you mind if I use your shower?"

"By all means, here come with me."

"Oh, I forgot—Adriano, can I have the keys to your car, my luggage is still in the trunk."

Adriano passes Jonathan the keys and looks at Sebastien. "Actually, this is Sebastien's car, he let me borrow it yesterday."

"Cool—that was nice of you, Sebastien. Be right back."

Sebastien follows Jonathan to the front door and opens it for him. "Can I give you a hand? I am pretty strong?" A grin crosses Sebastien's face.

"No, I got it—thanks, be right back."

Slightly disappointed, Sebastien returns to the living room.

"Adriano, do you think I should buy a new cell phone, since I lost mine? I assume in the accident," Rebecca asks.

The subject of phones pricks Sebastien and he casually walks over to the bookshelf. Adriano just watches as Sebastien opens up one of his cabinets from the bookshelf and pulls out a landline phone. He hooks it up into the wall jack and picks up the receiver. "Good—it still works."

Rebecca tries to smooth the obvious tension in the room. "Oh, that's good, they didn't cut you off then?"

"No—I was still paying for the service. I didn't bother to cancel it with *everything else* occupying my days."

"Can you give the number to Adriano so he can put it in his phone?"

At that point the front door opens and Jonathan comes in with some luggage and calls out, "Sebastien, can you show me where the shower is?"

"Yes, follow me, it's upstairs." Sebastien moves up the stairs using very little movements, then realizes is Jonathan behind him and starts climbing at a normal human pace. Jonathon was feeling dizzy again.

"Oh, sorry Jonathan—habit. Are you okay? You suddenly look dazed."

"No—no, I'm fine. It must be nice to move that quickly!" His smile is kind, his human eyes wandering curiously around the hallway. He notices the closed doors and the odd one painted with an X. "Wow, a lot of rooms. This is a really big place you have here—have you lived here a long time?"

"Yes—it belonged to Dr. Huntington."

Jonathan remembers the text from Adriano. All he was able to find out was Dr. James Huntington was a faculty member, but now is listed on their website as professor Emeritus.

"Here are some fresh towels, and there is soap in the shower." Sebastien's eyes stay on Jonathan, his curiosity building.

"Great, thanks, I won't be long."

"Take your time." Sebastien flashes a warm smile and moves downstairs towards the living room. He hears a question posed by Adriano.

"So what do you think, *mon amour*? Should we try to visit the art gallery? See if we can meet these vampires?"

Sebastien stands at the entrance to the living room, intrigued to hear mention of the gallery and meeting other vampires. It has been a long time since he went to a gallery. He and James visited them quite a bit.

"I guess we could try. I didn't realize you didn't meet other vampires in Toronto. Or did you tell me and I forgot?"

"I may have mentioned it in passing, it's okay—your memory is coming back better than we expected."

Sebastien jumps in. "No vampires in Toronto? Really?"

"I never met any back home. But that doesn't mean they weren't around."

Sebastien picks up the notepad and pen and writes his number down, then gives it to Rebecca. "Here is my house number."

"Oh, thanks, actually, here Adriano, put it in your phone." The subject of the phone still seems to leave a lingering sour mood in Adriano. He sits on the couch and starts entering the number in his cell phone. The room is quiet again. Rebecca is desperate to remove the tension, it is very uncomfortable. "Sebastien, yesterday you spoke about Count B, can you tell us of the other vampires James encountered?" She turns her face to Adriano. "We would really like to hear more, if you are up to it. Right Adriano?"

"Hmmm? Sure—tell us more."

"Okay, but I need wine!"

"Wine? In the morning?"

"Hazel Eyes, we are vampires. It has no physical effects. Be right back."

"Right, the things I have to learn." She smirks and gets up to browse the albums. She picks up one titled *Bach* and puts it on, the sound of a piano begins to play.

Sebastien suddenly stops in the hallway holding a tray of glasses and snacks. He just stands there, his mind travelling back, and he sees the image of James sitting in his chair, glass of wine in his hand and a book in the other, just listening to his classics. The memory strikes an unpleasant mood, but Sebastien composes himself. He returns carrying the tray. "Prelude Number One, nice choice, Hazel Eyes."

"Can you play this one too?"

"Yes, but I can see your mind thinking—don't get any ideas."

"Oh, come on? Please? I don't get it, if I could play the piano, or any instrument as well as you play the piano, I would be playing for anyone who asked."

"Oh—you play the piano, Sebastien?"

"Yes, but not as good as Rebecca is advertising."

"Oh, don't believe him Adriano, he's amazing! I hope he will let you hear it. Hint hint." "Maybe later." Sebastien smiles and pours the wine.

"I hope we haven't eaten too many of your snacks, Sebastien."

"Not at all, Hazel Eyes. Besides, I can always call Jacques now that I have the phone hooked up." A sarcastic grin splashes on Sebastien's face as he takes a sip of his wine, getting comfortable in his recliner.

Rebecca chuckles with a nervous twinge to it and places her left hand on Adriano's knee, squeezing it playfully. "So tell us about more of James' encounters with other vampires."

At that moment Jonathan walks in the room. "Other vampires?"

Sebastien looks at Jonathan; his hair is wet and combed back neatly. An unexpected flutter grows in Sebastien's stomach. "Please take a seat Jonathan. Can I pour you some wine? Sorry all I have are nuts and berries to offer you." Then suddenly Sebastien realizes, "Oh you must be starving by now!"

Adriano realizes too and stands up. "Oh man, sorry Jonathan!" He looks at Rebecca. "Why don't we go to a cafe, it will be good practice for you?"

Rebecca stands up too quickly, and everyone notices. "Oh shoot! I will never get this!"

"Of course, you will, beautiful—it didn't come easy for me right away."

"Me either, James really helped me."

"It's kind of cool, speaking as the only human in the room—that is, it really trips your eyes!"

"You're all very kind, thank you—I will keep practicing. So shall we go?"

Sebastien thinks quickly. "Why not."

CHAPTER 14

The Journal

All three vampires and one human arrive back to Sebastien's home, after lunch at the café and more hunting for Rebecca and Sebastien. The tension between Sebastien and Adriano has disappeared, which pleases Rebecca. They are all gathered in the living room. Adriano, Rebecca and Jonathan are seated on the large sectional and Sebastien is getting himself comfortable in his chair.

Sebastien comments, "That was a nice outing I have to say. I wasn't sure I would tolerate the green tea but it wasn't too bitter. How about you, Hazel Eyes?" Sebastien notices Adriano is still not comfortable with her nickname. "Oops, sorry, Adriano, I can't get used to calling her Rebecca."

"Oh, he doesn't mind the Hazel Eyes anymore—right Sweetie?"

Adriano taps Rebecca's knee with his hand, grinning slightly. "It will take some getting used to, my love."

"Am I missing something?"

"Oh, it's nothing Jonathan. Adriano is not used to my nickname." Rebecca looks over to Adriano, smiling.

"Okay, okay. By the way, Rebecca, I meant to mention to you, I thought I saw that gentleman Lucan in the cafe. He was with someone."

"Oh, too bad you didn't tell me then, I would have gone to say hi."

"Who's Lucan?" asks Jonathan.

"Oh, just some odd older man—"

"Odd? He wasn't odd, I thought he was quite charming. He looks quite good for his age."

"True. But there is something suspicious about him. Anyways, I would have preferred to encounter the two younger vampires I saw—Juliette and Veneur. Oh well—Sebastien, please tell us about the other vampires that James came across."

Sebastien looks over to Jonathan and can't help but chuckle. "Oh! Jonathan, this must be the most bizarre conversation that you have encountered. Hopefully this doesn't make you uncomfortable or uneasy once I start?"

"I just had breakfast at a cafe with three vampires, I think I can handle this."

They all laugh.

"This will probably be one for my memory—Adriano will agree that our conversations are about life in general, work, plans, the usual."

Sebastien smiles generously at Jonathan, getting so lost in thought that he doesn't hear Rebecca speaking to him.

"Sebastien, did you hear me?"

"Uhmm? What?" Sebastien turns back to Rebecca.

"I said should we bring out wine and snacks? ...You okay?"

Sebastien stands up, a bit frazzled and flushed. "Yes, oh—I forgot the wine." He moves quickly to the kitchen. Jonathan is suddenly dizzy, caught off guard by the speed he just witnessed. Sebastien is in another world, enjoying playing host to his guests, especially Jonathan. He returns to the living room. "Jonathan, please let me know when I can bring out the bread and cheese we bought earlier—we can't have a human becoming weak and starving among vampires." Just then an explosion of laughter suddenly fills the room. "Wine anyone? Jonathan?"

"Sure, why not, after all, I'm not driving." Jonathan watches Sebastien as he pours the wine, he turns to Rebecca. "So Rebecca, if you don't mind me asking, I know this is a lot for you to adjust to, but have you and Adriano thought of what you will tell your family? Adriano filled me in about the story you told about the hospital, amnesia, and tests, but what about you moving from your condo to a house?"

"Adriano and I are working on this. I hope our plan includes Sebastien too?"

Jonathan looks at Sebastien, who suddenly coughs. "Sebastien too? I don't follow?"

"Oh, Hazel Eyes has this idea that I should leave here. Come with them to Toronto, stay with her. I haven't decided yet, we were just discussing possibilities, but I can't imagine leaving my home to live with humans."

"Sebastien, we will figure this out, you know this is the best." Rebecca sighs. "I wish that day would come sooner."

Adriano turns to Rebecca. "What day?"

"The day when we can live among humans freely and without being feared. One day when I can finally tell my family, my sons, who I am. I know my truth has to come out for it to get better. I hate lying to them! But that day seems so far away." Rebecca sips her wine, the only sound coming from the song on the record player. The air in the room has somehow changed again, a cloud of deep thoughts resting over all three vampires and Jonathan. "Oh never mind all that for now, let's change the subject— Sebastien, please go on, tell us more about James's adventures—Jonathan, you have to hear this."

"Now I am intrigued, but who is James? I keep hearing this name mentioned."

Sebastien takes a sip of his wine, not sure if he has the energy to repeat everything. Jonathan notices the sudden melancholy look on Sebastien.

"Oh, sorry, I hope I—I don't need to know, it's okay Sebastien."

"Oh no, Jonathan, sorry, the question just caught me off guard. No need to apologize—after all, I am among friends." He pauses. "You see, James and I—he was a vampire too, very special to me."

Jonathan sips his wine and looks over to Adriano; he already knows what the other vampire is thinking: Sebastien is vague about James. But then his eyes move back to Sebastien sitting across from him. Sebastien can feel Jonathan's eyes on him and he blushes, feeling suddenly warm.

He is surprised at his schoolboy reaction, and adjusts himself on the chair, almost feeling guilty for the nice feelings he is having. He looks at James' recliner, but the chair remains empty.

He turns back to Jonathan then begins. "Oh right, yes, hmmm… Where to begin—you see, James continued exploring through the mountains and forests and in the countryside, and came across other vampires living in caves and churches and castle ruins. Oh, this is when he was a vampire, Jonathan, just so you follow. He learned some interesting history from the vampires who were willing to engage with him and also found writings on cave walls. He travelled through Poland and Ukraine, and he learned how to approach vampires cautiously and gauge which ones he needed to perform the traditional ceremony greeting that Count B taught him."

"Count B?" Jonathan looks to Adriano.

"Long story Jonathan, just listen, you will catch on."

"He was James's first sit down with a vampire—I can fill you in later, personally." Sebastien gives a warm and inviting smile. Jonathan smiles back. "Anyways, James soon learned that with Great Masters you don't make eye contact right away, it is earned. It soon became evident that James was not a threat, and he was welcomed into many caves. He also came across some vampires in old abandoned castles and church ruins. It disheartened him especially when he found some in old decayed crypts. James was very intuitive in knowing and seeking out their possible dwellings; these poor creatures lived in such horrible conditions. This saddened James so much. He said the stench at times was so unbearable that when he left he became violently ill. Some were receptive, and he enjoyed talking with them, while others he knew he was at times risking his own life just being there. But his research compelled him to carry on, despite the danger. Jonathan are you ok?"

"Yes, just stunned as to what I've heard so far. Is this for real?"

"Yes. Of course. I wouldn't make light of such conditions and suffering. If this is disturbing you, I can—"

"No—no, please go on." Jonathan takes a large gulp of his wine. He can't believe he is listening to real historical anecdotes about vampires.

"James noticed a pattern forming with the vampires. The ones who lived in caves were all male, Great Blood Masters. They shared common traits: they were more stoic and very traditional and private. They would never discuss the events around their rebirth. That was a taboo. James also encountered some who were extremely dangerous; these ones sent him running for his own life, afraid he would be their next meal. Thankfully they wouldn't travel far from their caves, but he could see such darkness emanating from their beings. Their souls were completely gone, and the sound and hissing they made was petrifying. James came across other vampires who seemed more open and wanted to share and had questions; they were more curious. Some of them risked going against the vampire traditional code and spoke about their experience of becoming a reborn, which was forbidden in centuries past. Some revealed they had pleasant memories of the vampire who turned them, but then there were cases of trauma relived again, and those vampires became very emotional. James just didn't know how to comfort them. It was clear they suffered PTSD and anxiety. James did his best to gain the trust of these vampires enough to engage them, and they wanted to learn about James. Many were shocked to learn that he became a scientist and went to University after he was turned. They thought it was unbelievable to study among humans, undetected, not feared or loathed. They couldn't understand how he could just be around them without drinking their blood."

"Interesting, so it was quite rare then for vampires to discover educated vampires?"

"Yes, Jonathan. You have to remember the generations he came across. Some were ignorant, satisfied with not advancing with society at the time, while others were absorbing the period of enlightenment. Advancements in society and science were felt all over. However, these unwanted creatures were not a part of the future, and they were forced to hide outside of society. For them, meeting James was a novelty." Sebastien pauses to compose himself, clearing his throat, which is becoming dry with all the talking he's done. He is beginning to look a bit frail.

"Sebastien, maybe we need to stop for now, I think this has been too much for you?"

A heavy sigh escapes Sebastien. "You're so kind, Jonathan. It's difficult to talk about the hardships of our kind, but it's important, since James discovered these poor souls. I'm okay."

For Adriano, this day has become mentally exhausting already, and it is only eleven a.m.. But he is learning and discovering so much through Sebastien, he is starting to feel that maybe they have more in common than he thinks.

Sebastien's spirit remains dim, but he nods his head, understanding that there is more he needs to share. He gets up to change the album that finished playing a while ago. He puts a Bach record on, hoping James's ghost might return for a little while. Sebastien sits back down, crossing his legs. "James feared that over time, our species would disappear because of the decline in vampires not turning humans. The risk and chaos of being detected if our population were to grow exponentially would be devastating. But he also knew that to have that kind of power over life and death was very dangerous. Even though he was a vampire he still wanted to keep his humanity, to be true to himself and who he was. If he could be a decent living vampire, he believed others could too. But many of our kind are not given a chance to grow in spirit and love."

"Fascinating, please go on," Jonathan says.

"Thank you. This is so refreshing, I must say, to have a human so mature and respectful to our history. It means a lot." His eyes caress Jonathan's thick dark hair in his mind. "James was still discouraged, though, about the one thing that spearheaded his quest: he still couldn't find any other vampire with our disease. Vamprogeria just was so rare, unique."

"Wait—what? Vampro—" blurts out Jonathan. His human mind is still trying to process everything he has heard up to this moment.

"Vamprogeria, Jonathan—this is the disease Rebecca and I have. It is a specific blood disease."

Jonathan remains confused. "Disease? Am I missing something here?"

Adriano leans quietly over to Jonathan. "I will fill you in later. It is very complicated. Sorry to interrupt, go on Sebastien."

"That's fine, Adriano. —Jonathan, have you heard of progeria?" Sebastien can see Jonathan thinking, and he can't help but smile. *He looks so cute as his mind is searching his memory data,* Sebastien thinks. Then he clears his throat, waiting patiently, curious.

"Oh, I think I've heard of that, isn't that when you age too quickly or something? I'm sure I saw a documentary on this."

A documentary, how adorable, Sebastien privately confides to himself. "Yes, Jonathan, \you're correct. However, a little more complicated. Basically, for Hazel Eyes and I, we need to frequently drink blood or we age rapidly."

"Oh—is it dangerous?"

"Yes," is spoken simultaneously by all three vampires.

Sebastien continues. "James didn't have medical information on our disease, vamprogeria. He couldn't apply for funding, obviously, because he couldn't provide the Ethics board with the details of his study, which involved vampire genealogy and medical history. This just made him feel so closed off from the medical and science community. It was difficult for him to accept. He needed funding for this study but that would mean he would have to lie, and he was not doing that! He was so passionate about our disease, he believed it needed a real name. He still dreamed that one day, future generations of medical scientists would discover our scientific historical notes and be able to properly and openly study vamprogeria with grant funding. He was a dreamer, my James. I loved this idealistic side of him. My life experience as a vampire cannot compare to his. I live a very quiet *life now.*" Those last few words struggle painfully out of Sebastien, and he fights back the tears.

"I'm amazed by all of this. I especially never thought vampires could have any disease."

Sebastien takes a large gulp of his wine, calming his intense emotions that are rising, and turns to Jonathan. "We are lucky. Look at you, Jonathan, friend of Adriano and Hazel Eyes. We are proof that humans and vampires can be friends...or more." He pauses, feeling flushed. "It's necessary to both our health and wellbeing."

"Yes, but Sandra and Jonathan are in a unique situation."

"Sandra?"

"Yes, she is our good friend, a human, back in Toronto. I've known Jonathan and Sandra for a long time. They are my two very first human best friends."

"I see. Trust, respect, and acceptance between diverse species can bring growth and harmony. Discussions should take place with both sides at the table, without either of them fearing that harm will come to them. Vampires have great ideas and gifts we can bring, and now we have a greater set of tools to work with, not weapons. Our tools are history, experiences, and education. Our unique powerful gifts can be an advantage for humans. But first they have to believe and know that we exist!"

"Sebastien, I know you're passionate about all of this, but try to stay calm."

"Hazel Eyes, it just is too much at times. The things that James revealed in his journal leaves a dark stain on humanity. As I mentioned, James travelled part of the world with the intention to study and encounter other vampires. Many vampires in the past suffered in order for the new generations to have a chance to trust and be trusted, but we still have a long way to go before we can truly coexist with humans. There are many of us vampires who are making a real difference in science, art, medicine, business, and so many other important areas that create a healthy culturally enriched society but they receive no recognition! As long as the majority of vampires see humans as the real drink of choice—no offense Jonathan." Jonathan nods his head that he is fine.

"And as long as the majority of humans see us as pariahs that need to be extinct, it will be difficult to create a world where two very distinct intellectual species capable of love and empathy and beauty can live amongst each other."

The record has already finished that one side. Everyone sits in their own thoughts. Sebastien gets up to pour more wine for everyone. "I am sorry, I can go on tangents sometimes, James used to say this too—I have done too much talking." He takes a sip of wine.

Adriano is feeling uncomfortable at having this conversation move to the subject of killing humans again.

Sebastien sits back down in his chair. "I haven't factored in the vampires with blood addictions, those who cannot stop from drinking. It is unfortunate for these ones, especially because unless they know of vampire psychiatrists or psychologists that specialize in a vampire's mental illness and addictions, how can they possibly get professional help? They will continue to kill humans because of their need for blood, even if they are not thirsty yet. They will not have self-agency to stop before they drink them completely. They don't get the same fix—if I can use that word—drinking from animals."

Just in that moment a dark memory shadows Adriano's present moment, and he remembers the last thing that Signore Domenico said to him when he was first turned. Thinking that nobody can hear him, he mumbles the haunting phrase out loud.

"Did you say something, Adriano?" asks Rebecca, sitting beside him. Sebastien stops talking.

"It's nothing, I just remembered something that was once said to me."

"What was it?" Rebecca is curious to know, but sees Adriano is troubled.

"The one who turned me, or as you say, Sebastien—my blood link. Although that term you give seems much more intimate, more connected. I don't feel any connection to him. I hate him! I wasn't given a choice." Adriano takes a deep breath. This is uneasy territory for him now, he's only spoken about the vampire who turned him and the horror of that event to Jonathan and Sandra. But not in detail. He isn't sure if he is mentally prepared to share the details that he has forced down in his mind.

"It's okay Adriano, you are among friends. I shared so much about James and—"

"This monster is not at all like James!"

Sebastien is alarmed by the loud outburst.

Adriano suddenly feels this heavy weight over his heart, this emotional boulder just landing there out of nowhere. "He killed my mother! In front of me!"

"Oh Adriano! How horrible." Rebecca puts her hand on Adriano's shoulder.

"Rebecca, I never shared about my mother or my family with you. Only a little to Jonathan and Sandra. But Jonathan, even you don't know the whole story."

"What was her name? Please tell us, we're here for you."

"Thank you, *mon amour*. Her name was Elizabetha. She was the gentlest, sweetest, most nurturing mother. She sacrificed herself—for nothing!" The room becomes instantly silenced. Rebecca takes Adriano's hand, which is a bit on the cool side. "I was deathly sick in bed, believing the vampire's word that he would not harm me. My poor loving mother died protecting me. He lied to her! He just drank her to her death. Then I heard this loud sound, I knew it was her dead body falling to the floor. He turned, and I could feel and smell his stench on me. I don't know what happened after that, it's still a blur. But obviously I drank from him—the man who killed my mother." Adriano's head collapses heavily into his trembling hands. "Why did I do that? What possessed me to drink his blood—*his* blood?"

Sebastien sits dumbfounded in his chair, not knowing what to say, but feeling such empathy for this vampire.

Rebecca grabs hold of Adriano tightly. "Adriano it's okay, I'm here. I can understand why you never talked about this part of your life. That is so cruel of him."

"He just left me lying there. I'm haunted by the vision of my mother's dead corpse. I was so confused. I remember suddenly feeling this unbelievably excruciating pain spreading through my bones and joints. I felt like my blood was boiling, I thought my bones would burst out of my skin. It was horrible, frightening, and I was alone! He didn't stay to help me through the death of my body. He just turned me, and his last words to me were a cryptic warning. '*Do not drink unless drinking to the very end, or it is your responsibility for the life you hold in the balance.*' I will never understand why he didn't just kill me like my mother. Why did he turn me and leave? His message to me was basically go ahead and drink to completion, to kill."

Sebastien gasps in horror. "How awful! Oh my God—what kind of monster tells his own innocent blood link to kill humans, and then leaves him to turn on his own? That can leave such emotional trauma."

Adriano feels panic rising within. He can't stop his hands from shaking, and he tries to cover his face like a shield for his own mind. The horrible memories flood in, images coming in and out of the moments before and after his rebirth. It's as if the room is struggling with the eerie silence.

"Adriano, my God, what you have been through. Your rebirth, such a horrible experience—no innocent reborn should go through such unspeakable events as you did. Oh, this is so upsetting. But just know—whatever you have done—it's not your fault, you were taught wrong."

Adriano looks up immediately to Sebastien, his expression turning from sadness and guilt to anger and worry. He is aware now that he has revealed too much, letting Sebastien realize that he has killed humans. Adriano abruptly stands, and a low growl rises out of him. "What I have done? You judge me!" He glares at Sebastien.

Sebastien swallows. Fear, mixing in with a need to survive, travels through his body. He holds back a growl that wants to emerge.

Rebecca speaks. "No one is judging you, Adriano. I'm sure Sebastien—"

"What I have done saved lives! What I have done gave me a purpose! And I don't need either of you to feel pity for me, ever!" Adriano is in a rage of emotion. "Hear me—I chose this path and I have my damn reasons, which you will never understand! There are monsters out there—human garbage, rapists, drug dealers and pedophiles. I feed from them. I kill them! Yes, Sebastien, you heard me! Does that make me an evil seed!? I wonder. Am I still surrounded by trusting friends?" His eyes are throwing daggers, mostly at Sebastien. He feels judged, all the eyes staring at him. Sebastien is so nervous, shifting in his chair, that he just wants everyone to leave. Especially Adriano.

Jonathan stands up immediately. "Adriano, calm down! No one is judging you."

Adriano can't help but feel out of control and embarrassed. "Excuse me, I need some air." Adriano immediately stalks out of the room, out the front door, slamming it behind him. Rebecca's doing her best to hold back any emotions, but her heart is breaking, and she turns to Jonathan.

"Jonathan? Did you know? Did he ever talk about this with you?"

"About his mother? I mean, we knew that his mother died, and we saw every year on July ninth how that date really affected him, but he never told us the whole story."

"No—I mean, about killing humans. Did you know?"

Jonathan looks puzzled and disappointed. "Yes, but don't paint a picture so quickly in judgment, Rebecca!"

"Oh, Jonathan! I'm not judging—I'm just trying to process this!"

"Rebecca, I need to tell you this—brace yourself—you knew about the human killings. You just don't remember the conversation."

"What? I knew? That can't be!"

Sebastien leans forward in disbelief.

"Yes, it took you awhile to accept it, but you did, because you loved him. He feels very strongly about the type of evil he goes after. It's not about a craving for blood. This is different, it goes so much deeper. It is very personal for him. But he also feels remorse after. This is what I hold onto about him. He is not evil. I hope you can accept this, you once did. Adriano needs to know you still respect him. He is torn by his need to do good and his need to remove evil. Rebecca, he has so much love to give, but he has deep hate for human predators. I know it sounds wrong hearing this from a cop, but honestly if you saw some of the things I've had to stomach in my job, the things that some humans are capable of, it would haunt you forever. When he met you, it was like a light went on inside of him, he trusted you with this part of him. Don't abandon him. He needs you. This is the most troubling secret he carries with him."

Sebastien moves more forward in his chair. "I am stunned-- I can't believe this."

"Sebastien, you don't know him like I do. He is not a monster."

"Please—don't misunderstand my reaction, Jonathan. I am not judging."

"You're not?"

"No, I stopped judging people *a long time ago.*" His voice dips very low and private guilt crosses over his heart. "We all have our crosses to carry."

"So it doesn't bother you either the fact that I accept this, as a police officer?"

Sebastien doesn't respond right away; he takes his time, gathers his thoughts, "I don't know you well enough yet, Jonathan, but I am a good judge of character, and I do know that life is not black and white. Humans or vampires, both have good or evil amongst them, both have good and not so good inside them. Good people can do bad things. It is very rare that bad people can do good things. Big difference. I would not surround myself with anyone who is evil or share what I have shared if I didn't absolutely trust you all. There are things I haven't yet—" He pauses, panic rising at the near-slip in his words. "Sometimes, we do things that we would never have thought we could do, but until you're faced with that moment, you don't really know what you are capable of, what your mind allows you to accept. I didn't realize until I met James, until I became a vampire—until I read the journal."

"What are you talking about, Sebastien?"

"Jonathan, I can't talk about this now."

Jonathan sees the upset in Sebastien, and he doesn't want to push. He gets up. "I'm going to go check on him."

"Jonathan, let me go, please."

"If you don't mind Rebecca, I think it would be better if I go, okay, I think Adriano needs a human this time—I mean no disrespect."

"But he needs to know I'm here for him."

"I will tell him, but he's really upset. I don't think he can face you right now. I know he feels really bad about his outburst and what just happened—Rebecca, trust me, okay?"

"Please, tell him I'm here for him, please let him know."

"Of course, I will. He loves you."

Jonathan grabs his winter coat and opens the front door. The evening winter wind is biting at his face already. Adriano is just sitting on the porch step, coatless. He hears footsteps on the porch. "Came to check if the vampire has cooled down?"

"Yes, but mostly I came to check on my friend, I hope he is okay?"

"Oh Jonathan—I'm not sure. If I am honest—I feel so overwhelmed. I don't know what happened back there. I felt so—so out of control. It scared me."

"To be expected. A lot has happened in the last forty-eight hours. Hell, the last two months you've been going through hell. I could tell from your voice on the phone when you called me to come to Paris. My friend, you can't control everything. I know you think you can. I can see how much you're trying to hold it all together for Rebecca. She has a difficult road ahead of her. I can't imagine what you are both going through. This is a complicated situation and having Rebecca lose parts of her memory, well, it can't be easy."

"She must hate me now. Rediscovering that I—I kill. Is she okay?"

"You're wrong, so very wrong, she loves you. She's sitting in there desperately trying to remember that conversation when you told her that you have killed, but buddy, you have to give her time, she has to process this, *again*. Give her time. And Sebastien—"

"Oh Sebastien, I can imagine his reaction."

"No, I don't think you can. Adriano, you're surrounded by friends, no one is judging you—you are your worst enemy sometimes. I wouldn't have given you those files to these predators if I believed you were evil. Maybe that makes me just as guilty or bad in society's eyes. But damn society! So many bad seeds out there. I see such horrible things that humans are capable of, and you wonder who is really the monster—the human or the vampire? I'm not a soldier in a war zone either, they see the worst of humanity."

Adriano turns to Jonathan. "I don't kill for pleasure, you know that, right?"

"Of course, I do—how can you ask?"

"I just needed to hear."

"Come back inside, it's freezing out here. And you have no coat on."

"Jonathan, really?"

Jonathan smirks. "If Sandra were here you know what she would say. 'Adriano! My God, are you deliberately trying to see if you can get pneumonia, just for the fun of it?'"

"Aww yes, she probably would say something like that, how is she?"

"She's good, she's worried about you. She wanted to come but she just couldn't get the time off."

"Oh, before I forget, did you get my text?"

"Yes. All I could find is that he was a professor at *l'Université de science et médecine*, in the clinical biology department. He retired, according to the website."

"I see. Something just seems off. I mean, Sebastien shared everything else about James, but he is deliberately careful what he says."

The winter wind is picking up. Jonathan is shivering now, his teeth chattering. "So-o wh-ha-at is-s your-r plan-n-n when-n you get-t back-k to Toronto-o-o?"

Adriano chuckles. "Let's get you inside. We don't want you catching pneumonia—that's all I need, two vampires on my back after." They go inside. "Hey Sebastien, you wouldn't happen to have tea or coffee in your cupboards?"

Rebecca responds. "Sebastien went upstairs for a minute. I will check, but highly doubtful."

Jonathan sits on the couch, shivering to the bones and with chattering teeth. "I don't know-w how y-you vamp-pires can stand the cold-d-d!"

"We adapt better than humans, perks of being us. Let me go grab some more firewood—here human, wrap this blanket around yourself." Adriano smiles warmly as he leaves the room.

Rebecca returns to the living room and sits beside Jonathan. "Oh, are you okay?" She hesitates if she should rub his shoulders. But she feels confident, no craving rising.

"Yeah, I'm tough." He coughs.

"Is Adriano, okay?"

"Yes, he's okay. Don't worry, he has Sicilian blood in those vampire veins, you know how they can get, hot headed and then cool as a cucumber—man, it is c-c-cold-d out there."

Sebastien returns to the living room carrying the journal, but notices the state that Jonathan is in and puts the journal down. Quickly, he moves to the cabinet and pulls out a bottle of whisky. "You humans, so fragile." He grins wickedly, his eyes twinkling,

"Ha ha, you vampires so-o—so—ah, forget it, my brain is froz-z-zen." A burst of laughter covers the room like a warm and cozy blanket. Sebastien pours Jonathan some whisky in a glass.

"Than-n-nk you-u." Jonathan takes the glass, his hands shaking.

Adriano returns, carrying a few pieces of firewood, and places them in the basket near the fireplace. Sebastien clears his throat and awkwardly takes a seat in his lazy boy. "Thank you Adriano, for the firewood."

Adriano places some wood in the fireplace, he then stands up and faces Sebastien. "Listen, Sebastien, I'm sorry for—earlier."

"I understand. Just realize, we are all on the same side. Even angels can experience darkness sometimes. Life is not without light and dark." He picks up the book. Adriano is puzzled by the comment. *Who is the angel in this scenario?* He lets it be.

Rebecca notices the leather book. "Oh, is that the journal you mentioned?"

"Yes—I believe James meant for me to share his story, I know it."

"Hey, look, the candle is flickering again." Adriano looks behind them. "There must be a cold spot above us, probably some outside air is getting in somehow. Sebastien, I noticed you have some deep scratches on some of your walls? Like an animal did it."

Sebastien doesn't respond.

Adriano becomes more curious, his mind collecting more data. *Another omission, what are you hiding?*

"Listen to the wind blowing out there, the windows are rattling more than my teeth were earlier," Jonathan says, and they all laugh.

"Oh Jonathan, you are so funny. Feeling much warmer now, I hope?"

"Yes, thanks Sebastien, so are you going to read it to us?"

Sebastien looks across to the recliner in the dark corner. The ghost of James is beginning to vanish. *Go ahead, Seb, tell my story.* Sebastien's eyes turn to meet Jonathan's. "Yes, I would like to. James went through some horrific events in the days leading up to him becoming a vampire. They at times haunted him in his dreams. I didn't realize how horrible it was for him. He would wake up screaming, and he would jump out of bed and in little movements would land at the bottom of stairs and then race out the back door into the woods. I would be running after him, calling out, but his mind would be back to that day and it was hard for me to reach him. When I caught up to him I would hold him tightly, kissing him, trying to reassure him it was just a dream, he was safe, he was at home with me. Eventually he would be calmer." Sebastien takes a sip of his wine, "What I am about to read you is quite compelling, a part of World War Two history never revealed. This shows the heroic side of my *James*." Sebastien opens the journal and flips the pages to the passage from James that he doesn't mind sharing and he begins.

If my memory hasn't failed me on this, I believe it was a few days after I became a vampire that this next event occurred. All that is important for me to remember is that I met this remarkable vampire, Xavier. My mentor, my dearest treasured friend.

I was still adjusting to my cravings for blood. I was naturally acquiring a taste for it, and was instinctively hunting all kinds of animals along the way. I mainly kept to the woods to avoid detection from humans. I never did encounter the vampire who turned me, and maybe just as well, I had a few choice words for him!

I was sitting on top of a tall tree, just thinking. I used to do that a lot; since I was alone, I thought I might as well enjoy this new ability to climb trees faster than a monkey or tiger, and leap down just as grace-fully as a cougar. So I was contemplating what I would do with my life. How can I help society, how can I help stop the Nazis! I suddenly heard the sound of a motor. My ears did not fail me, and sure enough a large trailer truck was coming down the dirt road. I watched it carefully with my vampire eyes, and something caught my attention immediately. The sides of the truck were painted, showing scenes of people laughing and drinking merrily. I heard voices, or more like screams, calls for help. I leaped down from the tree and ran as fast as my vampire speed allowed, and slumped down behind a large rock. The screams became louder, and to my complete horror I realized there were people in the back of that truck! Suddenly, the truck abruptly stopped, and I heard horrifying high-pitched screams coming from the front of the truck. Without warning the back door opened, and a soldier was standing there with blood dripping from his mouth. His eyes were glowing.

The people at the front of the trailer could see him, and once the shock wore off it soon became clear to everyone at the front that this was not a soldier, not a human! He suddenly spoke, saying he was there to rescue them, and people started jumping out of the truck. Some were injured as they fell out, terrified people escaping from the truck. I watched in horror, frozen, as people were running up the hill, mothers and fathers carrying their children or holding tightly to their hands. Then I realized he was telling the truth; he wasn't chasing after them, he just he watched them. He ran up to the ones who were in shock and pushed them gently, telling them to run. He was rescuing them! I leaped down and ran towards the civilians, helping to guide them out, calling out to the people, letting them know that they were safe but had to run away from here and to stay away from the town and city. Suddenly, the vampire came running towards me, and we both stopped a few feet away from each other. Like two Alpha males mentally gaging the other's powers. Then he spoke to me. Where did you come from?',

'I answered, 'the woods,' and he laughed. 'Okay, let's try something simpler. What is your name?' I said it was James. 'Well James, I am Xavier,' he said, 'but I prefer you call me X, okay? So are you ready to do what is necessary?' I didn't know what he meant, but I was taken in by this tall vampire with brilliant green eyes and charismatic aura, and I think I said yes, I must have. All I remember after that is we spent the next few months together finding Nazis and killing them.

We didn't suck their blood, X refused to have their blood in his body and I agreed. We preferred to just break their necks, throw them fiercely against tree trunks. We could hear their frantic screams, but waited for the sound of their bones breaking at impact. We found all kinds of ways to dispose of them. We felt empowered, we felt we were doing good—I still believe to this day we helped, in our own way, to save many lives from reaching terrible unspeakable deaths. We had vowed to never feed from humans, only animals."

Sebastien stops reading and closes the book. "Sorry, this is just too difficult all at once, I have read this over and over and it still affects me every time, crazy isn't it? I just need a little break, I promise I will continue, if you would like to hear more?"

Three voices simultaneously speak. "*Yes.*"

Sebastien is pleased. He wants to share.

"Adriano, may I borrow your phone, I'd like to call the boys in the meantime."

"Sure, here." He hands Rebecca the phone but then he pulls her aside. "I'm so sorry, *mon amour,* for my outburst earlier. I—-"

"Shh... It's ok, you're back here, you're among friends. Poor James, what he must have gone through. I really need to hear my sons' voices." Rebecca kisses Adriano on the lips. "Be back shortly." As Adriano watches her, he sees her as his own angel moving to the bedroom and shutting the door.

Sebastien hollers out from the kitchen. "Jonathan are you hungry, could I fix you a snack, the bread and cheese?"

"Sure, but let me come and help." Jonathan leaves the room.

Adriano moves the wood around the fire and then sits back on the couch. Rebecca comes back in the room. "That was a quick call. Is everything okay?"

"There was another call on the other line, for you, from a Richard?"

Adriano takes the phone and whispers, "He is my real estate agent. I asked him to do some searching for you, are the boys still on the phone?"

"No I told them I would call them back."

"Richard, hey, it's Adriano—no, that's okay, that was Rebecca, yes she is doing well. So tell me, anything—uh huh—okay, uh huh, I see, okay—yes."

Both Sebastien and Jonathan return to the living room, and Rebecca whispers, "It's his real estate agent."

"Okay, yes, send me the listings, I will take a look, sounds good, okay, I will be in touch. Yes, good, I will, thanks, bye."

All eyes are on Adriano, "Well, he has two possibilities and will be sending them shortly. Sebastien, do you by chance have a laptop, or did you disconnect that too?"

"Adriano!"

"What? Just having a little fun, my love. Sebastien knows I'm over the phone drama—right Sebastien?"

"Sure—I'll get you the laptop, it's upstairs." He moves quickly out of the room, leaving Jonathan's eyes crossing, the room briefly spinning.

"Okay, I will need your email address, if you don't mind. I will email these to you, so we can see it on your laptop," hollers out Adriano to Sebastien, who is already ascending the stairs.

"Sure, it's SebWoodsworth@gmail.com—that's S-E B—" Sebastien hollers back as he reaches the top step. A few minutes later, he is back in the living room. Jonathan is sitting quietly on the couch, dizzy, but he admires Sebastien's moves. This vampire looks so powerful at this moment, and something pleasant inside of Jonathan stirs. Then he thinks maybe it's the warm effect from the whisky and blanket cuddling his body. Or maybe it's the vampire stirring something different and welcoming in his body.

Adriano pulls up the listings and everyone gathers around the laptop to carefully view each of the houses. A half hour goes by, and Rebecca is starting to feel her energy going down. Sebastien and Rebecca head to the woods, hoping this time to find rabbits. The squirrels' blood just doesn't last long in their system. Adriano stays back with Jonathan and makes a call to Sandra to update her on everything.

Sebastien and Rebecca return after half an hour. They quickly go wash up, and return. The fire is crackling, the room is filled with friendly energy, anticipation brewing, waiting to hear more. Sebastien opens the journal and begins again.

X and I became really great friends that summer, and he taught me a lot about being a vampire. He told me that there was a group of

Nazis that were capturing vampires and using them for experiments. He warned me, they would bait them with corpses dressed in either civilian clothing or Allied and even Nazi soldier uniforms, and they would stage these corpses in different locations at night including park benches, standing near the Eiffel Tower, or against trees in the wooded areas. It was easy for Nazis to do this without anyone noticing, because there was a strict curfew in place from nine p.m. to five a.m., so no civilians were allowed out in the city. They knew the vampires would attack from behind mostly, so they wouldn't realize until it was too late that they had drank old blood from a corpse.

I learned a very important secret from X, and somehow so did these Nazis. The only way to capture or even kill a vampire effectively is to have them feed on dead blood. Once the vampire drank the dead blood they would immediately have a violent reaction, and would fall to the ground, instantly feeling violently ill. Their powers and gifts would weaken enough so the Nazis could approach and shackle their arms and legs and blindfold them. Then they would take them to a facility and they were placed into steel cages. If they didn't drink fresh live blood within the hour, they would die an excruciating painful and slow death, but the Nazi were not interested in killing them. It is hard to write this part down. They would capture civilians, mostly men, husbands, brothers, sons, all ages, and would throw them in the cage with the vampire so they could feed from them. Oh! The atrocities!

Some experiments involved electrocuting the vampires to see if they could recover, and the voltages used was in some cases so high that they became brain dead. Other experiments involved stabbing them in different parts of their bodies and watching and recording how long it took for their bodies to heal. They blinded them with pointed tools to see if their sight could be restored, they removed their blood and tried to inject it into prisoners to see if their blood wood react and accept the foreign blood. They wanted to create vampires that they could control. But what the Nazis didn't figure out was that a vampire's saliva is very powerful and unique, because it prevents infection at the moment the bite occurs, allowing their blood to enter and interact with the human's blood without infecting antibodies. So these prisoners became infected once the foreign blood was in their bodies, since they didn't have the saliva to protect the entry of this blood into their bodies, and they would die.

I was shocked further to learn that X was one of the vampires captured, but he managed to escape. They thought he was incapacitated from the corpse blood but he recovered his strength enough to pry open the back of the truck he was in and he jumped out. He followed the truck to see where they would have taken him. That is how he discovered the horrors taking place in that facility outside of Paris. He did his best to kill the guards and commanders there, and he rescued as many civilian and vampire prisoners as he could. He vowed he would search and kill any Nazis he could find, and then we met and I joined his fight.

I miss him terribly even to this day. It was a couple years after the war that something in him changed. He was struggling; the atrocities of the war affected him, haunted him for a few years, and he had recurring night terrors about the facility. He was spiraling into a deep depression filled with anxiety and stress from the trauma.

He was a restless spirit. He couldn't stay still, he always needed a challenge, and he wanted me to go with him wherever his mind pulled him. He was becoming careless in hunting, and would crave human blood more than animal blood. His heart and mind gradually became jaded about the kindness in humans, and he became less respectful of anyone in authority. He was growing more and more agitated, and it was becoming difficult for me to be around him regularly.

He was always trying to pick a fight, and sometimes he would leave without warning for days and then return. It was becoming difficult for me to control him; it broke my heart to see him fall into despair. I realized then that vampires can also suffer from different types of mental illness: anxiety, depression, and post-traumatic stress. I was starting to feel overwhelmed, lost. I didn't know how to help him. I needed structure. I wanted to go back to school and finish my medical science degree. I wanted someplace to call home. He continued down a dark path that I couldn't follow. The things we did during the war haunted me too; I needed to do something positive, and academia was always a positive outlet for me. Over time, I realized I couldn't continue worrying about him and letting my own well-being suffer. I was emotionally torn. So I decided *the only thing left to do was to go our separate ways, so I wouldn't resent him one day. It broke my heart to let go of that friendship; I had thought our friendship would carry on for many years into the future.*

To this day, I hope maybe I will receive a postcard, a letter, even an email from him, just letting me know he is okay, that he forgives me for abandoning our friendship. I just hope he found peace, and that his demons are gone—or at least he has power over them now. I hope he is living the life he was reborn to live, helping the weaker ones.

I don't know what more to write now. I don't know if there were other significant memories I am missing. But my heart tells me I captured what was the most important for me to bring to these pages. The rest, well—if it is really that important, I hope they will be in this journal another day."

Sebastien stops reading. He takes a sip of wine. Adriano, Rebecca, and Jonathan remain bewildered at what they just heard. This other historical account of atrocities taking place in World War Two, never to be known by anyone. They all look at Sebastien, who seems to be deeply affected. They remain respectfully quiet, each in their own thoughts. Sebastien has his head bent down, his eyes focused on the final private written words his beloved James wrote just for him. He rereads this once more to himself.

Sebastien, I am hoping you found my journal; it was meant for you to find after I was gone. Maybe now you will understand why I couldn't tell you about my past. I didn't want you to feel pressure or responsibility to carry my burdens with me from my dark past, and I couldn't let you see the side of me that killed humans, even though they were despicable disgusting Nazis.

Now I look back and see my mistakes with X, with my beliefs, and with you.

Forgive me my Seb.
Love James

Sebastien closes the journal and he closes his eyes, holding back the tears trying to escape.

CHAPTER 15

Revitalized

It's Monday morning. Sebastien opens the back door from outside and steps into the house, quietly shaking the snow off his sweater and pants. He tiptoes as quietly as he can into the spare washroom and rinses out his blood-stained lips and mouth, and washes his face. He glances into the living room; there is a chill in the air, so he decides to light a fire.

"Oh, I hope I didn't wake you Jonathan." Sebastien can't help but look at Jonathan's dark hair; it's disheveled, and there are dark stubbles peeking through on his face. *Not bad, kind of cute,* he quietly reveals to himself.

Jonathan stirs and stretches out his long legs, while lying on the couch. "No, no. I was already waking up."

"That couch can't be too comfortable, sorry about that."

"It's fine, Sebastien, trust me. I've slept on the police station couch many nights, this is heaven compared to that old springy thing! Thanks again for letting me stay over. I'm glad we sent them home last night, I think they needed some space, you know, alone time."

"I think we were all affected, I hope I did the right thing reading the journal."

"Of course, that was an incredibly powerful account that James experienced and revealed in his journal. Are you okay now that you shared all of this personal stuff?"

"Yeah, I think so. It was nice that you stayed over. I mean—I'm glad we also had a chance to get to know each other more, don't you think?"

"Yeah, we should really check out one of those museums you mentioned, I am in Paris after all."

"That would be great!" Sebastien's voice squeaks in a high pitch. "I mean—it would be nice to do normal things again. Even with a human. Such as you." A warm smile crosses Sebastien's lips, and he feels his face heating up. "I think you have bread left over. Sorry I don't have coffee or tea."

"Uhmm…yeah but actually, I have a better idea. How about we go out?"

"Out? Just the two of us?"

"Yeah, why not. Show me around. We can grab a taxi. Besides, I think Adriano and Rebecca need to spend some time together, we can always check in with them."

"Sounds good to me. Oh, that reminds me, I think it is time I get a new phone, maybe we could do that first—in town?"

"Sure, okay, let's shower—"

"Okay—I mean, yes, I will go into my room to shower and you will go to the spare washroom."

"Yes, right."

"Oh—I knew that's what you meant," Sebastien can't help the nervous giggle escaping as he walks awkwardly backwards out of the living room, almost walking into the wall.

"Oh, do you uhmm—need to hunt first?"

"Oh—uhm, no, I already did, earlier—but nice of you to ask."

"No problem, I got used to it with Adriano." Jonathan is folding the blanket neatly and placing it over the couch.

"Well okay, see you soon." Sebastien quickly dashes up the stairs, his heart racing with pleasant excitement. Jonathan's eyes cross, he takes a seat on the couch. *I've never seen a vampire move so quickly. Incredible, sexy.*

The taxi dropped them off in the 7th Arrondissement, near the Eiffel Tower. They spent a few hours together in the city. Sebastien purchased a new cell phone and immediately gave Jonathan his number. They stopped in at a corner café that Sebastien used to frequent when he was human. They spent a couple hours talking and sharing common interests. Jonathan talked about his work and how he was studying to become a detective. He kept ordering cappuccinos, and Sebastien sipped at the green tea that was now cold in his cup. It was turning out to be a nice crisp sunny winter day, and Sebastien was looking forward to showing Jonathan around. Now, their coffee done, he brings Jonathan through a street where many local artists come to sell their pieces.

Jonathan is interested in stopping at each artist's spot, admiring the different paintings, drawings, and the variety of crafts displayed. Sebastien occasionally stays behind and looks through antiques, but mostly he is just standing back to watch Jonathan move. Something is stirring inside of him; he hasn't felt this good in a long time, but the feeling kind of scares him. He feels a bit guilty. Jonathan, occasionally, looks back and smiles at Sebastien, who pretends to be looking at his phone or an antique. Another table catches his attention, and he casually makes his way towards the jewelry on display. The woman standing behind the small table is just finishing with another customer, handing him a blue small little nylon pouch carrying a tie clip shaped like a musical note that he has just purchased.

"It was so nice to meet you, Lucan, I do hope you come by with your friend." Lucan takes her petite hand and bends down to kiss it.

"*Tu est tres gentil, mademoiselle Juliette.*"

Juliette giggles. Lucan smiles his warm charming smile, and as Jonathan arrives Lucan greets him.

"*Bonjour.*"

"*Bonjour.*" Jonathan smiles. He suddenly smells chocolate in the air.

Lucan takes his cane and makes his way casually through the busy crowd.

Jonathan stands at the table admiring the delicate and interesting pieces. He looks up to Juliette, charmed immediately by her soft warm grey and violet eyes.

"*Bonjour, mademoiselle.*" He knows his French won't expand too much further. He only learned some words through Adriano over the years.

"*Ah, bonjour,*" the woman says in a French accent.

"These are beautiful, did you make these?"

"*Oui, merci,* are you looking for yourself or—? Here we have unisex pieces, let's see—if I may, I think this one would look very nice on your wrist. May I?"

"You speak English very well."

"Thank you, I speak English more than French, but we are in Paris." Her laugh is delicate and genuine.

Sebastien is suddenly beside Jonathan. He feels protective over him. He doesn't know if Jonathan is aware just who he is standing beside.

"*Bonjour monsieur.*" Juliette smiles.

"*Bonjour mademoiselle.*" Sebastien smiles, a little apprehensive.

"What do you think, Sebastien, she makes these herself—sorry, what's your name?"

"My name is Juliette."

Jonathan reaches out his hand to shake hers. Suddenly he feels he's heard this name spoken recently, but he is so mesmerized by her eyes the memory escapes him.

"Hi, I'm Jonathan—this is Sebastien."

Sebastien shakes her hand, both vampires aware of the other.

"*C'est un plaisir de vous rencontrer,* Sebastien."

"*Ravi de vous rencontrer également,* Juliette."

"Sorry both of you, my French isn't that good," chimes in Jonathan.

"Neither is mine," chuckles Juliette.

"Juliette, I am sold on this bracelet." Jonathan smiles warmly.

"Oh, very nice. Would you like to wear it now?"

"Yes." Jonathan shows it to Sebastien.

Sebastien smiles. He is a bit distracted. He can't help but notice the sketchbook on the chair behind Juliette. "You sketch too?"

"Yes, actually I have an exhibit this Wednesday, you should both come. It will be at the Coultier Gallery. Please, take a flyer." She points to the pile of paper on the corner of the desk in a small box.

Sebastien takes the flyer while Jonathan pays for the bracelet.

"Thank you Juliette, I will enjoy wearing this unique piece of yours."

"You're too kind, Jonathan."

"Well, have a great day Juliette, stay warm!"

She smiles kindly. "You too. I hope you will both come to the gallery. Goodbye Sebastien." Juliette's eyes express warmth and sincerity.

"Bye Juliette." Sebastien smiles.

Jonathan and Sebastien continue walking around. "What a sweet woman. Very talented."

"Jonathan…"

"Yeah?" Jonathan is busy admiring his hand-crafted leather bracelet.

"Did you notice anything about her?"

"Juliette? No, like what?"

Sebastien moves in closer to whisper into Jonathan's ear. His lips feel like a piece of velvet caressing Jonathan's ear. A sudden warmth and tingling sensation travels through Jonathan's body, while Sebastien soaks in the tantalizing scent of coconut shampoo and sweet cologne coming from Jonathan's thick dark hair and neck. He whispers softly, "She is a vampire."

Jonathan stops walking. "What! No way."

Sebastien looks into Jonathan's deep brown eyes. He wants to stay in this moment, bathe in their warm hue. Slowly he nods up and down. "Yes—she is a vampire."

"Wow. Amazing—she looked so—"

"Human?"

"Yes! There was something about her that was hard to stop staring at, but it wasn't a bad thing. Her eyes were spectacular; they had a violet hint to them."

"Yes, we vampires just have that charismatic appeal regardless of whether or not we can also instill fear."

"Did she know you were *one*?"

"Oh, yes I think so—maybe we should check out that gallery Wednesday? This is probably the same Juliette and the gallery exhibit Adriano mentioned. I think he—"

"Oh, yeah, but not sure I can stay all week, I have to see."

"Oh, right, of course." A hint of disappointment shadows Sebastien's tone, and Jonathan feels an urgent need suddenly to please him.

"But, don't get me wrong—I want to stay longer." His eyes are drawn in by Sebastien's. "I will find a way."

"Great! We will have fun!"

"Wait til Adriano hears this —I met another vampire, I mean besides you of course, well, you know what I mean."

"Come on, lots more to see, *Jonathan.*" Sebastien puts his long thin arm around Jonathan. Jonathan moves in closer, and their shoulders touch.

Meanwhile, Adriano is trying to calm Rebecca, who is in a frenzied state. "Rebecca, I am sure everything is fine, Jonathan is there, and he would call me if there was an emergency!"

"But why isn't he answering his phone? He connected it right? We saw? And Jonathan too? He's not answering?"

"Maybe he is hunting?"

"With Jonathan? I highly doubt that. He isn't reckless. Adriano, I'm worried, please let's go there."

"Let me try Jonathan again on his cell, if I don't reach him this time, okay, we will head there." Adriano calls Jonathan's cell again and it picks up after the third ring. "Jonathan—finally! I have tried calling a few times. Oh it was, well, is everything okay? Oh, I see—yes, we are fine, Rebecca is worried, Sebastien didn't answer his phone—you're not there? Walking around the Seventh Arrondissement?"

Sudden fear comes over Rebecca as she listens with her vampire ears to both sides of the conversation. "What! They are in the city?"

"Hang on Jonathan." Adriano covers the phone with his hand whispering, "They are both fine. Relax." Adriano returns to the call. "Sorry, she is just worried=uh uh —I see, no no, sounds like you guys are having fun. Sure, I will ask her and let you know. Okay, maybe, yeah, okay. Bye."

"See, everything is fine. It's nice that Sebastien is showing Jonathan around. I kind of feel bad I have his car—oh well, anyways, Jonathan seemed so excited. I haven't heard him sound like that in a while. Hmmm... I wonder if there is something brewing between the two of them?"

"Really? Do you think so?"

"Who knows—at least Sebastien is out of the house, and he is in good hands with Jonathan." Adriano caresses Rebecca's face and hair. "So Ms. Dimondo, we have the day to ourselves. Oh, actually Jonathan asked if we want to join them, but how about we explore a little bit of the city ourselves, we can meet up with them later?"

"I don't know—I—"

"I will be there beside you—it will be good for you. You will have fun, trust me. Every bit of exposure to humans, noises, and movements is important. I know you are nervous, but it's okay."

Rebecca's hands are shaking but after a few seconds to think, she says, "You're right, I need to do this. I trust you—let's go."

"Hang on, not so fast." Adriano pulls Rebecca's body into him. He starts kissing her and taking in deep breaths. "I need my fix first of your luscious scent."

Rebecca giggles, her body responding to his touches. "Didn't you get enough last night and this morning? Come on vampire, I have to practice."

Adriano moans in pleasure. "Mmm—just a little bit more, we have time, the humans won't go away."

"Oh, you sexy vampire, it will be hard to resist you."

"That is the idea beautiful, mmmm—you smell too good."

The next thing she knows, Rebecca is picked up in Adriano's arms and carried back to their bedroom. He lays her gently on the bed, lays on top of her, and begins caressing her neck with his tongue and lips while his fingers explore her body over her clothes. They reach into her V-neck top and inside her bra.

"Mmmm...this is what I wanted. I love how they get so hard for me." He moves his face into her top, pulls the bra down, and continues kissing and sucking gently on her breasts. Rebecca moans with delight as she reaches down and unzips his jeans. She reaches into his underwear, feeling his hardness, and she strokes him. Both vampires, moaning and teasing each other, slowly take their clothes off. They tuck inside the warm covers and their bodies move in a glorious rhythm up and down, slow then fast, Adriano thrusting and lingering.

After they cuddled for a little, Adriano notices that Rebecca is too quiet. "Hey you, you asleep?"

Rebecca responds, but her voice is low. "No, I just feel so tired, I don't feel thirsty though?"

Adriano immediately looks at her with concern. Her eyes still show their vibrant hue, but he can see the cinnamon and amber colour in her vampire irises are fading. He quickly gets up and dresses, followed by Rebecca.

"Sorry Adriano, I thought I drank enough this morning."

"Never apologize to me about this, *mon amour*! It's okay, we did use up quite a bit of energy the last twenty-four hours, I should be the one apologizing to you."

"No, no, I don't want this disease to stop me from enjoying sex with you."

"It won't. We just have to be a bit more careful, it's okay, don't worry about this—I can see that beautiful mind processing, worrying. Come on, let's go. We'll hunt, then come back and freshen up and we can take a walk in the city."

"Okay, it just seems like a lot."

"We will go at your pace, *mon amour*, no rush, I just want you to keep practicing." He smiles and kisses her on her lips and they head toward the car. Adriano drives to the woods and they walk deep inside and begin hunting.

It is now three p.m. Adriano parks the car in town, takes Rebecca by the hand, and leads her down the street. The air is crisp, but to these vampires it is welcome. Adriano whispers in her ear that she is doing fine. "Take deep breaths and just observe the humans." He tells her how to pick a noise that she hears, whether it be cars, voices, or music, and focus on one sound. She practices doing this as they walk along the busy street.

Rebecca mentions that she wants to visit some churches and at some point, the Notre Dame Cathedral, so they spend some time walking in different churches. She enjoys admiring the architecture of the buildings, and is relieved to know that she still feels peaceful in these settings. They also visit different perfume and clothing boutiques. She doesn't want to buy, but just practices going in and looking around and talking to the sales merchants. Some are patient speaking English, while others have an air of snobbery. In the latter case Adriano steps in and speaks French, but they leave soon after.

A few hours have gone by, Rebecca is starting to feel tired, but to her surprise her thirst is not rising. It is starting to snow, so Adriano calls

Jonathan and they arrange to meet at a bistro nearby. A half an hour later, both Jonathan and Sebastien walk in, and Adriano waves them down to their table. Rebecca is happy to see that Sebastien is smiling and looks healthy and vibrant. They come to the table and kiss both cheeks of Rebecca.

"Wow, you two have quite a few bags, you must have shopped all day?" she says.

"Sebastien brought me to such beautiful men's boutiques, I couldn't resist. Adriano, you have to go and check them out. How about you guys, what did you do today?"

A few seconds later, the waiter drops by and sets down three glasses of wine and a tall glass of Stella Artois, which Adriano ordered as requested by Sebastien and Jonathan en route to the bistro. Rebecca scans the menu. She remembers when she was human how much she enjoyed onion soup and steak et frites, and for a fleeting second, she misses the taste of foods like this.

"I don't know what to order, it all sounds so good. Umm, could I have the onion soup but without the cheese and bread baked on top? Just the soup?"

The waiter frowns as he is writing down her request and moves on to the other patrons at the table, only to discover that Sebastien and Adriano also request the same. Jonathan goes all out and orders a steak with a mushroom bordelaise.

"So did you show Hazel Eyes around the city?"

"I did, it has been a busy and active day for us—wouldn't you say, Rebecca?"

Rebecca grins, trying not to blush. "Yes—I mean, Adriano brought me through some perfume boutiques, then we visited some churches—that was amazing."

"Churches? Really? I haven't thought of that."

"Oh, it was amazing Sebastien—I love the architecture and it was just so peaceful inside. Even with humans around, I was okay, wasn't I Adriano?"

"Absolutely, I think you managed very well, *mon amour*."

"Oh by the way." Sebastien reaches into his pocket. "Surprise—I got one."

Rebecca shrieks with excitement. "Amazing! Finally, I can reach you. Good for you. Give us the number."

"I don't have it memorized yet, give me a second, I have it in my contacts."

"Oh Adriano, I meant to tell you, you wouldn't believe who I encountered today." Jonathan looks over to Sebastien, grinning.

Sebastien waits for Adriano's reaction. "Oh right, yes, I'm sure this will be interesting, go ahead and tell them, Jonathan."

Adriano looks confused but curious. "Encountered, here in Paris? Who?"

Jonathan smiles. He slowly leans over the table and whispers very carefully, "A female vampire."

Adriano just stands still, his eyes don't blink.

Rebecca looks completely shocked, turning to Sebastien. "You're joking."

Jonathan shakes his head slowly side to side followed by Sebastien.

"Where?" Adriano asks.

"I can't remember the street, do you Sebastien?"

"No, but it was about a block away from the Eiffel Tower, there was a line of street artists out. I'm surprised you didn't see them?"

"Oh, Rebecca and I were in and out of shops and churches—tell me more, did she know you were a vampire, Sebastien?"

"I think so but she was friendly, quite talented."

Jonathan shows off his bracelet. "She made this, cool isn't it."

"Oh, I like this. This is something I would buy you, Adriano. Does she have items for women too?"

"Yes, lots of rings, bracelets and things. Her name is Juliette."

"That's her! It must be," Adriano shouts out in excitement. Then he realizes other patrons staring in their direction. He waves an apology to them.

Rebecca is startled. "Who?"

"The vampire I noticed the day I found you, remember, I mentioned to you that I wanted to visit a gallery this Wednesday."

"Oh--I almost forgot." Jonathan reaches into his pocket and pulls out a piece of red paper, which he gives to Adriano. "She gave us a flyer."

"Well, I guess this Wednesday we are all going to this gallery. That is, hopefully Brown Eyes —Jonathan—umm if you will still be here?"

"Brown eyes?" smirks Adriano teasingly. Jonathan squirms in his seat. Adriano turns to Sebastien. "Do you call anyone by their actual name?"

Sebastien doesn't miss a beat. "Yes, I call you Adriano."

"Now, now you two. Play nice."

"Don't worry Hazel Eyes, I will grow on Adriano yet."

"Oh Sebastien, he likes you, he's just teasing you—right Adriano?"

Adriano smiles. "He is growing on me."

"So Jonathan—can you stay?" Sebastian's dark brown eyes can't help but seduce Jonathan, drawing him in.

"I will do my best to extend this trip. I'll check in tomorrow with the station. I think it should be okay—oh Good, the food is coming—after all, I have to clear some loose ends up with the police about Rebecca's case."

"Oh, I forgot about that."

"Not to worry, I'll handle it. But they may want to meet you, Rebecca, just to be sure you are okay. I'll try to convince them that you're just anxious to get home."

The waiter arrives, distributes the plates, and leaves. Adriano raises his wine glass. "I would like to say a toast." Everyone raises their glasses. "To my beautiful Rebecca, thank God she is back with me. And to our new chapter ahead, may our lives be rich with love and friendships! *Salut* and *bon appetit, mes amis!*"

"*Salut!*" echoes back all.

They linger at the bistro, enjoying each other's company and sharing anecdotes, and then Adriano drives everyone back to Sebastien's home.

Adriano encourages Rebecca to hunt again, quietly privately hinting that she may need her energy for later if she is up to it. Meanwhile, Sebastien privately whispers in Jonathan's ear to stay another night. Both vampires take off for the woods, while Adriano remains in the living room with Jonathan sitting on the couch, the fire is keeping the room nice and warm.

"So Brown Eyes—" Adriano teases.

"Ha ha, funny."

"Just kidding, but I have to say you two seem quite comfortable."

"And?"

"And nothing, just curious."

"He's nice. We have a lot in common— he's quite the intellectual."

"Yes, that he is. Totally your type."

Jonathan doesn't respond, but his smile reaches from ear to ear.

Adriano looks around and then remembers something odd in this house. "Hey Jonathan, did you notice the X painted on one of the doors upstairs?"

"Oh yeah, you saw it too?"

"Yeah, I wonder if it had to do with James?"

"What do you mean?"

"Not sure, but I have a feeling, I would really like to go check it out."

"Oh, you shouldn't, Adriano."

"I know, but I'm not sure he will tell me if I ask."

"Better to ask then snoop."

"You're right—but it does seem odd that in this huge house there are only two bedrooms and very minimal furniture pieces."

"Well, from what Sebastien shared with me today, they seemed to be preoccupied with their research, so maybe they just didn't have time for furnishing the other rooms with beds?"

"Maybe."

"You're not going to let this go, are you?"

"Probably not—but I am surprised at you. A cop, you want to become a detective, and here's a chance to practice your skills."

"Nice try. I can't snoop, now that I know him, like him—"

"I hear you, I get it."

"It must worry you now about Rebecca and this vamprogeria?"

A burdened sigh escapes Adriano. He stands up, walks to the fireplace, and adds more wood to the fire. "Yeah, it really does. This is going to be such a complex challenge. I mean, how the hell is she going to manage her disease and still look after her sons? They are still too young." His voice sounds a bit strained, frustration building as he crumples some paper and places it on top of the fiery logs.

"I know, it's already tough enough trying to hide so many secrets, now this? I feel for both of you, Adriano."

Adriano remains standing, leaning against the bookshelf, "I've been thinking a lot. Rebecca can't rely only on hunting animals when she returns home, especially if she has to go back to her apartment until we move her into a new home. We need a regular emergency supply for her. I may need to ask Sandra to get me access to blood from the hospital, but I don't want to jeopardize her career."

"You know Sandra and I will continue to supply our blood, no question—did you use up the blood that we had shipped? Did it arrive?"

"Yes, those bottles are gone. These last two months have been hell, so I needed to drink more, to calm my nerves, mostly. I wasn't even that thirsty. But that was really risky, I am truly grateful to both of you for all the help and support. The problem is, we would need more blood. Those tiny glass vials are fine for me, but Rebecca needs more. We will have to build a private storage for her with a small fridge. Her apartment is small, I don't know how we can do this. Maybe in her closet? Oh, damn it!" Adriano suddenly looks panicked

"What is it?"

"Jonathan, how the hell are we going to get her and Sebastien through the plane ride? It's at least a six-hour flight, more if there are delays. How am I going to do this? We only have a few more days. She is so anxious to get home, but does she really understand what she is facing?"

Jonathan stands up and approaches Adriano, putting his hand on his shoulder. "Hey relax, your mind is racing, we'll figure this out. No use stressing out, we just have to think and strategize. Sebastien is a pathologist, so maybe he has ideas about transporting blood safely but hidden? I will give her blood this week, that's not a problem."

Adriano hugs Jonathan. Sebastien and Rebecca are at the entrance of the living room, and Rebecca approaches Adriano. "Everything okay?"

"All good, Rebecca. Jonathan and I were just talking, you know—guy stuff. Hunt okay? Did you get enough?"

"Yeah, but we had to go a little further out tonight, the animals are just not around as much—too cold. But we did good."

"Shall I bring out the wine and berries, I think I have some left? Jonathan, if you're hungry there is still some bread and cheese?"

"Oh—thanks Sebastien, I'm full from the steak, but good to know."

"Hazel eyes, Adriano, wine?"

"Sure, Adriano too. Thanks Sebastien—can I help?"

"No, thanks."

Sebastien returns minutes later with a large tray carrying two bowls, one with nuts and the other with the last of the berries, four wine glasses, and a bottle of Pinot Noir. He places it on the coffee table. He is feeling so relaxed and happy from the days outing with Jonathan and now he is entertaining again. He realizes that today was the first day he went a whole day without thinking about James. He still misses him, but it is not too difficult today. He looks across the room; the ghost is not there, and there is no feeling inside of him that James is around. He sits in his chair. He isn't sure how to process this, but puts it aside for now and just allows himself to enjoy the company of his friends. Deep down he knows that a part of his joy is due to the friendly human with the deep brown eyes, wearing a warm and tender smile and sitting on his couch gazing at him. Sebastien feels revitalized again.

CHAPTER 16
Behind the Curtains

The sound of Sebastien's new cell phone alarm is ringing. Sebastien picks it up, the display reads, 6:30 am, Tuesday February 19. He quickly turns it off and turns over looking at Jonathan lying beside him. "Sorry, did I wake you?"

A groggy Jonathan opens his eyes, yawning. "No, not really, what time is it?"

"It's still early, but I set the alarm, I need to—*go out.*"

Jonathan turns his body toward Sebastien. "You can say it, you know, it doesn't bother me that you need to go hunting, honestly."

"You're sweet. I guess it just hasn't set into my consciousness yet—you, a human, and me—together, in my bed. I never thought I could feel so alive again!"

"Well, the feeling is mutual. And this human can see that your eyes are fading, go hunting! I'll go and shower in the meantime."

Sebastien leans in and kisses Jonathan on the lips. He gets up and quickly puts on his dark blue jeans and a thick black sweater. "Be right back, Brown Eyes."

"Oh and wear a winter coat this time for God's sake."

Sebastien is at the archway of his bedroom door. "You're kidding, right?"

"It's still winter, besides you never know if someone could be in the area, we don't want attention drawn to you."

"In these private woods? At six thirty? In this winter air? Jonathan, if there is anyone in these woods at this hour, in this crisp temperature, they are probably up to no good, like hiding a body or something."

Jonathan bursts out laughing. "Get out of here, you crazy vampire."

"I'm crazy? You're sleeping with a vampire." They both laugh, and Jonathan throws his pillow at Sebastien. "Oh, you are asking for it."

Jonathan grins. "Stop teasing me—besides, you need to hunt first."

"I have time." Sebastien walks back to the bed like a prowling lion. He slowly moves his face down Jonathan's bare chest. He takes in the sweet masculine aroma as he climbs with his lips upward from Jonathan's thighs, making Jonathan moan with delight as Sebastien's tongue lingers tenderly and strokes him as he grows firm with every tender stroke motion from Sebastien's hands. They spend the next hour pleasing each other, exploring and discovering the intimate touches that each becomes aroused by. Sebastien's thirst wakes him from this pleasant feeling that his body is still experiencing. Sebastien leans in for another quick kiss and Jonathan accepts it teasingly.

"Round two?"

"You are insatiable—don't you need to drink?"

"That is true—but you bring out the animal in me."

"Good to know."

Sebastien gets up and quickly dresses in jeans and a thick sweater. "Be back soon—*sexy* human." He moves quickly out of the room.

Jonathan can hear Sebastien already descending the stairs as he hollers out, "Happy hunting!"

Sebastien leaps down the stairs in two movements as he hollers back, "Thanks!" Sebastien dashes out the back door and practically leaps towards the woods, feeling so jubilant and energized. Jonathan meanwhile is at the bedroom window admiring this vampire as he disappears into the woods.

"He forgot his coat, I knew it." Jonathan springs out of bed, energized. He heads to the en suite shower and runs the water. A song pops into his mind by George Michael as he enters the warm shower, he starts singing. "That's all I wanted, something special, something sacred in your eyes. For just one moment, to be bold and naked at your side."

Meanwhile Adriano is driving Rebecca back to the woods nearby, and they both spend the next hour hunting. Rebecca manages to find two rabbits and a squirrel, and she subdues each of them to drink, while Adriano is busy running at vampire speed to catch his breakfast. Rebecca almost feels sorry for him that he has to work so hard, but he insists, "The thrill is in the chase, *mon amour.*"

After they satisfy their thirst, they drive back to the apartment to shower. Adriano is planning another outing for Rebecca in the city, encouraging her that it is necessary for her to practice her movements.

"Are you sure I'm ready for this? What if I slip up? Then we will have humans freaking out."

"No one is going to freak out, you are ready *mon amour.*"

Adriano drives Rebecca into the 9th Arrondissement and parks near Galeries Lafayette. "I thought I would bring you to this famous upscale department store."

"Department store? With all those humans in one place? Oh, you are really testing me today."

"I know you can do this, *mon amour.* Take a deep breath, you got this." He walks to her side to open the car door, takes her hand, and leans in and gives her a tender kiss. "For good luck—ready?"

"I guess."

Adriano's smile reassures her, and they walk hand in hand into the mall. "This is a department store? Adriano, this is huge. Beyond anything I've seen."

Adriano lets go of her hand slowly and softly whispers into her ear, "Look up."

Rebecca slowly raises her head upward, and her eyes are instantly dazzled by the sight of the most spectacular elaborate scenery of carved and painted floral depictions on glass. As her eyes travel across and down she sees several pillars. Her senses are overstimulated since they are in a closed space, although the air remains fresh.

As her eyes move around the whole area, she spots new and different things. The noises of the humans walking by, including cries or laughs from children, the vibrant array of colors, and the different smells coming from perfumes, restaurants, and humans shock her senses. She quickly grabs onto Adriano's arm. Adriano can hear her heart beating faster.

"You're ok *mon amour*, take a few seconds, breathe in, just observe. Let your vampire eyes, ears, and nose adjust to everything, their natural instincts will guide you, trust them." He gently releases her hand from his arm and continues whispering softly into her ear, staying very close to her. "Breathe, now slowly try to focus on the ones walking slower. Study their movements, you can do this. Focus on the movements for now, let the different voices and sounds just fade into the background, they are not important. Tell your mind, they are there but they are not a focus right now."

Rebecca listens very carefully to Adriano's reassuring voice, and she focuses all of her attention on a woman strolling a buggy with a sleeping baby inside. She just concentrates on the women's legs as they move and before she realizes it, the sounds of the busy active mall fade into the background. She takes a step forward and then another, and notices her arms and legs are moving slower. She continues practicing this, walking a little further away from Adriano. She then turns around and walks back to him, smiling, feeling confident. "I did it."

"Yes, you did, *mon amour*."

Adriano embraces her tenderly, then Rebecca releases and tries again. She walks further this time, and her movements are a bit faster, but still in pace with a human. She turns around and then walks in a different direction, and turns around and stops and listens. She looks up to the ceiling and looks back to Adriano. Humans are passing her by, but she doesn't notice their eyes on her. She can smell all the different aromas and scents.

She walks at a human's pace back to Adriano, whispering, "It's happening—I'm doing it. Did you see that? I walked right by that human couple and it was normal."

"I told you you could do this, *mon amour*. Let's go on, keep walking and talking to me quietly, like a whisper, I can hear you, describe what you see."

Rebecca feels in control. It is the most amazing sense of accomplishment for her as a vampire. She is determined now to challenge herself further, and she walks into a clothing store to browse on her own. She is hoping a salesperson will approach her, and she moves with the pace of a human around the floor admiring the different dresses. She's pleased with herself that she is learning how to keep a human pace. She glances at herself in a mirror; she sees Rebecca in her reflection, not a pale vampire. She looks back at Adriano, who is just watching her from outside the store. He feels elation and satisfaction for her achievements today. Rebecca signals for him to stay there, and he nods that he understands.

Suddenly a woman approaches her, speaking in French. Rebecca takes a deep breath, and Adriano's eyes are like lasers watching. "*Pardon, mon francais ne pas bien*, do you speak English?"

The woman responds in a French accent, "Yes of course, where are you from?"

"Canada."

"Ahh, Canadian, how nice. Do you see something you like?"

"Yes, could I see this dress in a size—sorry I don't know European sizes."

The woman looks Rebecca respectfully up and down, pauses, then nods and quickly searches through the dresses on the rack. She finds one and gives it to Rebecca. Rebecca looks back at Adriano, she smiles and mouths to him, "It's okay."

He understands and stays back. A few minutes later, Rebecca comes out into the hall of the fitting room and Adriano is standing there.

"Beautiful—" Adriano admires her. Rebecca is happy to see him.

It is now just after lunch, and Sebastien and Jonathan arrive back home by taxi. They spent a few hours in St. Denis exploring, and picked up some groceries for the human and the vampires. They unpack the groceries together. Jonathan is feeling more and more at home in Sebastien's kitchen and space and with Sebastien. "Sebastien, something has been on my mind, I hope you don't mind me asking?"

Sebastien is busy washing more berries. "What is it? Ask."

"Why is there an X painted on your bedroom door, and another door is painted in red?"

Suddenly Sebastien's shoulders droop, his head remains bent down. He shuts off the running tap but doesn't respond. He shakes out the berries in the strainer, places them on the counter, and wipes his wet hands on a tea towel. Jonathan can see his question affected Sebastien. "Sorry, if this is too personal or if you aren't ready to share, I—"

"It's okay. I don't mean to be mysterious or secretive. You just caught me off guard. It's just that, well—I never expected that I would have this conversation with anyone, it is difficult to talk about this." He sits down at the kitchen table and Jonathan takes a seat beside him. "I don't know where or how to even begin, it was a very difficult time in my life, one I can't forget, but I wish never to remember parts of." Sebastien's brown eyes seem to turn sad.

"I'm sorry, whatever it is—I can see it has really affected you."

"Yes." Sebastien places his head in his hands for a second or two, then he pushes his hair behind his head. "*Mon dieu—est-ce difficile.*"

"Take your time. Do you want a drink? I mean wine—"

Sebastien manages a grin. "Yes, I know."

Jonathan opens up a bottle of Pinot Noir and pours a glass of wine for each of them. They click their glasses together and each take a sip. Then Sebastien clears his throat. "Remember I mentioned to you about vamprogeria."

"Yes."

"Well, this disease really began to affect James." Sebastien takes another sip of his wine. "The disease transformed him and altered his mind in the process."

"Transformed? What do you mean?"

"*Mon dieu*—I don't know how to say this." Sebastien pauses, leans back in the kitchen chair, and turns to face Jonathan. "You see, vamprogeria progressed to a dangerous level for James, and we really didn't know why. Why did the disease not progress rapidly for me, too? It had been the question disturbing our minds. He was my blood link donor, but I called him my blood link *lover*." Sebastien looks at Jonathan. "Sorry Jonathan, but you wanted the truth."

"Of course, he was your lover, you don't need to hide that from me. I can see anytime you talk about him that he was a very important man to you. We're not teenagers, I know you have a past, as I do. But what do you mean by blood link lover—Adriano mentioned it too?"

Sebastien takes the time to explain to Jonathan about this concept.

"So then, you're Rebecca's blood link?"

"Yes, but don't repeat that too much in Adriano's presence—is he the jealous type?"

"I am starting to think so. You see, since I've known him I haven't seen this extremely protective side of him. So I am learning about him in a new way. But he is a caring soul even though he acts tough."

"Oh, don't get me wrong, I think he means well, even if he only tolerates me." Sebastien smirks.

"Oh, don't misunderstand him Sebastien. He likes you, he's just dealing with a lot. Now I understand his reaction to you at times. You see, he wanted to be the one to *turn* Rebecca. It really scared him when he thought she only had months to live because of the tumour, so he begged her to let him turn her, but she didn't want to become a vampire. She was always afraid of the fact that she would watch her loved ones die."

"I see. I can understand that. Oh boy. And now she is my blood link—I hope Adriano will eventually come to terms with how it happened. I mean I saved her. She is my blood link, but not lover. There is a big difference."

"But you and Rebecca will always share this linked bond—that is difficult for Adriano to accept. Just give him time. Anyway, go on, we got sidetracked."

Sebastien strokes his trimmed goatee. His mind suddenly cannot help but wander back to special intimate moments with James. Then Sebastien wakes himself from that reverie and runs his fingers through his neatly combed hair, feeling a bit exposed and vulnerable sharing as much as he has. But he continues in a serious low voice. "James started to notice some changes to his body, his mind, and his mental state but it was so *gradual* at first. His mobility started to challenge him but his mind was sharp. He refused to use a cane at work, and suffered through the pain, but that just agitated the disease. He told me that one day he was in a meeting with the dean and three other colleagues, and suddenly one of the colleagues got up to get a glass of water and unintentionally brushed against James's shoulder. He was suddenly aware of the scent coming off of the human colleague, and out of nowhere, James felt this instant craving for his blood. The feeling was so intense that James had to excuse himself and go to the bathroom to splash water on his face. He was sweating, and his eyes turned very dark. He stayed in the bathroom until the thirst subsided and he left early that day, explaining he felt flu-like symptoms. He told me that evening that he knew it was time to face the inevitable truth: he was entering a new uncharted stage of this disease, and we had to document everything." Sebastien stops talking and looks at Jonathan. He sees a bit of concern cross over Jonathan's face. "Does hearing this worry you? Be honest, Jonathan."

"Not sure I understand your question?"

"I just told you that James suddenly craved human blood."

"Yes, but he was sick. It was the disease? Right?"

Sebastien looks down and takes a sip of his wine before he responds. "Yes, but I have the same *disease*. And you are a *human*." Reality comes crashing down on both of them, leaving their spirits troubled. Sebastien puts his head in his hands, but Jonathan reaches out for his hand and pulls it away from his face.

"Like you said, you didn't get a chance to research this condition thoroughly. You have no other studies to compare with, so how can you be so sure the same will happen to you? Or Rebecca?" It's like a light just turned on very bright in Jonathan's mind. *Oh no, Rebecca too. Adriano.* His facial expression turns very serious, alarmed.

Sebastien notices as he looks into Jonathan's eyes. "Are you okay? I realize this is upsetting."

"No, sorry I want to hear more. This is what's troubling. There is so much we just don't know."

"Okay, but let's go to the living room, I'm not comfortable here—I mean on this chair."

They bring their wine and move to the living room. Sebastien is about to sit in his usual chair but then decides to sit on the couch beside Jonathan. Sebastien looks towards the far corner to see if the ghost will appear. It catches the attention of Jonathan, and he too looks where Sebastien's eyes are directed.

"What are you looking at over there?"

"Hmm? What? Oh, nothing, just thinking." Sebastien adjusts himself, curling his legs inward on the couch. He faces Jonathan, who is also curled up, a pillow is between them. "James was forced to stop travelling for medical conferences, and within a month he gave the dean his resignation letter. But he had to come up with a valid reason—my James was all about integrity. He told the dean that his heart and soul were not into academia anymore, that he needed a change and wasn't sure yet what that looked like, but he knew he couldn't continue giving the University the best of him that it deserves. This sudden decision shocked many of his colleagues at the University—he was one of their esteemed colleagues, and very well respected at the hospital where I worked; he was a collaborator with researchers. I am sure you can imagine the ridiculous rumours and specu-lations that surfaced, with some university community members saying maybe he came into some money, or maybe he was having a nervous breakdown—they assumed by his appearance that he was too young to afford to retire early without his university pension, and he didn't look sick. At least James left with integrity and respect—that is what I believe."

Jonathan understands now the Professor Emeritus status beside Professor James Huntington's name on the faculty website.

Sebastien takes a gulp of his wine this time, he feels his energy fading. "It came to a point that I had to abandon travels for medical conferences and stopped the after-work social gatherings with my own colleagues. I didn't miss it too much, if I am honest, only because I was tired of the questions that I couldn't answer. Lying to people who I respected was taking its toll on me mentally. I guess over time our world became smaller, eventually isolating both of us. But neither of us complained. We still had each other and this home that James proudly purchased with no mortgage. But as his body could no longer fight the growing frequency and rapidness of his symptoms, it became more difficult for him to shower and dress himself without using up his energy. I took over, but he still had some control, he knew how he wanted to be dressed and groomed. Are you sure you want to hear this? I mean, I am talking about the man I loved?"

"That is precisely why I want to hear this. I am trying to learn about you, your life; who you loved is part of it. It doesn't bother me. I can't imagine what you went through, but I need to understand it, it is important. By the way, you look a bit tired, is it time?"

"Oh Jonathan, you are so amazing. In such a short time you really are learning, yes, it has been a few hours, I do think I need to go. I feel bad leaving you like this."

"Why? You need to hunt, you need to look after yourself. I will be here."

"*Eh bien*, I will go, feel free to put some music on."

"This time—wear your coat. Please."

Sebastien leans in and kisses Jonathan. "Okay, okay—you humans, so demanding." His smile melts into Jonathan. Sebastien walks briskly to the hallway, grabs his winter coat, and puts it on. He heads to the back door, passing the living room entrance on his way. "See, I am wearing it."

"Happy hunting."

Jonathan gets off the couch with his glass of wine and casually walks around the large living room, observing it with more attention to detail. But it feels dark and stuffy, so he thinks to open the curtains behind the piano to let in some light. He instead finds closed shutters, and opens them. He is shocked suddenly; the large full-length window is black. He touches the window and scrapes at it; the black substance gets under his nails. "Paint?" He moves the curtains further apart and sees more shutters on the other window, and opens them to discover more black paint. He moves quickly to the other curtains and moves them apart to find the same. All the windows in the room are painted black.

Jonathan quickly moves to the kitchen and opens the curtains over the sink and finds the same. He goes into the hallway and opens up the door into the dining room. It is dark. He feels for the light switch and turns it on. The light is very dim; the ceiling chandelier has some broken bulbs. Jonathan sees a long oblong dark wooden table in the center of the room. As Jonathan observes more closely he notices deep scratches on it. Then his eyes move to the walls; they too have similar scratches on them. He thinks, *did they have cats?* He notices there are no chairs around the dining room table. He sees more dark curtains but they are torn severely. He can see these windows are also covered in black paint. His cop instincts are kicking in, he is curious why all these windows on the main floor are painted black. He remembers that Sebastien's room's window is not.

Jonathan quickly runs upstairs and passes Sebastien's door, which is marked with the X. He sees the curtains in the hallway at the front of the house, and opens them to find the black painted windows. He is puzzled. He walks into the next room and sees the wooden floor is stained with paint. There is a table with many tubes of paints and brushes, and near the wall he sees many blank canvases and an easel. He opens up the curtains and is relieved to see the snow-covered backyard. He looks to see if Sebastien is returning, but there is no sight of him coming from the woods. Jonathan looks around this room. He notices several other canvases in a corner. He takes a closer look at these and discovers some of the paintings are portraits of James. He is dressed in different stylish outfits, including blazers and sweaters, and wearing a sapphire ring on his middle finger.

Suddenly, something in the corner catches Jonathan's eyes. He walks towards a grey sheet covering something. He lifts the sheet and discovers other portraits. They are disturbing to look at because they are paintings of some kind of beast or creature, yet even more peculiar is that they resemble James in some uneasy way. He focuses on the eyes especially. All these portraits have James's eyes. There is no mistake, these paintings are of James, with one significant difference in detail. These painted eyes are glaring in red, and the smile is menacing.

Jonathan flips through each painted canvas carefully, observing the details, each one portraying even more disturbing images of a creature resembling James. The more Jonathan observes and examines each of these unusual painting, the more troubling details he finds painted in the picture. The teeth are menacing, very long and jagged, and the hands are like the ones showing in James's portraits with the same ring, but curved like claws.

Jonathan is impressed by the talent and skill of the paintings. The colors, the light, shadow, and texture techniques truly capture the depiction of this ferocious creature. However, he is very troubled. Why Sebastien would paint portraits of James as an ugly menacing creature? To Jonathan, this is not a nice and respectful thing for Sebastien to do involving his beloved James. Jonathan is growing more curious by the minute; he hesitates slightly but then he decides to investigate further.

He walks to the room further down the hall with the red painted door. He is suddenly confronted by a revolting odour. He sees a deadbolt lock on the door, but to his surprise it is unlocked. He instinctively covers his nose with his sleeve, then opens the door and turns the light on. He suddenly feels uneasy as he enters. His eyes don't know where to look first. The floor has blotches of dark red stains on it near the bed, and the bed is fitted with steel bars on each side. The mattress is torn and covered in bloodstains. Jonathan sees thick chains and shackles attached to the bed bars. He then scans the room further. The walls are scratched all over. The curtains are barely hanging on their rod, badly torn, and again the large window is painted all in black. His eyes adjust further and notice a long tube connected to some device near the side of the bed. A large crucifix is hanging over the wrought iron bed post. The entire room leaves Jonathan very disturbed emotionally. *What the hell happened in this room?*

"Jonathan! What the hell are you doing in here? Get out! Now!"

Jonathan feels powerful fingers digging into his shoulder and pulling him back out of the room, with such speed and force that he almost loses his balance in a brief moment of vertigo. Sebastien lets go of Jonathan, but he is growling fiercely, his mouth slightly open revealing the hidden sharp teeth. "You had no right to do this to me! I trusted you! You betrayed me!"

Jonathan is stunned and feeling quite nervous and guilty. "Sebastien, calm down! Let's talk about this."

Sebastien has his hands on each side of his head, pacing frantically up and down before approaching Jonathan again, "I can't believe this! Why did you do this? I trusted you, I trusted you!" He moves threateningly closer to Jonathan, his eyes full of anger. They are very dark and intimidating. There is still a low growl remaining in his tone. "I'm trying to control my temper, go downstairs now—slowly! I don't want to smell your fear. I can hear your heart beating rapidly—and that is not good for you, human."

"Sebastien, wait—"

"Damn it, Jonathan—I mean it, get out of my sight! I can't control this much longer."

Jonathan looks directly into Sebastien's eyes, and shakes his head. In a calm but angry tone, his mouth barely open, he says, "That's not fear you smell, it is disappointment. Trust goes both ways, Sebastien. If we can't even talk about this, well then, I was wrong about the man I thought you were. I don't need this. I'm out of here." He storms quickly down the stairs.

"I said slowly! Dammit, are you trying to tease the thirst of the vampire? Not a good idea."

"Whatever." Before Jonathan finishes descending the stairs, Sebastien moves at an alarming speed passing Jonathan and reaches the bottom of the stairs, waiting. His expression is firm and serious.

Jonathan recovers from the dizzy vertigo and stops before he reaches the last few steps. "What the hell, Sebastien? I could have fallen down the stairs!"

"You want to talk? Let's talk." Sebastien's tone is curt and crisp.

Jonathan shakes his head in frustration as he reaches the main level. His heart rate slowly returning to its normal beats, he takes a few steps toward Sebastien. He is not going to show fear. He can feel the vampire's warm but wild-smelling breath almost touching his face, and he looks directly into Sebastien's dark brooding eyes. "Fine! I will give you the opportunity to explain the windows and that room! But let me be clear—if you ever try to threaten me again, it will be your last time—*vampire*."

Sebastien is taken aback by these threatening but courageous words, and he is struck with a tingling sensation in his extremities, overtaken with incredible respect and admiration for this human's fearlessness. Sebastien wants to grab Jonathan and kiss him passionately, but after all Jonathan did invade Sebastien's privacy, his anger and pride hold him back. Jonathan takes a seat on the couch and Sebastien approaches.

"Would you like some wine first?"

Jonathan just looks at him, shaking his head in disbelief. "No! Just sit down and explain to me why the hell you have black painted windows and what the hell I saw upstairs in the red door room."

Sebastien remains standing, facing Jonathan. "First—I would appreciate an apology for invading my privacy. At least admit that."

Jonathan sighs heavily and scratches his head, his arms briefly extended in the air. "Alright, I'm sorry for snooping, but it wasn't like you think—I didn't deliberately wait for you to leave. It was dark in here and I wanted to open up the curtains, let some light in. It's always so dark in here, like a cave. So I pulled the curtains and shutters back, then I saw the black painted window. Come on, you have to realize that is odd and would peak my curiosity. So I checked the other windows on this floor. They're all painted in black. My detective instincts kicked in. You can't blame me for that—I will not apologize for being a thorough investigator. So now you know, I wasn't snooping. Tell me, what's up with all of this?"

Sebastien's angry demeanor changes. His eyes return to their dark brown hue, and his teeth are back to normal. In a calmer, softer mood, he walks onwards the fireplace mantel and just stares at James' photo. "I didn't want you—or anyone—to know this, especially not yet. I was afraid that if you or Rebecca or Adriano found out, you would *desert* me."

Jonathan hears this heavy sigh escape Sebastien, and his heart pulls closer to this vampire. Jonathan's voice is gentler but curious. "Desert you? Why? I don't understand. Turn around, Sebastien, as much as I enjoy looking at you from behind, I need you to face me."

Sebastien turns around, feeling awkward and embarrassed for his outbursts and actions earlier. He chooses to sit on his La-Z-Boy instead of beside Jonathan on the couch. "Jonathan—James' disease drastically transformed him. It was awful. It was just the most terrifying, heart-wrenching experience I went through. There is something I haven't shared yet with Rebecca, or any of you, about vamprogeria. I know I need to tell Rebecca."

Jonathan leans forward on the couch, his arms resting on his knees, his hands resting on his chin. "Tell me."

Sebastien stand up quickly. "I need some wine first."

"Dammit Sebastien, forget the wine."

"Give me a second—please. This is not easy for me." Sebastien quickly moves to the kitchen, pours some wine, and gulps it down. He pours himself another glass and carries it to the living room. He takes a sip and sits on the couch beside Jonathan. "Before I tell you, I just need to make sure you understand I am not trying to frighten you."

"Oh, I see, the vicious vampire I saw earlier is gone? Well, thanks for letting me know I am not in danger of attack."

Sebastien feels this deliberate sting of the arrow thrown towards him in Jonathan's words. "I deserve that, I'm sorry I threatened you earlier. I was just hurt —okay?"

"Go on."

"Anyway, there is still so much about vamprogeria that is unknown. There's no conclusive evidence to suggest that every vampire with vamprogeria will experience the same final stages."

"Final stages? What do you mean by final?"

Sebastien remains silent, and the room becomes very quiet.

"Sebastien! Dammit, tell me." Jonathan is struggling to contain his frustration.

Sebastien's eyes look so sad suddenly. Jonathan can see Sebastien is struggling with something he wants to say, but he remains quiet, and his eyes look afraid. Jonathan notices, and as if a light bulb is going off in his mind, his eyes widen.

He gasps in disbelief. "Oh my God— are you saying that Rebecca will die from this disease? That it is just a matter of time? That means you, too?"

Sebastien puts his hand on Jonathan's knee. He still doesn't respond, and the dreadful silence and gloom in his demeanor fill the room momentarily. Then he opens his mouth. "I don't know. We found that our blood had been showing signs of inconsistencies, the production of healthy cells and enzymes levels were up and down, but especially in James. We were stunned to see that his were decreasing. The disease was slowly taking over his healthy vampire systems, including immune, nervous, and rejuvenating systems."

"Oh my God."

"The disease was mutating, and somehow it was showing similar traits to symptoms humans experience if they have leukemia, dementia, and Parkinson's disease. James couldn't get enough blood intake. I went to the hospital one late evening and broke into the blood clinic and stole three bags of blood, and intravenous fluid pumps, blood warmers, and plasma thawing devices. I thought maybe human blood was our only chance—we were so desperate. I gave him the blood transfusion and one bag seemed to calm him down, at least for a day or two. We noticed he was regaining his complete vision, his hearing improved, and he was walking without his cane. We even left the house and went to the woods to hunt, just to keep his nourishment up. The nourishment of animal blood and human blood seemed to give him extended days of strength and sustainability. So I gave him another transfusion with the second bag, and I hunted down an animal for him and brought it to him so he could conserve his energy. This seemed to help."

"I take it—it didn't?"

"At first it did. We both thought we could fight this with human blood and animal blood. I needed to access more human blood, so I contacted my friend Jacques, hoping he could use his networking street skills. Through his girlfriend, we got connected to someone who could get us human blood bags, but for a price of course. And we paid! For a few weeks we were enjoying life again. James and I monitored and recorded his progress, but his progress didn't last long. We started to notice symptoms resurfacing again, and his need for blood became more frequent. He digested the human and animal blood too quickly, so we couldn't keep up with his feeling of thirst. But then it got worse. Our blood supply stopped because our dealer couldn't keep up with our demand. He was worried he would get caught. So I had no choice but to manage hunting for both of us!"

"How? That must have been difficult?"

"Yes, and exhausting. I was alarmed for both of us. Within a couple of weeks we could see *other* changes happening." Sebastien pauses and gulps his wine. "He was losing his appetite to hunt for blood. His mind was tricking him to think he was full, but his body was telling him differently. He experienced tremendous abdominal and throat pain. Then I started to see *changes* in his behavior and his mental state."

Sebastien stands up. Feeling very restless, he tears up some newspaper, crumples it, and throws it into the fireplace. Clearing his throat, he picks up his wine glass from the coffee table and just remains standing, looking at the fire. "First it started with James's memory and his identity. He was struggling to remember that he was a vampire and not a human. He was confused and very troubled by the reality of who he was. I had to remind him of his travels in Europe to find other vampires, but these memories and his memories of Count Bernard were fading. He thought I was tricking him, he thought I was mocking him. He was angry and hurt that I was telling him that he was a vampire!" Sebastien picks up the framed photo of James from the mantel. "I had to console him, remind him how much I loved him." He turns toward Jonathan. "But James wasn't trusting me."

Sebastien puts the frame back. "He forgot important dates. At times he would get phone calls from his closest university colleagues and he would not recognize them. I would take the phone and say he was on medication that had side effects. Eventually, I had to answer our phone and make excuses for him. I even stopped Jacques from coming into the house, he had to leave our groceries outside; I was concerned for his own safety. James would feel so lost at times, forgetting where he was or which room he came from or where the living room was." Sebastien takes a sip of his wine, rolls it around in his mouth, stalling, then swallows harshly. "I had to paint the X on our door so he knew this was our room, but gradually it got worse. He couldn't recognize his own furniture or artifacts he had collected. Then he started getting upset and agitated for silly things."

"Like what? Come sit down, it's okay."

Sebastien moves to the couch and sits beside Jonathan. " If the TV or the record player was on, for instance. He hated any noises. I had to stop playing our albums, and I got rid of the TV, he hated the sight of it. It became worse, he started not to recognize me at times! It was so sad and hurtful, but I knew it wasn't him, it was his brilliant brain dying." Jonathan is shocked and saddened to hear what transpired. He sits motionless, listening to this frightening detailed account, every word trying to be processed and digested, and panic rising as it sinks in.

Sebastien stops talking. He takes in a deep needed breath and his eyes slowly travel to the other chair, he is almost afraid to look and see if the ghost is sitting there listening to his own horror story be retold. But the ghost has not come back. Sebastien composes himself. "My James was the calmest, loving, passionate, caring man. He never yelled at me, we always discussed like adults—and he usually gave in to my whims. He said I made him feel so young and alive—but even my love for him could not overpower the disease. James was becoming more agitated, especially at night during twilight hours—it's like he just became *unrecognizable* at times. I had to remind myself it was James staring back at me. At times his eyes were black as coal or red as blood, glaring at me, his teeth protruding and violently snapping into the air, growling ferociously! I discovered that when I played the piano, he calmed down, it soothed him somehow. I played every night for him."

Jonathan leans back on the couch, momentarily in a daze, astonished, horrified by what he is hearing and learning. Then he suddenly remembers the painted portraits he discovered in the room upstairs. The creature painted in portrait style, in different outfits. Jonathan suddenly becomes horrified in disbelief, asking himself privately, *Was the creature James? Nah, it can't be—oh my God.* "My God—I can't imagine the horror you both experienced. Oh Sebastien, I'm so sorry."

Sebastien takes another large gulp of his wine and speaks in a solemn deep *affected* voice. "Jonathan—what I am about to tell you next is so di-ff-ic-ult." He chokes back tears.

Jonathan takes Sebastien cool hand, his mind racing with the worst feeling of anxiety, not sure he was ready to hear anything else disturbing.

"Jonathan, I have to tell you—oh God, I have to tell Rebecca. But how?" Suddenly Sebastien's cell rings and it startles both of them. He reaches into his pocket and pulls it out, his eyes widen in shock. "*Dieu*! It's Rebecca." He composes himself and takes a deep breath. "Hi, Hazel Eyes." He puts the phone on speaker.

"Hi Sebastien, just checking in, now that you have a phone." A playful giggle is heard from Rebecca. "So how's it going? I hope I am not interrupting?"

Jonathan jumps in, "Hi Rebecca, you're on speaker phone."

"Oh, hi Jonathan. Listen, Adriano and I would like to have you both over for dinner."

Sebastien isn't sure if he heard Rebecca properly, he looks puzzled and mouths silently to Jonathan, *Dinner?* Jonathan shrugs his shoulders in confusion.

"Hello, are you guys still there?"

"Yes, sorry Rebecca, bad connection suddenly, did you say dinner?"

"Yes." She smirks. "I know it sounds crazy to hear this, but I couldn't stop thinking about that restaurant meal we had at Le Miaou du Chat, it inspired me to try something, you know—for us vampires! Oh, and I will have a nice meal for you too Jonathan! So please tell me you will both be available tonight? I know it is very short notice, but please come over, I miss you guys."

Jonathan looks at his watch. It is six p.m. "Hang on Rebecca, okay?"

"Sure."

Sebastien puts his phone on mute. "We can't say no?"

"No, we can't, she seems so excited. Besides, she needs to know. Adriano needs to know."

Sebastien nods his head slowly in agreement, he unmutes the phone. "Rebecca?"

"Hi, I thought you hung up. Is everything okay?"

"Sorry—we would love to come."

"Fantastic. Okay, call me when you're about to leave."

"Okay, we will see you soon, bye."

"Bye Sebastien."

Sebastien puts his cell on the table. He runs his fingers through his hair and slumps back into the couch. Jonathan can't help himself and grins suddenly. "My life gets stranger and stranger. So I am about to have a meal cooked by an Italian vampire, this should be interesting."

Sebastien just sits quiet, the humour lost on him; he is deep in thought.

"Hey Sebastien, you okay?"

Sebastien can feel his energy fading; this conversation has taken its toll. He stands up. "I need to hunt, but since we are dining at Rebecca's, maybe I just need to rest."

"Oh, sure, okay, I'll just go get ready in the meantime." Sebastien looks at Jonathan. "I promise, Sebastien, I won't invade your privacy—are we okay now?"

"I trust you. It's not that—I feel so overwhelmed, I haven't told anyone what I told you just now."

Jonathan holds Sebastien's hand. "I know, it's not going to be easy tonight, but it is important for all of us to understand what may lie ahead. We just need to be prepared mentally, if that is possible. You can't keep this from her or Adriano."

"I know." Sebastien releases his hand from Jonathan's. and abruptly stands up. "I need some air." He stalks out of the room with a wilting demeanor.

Jonathan remains on the couch, his hands covering his face. Sighing heavily, a feeling of doom travels through his mind. He looks over to the open curtains, and everything that Sebastien revealed to him came rushing in like a jolt of lightning as he stares at those black painted windows. The scratches on the walls and the bookshelf and the missing TV are evidence of secrets now revealed to him, truths he wished he didn't learn. *Oh Adriano, my dearest friend. This is going to break your heart.*

CHAPTER 17

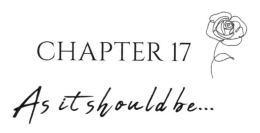

As it should be...

"Now Rebecca—that was an incredible dinner! I'm impressed, how did you get the recipe?"

Adriano jumps in feeling proud for Rebecca. "This was all Rebecca, she just used her skilled creative cooking knowledge and techniques."

"Aww...you helped too, my vampire."

"Thanks—all I did was ask the butcher for a piece of fresh venison and some steak. But it was your creativity with the spices and lemon and wine that made it delicious."

"Sshh...don't give away all my secrets about the marinade." They both laugh, but awareness of the strange expressions of Sebastien and Jonathan, who are looking at each other, triggers a discomfort. Rebecca becomes concerned,

"Hey, you both okay? You both seemed kind of quiet this evening, and Sebastien you were a bit distracted or something?"

Sebastien takes a sip of his wine, failing to keep a painted smile on his face.

"I hope the steak was cooked enough for you Jonathan?"

"Yes, it was delicious Rebecca, thanks for cooking my favorite Italian dish, see all the spaghetti and meatballs are gone."

Rebecca feels pleased, smiling so warmly. "Oh, it feels so amazing to entertain again, to cook—thank you both for coming tonight, it really means a lot to me. It's special too since I got to cook a meal for my dear friends in Paris. Too bad Sandra is not here."

Rebecca gets up to start clearing the plates.

"Oh no, you sit, I got this. Go in the living room, I will be in shortly."

"Thanks Adriano."

"Here let us help," is simultaneously spoken by Jonathan and Sebastien.

"No, no, I got this, you guys go join Rebecca. I'm just going to put these in the dishwasher. Oh, Jonathan do me a favor, bring the wine and glasses to the living room, help yourselves okay?"

Jonathan grabs the bottle of Cabernet, and Rebecca puts the wine glasses on a tray and carries it to the living room. Sebastien slowly moves away from the dinner table to join Rebecca and Jonathan.

"Dessert is just fruit, sorry, I haven't yet figured out other desserts that may please a vampire's taste buds without causing major indigestion!" She chuckles.

"No apologies, Hazel Eyes. Fruit is fine with me."

"Me too, I'm stuffed anyway." Jonathan is trying to keep the air light but it is obvious that Sebastien is struggling to appear in good spirits; he is overburdened with thoughts, and this is not lost on the worried Rebecca.

"Sebastien? I know something is troubling you. You're among friends."

Sebastien runs his fingers through his hair, an action Rebecca is learning means that he is nervous, worried, and frustrated. "Hazel Eyes, I need to talk to you."

"Ok, do you mean privately?"

Sebastien shakes his head. "No, Adriano needs to hear this too."

Rebecca's demeanor shows alarm. "Okay." She calls out to Adriano, who has the water running and is just wiping down the counter. "Adriano, can you please come in the living room."

Adriano hears Rebecca's voice full of sudden tense and worry, he puts the cloth down and moves quickly to the living room. "Is everything okay?"

"I don't know? Is it, Sebastien?"

"Adriano, please, sit down, there is something—" Sebastien turns to Jonathan for moral support, and Jonathan nods his head in reassurance. "There is something I need to tell you both, I can't put it off any longer."

"What is it? You're worrying me."

"Sorry Hazel Eyes, I don't mean too, but—"

"Just tell us Sebastien, obviously something is on your mind."

Jonathan interrupts. "Adriano, please, just give him a chance."

Sebastien begins. "It's about James."

"Okay, we're listening." comments Adriano, thinking, *maybe finally he will tell us the truth.* He looks over to Jonathan, but Jonathan doesn't look his way. Adriano can see expressions of concern and worry and even sadness on Jonathan's face.

"The James I knew and loved was disappearing."

"Disappearing?"

"Please, Rebecca, let me get this out."

"Of course." Rebecca and Adriano both aware that Sebastien used her real name and not his playful endearing Hazel Eyes.

Sebastien spent the next half hour telling Rebecca and Adriano everything he shared with Jonathan about the symptoms growing, the human cravings, James having to quit the university, and more information that Jonathan too was now just learning.

"James's heart and body and soul were changing. It was becoming increasingly difficult to keep him calm and peaceful, even with the sound of me playing his favorite piece Nocturne Twenty. at first it used to soothe *him,* but as time went on, even that was no comfort to the *creature.* With regret I share that I was becoming afraid for both our safety." Sebastien becomes silent again, his hands begin to tremble. "Sorry, just give me a second."

Adriano's heart is beating quickly; he swallows the lump in his throat. His panic is rising, but he forces it down. He isn't sure yet if his panic is justified. He remains calm, listening.

Sebastien regains his strength. "You see, I couldn't have him in our bedroom anymore, he would *terrify* me, waking up in the night just staring at me with glaring red eyes, not recognizing me, growling a low guttural sound, and it was intimidating. So I couldn't take it anymore, I needed to have a restful sleep in order to have the strength to hunt for both of us. It was so physically demanding on me to keep doing this day and night. I don't know how I lasted as long as I did. But I loved him, he was my James. I decided to put him in the room across the hall, and I painted the door red so he would know that this is his room. I attached a dead-bolt to it. James was still suffering disorientation and confusion, and I thought it would help guide him if he saw the red door, give him some control and dignity still to know his room. But it broke my heart to lock him inside alone, confused, probably feeling so emotionally hurt by me doing this and frightened." Sebastien stops talking,

"Sebastien, are you okay? Do you need anything?"

"I just need a minute, and more wine, please."

Rebecca quickly goes to the kitchen and returns with a bottle of red wine and refills Sebastien's glass. He takes a large gulp; his hand is still shaking slightly.

Jonathan feels so bad for him. "It's okay Sebastien, take your time."

Rebecca's hands are gripping Adriano's tightly as Sebastien continues on. "There is more you need to know."

"More? I'm afraid to hear this." Rebecca stands up nervously.

"Rebecca, stay calm, it's okay whatever it is, and we will face it together, *mon amour.*"

Jonathan holds Sebastien's hand, he too is dreading what next will be revealed. What more he might have to accept. "Go on Sebastien."

Sebastien takes a deep breath and continues. "Vampires may have stronger rejuvenating mechanisms to keep from aging and prolong our longevity. But in our case, with vamprogeria, we may not have the same powerful healing mechanisms long term. I'm afraid that eventually this disease will most likely accelerate and take over our healthy immune system, nervous system, and entire wellbeing, as it did for my James."

"There is more, I can see it in your eyes, tell us Sebastien. We deserve to know. Rebecca deserves to know."

"He's trying, Adriano, can't you see that? Look at him!" Jonathan's outburst catches Adriano off guard.

"It's okay, Jonathan, I'm alright to continue. You, Adriano, and Rebecca deserve to know everything now. What really happened to my *James*."

The room is silent as if it is waiting patiently, respectfully for Sebastien to speak. "It was an evening in early March, two years ago. I had just finished dinner with James. I brought him a fox to drink and I tucked him into bed after. I went downstairs and played the piano for him. I knew he could hear it from the room he was sleeping in, so I assumed he was calm and hopefully falling asleep, even if it would only last a couple hours. I remember feeling very sad and restless that evening. I just wasn't in a positive state of mind. It had been a very long and strenuous week trying to manage this difficult situation on my own. I went into the kitchen to pour myself a glass of wine and opened the fridge to pull out some berries. I suddenly felt James behind me—I was shocked because he was barely able to do the stairs anymore without great difficulty and concern of falling. And there he was standing behind me. I had a great smile on my face, thinking that he was turning a corner in the disease once again—thinking maybe the increased rest he got helped. Maybe we just had some good days still to treasure. I was naive. I turned around—" Sebastien pauses, the energy in the room tightens with every passing second.

"And? What happened?" Rebecca could not contain the anxiety and upset, and Sebastien felt so horrible knowing he was causing this.

"Then he—he—he—forgive me James for telling this—oh God! He lunged at me, grabbed me with his claws! those beautiful strong hands were gone, replaced with—with—"

"Oh Sebastien—how terrifying!"

"He held on so tight, Hazel Eyes, and his growl—I won't forget it, ever. It was so disturbing and ferocious. I could smell the foul wild stench coming from his breath that used to smell like sweet apple cider. I wanted to believe with everything in my soul that James was in that body, somewhere, but all I saw and heard was the sound of a creature, not James! Not my beloved vampire."

"Sebastien, I can't hear any more, this is so upsetting!"

"You have to Rebecca. It's important to you."

"Why, Jonathan? Why is this important to Rebecca?"

"Sebastien, continue, tell us—it's okay."

"The creature was trying to attack me. I shoved it forcefully. He fell back and I heard this cracking sound. I realized he hit his head on the corner of our table. He fell to the floor and he was unconscious and bleeding." Sebastien pauses, tears forming in his eyes, and he sniffles. "I screamed for James to wake up, but he didn't. I don't know how I did this, but it was like suddenly I had an out of body experience or something. I found myself lifting this creature into my arms—I'm not that strong as a vampire to carry another vampire. I carried him upstairs with ease into his room and placed him on the bed, and I just ran to the shed and found chains and ran back and tied this unconscious being to the bed. I was shaking, I was petrified. Then a few minutes later I heard the most beastly sounds coming from *it*. He was struggling to get free but I couldn't—I couldn't free James! I kept him bound in chains. For days. I couldn't hunt fast enough for him anymore; his body was absorbing the blood by the hour. My body couldn't do it—I was exhausted. Oh God, he died three days later of severe malnutrition. He died in chains. I killed him!" Sebastien breaks down weeping in floods of tormented tears. Rebecca dashes to his side, wrapping her arms around him. Sebastien pushes her away but she returns to him. Adriano stands up immediately but Sebastien is distraught.

"No! Get away Rebecca! I don't deserve your caring! I don't deserve empathy after what I did. I killed him! I killed my James! Oh God, forgive me James, I was just too exhausted to hunt anymore for the *creature*—his thirst was unstoppable. Oh God, forgive me, my James." The room is immediately altered to a dark and despairing state, filled with the weeping sound of Sebastien's heart breaking over again. His body wilts in a deep inconsolable storm of tears.

Later, Adriano and Rebecca walk out of the woods and back to the car. Both of them are distracted in their own private thoughts. Rebecca found it difficult to subdue her prey, and Adriano had to help her hunt. He managed to find a small rabbit and an injured fox for Rebecca to feed from. The beautiful dinner that she prepared earlier didn't manage to sustain her as originally hoped. The overwhelming emotional stress just overtook Rebecca after the shock of learning that this disease could ultimately kill her and Sebastien, or turn them into a creature that not even a vampire could control. Adriano is consumed with worry that Rebecca could faint like she almost did earlier in the living room.

"How do you feel? Did you drink enough? I can try and find more if—"

"I just want to go away. Far, far away." Rebecca's voice carries such strain and sadness. It pains Adriano to hear her talk this way. "My beautiful sons, my dreams, and my hopes, all gone—I have no future. I can't be with my sons—I can't risk harming them!" That is the moment that set apart all other troubling moments; she is mentally processing the agonizing reality that her mind refuses to travel to or accept, and she falls to her knees on the ground, weeping hysterically. Adriano quickly bends down beside her, embracing her tightly, afraid to let go as if she might wilt away emotionally. Adriano is struggling himself to keep his emotions from escaping. He can't break down now, not in front of her, not when his beautiful vampire is losing her spirit and her hope is despairing in front of him.

Adriano searches his mind for the right words to bring Rebecca back into the light, but he knows there are no words to say that can hold her spirit. The terrifying story that they all heard invades Adriano's mind in a loop of chaos and anxiety. Knowing Rebecca, this beautiful loving woman, vampire, and mother could lose her memories, decline in cognitive functioning, transform physically to a creature, horrifies Adriano. His mind is screaming, begging, praying. *Oh God! Tell me what to do—tell me what to say. How can I help this beautiful soul? She is kind, she is a mother who loves her children. She needs to be here for her children! Please don't destroy her! Give her some years with us. Please give her some joys to experience, give her wisdom. Give her courage to fight! Please don't abandon me now. Please give me her pain, give me her disease—I will take it. Take me instead—I am not worthy. I know my sins—protect her! I beg you, don't do this to me. Don't take away the love of my life, she is the air that makes me breathe.* Adriano's emotions are trying to escape out loud and he just can't do that to Rebecca. He collapses into her body silently, weeping in his heart, his soul crying in pain.

While Rebecca, in the meantime, remains tightly still in his arms, but praying silently. *God, I know that I have a difficult road ahead of me. I know I am not ready for this, but I know you understand my fear of the progression of this disease and you don't hold this against me. But you will be with me. I trust you. You have been with me all along; even as a vampire, you gave me the strength to overcome, you showed me experiences of unconditional love with Adriano, you brought into my life a new and amazing caring vampire friend Sebastien, who helped me understand who I am. I will not be afraid. I will enjoy my time with my sons while I am in my right mind. I know at this moment right now you are here, I can feel a peace come over me. I feel it, it is beautiful, just knowing that the worst fear I had is now further from becoming reality—you know what I am talking about, thank you. I know that it was meant to be to have this particular disease as a vampire, I understand why now, it is because you heard my secret prayer, you are doing everything in your power not to let me suffer the most unbearable pain and agony a mother could face. This disease will save me from living longer than my sons, my family. That is the one thing I begged you when I became a vampire, and you answered my prayer, I know you did. I will die before them, as it should be. Thank you!*

They both remain woven into each other's arms a while longer. Then an owl hoots and breaks the woeful silence. Rebecca looks up at Adriano, her eyes now vibrant, appearing to show an expression of clarity. She looks peaceful. Adriano is struck by this change, not sure what to think. Rebecca takes his hand. "Adriano, I think it's all going to be okay."

Sebastien and Jonathan took a taxi an hour earlier back to St. Denis. Sebastien was too restless to sleep, the difficult conversation staying with him. He tried to reassure everyone that the disease might not progress the same as it did for James, but everyone was too upset and emotionally charged. He was relieved when Adriano took Rebecca out to hunt, at least he only had to be concerned about himself tonight. His mind is now repeating the images of sadness and fear in Rebecca's eyes, and anger in Adriano's. Jonathan and Sebastien are in the living room. Jonathan is sitting on the couch reading emails from work on his phone. He glances over at Sebastien, who is sitting on his chair and appears to be reading from a medical text. Something pops into Jonathan's mind.

"Sebastien, have you given any more thought to my suggestion to ask Sandra if she can talk to her colleague in pathology?" Sebastien doesn't respond right away, in fact he just continues reading the journal, but Jonathan is pretty sure he is just reading words. Through his keen observation, he can tell that Sebastien is not truly absorbed in the reading. "Sebastien, did you hear me?"

Sebastien looks over to Jonathan; his eyes are dull and responds in a dry manner. "It won't be necessary."

"What do you mean?"

"Just what I said, I don't need a job in Toronto, since I will be here." And he returns his eyes to the words on the page, his mind far, far away.

"What? You changed your mind? Why?"

"Isn't it obvious!?" he snaps. "The plans to have me live with Rebecca are over." He abruptly shuts the book and slams it down on the coffee table. He stands up with such uncanny speed that before Jonathan can blink, Sebastien could be heard in the kitchen.

Jonathan recovers from the dizziness and walks to the kitchen. "The plans are over? Since when?"

"Since tonight. Come on, Jonathan it's not rocket science. Rebecca hates me. Adriano *loathes* me, which is not that far of a stretch for him, since he already disliked me from the beginning because he wasn't her blood link!"

"Where the hell did you get that idea? What is going on? No one hates you. It was a difficult subject tonight, I get that, and you had to let them know, that was not fun, but it's not your fault."

"Really? You sure about that? Don't forget—I made Rebecca a vampire. She is my blood link. Adriano can't stand the fact that Rebecca and I share this special bond, he knows it connects us. You have to understand this is a unique unbreakable bond shared between a vampire and his or her blood link. This bond lasts forever, whether they embrace it with all heart or despise it. So Adriano, who seems kind of the jealous type, hates this truth! And now the reality that Rebecca carries this disease because of me just adds to his hatred! So I'm pretty sure *it is* my fault." He takes a huge gulp of wine and pours himself another one, and then another. "Dammit! I wish I could get severely drunk out of my mind."

"You would need something a lot stronger for that."

"Did you forget, I'm a vampire, I could drink a hundred proof and not flinch." Sebastien suddenly stares at Jonathan. "Jonathan? Why are you here? You could have stayed back at Adriano's apartment, you should have—I'm sure they need you."

"I am where I want to be. I know you are upset, but—"

"*Upset*! I don't have a right to be upset. I don't have a right to be here with you Jonathan. I—"

"Stop! I have heard enough. Stop feeling sorry for yourself—you are wrong about Rebecca or Adriano hating you. Pick up the phone and stop this nonsense."

"You have no clue Jonathan—I ruined her life."

"No you didn't. She was going to die, for Christ's Sake! She had cancer! This was supposed to be her last trip before she died! *You* brought her back. She is going to see her sons, raise them, live as many years as she can, don't underestimate her. Like you said, you don't know enough about vamprogeria, so how can you assume it will be the same outcome for you and Rebecca! What if James had a precondition that you or he were not aware of? Did he ever tell you about his family history as a human? I don't know, just, couldn't it be possible that there was something in his medical history that might have influenced or exasperated vamprogeria that made it progress to a final stage? You're the scientist, isn't it possible?"

Sebastien puts his glass of wine down. Jonathan sees a shimmer of light of thought forming in Sebastien's expression. He knows Sebastien is pondering this idea. Sebastien walks slowly and pensively through the kitchen into the hallway, mentally opening up his scientific mind. Imaginative graphs and diagnostic diagrams are moving through his mind as he processes this possible truth suggested by Jonathan. But then the light dims again in his mind, the image of medical charts vanishes. Frustration grows as he realizes that he doesn't know the medical history of James, and without this history how could he research to see if there are any correlations between vamprogeria or any of its symptoms and any medical preconditions found in James' human family history?

"Sebastien, did you hear me? Can you think back to your family history?" Sebastien hears. He reaches far into his own private personal memories.

"I know that heart disease was evident on my mother's side. I lost her and one of my uncles to heart attacks. My mum died while on her daily jogging regime, she was only thirty-seven. My uncle Patrick, who was her older brother, died a few years later of a massive heart attack. I never met my grandparents. But—I was born with a heart infection, I was quite vulnerable as a youngster to fatigue, shortness of breath, and dizziness, and I always sounded like I was sick, coughing a lot, a dry irritating cough. Since I couldn't perform highly active activities I turned to books as my outlet." Sebastien stops talking, running his fingers through his hair. "Sorry, I haven't told anyone this about my life, not even James knew, it just never came up."

"I'm sorry to hear about your losses—that must have been devastating. Thank you for sharing this with me. So when you became a vampire, did anything change in your health? I mean, I know you become stronger and can heal faster than a human, but did you notice anything different with your heart condition, for example?"

"Absolutely. I could never run or do anything strenuous as a human, but as a vampire, the coughing stopped completely, and the fatigue became less frequent. Now I can leap as high as a tree and land precisely at the target I desire without breaking a sweat. I can climb trees, something I envied other kids my age growing up. If they saw me now, climbing like a cougar... However, this mostly occurs when I am not severely dehydrated—thirsty."

"And what about your father's side?"

Sebastien pauses, stroking his goatee. "I didn't learn anything about my father's side, he died when I was very young; I hardly remember him. My mum didn't want to talk about him, I think his death affected her too much."

"That's too bad. Do you mind me asking, how did he die?"

"Well the story that was told to me over and over when I asked as a little boy, was that he was a soldier in the British Army, out on a mission overseas, and he died trying to save a little brother and sister from a terrorist. He got them to safety in the mountains but he was wounded in the process, and died on the mountain. My mum made my father sound like a hero, and that is how I pictured him in my mind, but something in her voice always seemed like she was overcompensating. I only remember one photo of him she showed me, she kept it very close to her. He was in a British soldier's uniform, though. It sounded pretty cool as a young fatherless boy to know that you had a soldier for a father.

"The story seemed to get larger at times, it seems he also saved their German shepherd too—that was the version my Uncle Patrick used to tell me! I'm sure he included this detail since I had a German shepherd as a pet. He was my favourite uncle, great guy. So unfortunately, I don't know my father's medical history. But vamprogeria is its own disease, with its own unique symptoms that somehow mimics traits of progeria. Neither of us had progeria in our medical history. I'm sure James would have told me if this was the case in his. James didn't have a heart condition, yet he suffered fatigue and dizziness, and his body aged further as the disease took over, especially when he was not nourished enough. So this disease has a mind of its own. There is no other connection other than progeria! So how the hell did the other symptoms come into play in its later more severe stages? It's like he developed traits you find in dementia or Alzheimer patients, even Parkinson's Disease. I am so damn frustrated! It just doesn't make sense. I see where you were trying to lead me, Jonathan, and I thank you for your insight. However, I just don't think any precondition connects to this debilitating fatal disease."

Sebastien takes his wine glass and puts it on the kitchen counter, turning to Jonathan. "It's getting late, my mind is too tired to think anymore scientifically or anything else. I'm so confused, all over the place, tonight was just not a good night. I still feel Adriano's anger all over me—*dieu!* I want to scream."

"So scream, no one is here, we're isolated, who else will hear you?"

"Have you ever heard a vampire scream?"

"No, can't say I have, Adriano is not the screaming type. He shouts at times."

"Yeah I noticed. Trust me, it will be painful to your sensitive human ears if I scream, I'm not joking, it could cause damage, seriously."

"I will plug them."

"You're cute and persistent. Thanks for listening, it does feel really good to have someone to talk to again."

"Sebastien, I don't want you to go to bed blaming yourself for Rebecca's condition. I am sure she will want to hear from you tomorrow! Adriano was just upset, he blows up in the moment, but then once he has time to process, he becomes rational again. You have to understand that about him. Maybe it's his Sicilian blood that triggers these outbursts at times. He used to tell me that Sicilian blood triggers a powerful emotional response. Of course, it is nonsense—and he knew it, but liked to tease me and Sandra. He is a good friend, and I know he will do anything for Rebecca and his friends. I'm sure now that includes you too, whether you believe it or not right now. So I hope you will reconsider and come to Toronto."

"Jonathan, I can't think anymore. I need to rest, as I'm sure my thirst will rise soon from all of this emotional stuff tonight. Stress and heavy emotional feelings can trigger the symptoms, I know you realize this now. Are you coming? I mean, would you like to come up, just to cuddle, I don't mean to pressure you."

"Oh, I didn't think we—umm. Sure—but I'll be up in a minute, okay?"

Sebastien suddenly wears a trace of a smile, but his brooding brown eyes overpower any resemblance of joy. He moves quickly upstairs to his room and shuts the door.

Jonathan looks at his watch. "He'll be up." He dials Adriano and walks into the living room.

"Jonathan? Everything okay? You know it's midnight?"

"Yeah, sorry, I know it's late—how's Rebecca?"

"Why are you whispering? You don't sound good, you sure you're okay?"

Jonathan pauses. "Sebastien thinks you and Rebecca hate him."

Adriano smirks briefly then becomes silent.

"Adriano, he doesn't want to move to Toronto now."

"I see, well that's his choice."

"Come on, I'm serious. He can't stay here by himself anymore, not like this. He needs to know that he is still welcomed."

"Jonathan, I can't force him."

"Adriano, I hope he is not right? You don't hate him?"

"Hate, no, but am I angry? You're damn right! Christ Jonathan! He is responsible for giving this fatal disease to Rebecca—you expect me to thank him? Welcome him into our family?"

"That's not fair, and you know it—you can't blame him for this. He did what he had to—to save Rebecca. He brought her back to you, to her family, her sons—I know what you heard tonight scares you."

"I'm not scared!"

"Right, okay, well regardless, he needs us. He needs a place where he will be safe, this is not safe for him, mentally or physically. He is isolated—I can't believe I have to convince you? Is Rebecca listening, does she feel the same?"

"Rebecca is sleeping, but—no, she still wants him to live with her, but knowing what I know now, I am not convinced anymore. Why do you and Rebecca treat him like he is fragile? He is an adult, for God's sake, he has lived alone since his partner died, that was over two years ago. He can survive on his own—I don't get this over protectiveness for him, from Rebecca or you."

"Adriano, I'm not going to explain to you again. A vampire friend needs help. Get over the fact that you weren't the one to turn Rebecca. You have held this grudge against him, and he feels it—this is not the Adriano I know." The phone becomes awkwardly silent. Adriano feels the sting of those words and he can hear the disappointment in his friend Jonathan; he suddenly feels this heaviness.

"You're right—I am angry still. I can't help it. It's something I have to work out, I'm sorry I disappointed you. Christ! I'm overwhelmed. I just want to go home and put our life back on track, and I just don't know how to do this and include another vampire with the same disease that needs careful attention. I don't hate him, I know he needs us, but I am also worried about the humans in this picture, especially the children. What if it doesn't work out? Then it will be hard on Sebastien and Rebecca. Or worse, and I hate to say this, but we need to be real about this Jonathan— what if one day something in him changes and he craves them—her sons? There is no going back at that point. He would have to leave or I would kill him. You know that. So you see, in a way I do have Sebastien's welfare in mind." The phone again becomes silent, then Jonathan hears a heavy sigh escape Adriano. "I am trying my best to do the right thing for all involved. We have two vampires with a difficult and dangerous disease that needs to be carefully monitored, and we have humans we need to protect too. So what the hell am I to do? In three days, Rebecca expects to be on a plane back to Toronto, and I don't even yet know how to get her safely home. She can't go six or eight hours without blood, and we can't guarantee there will be no delays or stopovers. I can't control this, I can't control anything to keep her safe—that is what scares me deeply, Jonathan."

"I know, I get it. Trust me. We have a unique life, with complicated circumstances. I don't have any answers. I wish I did. As far as the flight home, last night Sebastien and I were running through ideas, he thinks there might be a way of carrying the blood on us in our carry-on luggage, so if she or Sebastien needs it, they can privately drink. But we can talk about this tomorrow."

"Seriously, he has a way to carry the blood?"

"I'll let him explain it. But back to your fear of cravings, I believe in my heart that if Sebastien ever in one moment felt a craving for Rebecca's sons or anyone close to her, he would immediately vacate. He would never do anything to harm Rebecca or her family."

"Jonathan, I understand you have grown fondly of him, but you can't be that sure, a craving can be so powerful to a vampire. It takes a lot of discipline for a healthy vampire, trust me. So imagine the extreme strength and will it would take for one with a disease that weakens them."

"Well, Sebastien and Rebecca are unique. I know they are powerful, mind, body, and soul. I hope you will believe this. You know Rebecca would kill herself before she allowed any harm to her sons, either by herself or anyone. So why wouldn't Sebastien be the same? He is a good man, he has a kind and caring soul." Jonathan pauses. The phone is eerily silent, he can hear Adriano breathing. He continues. "I have an idea. I've been doing some thinking, maybe Sebastien should come and stay with me, at least for now."

"Live with you?"

"I'll work it out somehow. I can change my hours so I can be home more, if that is what is needed. But we are getting way ahead of ourselves, we still have two strong vampires who are capable of many things. We don't know what our future will be, all we have to worry about is now, plan for now."

"Oh, have you discussed this with him? That's kind of a big step, living together. You just met."

"I would be helping a friend, that's all. Besides, I have the room, and I don't have other humans to worry about. I didn't want to mention any of this earlier, until I thought it through myself, but now I am even more convinced, Sebastien should live with me! Problem solved."

"Friend huh?"

"…Yes."

"Okay, keep convincing yourself, Brown Eyes." Jonathan can hear Adriano smirking through the phone. "By the way, Jonathan, whispering doesn't work, you are in a home with a vampire, his ears are very keen, remember that."

At that moment Jonathan is suddenly convinced he hears a creak on the stairs, and the sound of feet ascending upward again. Then he hears nothing, but then he definitely hears a bedroom door close again.

"Jonathan, you still there?"

"Yeah, sorry, thought I heard something. Anyways, tomorrow we all need to sit down and talk like adults and not gorillas thumping their chests."

"You're hilarious—okay, okay, it's late, go to bed."

"Later."

"Good night, *mon ami.*"

CHAPTER 18

Iceberg

Adriano's cell alarm rings, the display reads 8 a.m. Wednesday, February 20. He turns over and discovers that Rebecca is not beside him, then he clears the early morning fog from his mind and hears the water running in the shower. He gets up and goes to knock on the bathroom door in their en suite. "Good morning."

Rebecca responds that she is almost finished. Adriano goes into the kitchen and starts emptying the dishwasher from last evening. He is remembering the last conversation with Jonathan, and is curious to find out what idea Sebastien has in mind for carrying blood in their carry-on luggage. He also remembers that tonight is the art exhibit, and he is anxious to go there and hopefully meet the vampire Juliette.

Rebecca appears suddenly at the entrance of the kitchen, wearing her housecoat and towel over her head. "Shower's all yours."

"Actually, thought we would hunt first, then I will come back and shower. I'm just going to go wash my face and brush my teeth, be back shortly." He kisses her on the lips and heads toward the bathroom.

Adriano drives to the same wooded area they've been frequenting lately. Rebecca skillfully subdues a brown rabbit and then a fox. Adriano is satisfied with just drinking from one rabbit. He is relieved that Rebecca is able to drink from at least two animals this morning. Rebecca continues to practice concentrating on one sound at a time. In this case, her attention is focused on a nest of baby birds squawking. She manages to block out loud chirps from adult birds who are circling the tree with the nest. Adriano and Rebecca leisurely walk back to the car, enjoying the fresh winter morning air as if all the drama and anxiety from last night is temporarily out of reach in their minds.

But then parts of last night came back to Adriano's mind. "So Rebecca, I was talking to Jonathan late last night, and apparently Sebastien is upset. He thinks you and I hate him because of the things he told us about the final stages of vamprogeria."

"Oh—of course not! I hope you made that clear?"

"Well, I think you need to call him directly. Anyway, besides that, Sebastien has an idea as to how to transport blood so we can carry it in our carry-on luggage, so let's meet up with them and find out about this. We only have three days left before we head back."

"I know, this week is going by fast. We've been so busy. But—I am ready for this. I feel it." Rebecca is determined to just live and not focus on if and when the vamprogeria changes.

Adriano can see this new confidence and determination in Rebecca. "I know, I'm looking forward to going back to work, but there are still complexities we have to figure out."

"Did your agent Richard get back to you?"

"Yeah, he has a few houses lined up for us to see next week."

"Okay."

"By the way, I hope you are comfortable with us going to the gallery tonight." Adriano reaches into his pocket and pulls out a tissue. He wipes Rebecca's mouth, then his, and they continue walking towards the car.

"Oh right, that's tonight. I'm curious to meet this female vampire that seems to have caught your attention."

"She has—but not the way you might be thinking."

"I see."

"Anyway, there is something about her that struck me, when I saw her a few days ago. It's silly, but she reminds me of my little sister Maria, but an older version. If she would have been given a chance to grow into a beautiful young woman, I can imagine her looking something like this vampire."

"Maria? I don't think I know about her. Did you tell me about her and I have forgotten it because of my amnesia?"

"No, no, don't worry, we never discussed this. I didn't really share about my family. It's not a topic I feel good talking about. But I don't want to put walls up like James did with Sebastien, that's not a healthy relationship. I just need to do this at my own pace, share when I feel it is time. I hope you understand?"

"Yes, of course Adriano, I don't want to pressure you. I appreciate that you're even willing to take this step with me about your sister." They keep walking slowly, almost out of the woods now.

"Maria died, she was —"

Rebecca stops walking.

"*Sexually assaulted and murdered.*" His voice is deeply lowered, his expression troubled.

"Oh God, Adriano, how horrible." Rebecca instantly hugs Adriano tightly.

"Thanks, *mon amour.* I'm glad I'm sharing this with you. It was a very difficult time. Anyway, Maria had such a sweet and kind spirit and demeanor about her. She was so much like my mother that way."

"Did they ever find who did this?"

"No, and this haunts me to this day."

They keep walking, holding hands. Rebecca is beginning to realize there is so much more that she doesn't know about Adriano. "Understandable, I'm so sorry Adriano. My God. You have suffered so many losses in your life, so violently. Your mother and your sister." Rebecca leans in closer to him. She just wants to help him, let him know he is not alone.

"Thank you, one day I will share more of my losses."

"More?" Rebecca stands still again, she sees more sadness shadow Adriano's eyes. But Adriano doesn't elaborate. Rebecca is not sure if she should push him; her heart feels like it is sinking for him, but she can feel a distance coming from him. She has to trust he will tell her when he is ready. Rebecca just wants to help carry his burdens, but doesn't know how. Adriano is always so emotionally strong, and sometimes feels he has to carry everything for everyone, which also creates a distance that can be felt by those closest to him. She knows Adriano loves her, but she feels weary of the walls she sometimes feels with him. Suddenly, an image of a man surfaces in Rebecca's mind. She can't recognize him yet. But her heart is poking at her, quick fragmented scenes, conversations coming into view then fading. Her mind is letting her know that at one time this other man was very significant to her, and soon she will remember him and the history they had. She is confused by this.

Then a disturbing image suddenly invades Adriano's tired mind. He sees his father Massimo run out of their barn, and he sees his older brother Giacomo lying in the barn bleeding and choking on his own blood. Then a memory takes him back to the rake lying in the hay, drops of blood dripping down from the top, and Adriano quickly shakes his head, trying to remove the disturbing memory from his mind.

"Are you okay?"

"I'm fine, but we need to get going Rebecca—we have a busy day ahead of us." He grabs her hand and runs out of the woods to the car, then opens the door for her. "I will call Jonathan and let him know we are coming there soon." Rebecca enters the car, feeling the weight of heavy challenges ahead of her. Adriano's cell rings, she quickly realizes it is his real estate agent. He remains outside of the car. Rebecca closes her eyes, she can feel the walls within Adriano building—she knows it is not going to be easy for him to let her in further to his past. She is not sure why this worries her, but it does. She asks herself privately, *will his past create a distance between us? I can't let it interfere with us. I don't know if I can handle another relationship like the one with Olivier—that's his name, I remember. All those secrets. No—Adriano is different. I love him and he needs me, I just have to be patient.*

Adriano enters the car and starts the engine. He looks over and sees that Rebecca's eyes are closed.

"Hey you, is everything alright?"

"Yes. Any news from Richard?

"He is trying to set up appointments for us next week."

They drive towards St. Denis, back to Sebastien's home.

"First, I can extract the animal's blood with the syringe and transfer it to the perfume bottle refills, and store them in the cooler. We can keep them like this until we arrive at the airport, and then we'll remove them from the cooler and let them come down to room temperature before we go through check in. Lucky for us, they can stay out at room temperature for longer periods of time without health risk if we drink it."

"Thanks Sebastien. This might work, but I see one issue, we cannot carry lots of perfume bottles in carry-ons, as this might cause some suspicion as to why we wouldn't pack these in our main luggage. I have an idea, what if we use some small bottles of contact lens solution too, since they wouldn't show the liquid contents? Probably even better than the glass perfume bottles, unless we can find non-glass ones?"

"Great idea, *mon amour*—Sebastien, how much blood do you think you and Rebecca will need during the flight?"

"Well, if we drink from at least three animals each on Friday morning, and hopefully we can find foxes or large rabbits, we should be okay while flying if we have two bottles each of blood with us. So if we use contact lens solution bottles, we can all carry one of these—let's buy different brands so we each have different ones, probably less suspicious."

"As I mentioned earlier, I will be happy to donate my blood, too. I'm fine with syringes. I've donated blood for Adriano many times. Maybe it will sustain you better?"

"Thank you Jonathan, so kind of you. Sebastien and I might be okay with just animal blood. Sebastien, what do you think?"

"I think so but we must conserve our energy once we get on the plane, rest a lot."

"Okay, then I think we have a plan. Let's just hope there are no major flight delays or redirects. I booked us all first class."

"First class? I don't know what to say, Adriano. That is very generous of you, but I can go economy."

"Don't be ridiculous, Sebastien. We are all sticking together, and Rebecca flies first class, I wouldn't have it any other way." He leans over on the couch and kisses Rebecca on the cheek.

"Sebastien, I know this is a difficult subject and I don't mean to pry, but well, we only have a couple days, have you figured out what to do with this home? Will you just lock it up?"

"Yes, I have thought very hard about this. The only person I can truly trust with my home is Jacques. I know he will look after it, at least until I'm ready to sell it." Sebastien looks thoughtfully across the room to the recliner; the ghost was not there.

"Sebastien, that is such a huge responsibility, are you sure? He is so young, will he be able to manage this huge home?"

"I understand your concern Hazel Eyes, but I have thought hard about this. I know it is risky but all he would have to do is look in on it maybe every other week, it will be locked up. Jacques is a good guy; besides, would he really want to disappoint or anger a vampire?"

Laughter fills the room and Sebastien feels pleased, he needs to stay positive.

"Okay, now onto the next item, I would like to be at the gallery by seven tonight. Shall we all go in your Mercedes, Sebastien? You okay with that?"

"Yes, whatever, Adriano." Everyone could hear this sudden drop of spirit in Sebastien's voice.

"Sebastien? What is it?"

"Hmmm? Oh, nothing, Hazel Eyes. It's just hitting me. This is really happening—I'm really doing this. I'm leaving my home. If you will excuse me, I better go and find my passport and start packing some things."

"Sebastien, we are all happy that you are coming back with us."

"Hazel Eyes—I hope this is the right decision."

"It is, my friend."

"I need to decide what items I want to take with me. I know I can't take a lot, the rest will have to be shipped to me, in time." Sebastien's voice remains a bit distant, and he leaves the room looking and feeling drained of spirit, heading to the stairs.

"Sebastien, can I help?"

Sebastien hollers from the hallway, "No, Jonathan, this is something I need to do alone."

Within seconds a door upstairs is heard opening and closing.

"I hope Sebastien is really okay with this. This is a huge step for him, I just want him to know we are here if he needs us. By the way, Jonathan, Adriano mentioned to me that you had offered to have Sebastien stay with you, but I hope you understand why it is best he stays with me? We are the only ones who can truly hunt for each other, if necessary."

"Yes, Rebecca, Sebastien and I talked it over. I understand the concerns, and we agreed it would probably be best he stay with you. We need to find a suitable private property for both of your hunting needs."

CHAPTER 19
Mystery Man Collection

Adriano parks the Mercedes across the street from Coultier Art Gallery. All three vampires and one human exit the car and cross the street. Adriano is holding Rebecca's hand, he can sense that she is nervous. Sebastien and Jonathan are walking side by side, very little space between them. Their shoulders rub at times in a playful touch. As all of them are walking towards the entrance they are suddenly confronted by a very strange scent, and all three vampires sniff into the air simultaneously.

Jonathan notices this action and curiously queries, "What's up? You guys smell something?" Jonathan sniffs into the brisk crisp winter air too and then *he* gets a whiff. "I've smelt something similar to this before, mmm...delicious aroma, like roasted chestnuts or almond flavored coffee, makes me want to curl up near a fireplace."

Adriano comments, "What? It sure doesn't smell anything like that to me. I smell something that is hard to describe, kind of musty or like moth-balls? Is there any animal near-by? It almost has a strong wild smell?"

"Really? To me, it smells more like dark chocolate. It doesn't smell anything like a dog or cat or any wild animal for that matter, or I would start to feel thirsty." Rebecca smirks.

"Actually, I agree with Rebecca, but strange, we all seem to have a different interpretation of the smell," comments Sebastien.

"It is definitely not chocolate or almond coffee—whatever it is, it is becoming potent, wow, what is it?" Adriano scans the area. Sebastien, Rebecca, and Jonathan are puzzled by Adriano's disgusted reaction. At that moment, two men approach the entrance of the gallery, and Adriano recognizes it is Lucan and another younger man. Lucan quickly recognizes Adriano and Rebecca and greets them by tipping his Fedora hat. He holds the door for everyone and they all enter. They all check their winter coats at the coat check and Lucan approaches Adriano and Rebecca with his companion Nathan.

"How nice to meet you both here again, you look stunning Hazel Eyes."

Sebastien and Jonathan look at each other, confused.

"Actually, my name is Rebecca—it's nice that you remembered, though." Rebecca smiles warmly.

"Well, hello Rebecca, by the way this is Nathan."

They all introduce themselves, then Adriano politely wishes them a nice evening, takes Rebecca by the hand, and leads her away. Lucan and Nathan look at each other.

"I know Nathan—don't say it. *They* may hear you. They are a fascinating group. Shall we mingle for now?" Lucan and Nathan walk towards some art pieces hanging on the wall.

A few feet away, Adriano kisses Rebecca tenderly. "Ready beautiful? By the way, I love this red dress on you."

Rebecca nods a bit nervously as she adjusts her red dress one last time, noticing human eyes suddenly turning toward them. She is still not completely skilled in blocking out sounds, voices, or smells. She is struggling to block out what she doesn't want to focus on, but she can't manage to block out the human chattering. "As ready as I can be, if they would just stop whispering. I can hear bits and pieces, but it's all jumbled together. And I smell that delicious scent of dark chocolate, it somehow followed us in?"

"The smell is sticking to me, now it carries a bit of a wet dog smell, but not as strong as before." Adriano smiles and whispers in Rebecca's ear, his seductive natural scent of lemon and ginger penetrating throughout her body, "Don't worry about the whispers from the humans, your ears will soon adjust to the different noises and sounds. You have to keep in mind, vampires captivate them, and they just don't know why they feel so drawn to us even as they are unaware of who we are. And you are beautiful, *mon amour*, they can't help but be transfixed even more." Adriano kisses Rebecca tenderly on the cheek.

Meanwhile, Lucan is attracting attention from many of the women in the room, single or attached. This evening he feels and looks younger, carrying an air of eloquence in his demeanor. He is dressed exquisitely in a stylish dark navy-blue suit. He walks with his cane towards a tray filled with champagne, takes a glass, and then asks the waiter to bring the tray over to the ladies he is now walking towards with Nathan.

Rebecca realizes the sweet aroma is coming from the direction of Lucan, and is intrigued how he can smell so amazing, like sweet caramel mixed in with chocolate. Lucan is aware of many eyes observing him, he knows his natural body scent is alluring and brings different reactions depending who is taking in his scent; human or *others*. A few women approach him slowly, looking him up and down. It is obvious that these women are trying to get his attention. Nathan is close behind, also attracting some attention from women.

Lucan carries himself confidently, and with an air of traditional class. His abundance of chestnut hair reaches just above his ears, cut and combed neatly, with streaks of grey visible on the sides along with his neat and tidy goatee. He has one hand holding his glass of Pinot Grigio and the other hand is resting on the emblem of his cane. Soon more women ages thirties to ones in their fifties or older, slowly circle Lucan and Nathan. They try to seem inconspicuous, but they are like female wolves observing their prey. Both gentlemen are aware they are being admired, so they engage the group of women, and soon giggles and laughs are heard around them and flirtatious gestures are exchanged back and forth between these two men and the ladies. The women are finding any opportunity to touch either of them, especially Lucan, brushing against his shoulder or nudging against him, smiling and batting their eyelashes.

The room is filled with approximately twenty humans, both men and women; music is playing in the background, but not intrusively enough to hinder small chatter and the conversations taking place among the guests. Some guests are nibbling on crackers and cheese, while others walk around, glass of wine or champagne in their hand, stopping at a painting or photograph displayed on the walls. Adriano and Sebastien are already are aware of the scent of other vampires in the room. Rebecca is not yet experienced in detecting a vampire's scent immediately, as her senses are too focused on the humans right now.

"Oh, so it's not just paintings, there are also photographs being exhibited, very nice. Who knows, Sebastien, maybe one day you will have an exhibit of your paintings? Maybe one day you will actually show some of them to me?" she says.

Sebastien forces a smile and looks away, as if a painting caught his attention. He knows he can never show Rebecca the paintings he did of James in his final stage; it would destroy her hope of not reaching the same fate. But Sebastien can't destroy these portraits; they are a part of his history. As terrifying and disturbing as they are, it is still James inside the creature's body. He would have to find a way to pack these up and have them shipped to him. Lock them up.

Adriano scans the room, trying to locate the vampire Juliette, but she doesn't seem to be around. He takes Rebecca's hand and they start walking around the room, admiring the different pieces from different artists. Rebecca is still nervous, her hand holding tightly to Adriano's own warm hand. She is surprised at her nervous reaction, considering she managed to overcome her anxiety around humans when she was at Lafayette. This art gallery is small and intimate, she isn't sure if this is the reason that she is feeling so self-conscious. She takes deep breaths and walks with Adriano past each painting displayed; they are all by different unknown artists. They stop and read each of the artist's art stories printed on the wall; some artists are hanging around, eager to answer any questions.

Adriano and Rebecca follow the wall that curves into a niche, and then they stop to read the artist's story and realize this is Juliette's. The title is, "The Mystery Man Collection." This really grabs their attention, and they read her art statement. Then they look at the first painting. It is of a shadowy figure in the distance, the setting a street in Paris near the Eiffel Tower, which is painted as a silhouette in the background. Then they move onto the next painting, which has a silhouette of a figure standing closer to the Eiffel Tower. Their curiosity is building and they move to the next one and they discover it is a male figure, but he is facing away. They continue on to the next and the man painted on the canvas is now much closer, and glimpses of his stature more visible, familiar. "Oh my God—how strange, if I were not mistaken he resembles you, Adriano?"

Adriano looks more closely. "Hmm…there does seem to be somewhat of a resemblance, but this could be anyone."

"I don't think so. Look at his hair, it's styled just like yours; the length, the curls, look at his facial profile! His lean body, his long legs, the way he is leaning against a streetlamp. I'm telling you, this is you."

Adriano can't help but chuckle in his charming manner. "Rebecca, how can this be me?"

"I don't know, but I'm telling you, this is you."

Then suddenly a faint delicate feminine voice is heard in the background behind them. "Jonathan, how lovely to see you, both of you." Juliette's smile warms both Jonathan and Sebastien.

They both turn around. "Hi Juliette, you look absolutely stunning." Jonathon reaches in and kisses her on both cheeks, and she doesn't flinch. He is impressed now that he reminds himself she is a vampire. "We couldn't resist the invite from you. Look, I'm still wearing the bracelet you made me. Oh, you remember Sebastien?"

Juliette has a great smile on her face approaching them with a glass of champagne in her hand. Humans can't help but turn their heads, her unusual but graceful movements giving the illusion that she is floating. She is dressed in a classic, slim, deep purple, long, fitted gown that her brother Veneur surprised her with at the gallery before it was open to the guests. He knew she wouldn't have been able to have such a tasteful elegant dress in her closet at home, filled with the tacky loud outfits that she would be forced to wear as Paula. The deep purple accentuates her grey and violet eyes, and a slit accentuates her thin long legs. Her small neck is wrapped in a beautiful soft cream pearl choker necklace with matching pearl earrings, also a gift, from her other sibling Gabriel. Her blonde hair is pinned half-way back on each side, leaving some soft curls dangling at the sides, complimenting her flawless porcelain facial features. Juliette is accompanied by Veneur, who seems to bewitch the human females unintentionally, with his attractive features and alluring emerald eyes. He is wearing a sharp black suit, deep purple shirt, and bright burgundy tie. The contrast of his winter white skin and jet-black hair against the dark suit are striking.

Meanwhile, Adriano takes Rebecca by the hand and they walk casually towards Jonathan and Sebastien. Adriano and Rebecca are now standing beside them.

"Oh, and these are my friends, Adriano and—" Suddenly Juliette drops her glass of champagne, which she never tasted, and the room becomes instantly quiet, except for the music still playing. Juliette stares at Adriano, her expression of shock and bewilderment concerning Veneur and some of the guests nearby.

"It's you, my God, it's you!" she screams. Suddenly Juliette faints, and Veneur quickly catches her. People clear the way as Veneur carries her to one of the small couches. The gallery owner, Monsieur Coultier, approaches frantically to see if he can assist, and is asked to get some water. He quickly leaves and speaks to the guests telling them not to worry, everything is fine. He approaches one of the waiters and instructs him to bring the tray of food around, he needs to distract the crowd that is gathering around Juliette. He wants their eyes and attention back where they should be, the paintings and photographs on the wall. He needs to make sales, he has a business to run. Meanwhile Jonathan, Sebastien, Adriano, and Rebecca remain with Veneur and Juliette.

"Jules, Jules, sis—wake up."

"Is she okay? How can I help?" says Jonathan.

At that moment Juliette's eyes open and Veneur slowly sits her up. "Jules, you okay?"

"Yes, I'm fine—Veneur? What happened?"

"You fainted." He lowers his voice to a whisper. "Are you *thirsty*?"

Just then Monsieur Coultier returns with a glass of water. Juliette looks at the clear liquid, confused, then realizes the human gesture and takes it and looks at her brother. He nods and she takes a few sips, slowly, trying to appear as if the water was helping her. She forces a smile, but with each sip, her vampire body is not welcoming this cold unsatisfying liquid into her throat and stomach, and she stops drinking and gives the glass to Veneur, who understands immediately and casually gives the glass of water back to Monsieur Coultier, thanking him.

Monsieur Coultier looks at the water in the glass and scoffs. He walks away, mumbling to himself, assuming that no one could hear, "These amateur artists and their delicate nerves!"

He walks towards the nearest hostess and places the full glass of water on the tray. Suddenly Monsieur Coultier's voice is heard, and he quickly addresses the crowd that is still surrounding them. "Not to worry everyone, this happens sometimes with new artists, the excitement gets to their delicate nerves—please let's continue on with the exhibit, more wine and champagne coming around."

All five vampires look at each other. "Funny! If he only knew—I think he needs some valium for his delicate nerves," Veneur whispers, quietly enough that only the vampires can hear. Jonathan hears all vampires giggling and smirking.

"Did you say something, Veneur? What did I miss?"

"Nothing. Jonathan—is that your name?"

"Yes, that's right."

"Right—well, some communications should be reserved between vampires only—it may offend *humans*. No disrespect, *of course*."

Juliette slowly composes herself and stands up, giving Veneur a scornful expression. "Never mind my brother, Jonathan."

The crowd disperses and begins to mingle again and walk around the room, while Adriano, Rebecca, Veneur, Sebastien, and Jonathan remain beside Juliette, who can't stop looking at Adriano. Juliette is still processing the Mystery Man from her collection standing beside her.

"I still can't believe it's you, my Mystery Man. What is your name?"

"I'm right—see Adriano!" Rebecca says with excitement in her voice.

"I'm sorry, but do we know each other?" Adriano looks at Juliette, puzzled.

"Mystery Man? Can someone please explain this to me, the human?" Jonathan whispers so low.

"Jonathan, go look at Juliette's Mystery Man collection, then you will understand."

And so still confused, Jonathan and Sebastien listen to Adriano's instruction and move towards her collection on the wall. Juliette turns to her brother, her voice filled with excitement. "Veneur—can you believe this! I found him. He is real, he isn't a dream or a creation in my mind."

"Juliette, please tell me what is going on. How do you know me?"

"But that's just it, Adriano, I don't know you. And yet I feel like I have known you for ages! For some reason you have been in my mind, in my dreams, for a few months."

"I don't understand, how? We have never met before. I'm sure I would remember."

"We've never met, I would remember if we did too. This is incredible."

"But there must be some connection between you two?" Rebecca sounds bewildered. "Maybe you met through someone else? How can you just paint Adriano in such detail, without knowing him? It doesn't make sense."

At that moment both Jonathan and Sebastien return with an expression of surprise and confusion. "We understand now. Quite a resemblance for sure."

"Not a resemblance, Jonathan—this is Adriano, this is the man I saw in my mind and painted!"

Jonathan and Sebastien remain confused. Veneur steps in. "You see, my sister kept seeing this image of a man in her mind and in her dreams, for a few months now. She never knew where he was coming from. I don't understand this either, but for some reason you, Adriano, were meant to meet my sister Juliette."

"Interesting—I too felt this need to meet you, this is why we are here tonight. You see, I saw both of you a few days ago, on the street—the name escapes me now, but where the artists have booths."

"Oh, why didn't you drop by my booth?"

"Rebecca and I, well, we had to get home. But well, my apologies, but I overheard Veneur mention the gallery, so I wanted to make sure we could come."

"But why—Adriano, this is so strange! I mean, what makes the Universe bring us together like this?"

"Excuse me, but—what do you want with my sister?"

"Don't get me wrong Veneur, please, I mean no harm. It's just that you were the first—" At that moment Adriano lowers his voice to an impossible whisper and scans the room to make sure that no one else is paying attention to them. He leans into Juliette's ear and Veneur moves in close. "Other than Sebastien, you both are the first vampires that I have encountered face to face in a very long time. I just had to meet you." His eyes glance between Juliette and Veneur.

"Oh, really? That just seems hard to believe…" Her eyes move from Adriano to Rebecca and then to Sebastien, but still talking very close to Jonathan so he too can hear and not feel left out.

"I realize this, but it is true. My path did not cross with our kind. I moved around a lot, then I came to Canada and have settled there for years. Oh, this is Rebecca, my girlfriend."

"Nice to meet you, Rebecca."

"My pleasure, Juliette and Veneur."

At that moment, Monsieur Coultier approaches, asking in his thick French accent, "Juliette dear, are you feeling better now? Are your nerves calmer now?"

"Yes, thank you."

"Great, well then, shall we get back to the exhibit? After all, I dedicated special space just for you, my dear. There are others here who are eager to meet you. We mustn't ignore our potential paying customers." He glances at the vampires staring at him with an expression of frustration and curiosity.

"Yes of course, sorry, I will be right there, Monsieur."

"Please hurry!" Monsieur Coultier shouts nervously, as he quickly dashes back to greet more incoming guests at the door. "Welcome to my gallery, please have some champagne, mingle with our artists, they will be happy to meet you."

"Oh, Monsieur Coultier needs to calm down. He is exhausting me."

"Don't worry Jules. Just enjoy the excitement of it all. Try not to absorb his emotions so intensely." Veneur whispers into Juliette's ear, "Go on, I will be there shortly. You're just not used to all this attention just for you sis. Enjoy this time as you, Juliette Dubois, and not *Paula*."

Juliette looks at him and unintentionally cringes. Hearing the name Paula, she thinks, *this is my time to be Juliette—these are my paintings.* She feels almost like Cinderella at the ball; this is her magical night. She must not waste it—there are only a few hours left before she has to return to the role of Paula. "You're right Veneur. Please excuse me everyone, I must mingle while I am still—I mean—" Juliette smiles nervously and excuses herself again. "Enjoy your evening." She then walks towards two humans that are waving her down excitedly.

"Is she okay? She seems out of sorts or confused suddenly. What did you mean absorb his emotions?" Adriano's eyes follow Juliette then return back to Veneur.

"It's nothing, she is fine. I should go and be with her, she is very shy. It was nice meeting all of you, please feel free to stay and mingle."

"Before you go, Veneur, if you don't mind, I would really like to connect with both of you again, perhaps later after the exhibit? We could meet at a café or you can swing by my place?"

Veneur looks completely shocked and bewildered. "Meet at a café? That's funny."

"I wasn't joking. If you prefer to meet somewhere else?"

Veneur is confused at Adriano's proposal. He looks at Adriano and the other vampires. "Adriano, I don't mean to be rude, however, that is not possible."

"What? Why?"

"Excuse me, but I must go back to Juliette now."

"Wait, am I missing something?"

Rebecca sees Adriano's puzzlement, she too is now interested. "Veneur, we would love to have you both at our place, if you don't have a car we can drive you if that is your concern? Please come, Adriano has been so anxious to meet the two of you."

"Thank you, Rebecca, it's not that we don't want to come, we can't. It's not possible. I'm sure you understand." Veneur's eyes lower, his expression solemn. This is confusing Adriano and company.

"Actually, I don't understand." Adriano is losing patience.

Sebastien jumps in. "We don't want to intrude on your privacy, Veneur, but it is so rare to find more of our kind that you actually want to be around, and well, we all seem to be getting along nicely, so we should try and stay in touch. I know what it is like to be on my own without my own kind. Why not just come over and stay a bit, and if you're not comfortable then leave?"

"I must say, you are all very persistent?"

"We mean well, Veneur. We are just excited to meet more of our kind."

"I appreciate the flattery, Rebecca, however this is truly odd to hear that none of you have encountered more of our kind. Do you not leave the house?"

"It's not that. It's complicated."

"I see, well, Adriano I too have a very complicated circumstance and I can't possibly risk danger to Juliette or myself by socializing."

"Danger? We are not dangerous."

"That is good to hear, Adriano, however I am referring to the safety of Juliette and myself."

Adriano, Rebecca, Sebastien and Jonathan all look at each other confused.

"Sorry, Veneur, but we don't understand?"

"Jonathan, no offense, however I cannot explain this to you. You are human."

"Trust me, I know a lot more than you think. I'm friends with *your kind*."

"That is already blowing my mind. If you don't mind, I have to speak to your friends privately, no offense."

"Okay, you don't need to spell it out to *the human*. I'll go and mingle."

"Thanks Jonathan, sorry about this."

"No problem Adriano. Sebastien, are you coming?" Jonathan then realizes. "Never mind, I forgot, this is for your kind, find me later."

Once Jonathan steps away Veneur gathers the vampires in a closer circle. "Sorry I had to push away your human friend, but he wouldn't understand this. All of you must already know that some Masters are quite controlling, and believe they are the rulers. Well unfortunately for my sister and I, we belong to one of those extreme believers. He would not tolerate us mingling or connecting with other vampires unless he approved it first. I know you understand this, or perhaps you think it may be a bit stricter than you might be used to from your scion; however, the fact that you have a human in your mix, well, that would send him spinning. Do you see now why it is not possible for us to connect anywhere? The fact that you have invited me to your place or out to a café tells me that you all must be beholden to a scion that is more liberal—lucky for you."

An expression of blankness and befuddlement crosses over all three vampires. Veneur observes, and he isn't sure what in what he has said has confused them so or silenced the moment so oddly.

Sebastien scratches his head in confusion. "Scion?"

"Master?" chimes in Rebecca, bewildered.

"Why do you both sound surprised?" queries Veneur puzzled.

"This can't be true. You are joking, right?"

"Joking? I'm not joking, Adriano. Why would anyone want to joke about this? We are not all that lucky to belong in a group of our kind with a Master who is reasonably stable."

Adriano can't control his frustration. "But this is crazy! How can someone have that kind of control over you? I am confused—why don't you leave?"

Suddenly, a thought emerges and Sebastien's eyes light up. "Oh—it's just like how Count B explained it to James. This must be a Great Master. He must be ancient. How extraordinary."

"Great Master? Hardly. Ancient? No, but he is quite old—and extraordinary isn't the word I would use…Sebastien, is it?"

"Yes, I'm sorry, I meant no offense." Sebastien's demeanor droops, he feels embarrassed.

"Who are all of you? You seem like you are coming from another time or something. Like what I have told you is so unbelievable?"

"It is unbelievable."

"I'm living it, Juliette is living it—it is real. What business is it of yours, anyway? I mean really, Adriano, why so many questions?" Suddenly, as if

Veneur is tangled up in a long piece of rope, he feels stressed and trapped. Upsetting questions rise within. *Maybe this is a trap set by Enzo to see if I will take the bait and trust them, befriend them. Maybe these vampires are associates of Enzo.* His guard goes up. But as he observes each of them individually, their behaviour and their disposition seem so kind and genuine that he determines that these vampires are not a threat.

"You have to realize how ludicrous this sounds to us. No one should control you like this in this day and age. You are a vampire." Adriano's voice remains in a whisper that only they can all hear. But unbeknownst to them, they are beginning to attract the attention of some humans nearby, who are pretending to be interested in the wall art pieces but are really intrigued and curious about the intense expressions and demonstrations of outrage being displayed between these other guests who are gathered very closely together. Some of these curious humans are frustrated that they can't hear a word spoken from any of them. The music is not that loud, and they can hear bits and pieces of the other guests' conversations, yet nothing is heard from these ones. Their lips are moving but no sound is audible. How strange for these humans, and it causes more interest to stay nearby.

"Well this Master hasn't caught up with the era. He refuses to keep up with technology. He still uses a landline phone. I think he is dreadfully afraid of the advancements that have happened in communications. He depends completely on us. I think he has developed a severe phobia of the outside world. He doesn't leave the house anymore. Luckily for us, he refuses to learn how to use a cell phone or computer. At least we have some small window of detachment from him. You have no clue what Juliette and I have endured with his outrageous demands and expectations. I worry about Juliette mostly, she is more fragile than she may appear to be. It's complicated, Adriano, you need to understand the dynamics of this scion we live with. The roles we have, roles we are assigned to, that is. Our circumstances can be dangerous if not carefully handled—even just talking about this with you is risky! The Master has some connections to powerful vampires, he has verbally threatened us enough times. I've already shared too much with you." Veneur suddenly feels an overwhelming nervousness and scans the room cautiously in case other vampires are present who may report back to Enzo.

Adriano shakes his head in disbelief of what he is hearing. He is very troubled to see this young man feeling so afraid, anxious, and powerless. He thinks, *What kind of tyrannical vampire has them under his control?* He feels compelled to do something to help them, and yet he is fully aware that in two days they are booked to fly back home to Toronto. How is he going to accomplish both? He can't imagine leaving these two young vampires in such a state, and yet he can't keep Rebecca from her sons longer than she has had to already. Adriano feels the stress building and the panic rising; he takes a deep breath to calm his anxiety. He has to figure this out. He once again has this need to fix things. "Well this can't go on. You are an adult, and can make your own decisions, and he can't stop you. You just think he can. It's all in the mind game he is playing with you. He seems like a master manipulator. It won't be tolerated."

"You mean your Master allows you—?"

"Let me stop you, Veneur—I have no Master. I have no one telling me who I see or where I live or where I go. And neither does Rebecca or Sebastien. What's this vampire's name?" Adriano is becoming increasingly impatient.

"Enzo."

"Well, this Enzo needs an awakening. We live in a modern society. You and Juliette must leave him, it's that simple."

"Shh…. Please, this is none of your business. Simple? Hardly." Again, Veneur looks nervously over his shoulder.

Suddenly all the vampires turn towards the entrance. A distinct scent is now overriding any perfumes, hairspray, and colognes that are worn by guests. Soon after, the human guests cannot help but feel compelled to stop talking. There is a bit of uneasiness in the air even as the looped CD continues playing. The room is suddenly filled with curious eyes just watching as these two new guests walk in. Lucan is intrigued, thinking, *More vampires?*

A six-foot-tall muscular Gabriel walks in, and he is desperately and cautiously trying to make eye contact with Veneur without Bianca noticing. Gabriel carries an air of superior confidence about him, his milk chocolate brown eyes reasonably trusting. Bianca is beside him, and is enjoying the immediate attention falling upon her, aided by the black hat with a black lace veil trailing over her eyes. She commands drama. Just her lips painted in deep red lipstick are visible. There is a stern energy around her, and this seems to keep the humans on alert and she relishes in their unease, enjoying the control she has in their presence.

CHAPTER 20

Paradox

Suddenly these two new vampires who entered the gallery sniff the air, and they hold an unpleasant expression on their faces as they take in the musty smell. Bianca whispers very low to Gabriel, "Oh God—they need to open a window or something. What a stench. Is there a sick or dying animal in here, or are these humans just smelly?"

At that moment, Monsieur Coultier nervously approaches, and with clenched teeth he reluctantly greets them to his gallery. Bianca just walks past him as if he is invisible or beneath her, which he finds utterly rude, but then Gabriel greets him with a forced smile trying to use his gifted charm on Monsieur Coultier. But he is struggling, he can see the shock, disappointment, and fear on Veneur's face. He failed to keep Bianca away this important night, and now he is worried he has ruined Veneur's plan. He brings his own attention back to Monsieur Coultier, needing to ease the tension in the air. "We came to show our support for our sister Juliette— what a charming gallery you have."

"Oh, thank you. It is my pride and joy, I come from a family of—" Before he can finish the male vampire interrupts respectfully.

"Pardon me Monsieur, could I get a glass of that wonderful champagne?" The twinkle of mischief is coming through, manipulating Monsieur Coultier with his professional charming mannerism, convincing Monsieur Coultier that he is important.

Bianca, on the other hand, rolls her veiled eyes in utter impatience. She is restraining herself from pouncing on this human and ripping his throat out with her sharp canines. She amuses herself privately with the image of him flapping around like a rag doll, fear and shock cemented in his eyes as she sucks his blood. In her mind she moves onto the next human, and the next, creating a bloodbath in this gallery. She smiles to herself as the images move from one violent scene of the massacre she would have enjoyed creating to the next.

"Why of course, Monsieur! Champagne, quickly!" Monsieur Coultier snaps his fingers, commanding the attention of a waiter nearby, and then realizes everyone is now focused on these two strangers and not the pieces on the wall. "Carry on, everyone, the evening is still young, please drink, and eat!" He signals with a scornful expression to different waiters to move quickly around the room with their trays of food and beverages. Within seconds, the humans are distracted again, and some are resuming their small conversations with the artists. Other humans are admiring the art and making mental notes of which ones they would like to buy. Monsieur Coultier is about to call Juliette over to greet her siblings, but he turns around to find her standing in front of him, startling him. "Oh gracious, my dear, you mustn't sneak up on me like that!"

"Oh, I'm sorry Monsieur, I guess you didn't hear me approaching with the music."

"Well yes, of course!" Monsieur Coultier feels this sudden anxiety creep up inside, and all he wants to do is move quickly away from these two new guests. He is relieved to see a familiar face walk through the door, Monsieur Descartes, a known curator in his business circle, and he quickly dashes over to greet him. Other artists recognize this man too and move to greet him.

Veneur and Juliette are momentarily relieved to see that the humans are distracted; she doesn't need the extra stress and tension that is already present now that her unpleasant sister has arrived. Juliette whispers very low, failing to hide the upset revealed by her agitated tone, "Gabriel, Bianca, what are you doing here?"

"Yes Gabriel—I thought you and Bianca were having a night out?" Veneur struggles to remain composed when all he feels is anger.

"What? You think I would miss our sister Paula's first exhibit? Oops, I mean Juliette, is it Juliette now, for the time being? I get confused, Paula or Juliette?"

Juliette is feeling the wounds of these deliberate pricks, and Veneur is steaming.

Bianca eyes them both, wearing a cruel smile. "You think I would miss this exhibit? Don't be silly, Veneur. That wouldn't be to kind of me as a sister." Bianca then moves her cold eyes back to Juliette, "*Father* is disappointed that he could not be here to *witness* this, but well you know how he is around *crowds*. Father insisted I come. After all, he always wants to make sure he knows where you are, *Paula*—oops, there I go again. Anyway, there are a lot of influencers out there in the world—he wouldn't want you to get any ridiculous notions of taking this little exhibit further." Bianca's tone is charged with malice; she is hoping her verbal stabs wound Juliette. Juliette can feel her anxiety rising, her joy of the evening slipping away with this unexpected intrusion. Veneur takes hold of Juliette's arm, knowing she needs his support. Inside Juliette is screaming and begging to be released from this nightmare she is trapped in.

Veneur whispers abruptly, aware of the growing interest and curiosity coming from the humans in the gallery, "Bianca, we don't need you here, we have everything under control. Gabriel, please, take Bianca out for the evening."

"My dear Veneur, you seem stressed. What are you afraid of? You wouldn't dare be concerned about these *humans*? Or is it the fact that I saw you minutes ago socializing with those others, over there? I have keen eyes. Introduce me…or are you afraid father won't approve?" She smiles wickedly, her fangs visible to him, then turns her head directly facing the other vampires in the corner.

Her eyes quickly zoom in through her veil, and she lets out a low growl, aware that only these vampires can hear. But then suddenly her body shifts to the side and she spots Lucan. She is struck with confusion and alertness.

She snarls and a low threatening growl reaches Lucan's skilled ears. Nathan sees the rising expression of anger on Lucan's face, and he quickly recognizes this dangerous moment. He grabs Lucan's arm, redirecting his focus to the human women circling. One of the women reaches out to gently touch Lucan's tense jaw and guides his head back to look at her. He takes the cue and returns his attention to the women. But inside he is fuming. Meanwhile, all three vampires in the corner react in offense when hearing the growl from Bianca. Adriano is ready to move in but Rebecca holds him back.

"Wait, Adriano. We don't know what's going on, let's not attract any attention. Besides, Veneur is there, I'm sure he has it under control."

"We were just growled at, that is a threat, I don't trust these two vampires. I'm not so sure Veneur can handle this."

"Just hang on, we can't just interrupt. We may cause more trouble, and we're around humans, too. Let's just see what happens first."

Adriano is frustrated, but he agrees that confrontation with vampires is not safe for the vampires or humans; they could lose control of their anger and reveal their identity, or take out their anger on the humans. Adriano quickly scans the room to make sure the humans are not observing anything, and is relieved that no curious eyes are looking their way. He catches Lucan's eye, and Lucan slightly bows politely to Adriano, letting him know he is aware, which raises curiosity in Adriano. Lucan then redirects his attention back to the women.

"Gabriel, please, this is Juliette's night, take Bianca out of here."

Gabriel feels helpless in this situation, but he doesn't want further escalation of anger between any of these vampires, especially with the humans present. "Let's go Bianca, you have seen Juliette and where she is. You can report back to the Master that everything is fine."

"I want to stay, this looks like fun. Although it smells like pitiful humans here mixed in with some wild dirty animal."

"No, we must go."

"Stop pulling me, Gabriel!" shouts Bianca. The other guests notice; the conversations start becoming quieter, whispers rising from human guests.

"What's her problem?"

"Look at the veil, talk about the drama queen, who does she think she is?"

"She's odd."

The whispers are heard by all of the vampires and Lucan. Bianca snarls. She wishes she could move around quickly and slash the neck of every one of these humans.

"Let's go, Bianca—Master would be very disappointed in you if you caused a scene in front of these humans! You don't want to make him angry at you, do you? After all, he trusted you with this important task, and he expects you to do this safely and discreetly, without human eyes watching you. Do you want to risk our safety too? That veil only hides your eyes, it won't shield your identity if you get out of hand."

Adriano can't take it anymore. He takes Rebecca's hand and moves towards Veneur and Juliette and company. "Veneur, is everything—"

"It's you," screams Bianca in a high-pitched tone as she sees Adriano. The room becomes dead silent; the CD stopped playing minutes earlier. Bianca's screechy voice startles most of the humans; some spill wine on themselves, others drop their plate of hors d'oeuvres.

All eyes are on Bianca and Adriano.

"What is going on here?!" shouts Monsieur Coultier angrily as he approaches.

Gabriel quickly responds. "Oh, my apologies Monsieur, it seems our sister got a little excited." His voice is calm and endearing, hoping to ease Monsieur Coultier.

"Excited?! We thought someone witnessed a murder or something, that high-pitched scream, oh how frightful! Well, please control her—perhaps she needs air."

Bianca is about to rudely retort but Gabriel quickly interrupts, "Yes good idea, sorry everyone, please resume your conversations, nothing to see here,"

Monsieur Coultier aggressively pulls out a handkerchief from his suit pocket and wipes his sweaty forehead. He apologizes to his guests and signals to his waiters to quickly circulate the food and wine trays. He is exhausted and completely annoyed; he can't wait for this event to be over. These amateur night events are just not his cup of tea. He thinks, *there are always riffraff wandering in!* His nerves can't tolerate any more nonsense. He wishes he had taken that valium his friend suggested hours earlier.

Adriano lets go of Rebecca's hand and signals her to stay. He turns to Bianca, trying to see through her veil, but Bianca's eyes remain hidden. The veil just reaches the top of her lips, which are covered with red lipstick. "I'm sorry, do I know you miss?"

Veneur is anxious. "Bianca, it's time for you to leave."

"Not a chance, now that *he* is here." Bianca is staring at Adriano, standing inches away from him. Adriano has now learned her name, and he searches his mind, but he doesn't have any memorable data about any woman named Bianca. It puzzles him, and his curiosity is peaked. Veneur, Gabriel, and Juliette are confused.

Bianca's eyes are staring at Adriano through the black lace veil...

Rebecca steps closer to Adriano and pulls him aside, whispering very low directly into his ear, "Adriano? Who is this woman? You sure are popular tonight."

Sebastien and Jonathan are now walking towards Rebecca. "Everything okay?"

"I don't know! Who is this woman, Adriano?"

"I don't recognize her. You guys stay here, let me go find out."

In the meantime, Gabriel and Veneur have taken Bianca further aside. Juliette is standing away from all of them, anxious. Monsieur Coultier gives Juliette a scornful look of disapproval, then he moves on to talk to other guests. Juliette is left embarrassed and disappointed that she has left a bad impression on Monsieur Coultier. Her sad demeanor is noticed by Lucan and he approaches Juliette in concern, using the excuse that he admires her work and thinks she is very talented. Juliette responds politely, trying her best to maintain her professional composure.

Meanwhile Lucan's companion Nathan is preoccupied with the women who can't seem to leave him alone, especially now that Lucan has departed their company.

Adriano walks over to Veneur, Gabriel, and Bianca and smiles politely, thinking he can use his charismatic charm on Bianca; however she remains cool and distant. "Hello, my name is Adriano. You seem to know me, however, my apologies, I don't recognize you. Or at least I cannot really tell with the veil you are wearing. Perhaps you wouldn't mind lifting it up?"

"My name is Bianca. I know who *you* are, Adriano."

Adriano is a bit taken aback by the curt sharp tone expressed by Bianca. "I'm sorry, but I need you to remove the veil. You seem to be upset with me, and I honestly don't know why. Whatever this is, I'm sure we can resolve any misunderstanding." Adriano manages to hold a slight smile, but it is quickly leaving him with the growing cold look in Bianca's eyes.

"Really? Misunderstanding? Priceless."

Veneur is growing concerned; he doesn't know what is going on, however he and Gabriel both know Bianca enough to know she is stirring trouble. Veneur just wants Bianca gone from this venue.

Gabriel is aware and he has an idea. "Adriano, perhaps it would be best if you and our sister Bianca go outside and talk. You are attracting some unwanted attention. Bianca, this is not a good idea." His serious eyes signal towards some curious humans standing nearby.

Bianca reluctantly agrees and walks briskly past Adriano, with fury and crossness in her demeanor. Adriano shakes his head side to side feeling suddenly discontent, and he follows Bianca out of the gallery.

Veneur is frustrated and needs to think fast. "Gabriel, what am I going to do? We need to get Bianca out of here. This plan is going bad very fast."

"Maybe not, as long as she is occupied elsewhere, and she seems to be by this Adriano. Do you know what's going on there?"

"No. I'm more concerned about getting to the airport undetected."

"Okay—I think you should just leave now. The taxi I ordered has been in touch with me and is waiting as we planned. Just grab your luggage and Juliette and get going. Now is your chance."

Meanwhile Adriano is outside with Bianca. "Please, if you wouldn't mind, remove the veil."

Bianca obliges and slowly lifts up the veil. Adriano is suddenly struck with bewilderment and gasps.

"I don't believe it—it's you! I never knew your name. It's nice to meet you again, Bianca."

"Damn right it's me—and it is not a pleasure at all to see you!" Her aggressive curt tone takes Adriano aback, but he remains respectful.

"I'm sorry? I don't understand your reaction."

"I've wondered if I would ever run into you again—I have some choice words for you."

"You are obviously upset with me, however if you wish me to engage further than let's be civil and respectful. Why the hostility?"

"Oh man, you really are a piece of work. Okay, fine, I have one question. Why?"

"Why what—please be more specific."

"Why did you turn me? Was it just because you were thirsty? Is that all I was to you, just a thirst quencher? You ruined my life—leaving me to hide in the shadows like some freak of nature, a creature of the night, with no guidance, no—"

Adriano interrupts her. "Wait—that is *not* how it happened! You left me that night, I didn't leave or send you away. And you weren't just a thirst quencher—what a mean thing to say. I was alone and I saw you and—"

"And you decided to just turn me? You didn't know who I was, what life I had!"

"You were crying--."

"And that did it—that gave you the right to turn me?"

"Please let me finish. You were walking the streets alone, and I could just feel this enormous sadness coming from you, and all I wanted to do was help you. I just reacted. Perhaps my thirst took over, I admit that."

Meanwhile, Veneur and Gabriel have approached Juliette. Veneur is carrying two carry-on pieces of luggage and one large one. He was storing them in Monsieur's office.

"What's with the suitcases?"

"We are leaving." Veneur's expression is serious.

"It's okay, Juliette. Veneur and I have taken care of everything."

"What are you talking about, Gabriel? Both of you, what's going on?"

"We are packed and there is a taxi waiting for us to drive us to the airport. I've booked a flight to the United States. There's little time to explain further. We need to leave."

Juliette stands in shock. She sees the serious expression on both Gabriel and Veneur's face.

"I told you I had a plan, well it was for tonight. You never have to go back there. We are leaving; we can be free."

Meanwhile, outside, Adriano is stuck in a heated argument with Bianca.

"I'm sorry Bianca—I never meant to hurt you or destroy your life. My God—destroy your life? I just didn't think this would be so terrible for you, being a vampire."

"That's right—you didn't think, you selfish bastard!"

Adriano is taken aback and deeply offended and angry. "If you continue this I will leave. I'm willing to listen, but have the decency to show respect, as I have to you."

"Fine. Let's talk about the night you turned me."

"We just did. I told you, it wasn't coming from malice. I saw you alone, very sad, and I just reacted. I too was alone."

"Listen to me—you had no right. I was sad, yes, but I was going through a difficult time in my life. I was broke, I had split up with my boyfriend that day, then he kicked me out of his place. It just happened to be an extremely emotional day for me! I was walking all night through the streets trying to accept what was happening, and trying to figure out what to do—and then you suddenly came up to me, and all I remember is waking up feeling completely alien in my body, in my mind. Then a few minutes later, I felt this incredible pain inside my throat, like someone was taking a knife and just slicing into my throat, shredding it. And then I remember you cutting into your own arm, blood dripping out, and I was horrified by this. By you! I couldn't move, I felt paralyzed or something. Suddenly I felt this incredible sensation and desire rising inside of me, it was overpowering me and I was so afraid. I remember you said, *"Drink from me, the pain will ease very soon, trust me, your body is craving blood."* I was stunned, shocked, disgusted…but then I saw the blood coming up out of your skin and without thinking I was compelled to drink it. My God—I remember that first moment of my lips touching the blood, and it was so warm. I drank your blood, and it was so soothing to my throat, and I was confused, terrified by what I was doing, what was happening. Within seconds that excruciating pain was gone, and then you stopped me! I wanted more—I thought I was going crazy wanting your blood."

"I'm sorry, I had to stop you from drinking because I was getting weak suddenly, and I know that must have been difficult for your body to handle. But I must have passed out. All I remember after that is waking up and you were gone. Why did you leave?" Adriano carries disappointment in his voice. "You were my first to turn, to be reborn, and you were gone. I didn't know if something happened to you. If you were taken. I searched for you, but you were gone. I didn't even know your name."

"Now you do. Do you realize what I went through as I died as a human? The pain was unbearable, and the confusion in my mind! I thought my mind was shattering into pieces."

"I know, I know, I am so sorry for that, I would have helped you through the change, but you left."

"You are sorry? This makes it alright?"

"You have to understand, I was young, immature in so many ways. And so alone." Suddenly Adriano has a terrifying thought. "Oh God, did you change others?"

"What if I did? What— you can turn others but I can't?"

"I only changed you! I never planned to change others, at least not until I was really prepared. And stop being so rude and aggressive. This attitude will get you nowhere with me. I offered to talk, so let's be civilized."

"Fine, I changed some humans over the years. Why not?"

"Where are they?" Adriano's voice is so distraught hearing that other vampires roam the Earth with her blood. He fears that they could be as cold and dangerous. "How many?"

"I don't know, a few, I didn't keep track of them. It doesn't matter. We weren't suddenly this close loving family of vampires. There was upset and power struggles happening between all of us. We found dwellings and occupied them until we could no longer; some moved on, some stayed. I don't care."

"Oh my God, Bianca, there could be even more now— unguided vampires."

"So?"

"So—my God, don't you realize the danger you have—"

"Me? Not me—*you*. You did this. I didn't ask to be a vampire."

Adriano is getting weak, stress and anger rising, and then sudden fear comes over him as he realizes what danger humans could be facing if they encountered Bianca or any of her blood links.

"You have no clue how lonely I was these years. I had no direction, no connections, just on my own desperately trying to survive! I was torn and haunted by memories of when I was human, and had to bury these memories so I could forget I was human once. My mind was tormented by my actions as a vampire, but then I finally realized it was who I was. The guilt passed, and human blood was my right to have."

Back in the gallery, Veneur and Gabriel see that Monsieur Coultier is very preoccupied with two art dealers who have arrived. Veneur and Gabriel quickly escort Juliette to the back of the gallery, through the hallway, and into one of the storage rooms.

"Veneur, please, this is happening too fast! Veneur, this is dangerous, you haven't thought this through! We can't just board a plane, we don't have our passports."

"All taken care of—I picked them up today. Some clothes are packed from your room; I took things I know you would want to keep. Everything else we can buy when we settle."

"This is crazy—he will have us hunted down! His associates will come after us, or Bianca—"

"Juliette, please calm down. I know you are frightened, but Gabriel and I have taken care of this. Bianca has no idea of any of this; if she or Enzo's associates try to search for us, the breadcrumb of clues I left on my laptop and desk will falsely lead them to think we have fled to Eastern Europe." Veneur puts his arm on Juliette's shoulder. "We have set a fake destination trail for them, which is the first place Bianca will look. I wrote flight info about Budapest on my note pad. I don't know why I chose that city, it doesn't matter."

"It's true, Juliette. There will be no way they can find you. Veneur and I even discussed how we will communicate, at least for now. It may sound odd, but it will be a secret code between the three of us. Veneur will explain later. It's time you guys take off. I need to get back to the house before Bianca, so she thinks I left earlier."

"But Gabriel, you will be in danger now! Master will know you were involved in this too." Juliette's voice is cracking, she is overwhelmed and stressed.

"I know. It's a chance I have to take, it's the only way. One of us has to get away from this dysfunctional family. I will handle Enzo, he is old and paranoid. He still needs me, I make money for him. As for Bianca, I will keep an eye on her. Juliette—please, you need to go with Veneur—he will protect you."

At the same time, Rebecca is standing with Jonathan in the corner, near Juliette's paintings. Rebecca is worried; Adriano has been outside talking to that vampire for a while now. Jonathan tries to ease Rebecca's worries, but he is also observing Sebastien and Lucan—they seem to be involved in an enthusiastic conversation. They are exchanging cell numbers. Jonathan leads Rebecca to them. Lucan notices them; he smiles and continues speaking as they approach.

"Thank you. If I have time, we will drop by before you leave. Your house sounds just beautiful, Sebastien. All those private woods."

Rebecca and Jonathan approach Sebastien and Lucan.

"Hello Jonathan, Rebecca. My dear, is everything okay? You look concerned?"

"Adriano has been outside with that va-woman for a long time." Rebecca is relieved she didn't slip and say vampire. Lucan catches the slip, but plays it cool.

"I'm sure everything will be fine, my dear. Both of you, join Sebastien and I."

"Hazel Eyes, Lucan is a pianist, he is in Paris this week for a performance."

"Oh, how nice, you both play the piano. I would love it for one of my sons to learn to play."

Jonathan looks around, "Anyone see Juliette? I haven't seen her or her brother Veneur?"

"You're right, that's odd. I hope they didn't leave, that would disappoint Adriano."

"It's ok Hazel Eyes, I see them coming, look over there," says Sebastien.

Back in the storage room, Gabriel embraces Juliette for the very first time since he has known her and kisses her on the forehead tenderly. "I'm sorry for not appreciating more clearly how harmful this scion was to you, especially." He is filled with so much guilt and regret for not protecting Juliette. He turns to Veneur. "I hope one day we will meet again." Gabriel says good-bye and quickly makes his way to the exit, trying not to be noticed. He is successful.

He purposefully leaves the car behind for Bianca. It will be quicker for him on foot, since he can cut through the woods and use his athletic vampire legs and the aid of the cover of night to lead him back home in the 16th Arrondissement. His powerful legs sprint at speeds that seem impossible. His mind is spinning with all the different scenarios that could possibly await him when he returns without Veneur and Juliette. His heart is racing, and he suddenly realizes what he has agreed to. He has to believe that Enzo will need him still, and not want to destroy him.

He mentally prepares for the worst, even ready to kill if it means saving his own life. He has nothing to lose now; he lost the only two vampires that were family to him. He walks on; the wind is picking up from the north, but the cold winter air is giving him a fresh new perspective. He has his own dreams, his own desires and wants, and none of them involve interactions with the vampires he is now returning to.

A sad feeling enters his heart, and he feels alone. He has to trust and rely on his charm and business skills to convince Enzo to accept that Veneur and Juliette are gone. Gabriel tries to believe in his heart that this change will be okay. He thinks about the secret code he and Veneur came up with. At least he will one day soon receive a picture through text of a nature scene, a rock, a tree, and whatever it is he will know it is coming from Veneur. It will mean they made it, that they are settled somewhere. This picture will encapsulate his hope and trust in himself, that one day, he can also escape, have the life he desires. He just needs to be smart, patient, and a few steps ahead of Enzo and Bianca, from this moment on.

Before he realizes it, he is already a few yards away from the house. Gabriel's heart begins to race, his adrenaline gearing up, making him think he is thirsty; however he knows it is just his nerves and anxiety tricking him. His thirst normally stirs after a week at a time. He sees a rabbit running and it angers him; he should be able to just hunt it and drink from it in peace, without fear that he has broken a rule. He paraphrases in his mind, *thou shalt not drink from animals unless your life depends on it.* But the reality is that he is chained to a life filled with strict vampire codes, rules, and commands from Enzo. Gabriel approaches the backyard, and soon he is confronted with the harsh sound of Enzo yelling at Louisa.

"I told you this was not a good idea for many reasons! Where are they, all of them? Paula and the others should be home by now! Where are they? This is your fault if they ran into trouble with vamps or roamers! This is your fault for entertaining this ridiculous idea that Paula is an artist! Paula should be here. This is her duty. Your daughter Paula was not an artist. What possessed you to allow this other vampire this freedom? This is how it starts—they ask for one thing, then they are not satisfied and they want more. Just like you! I allowed you to keep Pietro, remember that—you broke the rule, you turned him. He is useless to me! And now you have influenced this female vampire to want more, to think she is an artist, a creator! Useless on all counts. These jewelry outings are going to stop, too."

"But Enzo, she is just a young girl. I didn't think there was harm in her little whims. Selling her homemade jewelry just lights up her up. This exhibit is just a tiny little thing. It will be out of her system. You have to agree, she *has* become my Paula. It's amazing how she has just absorbed the spirit of my dearest daughter—I just wanted to give her a little treat. I know you are our Master. My dearest Master, I appreciate all that you have given to me. I was not at all going against you. My sincere apologies if I have offended you." Louisa bows her head, hoping her carefully chosen words have reached this tyrant she has been tied to for several years now. How she wishes she belonged to another scion.

"Her duty is to me, I assign her the tasks. I run this scion. Not you! Look at me!"

Louisa slowly moves her head up and her eyes carefully reach Enzo's, but with a submissive action. Enzo is pleased at the continued power he believes he has over her. "You are just here because I need company. I can easily change this. I am getting fed up with your spending. How many damn dresses and gold pieces do you need? I need peace. Bianca is the only one I can rely on. She gets me. You don't. Sometimes I wonder if you and your pathetic Pietro are needed anymore."

Louisa swallows, her fear rising, but she manages to stay calm, she dares not speak.

"You are warned—I can easily have you dispensed of. Bianca and my associates are eager to be rid of you. Something to think about, Louisa. My patience is thinning with every moment these ungrateful vampires are not back home."

Gabriel stands perfectly still at the side of the house, listening to the drama inside. He suddenly feels he has made a terrible mistake, but it's too late. He has to confront this head on. He needs to mentally prepare first, so with stealthy movements he scales the brick side of the house and carefully opens the latch of his bedroom window. With slow methodical movements he steps in and just stands still, listening and keeping his breathing steady. Any odd sound could be heard if he is not careful. But the yelling and crying still happening muffle any other sounds. He is temporarily relieved at this moment. He needs to compose himself before he moves downstairs. His thoughts are spinning chaos and drama in his mind. *What will become of my life now?*

Meanwhile, back outside the gallery, Adriano is losing patience as his heated argument with Bianca seems to be endless. He still keeps his tone relatively steady, trying not to raise his voice like Bianca is.

"Bianca, I understand. I know the isolation and despair that can be felt. But when I turned you it was not out of spite or anger, it came from a different place inside—goodness and loneliness."

"Goodness?" she scoffs. "You are too much, Adriano. Do you hear yourself? You justified turning me because you were lonely? Well, I justify turning others too! You can't have it both ways! My life went to hell after you turned me. I found myself travelling back to my childhood neighborhood; I desperately wanted to see my family, thinking I was safe with them. I never expected that I would soon crave their blood. My own family. I wanted to die! I had to find shelter in abandoned buildings and trains. But my heart kept pulling me back to my home. I was worried, I felt I had been followed, and was afraid it might be the vamps."

"Vamps? I don't follow."

"Oh God, where have you been? Vampire terrorists, haven't you heard of them?"

"No."

"Of course not, you live a charmed life here in Paris."

Adriano doesn't correct Bianca; he is relieved that she believes he lives in Paris. That is a reassurance to him, that his private life is still intact. He is sensing danger with this vampire.

"Adriano, did you hear me? Are you listening? I told you I went back to my home and found my dad was killed, and the vampire that I turned weeks ago was now drinking from my little brother Tommy."

"Yes, sorry that is awful, I was just taking it all in."

"Right. I ran as fast as I could and broke through the window, grabbed a piece of glass, and stabbed that vampire over and over. I wasn't sure if it would even kill him, and he managed to break free and leap out of the broken window and take off. I followed him, and well, I got my answer. He was dying. It took him a while, but I waited patiently. At that moment, all my thoughts turned to you."

"Me? Why?" Adriano is puzzled and confused.

"Why? You ruined my life!"

"I didn't mean to."

"How you try to ease your guilty conscious."

"Bianca, I—"

"I don't want to hear it. I've survived all these years in ways you will never understand. I discovered that I have a power over vampires who are weaker, destitute. I was in command. They feared me. They obeyed me. I was even gaining some reasonable respect from vamps and vampire roamers—it may come in handy one day."

"I still don't follow, vamps, roamers?"

"You're pathetic. You live in this private little bubble. One day tragedy will hit you. I wish that with everything in me."

"That is unkind."

"Oh, am I to feel something? Look at you. It's as if no darkness has touched you all these years… How is this possible? How is this fair you ruin people's lives and you have everything you desire?" Bianca's voice stirs in cold and bitterness.

Adriano feels a sting of guilt pass through him; he feels responsible to some degree, and it weighs heavily on him. He understands her pain and the loss of siblings and a parent. He hopes he can reach her, bring her out of her bitter darkness.

"Bianca, I know that sorry doesn't mean anything here, but I am sorry for the loss you suffered, the darkness you have lived in; but things could be better, you could change your life. Evil and darkness touched me years earlier, many times as a human and a vampire. Please know, I would not have left you, I wish you hadn't left me that night."

"I was in shock—I was desperate to go back to my boyfriend, but when I got there he was gone. I looked for him all night…and then I saw you. You were holding someone firmly, and your face was on their neck. I saw them squirming, and as I got closer I realized it was Pierre. My Pierre."

Adriano struggles to remember so far back, but then he sees the image and the context comes into focus. "Bianca, you don't understand. He was robbing and threatening a woman with a knife. You must have seen this. Why didn't you help her? I had to react, I had to help her."

Bianca doesn't say anything, but her anger and hate for Adriano continues to be fueled by her rage. "I couldn't let him see me like this—you didn't have to kill him!"

"You're right, I should have just threatened him and let him go. That is on me; I'm sorry. I just reacted impulsively to save someone. He had a knife, and the woman was defenseless."

"Always with an excuse. Always justifying your kills."

"I will always try to protect those in need. I am not a monster. A monster made me, but I have spent my life now protecting as best as I can those who need help. I will not apologize for that—I'm sorry if that sounds cold."

"You had no right! I loved him, and he loved me—you bastard!"

Adriano is taken aback in offense, but understands that she is upset and full of anger. "He loved you? I saw the bruises on your face, the cut lip when I encountered you. Is that the love you are referring to? Is that the life you wanted for yourself?"

"It was my life! My choices. You took away my right to figure it out—you took away my right to be a human!"

"You're right. It was your life, your choices—for that I am sorry. But I gave you a chance as a vampire—a real chance, to live without fear. You walked away from me that night before I could show you. Again, I know sorry means nothing for what you endured. I'm sorry you had to witness Pierre's death, too. Knowing that he also hurt you just frustrates me; to see how you don't see that I gave you a chance at happiness and peace! But I didn't create you to be a monster. I take responsibility for not teaching you to resist to redirect the thirst, to feed on animals, but I do not take responsibility for you destroying the chances that were there for you. There are no monsters in my family. I live among loving vampires and humans—I fell in love with a beautiful human. I offer you kindness, Bianca, but you have to want it." He offers her his hand to shake and Bianca just stares at him in disbelief. Her eyes glaze over with shock, fuelling the resentment rotting inside of her.

"What? You fell in love with a human? That vampire with you tonight was human? You live among humans? If Domenico knew any of this he would—"

"Wait! What did you say?"

"Enzo would have you killed."

"Domenico? Enzo—it can't be the same person! He is your Master?"

Bianca is curious as she realizes that Adriano recognizes that name. "Enzo is my Master, and my mentor. When he finds out that you loved a human and keep human friends he will—"

"You live with Domenico?"

"Yes—but he prefers to be called Master, what of it?" Bianca pauses, observing the shock on Adriano's face. It is draining of blood, and he looks pale, angry. Bianca's mind pokes fiercely at her recent private discussions with Enzo, in the short time that she has lived in his scion. Then suddenly her mind finally reveals to her a memory of a particular discussion. "Oh my God—now it makes sense." She flashes back to the night Veneur brought her to Enzo's home and was introduced to him.

"What does?"

"When I was introduced to Master there was a look of complete shock on his face. I didn't understand why he had such a reaction to my presence; after all, he was the Master. Then he said he knew I belonged to him already, the moment I walked in and he saw me. He told me he sensed this familiarity, and he said he could smell my blood and it was part of his. I didn't understand. He asked me who turned me, and I described you to him. Suddenly there was something in his eyes, a memory that seemed to stir him. He shared with me that, years later as a vampire, he travelled throughout Italy and came across this small town in Sicily. The village doctor needed a temporary replacement. Enzo revealed to me that he had some medical training as a human, but stopped attending medical school. He didn't say why, and I didn't pry. After all, I was told you don't invade a Master's personal life."

"Go on." Adriano is already mentally prepared to hear what he already suspects.

"Anyway, he reviewed the patient files and came across one that intrigued him. He read that there was a single mother and her older son living outside town on a farm. He told me, always try to find isolated and fragile humans. These patients were quite ill. The son was dying of some kind of blood disease, I don't remember what he called it."

Leukemia, responds Adriano privately inside, his heart sinking as slowly learns of the moments involved before the horror of Domenico arriving at their front door.

"Go on—I want to hear more."

"I'm sure you do. Well, Master said that after he killed the mother, he decided not to kill the son but to turn him instead. He could see that the human was deathly sick already, and was going to die. But for some reason he decided he wanted to turn this young man instead of killing him. He wanted to know what it was like to create another vampire. He confided in me—imagine, a Master sharing that intimately with me—anyway, he said he was always nervous about such a powerful action to create another vampire. He took the risk and turned this young man, who I now assume is…you. Want to hear more?" Bianca is relishing watching Adriano sink in hurt and upset, the color continuing to drain from his face.

"Just go on."

"Okay. My pleasure. Master felt overwhelmed with this new creature he was now responsible for, and he said it was too much for him. He was so shocked after, he didn't know what to do, and he just needed to get away! Can you believe it? But he told me what he last said to this reborn. *"Do not drink unless drinking to the very end, or it is your responsibility for the life you hold in the balance"* Wise words, Adriano—you should have listened to him back then. But then again, I should have too." Bianca thinks of her little brother Tommy and her father, killed by one of her own reborns, and the anger in her builds. "Then Master went on to say the most unbelievable thing. It was odd, and he didn't elaborate too much. He said, 'Bianca, you belong to my son!' Well, I didn't know what he meant but —ha ha! I understand now. He is your Master."

The color drains from Adriano's face, and he gets a sharp ache in his head. "He is not my Master! He is nothing to me! Do you hear me—he is evil and you need to stay away from that bloody monster. "

"How dare you insult him like that? You are one to talk, you hypocrite. You are just as evil. I guess the fruit doesn't fall far from the evil tree! At least he wears it with pride and confidence. It all makes sense now. But listen to me carefully—I will never see you as anything but the evil you are, and the evil I am because of you." Bianca pauses and smirks wickedly. "Oh, you poor—foolish thing. Your precious life that you have created, surrounded by your friends and lover, is an illusion that you will one day soon realize will not last—I almost pity you, Adriano. You have trusted in a universe that has no mercy, and you have trusted yourself to believe you are good and that forgiveness is possible. Oh, don't look so sad, don't you see? Your true blood is Master's blood! Look at that! We are family after all. Oh—does this make *you* my real Master? Hmm…or my father? Well, definitely not my lover."

"Stop it, Bianca—I'm warning you—"

"I'm warning you! Time will show you who you are deep down. Keep fooling yourself by justifying who you choose to kill or turn. It was okay to turn me according to you, and okay to kill Pierre—according to you. It must have been difficult watching your mother die at the hands of a vampire. I know how it feels. And you were so young, too. But look at you now, you sure don't look eighteen. I guess life even wears down a vampire as pathetic as you. Oh! Does that mean you are with a much older female vampire? Does she know she is practically robbing the cradle? Ha! But strangely, you have aged—if I may speak frankly? You don't look eighteen at all. You have greys, and you just seem older. Odd. Maybe you are drinking too much of that disgusting animal blood? You should drink more from humans. They do keep me looking younger. I haven't aged at all." Bianca's rage and bitterness strikes emotional blows at Adriano.

"Enough!"

"I'm just getting started. Who knows how many more humans you have killed over the years for the good, as you believe. Actually, Master would be proud of you. Maybe we should all compare notes?"

Adriano can feel the guilt swelling inside, he can't take much more.

Bianca continues to antagonize him. "At least I have the honesty and integrity to say I kill humans for food, for my survival, and yes, I admit it—I take pleasure in watching them beg for their lives. It is a powerful thing to hold a life and to choose which fate they will have."

"That is the difference between you and I, Bianca—if I kill a human, there is a damn important reason."

"Really? What could that be?"

"It is complicated, but make no mistake, I don't feel pleasure."

"Right,and that makes you morally superior. You are delusional. One day it will all catch up to you when you discover that you have truly destroyed another human being. But you will do it again because it is in your blood, and always has been. You think you are above your kind. You justify your killings with your ridiculous excuses, so your guilt doesn't take over. Either you are in denial, or you are just a hypocrite—your instinct as a predator is too strong. Just like me—just like Master. Shame on you for disrespecting our ways as vampires, how dare you think you are above us. You are a disgrace to our Great Father."

"He is not my father! I will never be like Domenico. You know nothing of who I am."

"At least Master has the integrity to live his truth without compromise, and with honor. He is well respected among the other Masters. Masters don't respect their scion members, and yet I have managed to find a way up that secret ladder. I have proven to him that I am the vampire to make him proud. I will do what it takes, with no remorse. I have a lot of plans in store for this scion. Master will be elated. I'm going to make this scion even better. It is time for a female vampire to become a Master."

That last statement is an alarming thought for Adriano. She is more dangerous and power-hungry than he realized. Veneur and Juliette are in danger; he has to warn them.

"For Christ's sake! Just listening to you I can see that you are all over the place. On the one hand you are angry at me for turning you, on the other hand you are angry at me for caring for humans! Then you praise and admire a vampire for his ruthlessness, and yet you loathe me for trying to protect an innocent human because your Pierre was ready to kill. Your little brother Tommy was killed by a vampire who *you* made. So according to you, was it that vampire's right to kill Tommy? After all, he is the predator, it was in his power. Is that what I am hearing? Or are you so mixed up and blinded by rage and bitterness that you can't even realize how ridiculous you sound? Make up your mind. At least I know where I stand. I am a vampire, yes. I have made wrong choices with terrible impacts, I admit this. And I have killed, but it's not about power; you have no clue what you are saying. I've tolerated your ignorance and your spoiled behaviour more than enough. You hate me. Fine. I can live with that. You admire this cruel Master, as you call him? Well sorry for you, but that's your choice. However, I will not allow you or anyone to take away what I've built through joy, love, and friendship. Be warned, you have no clue what I am capable of."

Bianca's eyes turn a dark cold menacing hue. Her expression shows disgust and hate towards Adriano. Adriano accepts that there is no light to be redeemed in Bianca's heart. She is just beyond helping. Bianca steps in closer to Adriano, and Adriano is ready to grab her neck. How easy it would be to take it and snap it. She can't recover from that.

Bianca's cold stare angers Adriano more, he is so tempted to finish her. Bianca opens her mouth, her teeth showing, and she whispers, "I hate that I was made from such a weak creature." And abruptly she takes off before Adriano even responds.

"Whatever."

Bianca is far in the distance but purposely speaks out loud so Adriano can hear her still, "Just wait until Master hears about this. You better hope I don't encounter any of your family again, especially your precious Rebecca. There will be no mercy. Master, I, and others will tear her apart."

Suddenly Adriano lets out a fearsome growl and his fangs immediately protrude. He quickly he runs in her direction, but she is gone, and there is no trace of her scent in the air. She is the only vampire that he created. He believes this truth with all his heart and soul; he has no memory of ever creating any others after Bianca. But he knows the horrifying reality that he never ever wanted to admit or accept all these years, that deep down Domenico could have made others. How many vampires are from this bloodline? He is full of so much anxiety and guilt, but mostly worry, for he knows Bianca is a possible threat to his personal happiness, and to his friends and his family, if they stay here much longer. A chill travels down Adriano's spine; he made a monster from the monster who made him.

He feels he is falling, his mind collapsing into anxiety and rage. He is momentarily paralyzed in his mind. He stands like a statue. Seconds go by, and finally he returns to the present moment, his mind racing with what just transpired. He can't erase what Bianca said. Her words cut through him, and he questions his own goodness. Did he cause such damage to this vampire? Is she right, is he a fool to believe he is not evil deep down? Panic rising, he finds it hard to breathe. All these years he tried to forget the monster who made him, and now he finds out Domenico is alive and creating havoc for other vampires. Then the most terrifying reality hits him, like he just dropped off a cliff and hit rocks.

Bianca will tell Domenico, and they will hunt him and Rebecca and his friends. He feels he is about to explode, and he lets out a loud roar of anger and frustration. "Damn you, Domenico!"

Just then Adriano's cell rings; it is Sebastien in a panic. He says Adriano needs to get back here, Veneur and Juliette are trying to leave, for good.

Adriano returns quickly to the gallery and enters. It is nine-thirty. The last of the guests are making their way out of the gallery. The waiters are busy collecting the dirty wine glasses, empty champagne bottles, and empty food platters. Monsieur Coultier is already back in his office reviewing the sales of the evening.

Lucan spots Adriano immediately. He observes him closely; Adriano looks distracted and unhappy. He is pale, and his eyes are very dark and have fear in them. Adriano makes eye contact with Lucan, who is standing beside Rebecca. He approaches. Lucan whispers to Rebecca, "He's back."

Rebecca immediately turns around, followed by Sebastien, Jonathan, Nathan, Veneur and Juliette.

CHAPTER 21

A Night of Anxiety

Juliette is frantic. Everyone is now outside of the gallery, waiting in the parking lot for Adriano and Veneur to return. Adriano wanted to talk privately with Veneur so they took a drive. "Why aren't they back yet?"

"It's okay, Juliette, I'm sure they will be back soon."

"You don't understand, Rebecca, we should have been home by now. Bianca has probably already told Master everything about tonight, about all of you and us socializing. I pray that she didn't discover Veneur's plan. Oh, I can't handle this. Veneur thinking we can leave—we are now in more danger, we have to go back! We have to beg him to forgive us."

Just then they hear a car driving in the parking lot; Sebastien recognizes James' Mercedes.

"They're back," he hollers out. All of the vampires, plus Jonathan, Lucan, and Nathan, wait anxiously as Adriano parks the car and steps out with Veneur.

"Sorry we took so long, we just needed to run a quick errand."

"Veneur! We need to get back home," cries Juliette in an exhausted, anxious tone.

"No—we are staying with Adriano and the others." Veneur remains calm, determined.

Adriano approaches Rebecca, kissing her tenderly. "I'm sorry, Rebecca, that you've become involved in this. It's a long and complicated story, and there's no time to explain, not here. Right now we need to get back to Sebastien's. We assume Bianca has returned to tell Enzo everything about me and my life, and this is not going to sit well at all, apparently, with this crazy vampire. Veneur explained everything." Adriano looks to Juliette. "I'm so sorry that you have had to live as this Paula, that is so troubling to me. Don't worry, you don't need to say anything."

Juliette's eyes tear up, and her trembling lips express her gratitude for Adriano's empathy. The others all look confused, shrugging their shoulders and exchanging glances.

Adriano feels on alert. "Lucan?"

Lucan comes forward accompanied by Nathan. "Yes, hello Adriano, sorry to reconnect in such troubling circumstances. This is my good friend Nathan Jacobs." Nathan steps forward and extends his hand. Adriano doesn't reciprocate. He is just staring between Lucan and Nathan. He can't figure out what it is, but something makes him feel suspicious. Rebecca can sense he is agitated, and she moves beside Adriano, but in the tense atmosphere she slips back unintentionally into her quick vampire movements. Everyone notices this except her. Adriano takes her hand.

"Lucan and Nathan have been so supportive. Juliette was in such a frantic state."

"I see. Well, I appreciate you keeping Juliette company. I don't mean to be rude, however we are dealing with an urgent personal matter."

"Indeed, I understand. If there is anything I can assist with, please, I may be helpful."

"Thank you. But I don't think so Lucan." Adriano is growing irritated that these two strangers are still hanging around and are showing no sign of leaving.

"But I can see something has transpired that gives you cause for such alarm. I may be able to help—I know—"

"Adriano, Veneur, what's going on?" interrupts Sebastien again in frustration. Adriano pulls Sebastien aside to talk to him. Sebastien is stunned by the request from Adriano, however he can see the desperate situation at hand. "Of course, of course, they are welcome, but we must hurry, let's go."

Adriano drives Rebecca, Veneur and Juliette back to Sebastien' home. Jonathan and Sebastien take a taxi back since too many people in one car. All vampires except Adriano go out to hunt. The night's events really affect their energy. Juliette and Veneur are accustomed to hunting alone. so it is very strange for them to be in the company of other vampires. Adriano and Jonathan remain in the living room, busy brainstorming a plan of action.

"This is absolutely insane—all of it. I can't believe what these two vampires have gone through, I'm stunned. Imagine forcing this sweet Juliette to take on the identity of a dead girl named Paula—and she has been expected to carry this on for years? Enzo is nuts! And this vampire Bianca, what a piece of work, threatening me—Rebecca, my family? Oh I swear, Jonathan, a part of me wanted to snap her neck right there. Christ! I should have."

"Adriano, it's okay. Calm down. You had no clue where this was going with her. We will figure this out. This Enzo must really be a master manipulator—I've come across cases involving sociopaths, that's what he and Bianca sound like, only worse as vampires. I can't imagine Juliette and Veneur, these two adult vampires, afraid of their own shadows practically—brainwashed even. I never thought I would encounter vampires afraid of vampires. This is really unsettling."

"I'm still in disbelief. At least they are with us now, but I just don't know what more we may be dealing with. Like, these associates, who knows what powers they might have?"

"You're worried. So am I. I wish we could leave tonight."

"I know, but they might be thinking that too; we are safer here. This area is so secluded and far away from them."

"Adriano, you know I want to help, but I am human. How can I possibly lend any help when we are dealing with some odd vampire personalities?"

"I know, Jonathan, I know. I don't want to put you or anyone in danger. We just need to ride the next day out. Ohh, my brain is exhausted."

"You need a break, this night has been too much. Vampires cause more drama than humans." He chuckles, hoping to release some tension in the air, and in Adriano. "Listen, I don't mean to change the subject, but I am just a bit curious about these other two men, Lucan and Nathan, that we met this evening. Perhaps it's my cop instincts in overdrive with all that is happening, but what's your take on them? I mean they just kind of moved into our scene, but they're strangers?"

"I know. It's been puzzling me ever since I met Lucan. There is something definitely odd about Lucan."

"Odd? Tell me."

"Well for one thing—he isn't human, and he isn't a vampire."

"What? You're kidding me! Unbelievable—Nathan too?"

"No, Nathan is human."

"If Lucan isn't a vampire, then what is he? Now you're freaking me out."

"Honestly, I haven't the slightest idea. With everything else that transpired this evening, I put it out of my immediate mind. But make no mistake, I don't like knowing that there is *something* out there wandering about who is not human or vampire. I don't know if the other vampires picked up on anything. Oh God—I'm exhausted. This has been a crazy bizarre night." Adriano has a look of concern on his face and gets up. "Christ! What is keeping them out there so long?"

"Yeah, it does seem a while since they left to hunt. Maybe call Sebastien on his cell?"

"Let me go outside and take a look out back first, I don't want to spook an animal if they are still hunting. Stay here and call me if they come back. I will put my phone on vibrate." Adriano walks to the kitchen and out the back door, heading towards the woods hoping to spot them coming back. He just doesn't feel like himself; the events of the evening are really stressing him. He feels jumpy, and he can't shake the anxiety he is feeling. He is reacting to any slight movement or sound coming from the surrounding area with an unusually high degree of alertness.

Jonathan takes out his cell and is checking his emails when he hears a knock at the front door. He is alarmed, thinking maybe Bianca found them. But then he thinks, *would she really knock?* He wishes he had his gun on him, but he has it packed in his luggage still, which is now at Adriano's apartment. He calls out through the door, "Who is it?"

"Hello—it's Lucan and Nathan, is Sebastien home?"

Jonathan is surprised and he slowly opens the door. "Lucan? What are you doing here? How did you know this place?"

"Oh, Sebastien mentioned it to me earlier this evening. We are sorry for the intrusion, however we couldn't help but feel a need to make sure that everyone was okay. May we come in?"

"Sure, yes, umm—they are umm out right now, they should be back, uh, soon."

"That's fine, we can wait out here if you feel more comfortable."

Jonathan is panicking, not sure what to say. He can't get out of his mind what Adriano said. *He is not human or vampire.* Jonathan is worried if he is in danger. He has to try and reach Adriano on the phone to warn him and the others, in case they come home with blood on their mouths. He quickly texts Adriano and then opens the door and lets Lucan and Nathan in. He leads them into the living room. "Please take a seat, can I offer you something to drink?"

"No, thank you. We are fine. Relax, Jonathan, you seem tense suddenly. Is everything alright?"

At that moment all five vampires walk into the house. Adriano immediately smells a wet dog, and his protective instincts prick up. Veneur too smells something very wild, while Sebastien and Rebecca and Juliette smell chocolate and caramel. They quickly move into the living room. Sebastien smiles curiously,

"Lucan, Nathan? What are you doing here?"

"Hi Sebastien, please forgive our intrusion. As I was saying to Jonathan, I couldn't help but worry, and just wanted to stop by and make sure everything was okay."

Sebastien is suddenly feeling overtaken by all of these guests in his house, but then he quickly switches, becoming a gracious host, and runs into the kitchen to collect wine glasses and wine bottles. *Oh James, if only you were here to take part in all of this!*

Adriano is not impressed by the arrival of these sudden uninvited guests; however, this is not his home, so he goes along.

Veneur, Juliette, Lucan, and Nathan squeeze comfortably enough on the large sectional. Jonathan and Rebecca each take a large pillow and sit on the floor. Veneur and Lucan get up and offer their seat to Rebecca, but she declines as Adriano sits next to her. Adriano knows that Sebastien would prefer to sit on his own recliner. Sebastien returns and Rebecca helps pour the wine and serve. Adriano's phone rings and he passes it to Rebecca; she realizes it is her mom's house again, and she takes the phone and goes into her bedroom to talk with Ethan and Adam for a little while before they went to have their dinner with Nonna Catharina and Nonno Vince.

Meanwhile, back in the living room, everyone is gathered, the sounds of voices and brief mixed conversations taking place. For a few minutes there seems to be a mutual friendly and respectful air amongst everyone. Rebecca returns to the living room, her expression peaceful; for a few minutes she is able to forget the threats that took place a few hours ago.

Suddenly, the temperature in the room drops a few degrees; it is noticeably cooler, the lights in the hallway are flicking on and off, and everyone is taking notice. Juliette stands up.

"There is a presence here. I can feel it." Juliette looks toward the corner, where the other La-Z-Boy is. Sebastien almost drops the tray of glasses he is carrying. Everyone else turns their heads to see what Juliette is looking at, but they don't see anything. They start to think that perhaps Juliette is just over exhausted from the ordeal earlier. Juliette clearly sees James sitting in his recliner in the far corner of the room near the piano. James greets her with a friendly smile.

"Hello there, how nice of you to come to our home. I just wanted to visit for a while, don't mind me, it's nice to see my home filled with interesting individuals."

Veneur takes Juliette's hand and gently guides her to sit down again. "Rest Jules, it's been a long night. You are safe."

"But Veneur, I saw…"

"Shhh…it's okay Jules. It's your nerves, we are safe here."

Sebastien stays quiet. He is stunned that someone else has seen the ghost of his James. This was his secret, and now he just wants it to remain unknown to anyone else. Sebastien gives Juliette a glass of red wine, and his eyes and worrisome expressions convey to her to please let it go. Juliette respects his wishes and nods in agreement.

Meanwhile, Adriano is restless and can't help himself; he suddenly gets up and addresses everyone in a serious tone. "Okay, I hate to interrupt this nice friendly moment here with everyone. Thank you, Sebastien, for taking us all this evening. I must say, honestly, Lucan, Nathan—although unexpected and surprised to find you here, we appreciate your concern for our wellbeing. So now, I have been doing some thinking and before I begin I just have one important question to ask." His eyes immediately turn to Lucan. "Lucan, who are you? Or more precisely, *what* are you?" The energy in the room suddenly feels cringe-worthy.

The other vampires are stunned by Adriano's question. "Adriano, what in God's name possesses you to ask —" But before Sebastien can finish, Adriano speaks.

"Sebastien, he is not human—and he's not a vampire." All the other vampires look at each other in disbelief. Jonathan remains quiet, waiting, now in anticipation. Nathan just sits there drinking his wine, his eyes focused directly on Lucan. This was a question only asked of Lucan once before, and that was asked by Nathan years ago, so he is fascinated to watch the drama and hysterics about to unfold.

"What are you talking about? Of course, he is human!"

"No, Rebecca, he's not."

Rebecca turns to Sebastien, who nods and shrugs his shoulder in confusion.

"Adriano is right, I am not human and I am not a vampire," Lucan says.

The vampires look at each other, then at Adriano, then at Lucan.

"What's going on? Is this a joke?"

"Veneur, please sit down, I don't think they are joking."

"Jules, this is crazy."

"Veneur, please allow Lucan to explain."

"Thank you Rebecca. But before I answer your question Adriano, I must be able to trust all of you." Lucan's eyes move to each of the vampires, than to Jonathan who just looks so dazed and incredibly disheartened by all the supernatural he has witnessed so far. "After all, we should be united in the fact that we are not human—no offense, Nathan and Jonathan. Well—the truth is—" He pauses, his nerves reacting. "Sorry, this is only the second time in my life that I am revealing my truth. Remember, Nathan, a long time ago when you asked me this question?"

The vampires are growing impatient. "Lucan, just tell us, we have a right to know."

Lucan looks directly into Adriano's eyes and without blinking. "I am a lycanthrope, this is the term I prefer to use—it is much more distinguished." The blankness in everyone's eyes is evident, no one other than Nathan and Lucan know what this means. "I can see you are not familiar with the proper term." He sighs, shaking his head. "Oh, I do hate to use the *other* word, it has such a negative effect when it reaches *anyone's* ears, especially human ears, no offense Nathan and Jonathan."

Sebastien and Juliette suddenly are distracted by the ghost of James in the corner, he is slapping the lazy boy arm repeatedly, he seems very nervous and excited too. *"How incredible Seb—dear God—I can't believe this. He is a werewolf! Oh, how incredible—how dangerous! You must be careful."*

"Mon dieu! A werewolf!?" shouts out Sebastien in total shock and bewilderment; Juliette screams hearing the ghost too.

Instantaneously all eyes in the room are directed to Sebastien, and it is if time just froze in this chilling revelation.

"Sebastien! It's not time for joking—this is serious."

"Jonathan, I'm not joking—am I, Lucan?"

Lucan nods his head in agreement. "Ahh—you are familiar with the term." And a simultaneous gasp emerges into the room; cries of awe and astonishment echo through the living room. The vampires are noticeably rattled and stunned. Jonathan is mystified and dazed. Nathan continues sipping his glass of wine, taking in the drama unfolding, secretly relishing this moment. Finally, he is not holding this dark and isolating secret to himself anymore. Now others are given the harsh privilege of learning this unbelievable truth that he has carried for several years, alone. He takes comfort and respite knowing he is no longer alone in carrying this heavy burden. Within seconds the room is filled with shouting and gasps as vampires, humans, and lycan shout over each other.

"Stop playing around you guys—you had me there for a second. Ha ha." Jonathan laughs nervously, hoping the tiny hairs that are standing up straight on his arms are just a false alarm. But something unsettling in his mind is building, and it makes his heart beat faster.

"Is this real?" demands Adriano in a forceful tone.

"It can't be?" Veneur and Juliette are bewildered.

"You aren't joking?" remarks Rebecca as she looks into Lucan's troubled eyes.

"Fascinating, I would love to take a specimen of your blood!" says Sebastien. Lucan's expression turns to offense, and he quickly clarifies. "Sorry Lucan —I mean for study, with your permission of course, I mean, well, I am a scientist for God's sake."

"Tell us more, Lucan, what does this really mean? The only images coming to my mind, and I am sure I am not the only one, are those of films like old Abbott and Costello movies or horror movies like Werewolf in London!"

Lucan and Nathan chuckle mildly at Adriano's interpretation, although Adriano is clearly not amused at all. Seconds later, the laughter fades and Lucan becomes more serious. Nathan takes a large gulp of wine and calmly speaks. "Werewolf in London. You're not that far off, Adriano."

"Nathan—was it necessary to alarm everyone like that?"

"But it's the truth. *My friend*, let's not sugar-coat this."

"Explain," demands Adriano.

"Where do I begin? Why don't you ask me questions—but please one at a time."

Adriano immediately speaks out. "Okay—are we in danger? Can you control yourself when you are a—a—I can't believe that I 'm engaging in this conversation—a werewolf?"

"Lycan, please, I am more of a lycan. But to answer your question, it is *difficult*. Right now, you are not in danger, and—"

"*Now* we are not in danger? This is crazy! So what you are saying is that we *can* be in danger with you at some point!?" shouts Adriano angrily.

Lucan sighs heavily, desperately and carefully trying to find the right words; but what words can ease anyone finding out werewolves do exist? "Unfortunately, I cannot control myself once I have transformed completely. It is the grotesque truth, my cross to carry. But don't panic. Please! I don't transform just by the sight of the full moon. That is more of a trait of the werewolf. You see, I come from a lineage of lycans who have the capability to transform without the power of the moon; this makes us more powerful and unique within this species. My life would have to be physically threatened, or I would have to be under severe stress or anger, and trust me it takes a lot for me to get to that point. Or I can just will myself purposefully, and I can't imagine why I would want to do that. I have learned different practices over the years that keep me calm and tranquil, but of course life does throw us curve balls at times. But nonetheless! We, that is Nathan and I, have safety precautions in place, at all times! If this helps. You see, transforming takes a huge physical toll on my body, but unfortunately, I do have to transform at least once or twice a month, and I do so under controlled parameters. I can see the shock on all of you." Lucan's voice remains calm and steady.

"What safety precautions?" asks Veneur with growing concern. Just then he receives a text message on his cell. His focus has now turned immediately, and his ears tune out Lucan. He tries to remain composed. He doesn't respond to the text. He puts his cell back in his pocket. Then his ears slowly manage to pick up again on Lucan speaking. Lucan didn't even realize Veneur had trailed off in his mind earlier.

Lucan's voice drops. "Chains, locks, ropes—think about it. How else could one keep a Lycan bound? *Trapped.*"

Nathan joins in enthusiastically. "It's impressive actually—how much we have learned ourselves through the years. We have it almost precisely choreographed."

Sebastien, who is deeply interested in the science of this, asks, "How does the physical transformation actually happen? I can't imagine how the body can do this."

"Well, I am not a doctor, but basically my body and my bones break and rejoin, fuse somehow into the necessary shapes needed for a Lycan. It's quite remarkable."

Everyone cringes. "My God—isn't that painful?"

"Yes Rebecca, extremely, but that is the curse of the Lycan. It is not the lycanthropy itself that is the curse, it is the process of transformation into a Lycan. Our bodies and our minds have to adapt, and to this day, honestly, I can't say I have adapted to the excruciating pain during the change and transformation back to human. That is why I do my best to stay calm through the process. My bones have been tremendously affected by the changes over the years. Now this cane is my godsend!"

"So the moon has nothing at all to do with your transformation?"

"Not the way you mean, Veneur. The full moon does affect me; I become more restless and emotionally sensitive, but overall it's just a bad day for me, and I pamper myself to soothe the extreme anxiety. I guess my lineage was one of the luckier ones; I couldn't imagine living the way many of my other ancestors have lived, watching and waiting for the full moon every month, knowing they have no choice but to change. I choose to change every month because it keeps my aggression, anxiety, and mood swings down."

"Have you killed anyone?"

The room becomes awkwardly silent, all eyes directed at Adriano.

"Have you?" replies Lucan curtly. "I know I am in the company of vampires, your presence is unmistakable. Your glaring eyes and oddly pale yet smooth skin gives you away, no matter how much you try to look *human*. Vampires are just as dangerous if they don't control their thirst for blood."

"Vampires can control themselves. We can feed on animal blood, we can make choices. But we are talking about you!" shouts Adriano curtly. "We allowed you into this house, we are finding out that we could be in danger if you transform, so if you can't control yourself when you transform how do you prevent killing?"

"You don't understand, Adriano. I am not in my right mind when I am transformed, so how can I control what happens during that horrific time? Unlike a vampire, I am human until I am not."

"We vampires may not ever be human, but we can keep some human values."

"Thou shall not kill, right? Well, Adriano, am I to understand you don't kill humans?"

"I can control what I do—you are telling me you can't. That is alarming, to say the least!"

"Only when I am Lupo!"

"Lupo? Who is Lupo?" is spoken simultaneously by all.

"It is the name I gave to the other side of me. But understand, I am human most of my life. Doesn't that count for something? And it's not like we just let the lycan roam freely—I do care about humanity! So stop judging me as if I am some evil creature. Learn about me, understand me before you decide to condemn me." Lucan's eyes are glazing over, but he feels in control. He clears his throat and composes himself, feeling a bit embarrassed. "I apologize for that outburst, it is not like me to get that upset. But to be honest, I haven't had this conversation about who I am with anyone other than Nathan, years ago, so it is rather unsettling and upsetting that I have to justify my identity, my truth among, vampires." His voice raises higher, but is still steady and nonthreatening.

"Lucan, I'm not judging you. None of us are—I'm just trying to grasp the severity and danger of this situation. I mean no disrespect."

"Adriano, while he has been in my care, no one has been in danger," Nathan proudly remarks. "He doesn't travel alone, we live together, and I am very aware and alert to his moods."

"Thank you Nathan. I can see I've overwhelmed all of you. I'm sorry, I thought perhaps all of us creatures would understand and accept our individual truths. Well, it doesn't matter, I can see we have overstayed our welcome. Let's go Nathan."

"Oh—no, Lucan, don't go. We're sorry if we made you feel unwelcome, both of you," cries out Rebecca, giving a stern look to Adriano and the others.

"Yes, Rebecca's right, we just need to process this incredible revelation. Please sit down, stay. We are all unique and have a right to connection, belonging." Sebastien looks at Adriano.

Adriano doesn't know what to say at this point; he is alarmed and worried and exhausted mentally and physically. Hours ago, he was threatened by Bianca, and now he learns werewolves are real. Suddenly the most disturbing yet practical thought enters his mind, and he knows it is the only way to be sure. "Lucan, what I'm about to ask you is only asked because I need to truly understand what we are dealing with. I mean no offense but if you are sincere about wanting to associate with us, we need you to transform—safely."

"You're crazy!" simultaneously shouts Lucan and Nathan.

"Are you out of your mind!?" Veneur barks in disbelief.

"You are losing it!" shrieks Sebastien in panic.

Adriano gives Sebastien a stern look.

"Adriano, you're not thinking this through, carefully," Jonathan cries out in fear.

Rebecca and Juliette just stay silent, processing what Adriano just asked.

"Hear me out, everyone. I realize this sounds absolutely out there, but it's the only way. We need to know what we are dealing with. How can we allow anyone into our group without knowing as much as we can? We can't just ignore this. We have to do this. We have to know. We have to see. We have to be mentally prepared for what our eyes will see. I'm sorry to be so forward, but we are talking about lives. Lucan, if you want to be part of this group, then trust us so we can trust you."

Lucan turns to Nathan, who just shrugs his shoulders in disbelief. Lucan turns to Adriano, throwing his hands up in the air in defeat. "Fine, I'll do it."

Nathan stands up. "Lucan, maybe we need to discuss this privately. They really don't know what they are asking of you —of me."

"No, Nathan, it's time we take a chance on others." His eyes move around each individual. "I know who I am in my soul. I don't know why, but I just feel we are in the right company." His eyes turn to Juliette and Veneur. "I want to help Juliette and Veneur. I want to get to know all of you, especially you Adriano."

CHAPTER 22

Lupo

The anxiety, uncertainty, and tension are evident tonight, however individuals are doing their best to manage their own feelings. Juliette is suffering, and Veneur asks to have her lay down, so Rebecca brings her to her room to rest. Sebastien and Adriano walk the property, keeping their powerful vampire senses alert to anything unusual. Adriano's mind keeps reminding him they only have two days left in Paris, and there is still so much to do. Veneur is preoccupied in deep troubling thoughts. He quietly looks in on Juliette, but she is asleep.

Meanwhile, Nathan and Lucan are in the woods behind Sebastien's house, searching for a secluded area with many wild bushes and large trees to help muffle the sounds that will be heard once the change occurs. Nathan is carrying a large black duffle bag over his shoulder that he retrieved from their rented car earlier. This bag always goes with them no matter where they go.

He throws the bag down angrily on the snowy ground, shouting in frustration. "I wish you would reconsider, Lucan! This is not as simple as changing into a werewolf costume, for God's sake! They have no idea what

301

they are asking. You are not that young anymore. I know I am repeating myself but this affects me too." He unpacks the tools. "It's not fair—they have no clue the pressure and burden of responsibility I face, making sure nothing goes wrong each and every damn time! These chains and locks have to be so secure." He holds up the heavy steel chains and examines the locks, then throws them down on the ground.

"Nathan, calm down, please. We are surrounded by vampires—they will hear you."

"Good! I hope they do hear me. I hope they hear me say they are insane for wanting you to change, to bring Lupo out. Lucan—you never understood how traumatizing it is for me, watching you transform. The cries—the screams—the horrific sound of your bones literally breaking! The sounds coming out of you. Sounds like there are no words to describe. Sounds that make my heart beat so fast I feel it is going to explode—and I can't run because I have to make sure you—Lupo—is secure. Feeling the hairs on my body prick up because I feel dread and terror. The visual is no better—to actually see the creature emerge! That kind of image stays with you. You told me that just seconds before your body dies as a human, when you feel the first break of your spine in your back and your heart expand, you feel a sudden clarity that you could die in the next moment. And you experience this horrible reality seconds before every transformation. And now you just want to transform to this—this creature, again, without cause! Suffer excruciating pain? Just to satisfy these vampires? Why? In God's name, tell me. Don't they understand each time you change it could be the last moment you live? I don't want to be a witness to you dying in front of me." Nathan's face is hot and red, his eyes bulging, sweat dripping down his forehead; he is exasperated and mentally strained.

"Nathan, please, my good man—you're going to have a heart attack. Take a breath. I had no idea you felt so—so strongly about this. All these years, you seemed okay with all of this. I thought you had adjusted to our life. To me? To Lupo?" His eyes fill with hurt

"Lucan—be real. How can anyone adjust to this? I mean my God—he—you are a werewolf!"

"Lycan! Why is this so difficult to remember for everyone?"

"I tried, God knows I tried to accept all of this, but I'm human. I can't keep doing this. I'm afraid for both of us, that one day he will destroy you—or me." Nathan can see the hurt in his friend's eyes. "Don't get me wrong, I know you tried to balance our difficult life situation with the nice home we live in, the luxuries and comforts we have, the travels we have gone on—all amazing experiences I got to have because of you. But, I guess I'm just wanting more of the things that money can't buy. Lucan, it's taking a toll on me. I just needed to finally tell you how I feel. I'm sorry, I should have done this a long time ago. I realize that now. This wasn't the best moment to bring this all out—but I respect you. You have been a great friend and given me an extraordinary life, but I don't know how much longer I can live this way. I'm sorry, I just need to be honest."

Lucan stays quiet, just standing and staring out into the woods. His thoughts are racing, guilt creeping in. *Was I being selfish all these years?* He is mentally processing the possibility that he might be losing his only true friend.

"Lucan? Say something."

Lucan pauses for a moment, then his troubled eyes turn to Nathan. "I want you to know how much I appreciate that you sacrificed your own life to enter into mine. I know you are lonely. I know you wanted more than babysitting me."

"Lucan come on, it's not like that."

"Please Nathan, let me finish—I'm sorry for the burdens I've placed on you. I realize now, I depended too much on you. That isn't fair. These are my burdens to carry. I will find a way to ease this pressure on you. I will. I managed years on my own, I am capable of —"

"Lucan, I'm not saying I'm leaving you, it's just—"

"Nathan, I understand, really I do. You have given me more than any human could possibly give; time is precious, and you lent yours to me. But for now, I really need your support! If these vampires can trust me then my world will open up. Creatures need creatures just as humans need humans."

"I'm here, Lucan. Thank you for listening. Now—on the bright side."

"Bright side?"

"Yes." A mischievous smirk escapes. "I will finally have the chance to experience this transformation with others. I can't wait to see the look on their glazed eyes when Lupo comes out to play. This I must record—what do you say? After all, this is the first time anyone else will see *this other side of you.*"

"Oh Nathan, you are creepy and morbid sometimes."

"I have to have some fun. No offense, of course."

"None taken. Let's get on with this. I think I hear one of our audience members approaching—Adriano, is that you?"

Adriano is suddenly in view. "Yes, just came to see if you needed anything?" He notices the chains and locks lying on the ground.

Nathan bends down and pulls out a couple of long pieces of thick rope. "Damn it! I knew we forgot something. We don't have meat. We can't do this without food."

Adriano looks puzzled. "Meat? What do you mean?"

"We need a piece of raw meat so Lucan—I mean, the lycan needs something to occupy him during the hours he remains this way. After all, he will be hungry. He will need to eat. His instinct will be to hunt, but he will be bound. This will anger him tremendously. We don't want him howling all night and attracting unwanted attention. You see, I hang the meat from the tree just in front so the werewolf can just gnaw at it with his teeth. His claws will be tied behind his back, to the tree."

"Lycan!" shouts Lucan, exasperated.

"I see." Adriano observes and is growing disturbed at the image forming in his mind. He looks at Lucan; he suddenly feels pity and empathy for Lucan. "Not to worry. You are surrounded by vampires—we are the best hunters. We can find you something, a rabbit? Or bigger?"

"You mean a living one?" cries out Lucan in disgust.

"Yes, of course." Adriano is perplexed by Lucan's odd reaction.

"Oh God—how horrible! I can't eat that!"

"What? A werewolf can't eat a rabbit?" Adriano is baffled.

"Lycan, please. It will be hanging there, screaming, afraid—just waiting for Lupo to devour it. No. Too cruel."

"Lucan, it might work, actually, it will be better than the butcher's cut we always get. After all, it is for the werewolf—I mean lycan. You can't decide for him. It may sound disgusting to you now, but believe me when *he* comes *he* will be dripping saliva. We never did this, live meat. Ha ha! This is growing more exciting by the minute."

Lucan and Adriano both stare at Nathan in disbelief at his excitement. "Nathan! I am not here to amuse you with your macabre thoughts."

"Sorry, I guess I just—never mind."

"I will find something, let me know when you are ready." Adriano awkwardly turns to leave, thinking, *could this night get stranger and more disturbing?*

Lucan mumbles sarcastically under his breath, forgetting that Adriano can hear him. *"Huh! Ready he says? Oh, what am I doing?"*

The next few minutes are occupied with Nathan checking each lock carefully, and then the thick steel chains meticulously, and finally the ropes, making sure there are no frays. Once he is confident he asks Lucan to check them over too.

"They're good, everything is secure," Lucan says in a heavy troubling voice.

"Lucan, did we miss something, forget something? What's wrong?"

"I completely forgot. Oh God—I have to be —naked. How embarrassing. In front of these strangers, and women too! Just thinking about it is mortifying."

Nathan can't hold it back; he bursts out laughing, and carries on a few seconds further before realizing Lucan is growing irritated and annoyed, frowning, not enjoying this. Nathan quickly settles. "Sorry, I mean that. Don't worry, trust me, the only memory they will have is the one of the lycan howling ferociously and using its powerful strength to shake the trunk of this tree almost enough to pull the roots out from under the ground. That will be the memories they will keep."

Jonathan's mind can't take in more supernatural information, and he decides it is best not to participate in this disturbing event. He is feeling overwhelmed, his mind suddenly playing havoc with his psyche of what is real and what is his mind tricking him. He remains at the house, in case Juliette wakes up. Everyone else gathers at the tree chosen for the change to occur. Nathan is standing in front of Lucan, holding his winter jacket in front of his naked body. Lucan's thin ankles are already inside the cold steel shackles, and his body is pressed against the thick trunk of the tree. The cold steel chains are wrapped around him several times and secured with two heavy-duty locks and thick rope. Lucan's chest feels tight and constricted, and his hands are tied with more chains behind the tree; finally, a lock is secured around them. Only his head is loose.

Adriano and the others approach and suddenly they all become eerily quiet, feeling uncomfortable and disturbed at seeing Lucan bound this way. Adriano holds the squirming rabbit he found minutes ago tightly in his hands; the smell of fear is intoxicating to him, and unintentionally triggers thirst for him and the other vampires. But this meal is reserved for the new creature yet to make its appearance. They observe Lucan. His attractively older but toned body is now shivering, his feet cold as he stands bound to the tree on the snowy ground. There is a wind picking up from the north, and it stabs at Lucan's tender skin.

"Oh Lucan—you must be freezing! Put the winter coat on."

"I can-n-n-t-t-t -R-Reb-b-ecc-ca, it will get-t-t t-t-orrn of-f-f-f—I'm u-us-s-ed to th-his-s-s." Lucan looks at Nathan to continue; his teeth are chattering uncontrollably, the wind and cold relentlessly travelling over his exposed naked body.

"Just so you understand clearly—Lucan has to be naked for this. I'm sure you can appreciate how this must make him feel. He is a man with the greatest integrity! Don't forget this."

"Of course. We are all adults here, and we appreciate you trusting us." Adriano looks at Lucan with respect.

Nathan looks at Lucan; his body is still shaking fiercely. Nathan puts his hand on Lucan's shoulder and removes the winter coat, exposing his front to everyone. "I got you," he whispers. The vampires don't know what to do. They look around, trying to seem nonchalant. But they feel awkward as Lucan stands naked tied to the tree. Nathan directs Adriano to bring the rabbit over and tie it over a thick branch and position it inches in front of Lucan's mouth. Lucan is repulsed. Nathan asks everyone to step back a few feet. "It won't be long now." Then he climbs one of the trees as high as he can go. The vampires all look at him with curiosity.

"Nathan? What are you doing?" shouts Adriano up towards the tree.

Nathan shouts back down. "In the next few minutes or so all of you will understand. Let me remind you —a werewolf will emerge, and frankly I prefer to keep my distance. Thank God they don't climb trees."

Suddenly all vampires take a step back further from Lucan.

"We are here for you Lucan, it's okay," cries out Rebecca in a soothing voice.

"Let the pain take over, don't control it," shouts Nathan from the tree. His cell phone is in his hand, ready to record. Seconds go by, and the screams and cries of the rabbit echo into Lucan's ears, making him feel guilty and angry at himself for agreeing to this. He allows his anger to come forth, and channels all his negative energy. The growing winter wind aids in his increasing discomfort and pain. He suddenly lets out a loud sound of incomprehensible pain. All of the vampires cringe and take another step back; they are fixed on this scene, but compassion is mounted in their eyes. Then they hear Lucan struggle to speak.

"It's-s-s happpe-en-nin-ng —I c-can-n-n fee-el it-t-t—oh God-d-d! Help-p me-e-e! Ple-ease-e don't-t-t lea-ave-e me-e!" The words then change to sounds of groaning and whimpering, then unrecognizable sounds come out of his throat, and even the rabbit instantly stops screaming, frozen in its place. Its tiny eyes open wide and full of fear. All the creatures' mouths begin to salivate, their teeth protruding, as they hear its tiny heart beating so alarmingly fast.

Suddenly, a new and very disturbing sound escapes Lucan. The vampires hear the tiny bones breaking inside his jaw and they are shocked and stunned to see his jaw expanding and growing longer. With his mouth wide open, his teeth grow in length, curving and shaping into jagged sharp canine teeth. Then more bones break around his chest, which is now expanding and widening; and his legs, his feet, arms, and hands all break and reform. The vampires are grabbing onto each other, showing aversion as they freeze like stone statues in their spots, witnessing this abomination of nature emerge in front of them. The sounds are so unbelievably horrifying and painful to these vampires' ears, but they all stand there watching the horror unfold, determined to see it through.

Nathan meanwhile is staying quiet, just recording it all. Within minutes the growls resemble a wolf's, but there is a distinct difference in the growl, never heard before by these vampires. Lucan's body is filling in with thick dark brown hair all over his chest, arms, legs, and face. His eyes are turning from their beautiful grey to ochre, then deep crimson, then almost black. The rabbit is screaming for its life. There is no longer any trace of Lucan in that body. The wolf creature has emerged, and it is howling over and over. The vampires can hear echoes of wolves far away in the distance howling too. The creature is struggling to break free from the chains, and wild sounds are coming out of it. Then in a blink of an eye the rabbit is in its powerful open mouth, the long canine teeth are crunching down on its back, and blood is flowing inside the werewolf's mouth. He chews pieces of the rabbit as it swings from side to side, still tied up in the rope. The vampires are stunned beyond belief, cringing with every sound of tiny bones breaking as wild beastly growls in pleasure. The werewolf continues its wild behavior, desperately trying to release itself from the heavy steel chains.

Suddenly Rebecca can't anymore; she thinks her gift will work, so she lets go of Adriano's hand and slowly begins to walk towards the werewolf. All the vampires gasp, shouting out to her, and Adriano quickly is beside her.

"Rebecca, what the hell are you doing? Don't go any closer, *mon dieu!*"

"I'm okay, I have to try and reach Lucan, I know he is in there—"

"Rebecca, this is not an animal you can subdue! This is a devilish creature," cries out Adriano frantically.

"Stop yelling, it's aggravating him. I know what I'm doing, trust me."

Adriano is beside himself with fear and anger, and Veneur and Sebastien are still a few feet away.

"Adriano, let me do this, stand back."

"Christ, Rebecca! No damn way."

"Please, it won't work if you are beside me."

"I can't!"

"Trust me."

"*Mon dieu!* You are stubborn!" Adriano shouts out in frustration; he doesn't know what to do. If he pulls her back he might anger the werewolf further, but if he lets her go she could get injured or worse.

"Adriano, please, I need to try. It's my decision."

"A selfish one!"

"Let go." Rebecca insists. Feeling hurt by Adriano's words, she forcefully releases herself from his grip on her arm

Adriano is taken aback, and Rebecca slowly walks a few steps closer to the werewolf, who is growling ferociously, staring into Rebecca's eyes. There is no trace of the rabbit or even a bone fragment to be found.

Rebecca stands two feet away from the ferocious beast, and in her mind she works her gift and calmly and softly talks to Lucan in her mind. The werewolf is snapping his jaw and teeth ferociously, wildly into the air. "Lucan, it's Rebecca. I know you can hear me, don't be afraid, we are here, you are not alone, and this fear will pass. Stay calm, breathe deeply, and remember who you are; the kind and caring human, not the beast. You can change back, let Lupo go now. Allow yourself to come back. We understand now, we are here and trust you. Trust us! We are your friends, come back to us Lucan."

As Rebecca is mentally talking calmly and gently, she is affecting the werewolf, soothing the beast's soul. Slowly, to everyone's amazement, the creature stops struggling, the howling becoming lower. Everyone can see his chest rising up and down as he takes deep breaths. The vampires are astonished: the beast is subduing. The sounds of its ferocious growls are quieting, his powerful jaws are closing, and his long canine teeth are changing. The thick hair on its body is diminishing, slowly disappearing, as the bones and muscles readjust, realigning to his thin body. Rebecca continues to repeat in a trusting warm tone, "Trust us, we are your friends, come back to us Lucan. You are safe."

The beast's eyes are staring into Rebecca's, their cold blackness being replaced with a warm crimson hue and then returning to ochre. A few seconds more and Lucan's eyes are returned to their warm grey again and his body is human again. Rebecca slowly puts her hand on his face and gently caresses the cold skin. Lucan is back.

His head droops down, exhausted. A slight whimper can be heard. Nathan quickly stops recording and climbs down the tree carefully; he runs with the keys and unlocks Lucan from the chains, then unravels the knots from the ropes he strategically tied. Rebecca grabs the winter coat and quickly places it around Lucan but he is falling on her, he has no strength.

Adriano and Veneur rush in and pick him up, and they all run back to the house and place Lucan in front of the fire. Sebastien, realizing the urgency, runs to get some whisky he has stored away. Adriano gently places Lucan on a blanket near the fire and everyone gathers around him. He is in a deep sleep.

Nathan reassures everyone that he is okay and that this reaction afterward is normal. "He might be in and out of sleep and talking, and you may hear some screaming from the nightmares. But it's part of the trauma aftereffects from the transformation. I think he actually dreams of the event, it must be very traumatizing for him. The transformation takes a lot out of him. Now you understand his truth, and how it affects us both." But Nathan is still in shock himself, witnessing that for the very first time there is hope that the werewolf can be tamed; at least one person is able to reach the beast. Rebecca. Nathan has it all recorded for Lucan if he ever one day wants to see this remarkable connection that has been made, creature to creature.

The extraordinary events that took place just a few short hours ago have not been lost on the vampires. Sebastien and Jonathan are upstairs in Sebastien's room. Rebecca is in her room and trying to get some sleep beside the sleeping Juliette. A couple of hours ago, Nathan drove Lucan back to the hotel so he could continue to rest comfortably. Sebastien's house is just not equipped with more beds for guests. Unexpected exhaustion swept over Adriano, and he was unaware he had drifted off into a deep slumber on Sebastien's La-Z-Boy. Veneur is awake in the living room. He finds a notepad in a drawer and sits down at the kitchen table to write a letter.

Dear Juliette,

I am sorry but I have to go back. Gabriel texted me, and he is in trouble. I would not be able to live with myself if I was responsible for more damage to another vampire I care for. Enzo just wants me back. He promised he would not have you hunted. Gabriel said your departure has left a great hole in Louisa, and that is sitting well with Enzo. He is pleased. I don't understand this but Gabriel was insistent.

I know you will be safe and loved. I trust Adriano and Rebecca explicitly. Please go and live the life you deserve to live. I promise I will follow you one day, just not now. I will find you.

Remember the secret code Gabriel and I established to communicate, you and I can use this for us. Also, I was going to surprise you, but I packed some special little pieces in the large suitcase. One of my favorite memories I carry with me now, me and you sitting in my tree house, laughing. Find that laugh again.

So much more I want to say but I know this is a lot right now. Please I beg you, do not come back. It will irritate Enzo, trust me!

Love always and forever
Your brother Veneur (Ven)

CHAPTER 23

Going Home

Friday finally arrived. Adriano and Rebecca left early to pack up the apartment, with plans to regroup with everyone back at Sebastien's. Meanwhile, Juliette carried a heavy heart along with the letter left by Veneur. She read it over and over; parts of the paper were wet with her tears. Each time new tears would fall as she read it again. She would then pick up the pet rocks, Marcel and Henri, that Veneur packed for her and just stare at them. Then she would look at the marbles that she carefully washed. At times it took a lot of hugs and gentle words from Jonathan and Sebastien to convince Juliette that she had to stay with them. But they can see how difficult this is; her heart is breaking, pulling her back home.

For Sebastien, this day is measured moment by moment. And this is not lost on Juliette, who is so overly sensitive and can feel the mixed emotions of sadness, worry, excitement, and anxiety felt by Sebastien. His thoughts take him everywhere. *What life awaits me in a new city? A new country, away from the place I have called home for a few years? Away from the memories of my beloved James.*

He doesn't know if James will follow him to his new home, or remain locked up here. That thought alone makes Sebastien melancholy. Is he really prepared to leave this home, his James? He has to trust all these new friends completely with his life. Earlier, he contacted Jacques and told him that he was going on a lengthy trip and asked him if he could stay in the house, until Sebastien decided what he wanted to do. Jacques was thrilled; he couldn't believe the generosity of Sebastien. The vampire didn't tell Jacques where he was headed; Adriano explicitly instructed this. Jacques was confused and concerned but Sebastien insisted on letting it go.

Adriano calls everyone into the living room to go through a checklist of items and emergency responses if someone grows physically weak. Adriano is in full control mode; they are heading home. All the small sixty millilitre contact lens solution bottles have been replaced with blood that they collected earlier in the woods, from rabbits, and the full bottles have been placed in each of the carry-on luggages. They are now sitting on the porch to keep them cool. Before the taxi is due to arrive, Adriano insists that Sebastien and Rebecca hunt one last time in the woods before they head for the airport. Lucan and Nathan arrived a bit earlier, wanting to say goodbye to everyone. Lucan promises Adriano that they will be in touch once they return back to Guelph, and gives him his home address.

All the vampires start heading out, since the taxi is due shortly. Sebastien stays in. "I just need a few minutes, please." Adriano understands and departs the house with everyone else.

Sebastien takes one last long look around his home. He quickly moves through the upstairs rooms, taking a few minutes in each. Memories flood in. He left all the furniture behind for Jacques, but arranged for all his paintings to be shipped over. They are all wrapped up tightly in packing boxes and sealed. He is leaving all his medical journals and textbooks behind, but bringing James's journal. He walks through to the living room and looks at the empty mantel piece, his treasured photos all packed away. He looks at the scratches on the walls, taking in all the memories, good and bad, flooding in, and he sighs heavily as tears stream down his cheeks. "Goodbye my beloved James, I know you are happy for me! Come visit me, if you can." He knows James's ghost is not present, and this bothers him so much. This is when he really needs to see him, and he just isn't here. He can't understand it. But then he thinks maybe James knew it was best not to appear, it would be too difficult to say goodbye.

He leaves a sealed envelope on the kitchen table for Jacques. It is a thank you letter for all his kindness, acceptance, support, and friendship. It is a thank you for helping him during the difficult time before and after James's death. It is a goodbye and a take care letter. But the words that were most important, Sebastien could not write down. His hand would stop. His mind and heart could not cross over to that darkest memory and truth that he was sorry for killing his brother.

Sebastien releases a heavy sigh and drops the pen. His hand covers his face, covering the shame and guilt. He includes the keys to both the Mercedes and the house into the envelope. He hopes Jacques and his parents can at least have a beautiful home to enjoy, to mourn in. He opens the front door; Rebecca is standing there, and she can see the sadness in his eyes, mixed emotions coming through both of them.

"The taxis are here, are you ready Sebastien?"

Sebastien doesn't say anything; he just takes one last breath then closes the front door, dragging his three suitcases filled with treasured keepsakes from a life he has to leave behind. Two taxi vans are waiting on the drive-way, and Sebastien privately wipes away the tears still streaming down his face. All vampires and one human are off to Charles de Gaulle airport.

Anxiety is building in all of them as they go through the baggage check-point, watching each of their one-quart clear plastic bags carrying the contents of one small bottle of contact lens solution, each with a different brand, moving through the scanner. Rebecca is relieved that she decided not to include her small perfume dispenser bottles in her carry-on and packed them in her larger luggage instead.

As they all walk further away from that most stressful check point, a great sigh of relief showers all of them; they made it through this first stage. Time seems to be moving quickly, it is already time to board the plane. Rebecca and Sebastien are feeling quite full still from their hunt earlier, and perhaps the excitement of this journey preoccupies their minds so they are not thinking of thirst. Soon enough the plane is on the tarmac and ready to take off. Rebecca settles into her chair next to Adriano; Juliette is just behind them. Adriano was lucky he was able to get her a seat in first class with them. Sebastien and Jonathan are across from Adriano and Rebecca.

Adriano is feeling a bit restless though, he can't believe this day has finally arrived. All the running around, worry, and planning and threats are fading into the background of his exhausted mind. He tries to settle in, eager to rest for a while. There is still so much ahead to be prepared for once they get back home. He is looking forward to teaching again, he misses the students, the stage; the vibrant and fast-paced learning environment of the theatre keeps him moving. He misses the everyday life routine he became so adjusted too.

These past few months for Adriano were full of intense emotions, agonizing worry, moments of abandoned hope, and finally the unbelievable miracle of finding Rebecca and the surprising new connections that followed. It's time for Adriano to just stop and breathe and just be. He is always in control, and now he just needs a break from the stress. He just takes in this welcomed yet cautious calm, doing his best to drown out the thoughts of Bianca. He puts the worries and complexities around Ethan and Adam and living with vampires aside for now, too. He trusts that everything will work out; he can see and feel the goodness in all these vampires, and they know he will protect all of them and Rebecca's sons too. *"It will all be okay, we are a family, we are safe,"* he unintentionally mumbles to himself as he finally drifts off to sleep.

They are already a couple of hours into the flight. Everyone is either resting or watching a movie or reading. They all just need their own time. Adriano suddenly awakes to an unsettling feeling that is arising within. He looks over to Rebecca, who is fast asleep; her skin is still vibrant, and he is relieved that she is not thirsty yet. He looks back to Juliette; her eyes are closed, but he can see a tear strolling down the side of her face. His heart breaks for her. He looks across to Sebastien sitting at the window, and his color is a bit off, so he quietly leans over to Jonathan nudging him to wake up, whispering into his ear, "Sebastien is looking a bit pale, maybe he needs to drink?" Sebastien hears his name and opens his eyes. He feels the thirst rising and he quickly takes out his small carry-on bag and removes a contact lens bottle and heads toward the washroom.

Adriano can't seem to shake the uneasiness he is feeling. He leans over to the window to look outside, hoping to distract his sensitive nerves. He is starting to panic, an instinctive feeling of awareness that there is something nearby. But could it be true? Was there an unknown vampire on this plane? Rebecca awakes and senses the restlessness in Adriano, but assumes it is just the anxiousness of going back home. Adriano walks through the aisles and passes through the different sections of the plane, scanning everyone and listening intently for anything odd or a voice that has a tone in it that is very different from humans. His thoughts are racing with more questions, more doubts, and he has to catch himself and be mindful of what is happening. He is having an anxiety attack.

He begins breathing deeply and walks over to a quiet area; thankfully the plane is not packed. He finds a little corner of empty seats and just sits and tries to focus on his breathing. This anxiety attack is really trying to gain power. Suddenly, his eyes spot a woman walking up the aisle away from him and towards the front of the plane. He quickly moves his way through other people walking the aisles and then she is gone. He only saw the back of her but he thinks, *Bianca?* He has no time to think about why and how and all of that but just find her, find Bianca! He moves through each aisle; some passengers are standing around talking in the aisle. His mind is confused, and he thinks to himself, *where did she go? She couldn't just disappear.* Suddenly screams are heard coming from passengers up ahead. Adriano struggles to keep his movements normal as he pushes his way through the aisles. Suddenly, he is confronted by a scene of blood and horror. Moans can be heard, cries and whimpers. He runs past the injured and dead bodies.

Then he hears angry shouting coming from the direction of the cockpit. "How the hell did you get in here?"

Adriano quickly runs down the stairs and toward the cockpit corridor; he sees a male flight attendant on the floor near the door, with food scattered on him and hot coffee spilled on his uniform, the silver tray lying on the ground in the corner. Beside him lays another man in uniform, for a split-second Adriano doesn't know if this is the pilot or co-pilot. His neck is slashed deeply, blood splatter all over the wall and on his face.

In a split-second Adriano sees Bianca lunging for the pilot, who is desperately trying to control the plane. "May day, may day, we are under—" Before he can finish his sentence Bianca lunges for his neck with rapid speed, but Adriano, with even quicker speed, grabs her with such force that she lets out a small cry. He pulls her away from the pilot, who is in shock and trying to control the plane. Adriano snaps Bianca's neck instantly and she drops to the cockpit floor. The pilot, still trying to grasp in his mind what he just witnessed, manages to control the plane and radios the control tower for emergency landing.

Adriano sees another flight attendant approaching, screaming frantically, and he quickly pulls her into the cockpit and shuts the door, keeping his hand over her mouth. "Stay calm, please, I will let go of my hand, but you have to stay calm. The pilot is okay, he is in control."

The pilot's voice sounds in such distress. "Go back out and prepare everyone for emergency landing—please Jennifer! Stay focused, can I count on you?"

"The passengers, many are injured—dead!" Jennifer screams in panic and terror. The pilot is shocked but brings his focus on keeping the plane steady.

Adriano has to make sure Rebecca and the others are okay. He is desperate to reach Rebecca. He runs back to their seats. His eyes go directly to Rebecca; she is leaning against the window, her eyes closed, and he is astonished at how she could sleep through all of this. But then Adriano freezes in complete horror, he takes a closer look and sees something is not right with her neck; then he sees the blood splatter on the window. He grabs her and blood is dripping from her neck. It was slashed so deeply.

Adriano screams the most agonizing scream, and he looks over to Jonathan and Sebastien, but they both are slouched over and blood drips from their bodies, reaching down to the plane's floor in a puddle of horror. He looks around almost in a daze and sees Juliette's throat is also slashed. He whips back around back to Rebecca and he has no time to think, his instinct just kicks in to save her, and he bites into her veins, desperate for a pulse, but he can't feel one, the screams and cries of the passengers make it hard even for him to hear her heart beating.

Suddenly the plane violently banks to the right, and screams can be heard all around him from passengers. The plane is jerking uncontrollably into a downward fall. Adriano screams in terror and shock as he feels the plane falling from the sky rapidly. He falls onto Rebecca to protect her. His mind is in chaos.

"Adriano, Adriano, wake up, wake up." A faint but familiar gentle voice is calling Adriano from a distance; the more he hears it the closer it becomes, and the feeling of the imminent crash is fading as he opens his heavy eyelids, feeling a bit blurry still and out of focus.

"Rebecca," he cries out with tears in his eyes. He hugs her tightly, and the flight attendant stands beside him looking concerned; Sebastien, Jonathan, and Rebecca too. There are curious strangers watching, but still in their seats.

"You alright buddy?" asks Jonathan.

"You were talking in your sleep at one point, but then you screamed, was it a nightmare?" Rebecca wipes the sweat from Adriano's forehead with a tissue, caressing his hair.

Adriano still can't speak; he holds onto Rebecca tightly, hugging her and kissing her. He is shaking, they can see that the dream must have been extremely bad.

"What was it about?" they all enquire.

"Nothing I ever wish to bring up, please just let it go, it was a nightmare that's all, and I guess I am just overtired." He looks to the attendant. "Sorry for any trouble. I'm fine now."

The attendant asks if he needs anything and he shakes his head; he can barely get any more words out at this moment.

"Okay, but if you need anything just let me know."

Adriano looks to his watch; time has gone by quicker than he hoped. Rebecca doesn't push about the dream, she just holds Adriano's hand, which is extremely hot and sweaty. Adriano kisses her hand and he leans back into his seat, taking deep breaths; his body feels like he is on fire. The ordeal he just experienced seemed so real. He thinks, *that uneasy feeling was never really there after all, it was all a dream. Bianca has no idea where we are, she can't hurt us.*

Rebecca gets up to use the bathroom, Adriano is momentarily afraid to let her go, reaching out his hand as if calling her back to him, and Rebecca notices fear in his eyes; she's concerned by this peculiar behavior. Adriano composes himself and sits back in his seat and reassures Rebecca that he is okay. He privately talks himself back to a reasonable calm state. The rest of the plane ride goes smoothly; they are scheduled to arrive at Toronto Pearson airport at five p.m. Adriano already had a busy day ahead for tomorrow, he had to meet his agent as he had some houses lined up for Adriano and Rebecca tomorrow.

Adriano and Rebecca agreed it was best that they just go home from the airport and then call her family to let them know she was back. It was just best under the circumstances for everyone to not have a big commotion at the airport. Although Rebecca is struggling; she wants to see her sons so badly. Adriano knows how difficult it is for Rebecca to spend another minute without them, and he secretly contacted her parents and asked them to bring Adam and Ethan to Rebecca's apartment. Rebecca is exhausted but needs to see her sons. They would arrange for a family gathering in a few days. For now, Rebecca can only handle phone call conversations with her siblings. Rebecca's mom Catharina was a bit upset that she couldn't host a celebration, but Adriano convinced her that Rebecca's health is still fragile. She is still adjusting to a very strict new way of eating as instructed by the doctors at the clinic in Paris.

They arrive by van taxi to Rebecca's apartment. Rebecca opens the door and she is overwhelmed with excitement, exhaustion, and joy as she sees Adam and Ethan standing at the entrance. Her parents Catharina and Vince are standing behind them. She extends her arms and embraces her sons tightly, mindful of her new strength, kissing their foreheads over and over. Adam and Ethan are filled with warmth and joy, feeling the affection they are receiving from their mom. Adam and Ethan are young enough to not fully understand her lengthy disappearance, but old enough to recognize that there is something different about their mom. They can't yet figure it out, they just notice she is very vibrant and energetic. The next few hours are spent at Rebecca's apartment. Adriano is impressed and relieved to see how disciplined all the vampires are around Rebecca's human family and sons. An hour passes, and Rebecca is occupied with calls from her brothers and her two sisters-in-law, making plans to meet in a few days.

Juliette is managing her melancholy mood and is surprised and pleased to see how these two little humans, Ethan and Adam, quickly make her feel like an Aunt. Rebecca's parents Catharina and Vince offer their home to Juliette and Sebastien, assuming that there just won't be enough room in Rebecca's small apartment, but all the vampires know they will have to hunt soon so they decline gracefully. Adam and Ethan are anxious to stay with their mom but Rebecca feels she can't manage the needs of her sons tonight, she is feeling overwhelmed suddenly. She is torn inside; she wants to have her sons with her but she is not sure that she can manage her need to drink and her need to be home with her sons. Juliette senses Rebecca's apprehension and internal conflict. She can see how attached Rebecca's sons are to her and how it will cause such unnecessary upset to them if they had to leave her tonight. Her own emotions are being projected and triggered by her being separated from Veneur. Soon after, Catharina and Vince leave and now it is just Adam and Ethan among the vampires.

For Sebastien, these two little humans were just that, human, and he doesn't feel an attachment to them instantly like Juliette. Well, Adam and Ethan on the other hand are curious about their new uncle. He is only a few inches taller than Adriano, who is five foot eleven, but to Adam and Ethan's little impressionable minds, if you are taller than Adriano then you are a giant. They are so excited to have their mom back, and to have a new aunt and uncle, that they can't control their exuberance. They start crawling all over Sebastien, laughing, giggling, slowly breaking him down until he finally can't resist their innocent childish charms. Juliette smiles, watching these two little creatures playfully draw the serious scientist into their world.

Sebastien starts tickling them but is very careful of his strength. Adriano watches carefully and Sebastien at first feels very nervous, but the laughs he is hearing from Adam and Ethan melt his anxiety and he looks at Adriano, reassuring him that it's okay. Rebecca steps away into the bathroom carrying one of the contact lens solution bottles, and drinks lukewarm blood. She then quickly brushes her teeth and mindfully walks back to the living room slowly, aware of her movements. She looks refreshed, and smiles at her sons, who are now sitting between Sebastien and Juliette each with a game controller in their hands. Adam and Ethan are busy trying to explain each button on the controller and soon all you can hear is, "Get it, quick he's coming your way, shoot it."

Rebecca stands back just observing and she giggles, watching the intensity on Sebastien's and Juliette's faces as they try to kill zombies. Juliette is taking in these little humans so deeply. Rebecca and Adriano notice and look at each other. They know everything is going to be okay. Rebecca is so happy to see something has sparked a light in Juliette and knowing her sons are responsible just brings an elevated joy to her heart and spirit. Adriano winks at Rebecca and moves in for a kiss.

It is very early Saturday morning. All four vampires are up and strategizing coordinating their schedule around Adam and Ethan, who are still sleeping in their own room. It is decided that Sebastien and Rebecca hunt first, since it is more necessary for them. Rebecca drives to the Heart Lake conservation area, but both vampires are feeling the effects of these new surroundings of many houses and apartments, and it makes it difficult for them to feel comfortable hunting. This unease cements for both of them the fact that they have to find a property further out, more secluded. Rebecca is accepting more and more that her life and way of living as a human can no longer sustain her life and needs a vampire.

After a reasonably successful hunt, they arrive back at Rebecca's apartment and Sebastien goes to shower while Rebecca greets Adriano, who is on the balcony talking to Jonathan on the cell. She then goes to her sons' bedroom and sees Juliette is on the floor with them. She is drawing Spider-Man and they are just in awe watching him come to life so detailed on the page. They are anxious to colour him.

"Hi guys, do you want me to fix you breakfast now?"

"Hi Mommy, look, it's Spider-Man, Aunt Juliette is so cool."

Juliette smiles and continues drawing in the buildings in the background.

"I know, she is talented."

Ethan stands up, walks to Rebecca, and takes her hand. Rebecca doesn't want to let go ever. She looks down at him, mindful that her mouth is still stained with blood, and resists hugging or kissing him. Soon she hears

Sebastien come out of the washroom; he is dressed and is summoned by Adam to join them in their room. Meanwhile Rebecca takes the opportunity to shower. She has a busy schedule planned for today.

"If anyone else needs the shower, I'm done."

"Mommy, Adriano said we are going house hunting today." Ethan giggles. "He's so silly, isn't he?"

Rebecca laughs. "We are going to go visit some houses and see if there are any we want to buy—but first, I would like to bring Aunt Juliette to the mall."

"Yay, the mall, let's go!" cries Adam in excitement. And he and his brother run to their room to change.

"The mall?"

"Yes, Juliette, I thought maybe you might want to change your hair. But it's up to you, if you like the blonde—"

"Oh, I would love that! Really? Is it true?"

"Yes, of course, all of that is behind you now, you can choose what you want to wear, how you want to look, and most importantly, what you want to drink." Adriano, Sebastien and Juliette look at Rebecca in shock. But they realize it is true.

"There is a mall, not too big, just a few blocks away from here. If we go just as it opens, there will be fewer humans around. You and I can go to my hairdresser and Adriano, you can handle the boys?"

"Of course, Sebastien and I will be just fine."

"You mean just the two of us?"

"What's wrong, Sebastien, are you scared of little humans?"

"No. I just think that, well, they might get hungry, or—"

"Oh, you're right. Hmm…Sebastien, if they get thirsty make sure they only drink water or milk, no wine." Rebecca smirks, followed by Adriano.

"You're funny."

"Don't worry, Adriano will bring them to McDonalds."

A few hours pass. Rebecca and Juliette come out of the hairdresser and are quickly greeted by Adam and Ethan, who are captivated by the appearance of their mom and aunt. Juliette has a lighter air about her, even her tears are settled more. Adriano and Sebastien are also shocked. Juliette's hair is now black, with a few thick strands of a pink tone running through her shoulder length hair. Then they see Rebecca; her dark brown hair now has a thick red stripe at the front.

The next few hours are spent with Adriano driving everyone to the different houses lined up from Richard. There is only one of them that seems decent enough to meet their needs, but they are not feeling encouraged. They are now on the way to the last appointment.

"This next house that we are going to is located in Castlemore and is approximately fifteen minutes away from your parents and your ex-husband's home. So you are all still in proximity and there is a school bus that can take your boys to their current school."

"A bus? Oh boy, that will be interesting. You seem to know a lot about this particular house. You even know about the school bus?"

"What can I say, I am very thorough in my research." Adriano smiles. "I know it is important for you to have your sons stay in their current school. It will be good for them to ride a bus, gives them a little independence. Richard told me that this house has been on the market for a few months, the owners are desperate to sell due to a job transfer overseas. Rebecca, please read the listing out."

"Let's see, it's a thirty-six hundred square-foot old three storey Victorian-style brick house. It's move in ready. It has well maintained hardwood floors throughout and is listed as a five-bedroom home, four bathrooms, with a finished upstairs loft. It is fully furnished and it is located on five acres of beautiful wooded land that is fenced around the edges of the property, which backs onto a small forest. It is a very private location. This sounds amazing, too bad there isn't a picture of it?"

"Hmm? There isn't, that's strange. Oh well, we are almost there." Adriano smiles privately to himself.

They drive into the long private driveway. Right away their eyes move to the two tall twin towers on each side of the house. "Spectacular! This looks like a miniature castle!" cries Rebecca. Everyone is in awe, and Adam and Ethan are shocked to see such a beautiful home. They all exit the car and in their excitement Rebecca and Juliette move a little too quickly; Adriano grabs Rebecca gently but firmly and Sebastien holds onto Juliette's arm. Both female vampires realize what has happened and Rebecca sees Adam and Ethan just staring at them, looking dazed.

Adriano quickly speaks to distract everyone. "Look at how tall this is, Adam and Ethan, this is a huge playground for you!"

"Let's go inside, Mommy."

"Yes, once Richard comes out from his car to open the front door."

Richard exits the car and walks towards everyone. "Hi everyone, isn't this one a beauty! Let's go check it out."

As Richard unlocks the two large black double doors everyone walks in and can't help but gasp. The large foyer makes such an impression, with its cathedral ceilings that are highlighted by the beautiful array of light bouncing off from the stained-glass window feature to the left side. Then they all step on the warm dark hardwood floors. The focus of Rebecca's attention is drawn to a tall antique grand-father clock resting in the corner. Rebecca is so captivated by this rare antique and is thrilled to learn from Richard that all furniture and pieces are part of the sale.

Adam and Ethan run up ahead exploring. The vampires walk around the main floor. The same dark-stained flooring carries all through the main floor. They notice a staircase and look up and see the beautiful wraparound staircase. They move across the hall and to their left they see French doors and open them and discover an intimate living room. They open another door which leads them to a large dining room. They now walk back to the hall and to their right there is a door, and they see the powder room and another door leads them to a laundry room which leads to the double garage.

They move back into the hall and further in and walk into the family room with a built-in wall to wall bookcase and gas fireplace. From there they see the kitchen with white cabinets and white older appliances. Richard leads them to another door where they enter a small den. Rebecca is in heaven with all these rooms and large windows bringing in great light. She always wanted a house with all kinds of rooms. They climb slowly up the stairs, Rebecca and Juliette much more mindful now of their movements. There is a small landing area where a small wing chair is placed, and they climb past it up to the second level and walk around the spacious wraparound hallway and start entering the five bedrooms one at a time. They meet up with Adam and Ethan who have great big smiles over their faces, they are so excited running around into each room. They see a tall window located at the back of the hallway that looks over the front of the house. Adriano and Sebastien notice some of the bedroom windows are drafty and will need to be replaced, but the rooms are spacious with large enough closets and the master and two other bedrooms have their own en suites. The convenience of all these washrooms is very appealing to the vampires.

Adriano inspects them carefully. "However, the washroom cabinets are old and some of the hinges are loose. Hmm... The faucets are old too and need replacing."

"But I think overall it is just perfect!" Rebecca cries in joy.

Richard leads them to another set of stairs and they are pleasantly surprised to see the very spacious vaulted ceiling loft. He takes them through the two rooms on opposite sides of the house which are the towers. These two rooms are spacious enough to fit twin beds in each if they want. The windows in the main area of the loft are large so you can into the backyard and into the woods. Rebecca is already feeling at home in this house. They all move back down and descend to a semi-finished basement. There is one half-finished bedroom and a rough bathroom. The rest of the basement is spacious enough for a TV room.

"I love it!" cries Rebecca. "So much room for everyone." Her sons are already running around laughing commenting on how much room they have.

"Me too! I love the wraparound the porch outside," shouts Sebastien enthusiastically.

"There is a really warm and welcoming energy—I could call this a home," comments Juliette calmly.

They spend a few minutes more in the driveway just discussing. Richard asks if they might be interested enough to make an offer. Rebecca and Juliette can't contain their enthusiasm further, and speak simultaneously.

"I want this one!"

They all laugh.

"I know there is some fixing up to do, but we can do that in time. Adriano, this one just speaks to me! It is perfect for all of us."

Adriano chuckles. "I thought you might be drawn to this last one—that is why I removed the picture on the listing. It has style reminiscent of old Victorian, great character, and seems to be solid in structure."

"What do you guys think? It's amazing, right?"

"It's private that's important. Plenty of animals for us. Don't you think Hazel Eyes?" shouts Sebastien, then he realizes what he said and tries to correct himself. "I mean for us to admire, I love rabbits—nature that is, the trees, rocks." He is stumbling over his words, suddenly feeling very self-conscious, but Richard isn't picking up on anything odd and just agrees that they are surrounded with a great atmosphere of nature before looking at his phone. Adriano can't help but smirk, shaking his head, then he gives Sebastien a look that cautions him to be careful. They all look over to Adam and Ethan but they are too busy running around and chasing each other to pay attention to the adults.

"So is it a yes?" inquires Richard.

"Yes!" simultaneously is heard from all the vampires.

"This is the beginning of a great chapter for all of us!" shouts Rebecca.

Suddenly Juliette's eyes fill with tears. *Oh Veneur, I wish you were here, this is a real home.*

Richard is busy a few steps away on the phone talking to his office and setting in motion a new chapter for the vampires.

It is now Saturday at four thirty p.m.; the temperature is dropping and it is dark outside. The vampires and Adam and Ethan are back at Rebecca's apartment. Rebecca orders pizza for the boys and Adriano drives Sebastien back into the nearby woods to hunt. Adriano has already privately filled Juliette in about vamprogeria, and she is starting to understand how very complex this disease is for Rebecca and Sebastien. She is glad she is here now to help with all of this. She feels again this was meant to be. She was meant to come to Toronto to help with Adam and Ethan and be a part of this vampire family. Juliette doesn't need to hunt at all for a few days.

Hours go by at Rebecca's apartment. All the vampires are anxiously waiting to hear back from Richard. Adriano and Sebastien return from hunting and Adriano takes Rebeca out. He wants some alone time with her, and this is a perfect excuse. Adam and Ethan don't like their mom leaving again but Aunt Juliette and Uncle Sebastien quickly resolve their worries. Fighting zombies was a task only Adam and Ethan could do with some help. They are feeling very comfortable already with their new European relatives Uncle Sebastien and Aunt Juliette, who likes to be called Aunt Jules, when they remember to. Juliette is especially and quickly attaching emotionally to these little humans in such a short amount of time. She never had siblings, so this new protective role as Aunt Juliette is the best role that she has ever taken on, willingly, heart and soul. Suddenly Sebastien's phone rings, it is Adriano calling from the woods, they got the call that they were hoping for. They can move in two weeks.

PART 2

Heart-brake

CHAPTER 24
Woodland Heights

A month has passed. It has been a hectic time for all the vampires, adjusting to their new surroundings, organizing new hunting schedules around Adam and Ethan, and just learning to live with each other and respect habits and space. They already booked contractors to come in and do some renovations and add some unique features that Rebecca dreamed of having one day. Rebecca decides that she wants to give their new home a name, and the vampires are happy to agree.

"It is an important symbol to all of us, this is our special sanctuary. I've been giving this a lot of thought, I want something that incorporates the twin towers and our beautiful wooded landscape. I've been channeling my love of nineteenth century Gothic literature," she giggles, "and I am thinking—Woodland Heights!"

From that moment on they live at Woodland Heights. Adriano and Sebastien surprise Rebecca and Juliette a few days later with a custom plaque showcasing *Woodland Heights,* and they install it on one of the outdoor brick columns at the entrance.

The memories of Paris and the events that took place are slowly fading away in the minds of each of the vampires, but not for Juliette. Juliette occasionally can still be heard crying in her room, missing her brother Veneur.

It is early Friday March 14. Juliette wakes up from her accustomed light sleep, but she is noticing that her sleep pattern is slowly becoming better. Her nightmares are decreasing in frequency. She isn't waking up daily in an anxious fearful and despairing state like she experienced living with Enzo. The loud obnoxious voices of Louisa and Enzo are beginning to fade into the deep recesses of her mind. But Veneur's voice too is starting to fade, and this disheartens her. Juliette sits down at her vanity table and looks into the mirror. She sometimes needs that self-reassurance that she is not Paula anymore. She sees her black and pink hair and not the bleach blonde and her self-identity is again restored to a healthy state; she knows she is Juliette Dubois.

She then walks around her room and into the closet and sees everything that she has chosen, the styles and colors of dresses, jeans, shirts, shoes, boots, scarves, and belts, and she closes her eyes and breathes peacefully, trying to hold onto this feeling. But even though she feels blessed that she is in Woodland Heights with Rebecca and Sebastien, now and again she still suffers states of sadness and longing for Veneur. At least in Paris in that dysfunctional negative home she had the joy and connection of Veneur around her, and that was worth all the suffering she endured. Now she is in a beautiful home filled with so much love and joy and new experiences and relationships, and she fights the spells of sadness that stalk her.

She is learning to live a life without Veneur in her daily routine. At times she is frustrated; she doesn't even know if any of her Mystery Man collection pieces sold that night at the art gallery. Then she thinks of the jewelry pieces that Veneur could not pack and were left behind in the bedroom. Now, she hasn't had any desire yet to create new pieces. Her heart is just not into it. But then she walks over to the built-in bookshelf in her new bedroom and sees the pet rocks and marbles displayed on her bookshelf, and all of the negative feelings she woke up to are fading. *Come on Jules, snap out of it, Veneur would not want to see you like this. You are blessed now, you can do anything you want. Let's try again to find that creative spirit.*

Juliette goes to the upstairs loft, hoping she can distract herself with painting. The house will soon be busy again with sounds of hammering, drilling and voices of crew men. The vampires are trying to live with this chaotic construction happening, but the dust and loud equipment noises are just hitting at their extra sensitive sensory systems. But they are excited for the new custom design and features to come.

An hour goes by, and Juliette is just playing with colors on the canvas, no real inspiration coming to her yet. She is just allowing her brushstrokes and blending techniques to guide her on this moment's attempt of creativity. It feels good to just do this action. Suddenly, Rebecca can be heard, her voice is raised in excitement, then she hears her calling out.

"Juliette, Juliette, Sebastien, come here—quickly." Juliette drops her brush and runs down the stairs at vampire speed, aware that Ethan and Adam are not with them today and the crewmen are not here yet.

"What is it Rebecca, is everything okay?" As Juliette approaches she can feel such joy and happiness absorbed all over Rebecca.

"Where's Sebastien?"

"He's out hunting, he should be back soon—you're so excited, I can feel it, what's going on?"

"I wanted to wait for Sebastien, however, this is really a surprise for you. Adriano forwarded me this, look."

Rebecca shows Juliette her cell phone and Juliette's dull grey eyes widen and the violet specks brighten along with her smile. The long-awaited picture from Veneur is received. Juliette is ecstatic to see the picture of small spotted rocks on the ground. She now knows that Veneur is okay, and she is hopeful he will find a way out. But she doesn't know how he will find her.

"Oh, Veneur, you're okay." Juliette can't take her eyes off the rocks. "He's okay, Rebecca!" Juliette is jubilant.

"Yes, I'm so glad. I will forward this to you. Now you should send him a pic through your own phone, that will truly shock him with joy."

"You think so?"

The other vampires have been teaching Juliette how to use these devices, since she was purposefully left in the dark, as instructed by Enzo, when it came to modern communications.

"Of course. He will know you are okay, that you have choices, you have your own phone!"

Juliette quickly runs into the backyard and into the woods and takes a picture. She sees Sebastien coming towards her, just returning from his hunt, his lips still stained with blood. Juliette greets him excitedly and shows him the picture from Veneur.

"Amazing. Wow, this picture code system really works. What are you sending him?"

Juliette shows Sebastien the picture she just took of a beautiful snow-covered oak tree and she sends it to Veneur. She feels so liberated and free, and it is registering strongly at this moment, not just the fact that she has her own cell phone and laptop, but this is her first reconnection to her brother Veneur.

Three more months have passed. It is late Friday night. Juliette is in her room. The house is quiet; the crewmen left a few hours ago. The renovations never seem to end. Sebastien is hunting with Rebecca. Adam and Ethan are at their father's house for his custody week. Adriano is not due to come over tonight, he is busy marking final exams. Juliette is in her room. She has been feeling off today, spells of unfamiliar feelings interrupting her day. She has been feeling this strange anticipation like something is about to happen, all day. She looks at the wall she has dedicated to various five by seven photos of rocks, trees, the moon, and the sun that were sent through text by Veneur over the past few months. Tonight, she just misses him more, something inside her is making her restless. She moves out of her room and walks through the wraparound hall and descends the dark stained hardwood floors staircase. She moves to the family room and flicks on the gas fireplace and turns on the TV; she just needs some distraction. She isn't due to hunt for another few days and she doesn't feel like strolling for leisure in their woods.

Suddenly, Juliette's cell notifies her she has a text. She picks up her cell and her eyes light up and she screams in shock and joy, "Veneur!" She reads the brief message.

Hi Jules,
I'm at an internet cafe. Call me, now. :)
V.

Juliette's hands are shaking, her mind racing, thinking, *is this true, we can actually talk?* She pushes the receiver icon and hears the rings, then Veneur's voice.

"Jules!"

"Ven, is it really you?" cries Juliette in bewilderment, hearing his voice.

"Yes, oh Jules, how good it is to hear your voice."

"How is this possible? Are you safe?"

"For now. I'm in the city, at a café—I've been wanting to do this a while now, but I had to make sure first that I found the right café and this is the one. The owner Eddie and I have become good friends."

"Friends? Human? Oh, Veneur that's dangerous!"

"Don't worry, I am careful."

"Does he know who you are?"

"No. It's okay. Never Mind that. How are you? You sound good."

"I'm good, really good. Oh, it's so good to hear your voice—I can't believe it. I've missed you so much." At that moment Juliette just wants to capture the sound of Veneur's voice and bottle it so she can protect the memory of it.

"I've missed you too. But hearing your voice, I know I did the right thing."

"How's Gabriel?"

"He's okay. We have become much closer. We really bonded after everything went down. We protect each other."

"Protect? Oh Ven, it is bad, isn't it? You're not safe?" Juliette's voice growing anxious.

"No, no, we're fine. Really. I just mean we are there for each other—I'm okay. Gabe and I have made some reasonable peace with Enzo. Well, at times anyways. He has really declined in his mobility. Hard to believe that is possible with our kind." Veneur is careful in choosing his words while sitting among humans in the café. He tries to stir the conversation away from the home situation. "I can't believe you have a cell phone."

"And a laptop!" cries out Juliette proudly.

"Cool. Are you happy Jules, are you being treated well?"

"I'm happy as can be. I miss you. But yes, I'm treated amazingly. I have two little humans that have taken my heart. Adam and Ethan, Rebecca's sons. I hope you can meet them one day. They truly have saved me."

"I'm glad. Maybe one day I will meet them." He reaches inside to pull out positive spirit; he can't let Juliette know just how devastated he is that he couldn't escape.

"Really, Ven? Is it possible?"

"I don't know. Things have changed here." His voice drops a little; he looks around, and he feels safe enough to continue. "Bianca is gaining some respect with Enzo's associates, that worries me and Gabe. She is feeling a sense of power and entitlement, more than usual. But Enzo is still Enzo, he is still in command. For now."

"For now? What do you mean?"

"Jules, it's complicated. Anyway, I don't want to waste this time talking about him."

"How are Martha and Guy, are they bringing you snacks of mice, like they did with me? I hope so."

Veneur doesn't respond right away, there is an awkward pause, Juliette can tell something is off. "No. They…" Veneur pauses again.

"Ven, what aren't you telling me?"

"Things have changed. The servants are—not with us anymore. Jules, you need to forget this place and all of them."

"But what about moth—Louisa?" Juliette's anxiety is rising as she for a split second felt odd saying the name Louisa and not mother.

"Why the hell would you want to ask about her?"

"Ven, she is still a part of me. I don't have hard feelings for her. She is just a troubled soul suffocating in grief. I don't blame her for anything."

"You're incredible."

"How is she?"

"She's Louisa. I don't want you to waste another moment ever thinking about her or this place. Please, move forward."

"I am trying, but I can't just erase my life before Woodland Heights."

"Yes, you can. Wait—Woodland Heights?"

"Yes, the house we live in. Rebecca named it."

"Cool, I like that. Tell me, is Canada as beautiful as I imagine?"

"What? Ven, is that safe to ask?"

"On the phone, yes." Veneur's curiosity is fighting his moments of frustration that he is still under Enzo's command."

"Yes. We live in a beautiful home, with a private wooded area in back. I hope one day you—"

"Jules, listen, I've got to go, but let's try and coordinate this time again on Fridays—if possible. But don't contact me. Ever. Unless I say it's okay. I will contact you first."

Juliette can sense sudden tension in Veneur's tone. "Ven, what's going on? Are you okay?"

"Sorry Jules, but I gotta go. I will contact you soon. Don't worry. Be well." Veneur disconnects before Juliette can even say goodbye. He can't believe he saw Bianca walking on the other side of the street. Of all the times for her to come to the city. His heart sinks. He knows now that he needs to stay in touch with Juliette. He needs to know there are these kind and caring vampires in his life, even if he can only connect through incognito communications. It's a matter of his own emotional wellbeing now. He quickly deletes the text message he sent to Juliette and locks the phone. He gives it to Eddie, who places it in the black computer bag hidden under the counter which also has Veneur's new password-protected laptop inside. He gives Eddie some money that he got from Gabriel and moves to the back of the café and into the washroom, where he slides the window over and squeezes out before moving the window back to closed.

Veneur cautiously moves through the alley and onto the busy Parisian street, his anxiety at high alert. He scans the area, making sure he is not being watched or followed by Bianca, vamps, roamers, or any of Enzo's associates. He suddenly stops abruptly and hides inside a store. He sees Bianca on the other side of the street now talking to someone in a private laneway between two buildings. His heart begins to race wandering if his instincts are right, this is a vamp. They both look very suspicious; she has her cell phone out and is showing it to the male vampire. Veneur is growing more worried. His eyes are glued on them and then he sees her quickly move down the street at human pace and disappears. This was a close call for Veneur. Confident and secure that he is safe again, he moves quickly into the woods and back to the house and sneaks back into his room.

The Canadian vampires spent a lot of the first year at Woodland Heights in dust and construction renovating the bathrooms, upgrading electrical and technical cables. They even spent money upgrading the windows all through the house so they were properly insulated. However, in the loft twin towers, the shared bedroom of Adam and Ethan, these windows were all strategically customized with textured glass because they looked out into the backyard and woods. Rebecca and the vampires did not want little eyes accidentally or curiously spying as the adults moved through the woods to hunt. They replaced the chain-link fence with a ten-inch wooden fence around the property. Rebecca and the other vampires made this thirty-six hundred square-foot home a peaceful and cozy sanctuary for all, but mostly she made it a special home for her two sons.

The relationship between Rebecca and her eclectic menagerie of souls, including humans and her lycan friend Lucan, has grown very tight over time. Rebecca sees Juliette now as her little sister. Rebecca manages obligations dealing with human family and relative relations, but over time it has become too complex and stressful for her and the other vampires at extended family dinner gatherings, and she has started to decline invitations. Over time, Rebecca and her vampire family have become frustrated and feeling guilty for having to continuously lie and make excuses about their strict diet. Rebecca tried at first to host dinners at her place, but that too was a challenge that left her exhausted at the end of the evening and the other vampires frazzled and anxious. These extended family dinners at Woodland Heights eventually stopped. Soon after, invitations dwindled, including ones for holiday gatherings. At first this upset Rebecca because one of her favorite social pastimes was to bake, cook, and entertain, and she missed this part of herself so much. She was hoping to regain that part of her, and now that she lived in this beautiful grand house that they had renovated and customized with the fully equipped spacious kitchen she had dreamed of for many years, and the old white appliances are now replaced with high-end black appliances with plenty of room for all her vampires, it was hard for her to push down this dream.

Rebecca did her best to make her vampire family feel at home and loved, and she felt so loved and cared for too. Rebecca formed a family tradition; on Saturday evenings when she didn't have her sons that week, she used her creative cooking skills and explored with various spices and created a variety of fresh butcher-cut raw meat recipes that would suit the vampire palette. And of course, there was never a lack of nuts, berries, and wine in this household; Sebastien made sure of that. Rebecca enjoyed cooking and baking for Jonathan, who would call ahead and drop in frequently to visit with Sebastien or stay over on weekends. Sandra would come over too, sometimes. On the weeks that her sons were there the house was even more exciting and joyous. They would all pile into the large SUV that they jointly purchased and take short family excursions that included visits to the science center or farmer's markets or cinemas. Adam and Ethan were happy and thrilled for these outings.

Dinners were still a challenging ordeal for Rebecca when her sons were staying over on her weeks. Rebecca would cook just for them as they did their homework, and she would then sit at the table with them but not eat. Rebecca was very attentive to her sons; she knew she had to be mindful that they were at a young and impressionable age; all the vampires had to be alert and cautious of their behaviour, movements, and hunting times when the boys were around. Rebecca was determined not to let her confidence dwindle as a mother and wanted to make this a special home for Adam and Ethan, despite the complexities around food and her unique health condition. Adam and Ethan's perspectives and observations were difficult and confusing for the boys at times, as they watched and observed strange occurrences and behaviors from their mother and their European uncle and aunt. But they kept it to themselves.

Rebecca has decided it is time to attempt to fuse dinner-time meals. She dreams of having complete family dinners for both her sons and her vampire family, but she has to slowly adjust her sons first to the unique food requirements of their mom and their European uncles and aunt. Rebecca sits them down at the kitchen table and tries to explain.

"You see, Adam and Ethan, in some countries, eating raw fish or certain meats is part of the custom, insects are a delicacy, or the intestines of animals is a cozy meal. And you might not want to try any of these and that is perfectly okay, but we must respect customs and different food choices of others. Adriano, your Uncle Sebastien, and your Aunt Juliette and I have certain dietary needs. Very different from anyone else. Our diet is not safe for anyone else, it will harm you—it is dangerous. Remember this, it is very important—promise me!"

"Yes Mommy," says Ethan. He's trying to stay focused, but his mind is imagining the disturbing image of eating insects.

"Don't worry, Mommy, we won't eat your food. I like cooked meat," Adam says like a little adult.

"Okay, so now I think we need to start having some real family dinners! What do you say? We have this beautiful large wooden table for all of us. Can we try to all sit at the table and eat together, even with our different foods?" She smiles warmly. The boys don't respond right away, they are both thinking.

Adam and Ethan look at each other and then nod their heads. "Okay Mommy, we can try. But why do you have to eat like them too? You never ate raw meat before. Is it because of your illness?"

Rebecca's heart wants to crumble in that instant, as she is asked a very direct and sincere question from her oldest son and all she can do is think of a lie to tell. Her spirit drops briefly. *How much lying can I allow myself?* She hesitates then, slowly choosing her words carefully.

"Yes, Adam, partly because of my illness. You see, some adult's taste buds change as they get older. It could mean they start to like vegetables, or fish, eel, or even snails—"

"Snails! Eels! Ewww!" cries out Adam and Ethan in disgust.

"The point is, my taste buds have also *changed*, and what I eat now keeps me healthy. I'm sorry if my new diet bothers you, I understand, really I do. Hmmm…maybe this isn't a good idea, I don't want to make you feel uncomfortable at the dinner table. We can find other ways to have family gatherings—you guys are more important!"

"It's okay Mommy, it's not that bad. Right Ethan? We can handle it!" Adam is signaling forcefully with his eyes to Ethan to agree.

"Uh huh, sure." Ethan's voice has slight trepidation. "But, I won't get used to eating snails or eels, ever!" he shouts.

"Okay, no eels or snails for Ethan!" Rebecca chuckles. She leans in and gathers her sons in her open arms and wraps them up tightly, snuggling them with kisses. "I love you both very much, you are growing up before my eyes!" Adam and Ethan smile from ear to ear, feeling so mature and secure in their mother's arms.

It takes a few trial dinners before Ethan and Adam are not losing their appetite, and the vampires are not so nervous eating in front of them, but eventually, Rebecca's dream to have family sit down dinners at their table happens, albeit dinner time is an unusual experience for Adam and Ethan. They sit beside one of their uncles or their aunt, whose eyes would become so bright, licking their lips as the dish of sliced raw meat in some kind of red gravy was placed on the table and passed around between the adults. Rebecca could see through the expressions on Adam and Ethan's face that their curiosity was running high in their young inquisitive minds. Their bright little eyes expressed to everyone that they knew something was very different about their mother and these adults who lived here. This made the vampires more self-conscious at times, keeping them alert and aware of their movements and words around the boys. Adam and Ethan became very observant and watched carefully to see what other strange behaviors they would encounter.

As quiet and stealthy as they could be, sometimes the late-night outings into the woods of the vampires were witnessed by the boys. Adam or Ethan would suddenly hear a noise or movement downstairs and one of them would wake the other one up. Quietly, with sleepy eyes, they would press their faces to the rain-textured window in their bedroom, struggling to peak out into their backyard as they reached as far as their inquisitive eyes could travel to see into the distance and entrance of the woods. They would wait patiently but with excitement and with awe, witnessing dark blurry shadows rise up very high into the air. Sometimes they could identify the blurry figure or figures by the sound of laughter or talking and they see someone leaping over the ten-foot fence just like superheroes with special gifts; and then they would be gone. The boys thought they had the coolest group of super humans on the planet, and knew this was a secret they must protect. They were observant to anything that had to do with their mom and the others. The fact that when it was winter or snowing or below zero, neither their mom or Adriano, nor their uncle Sebastien and aunt Juliette, wore scarves, hats, winter jackets, or mitts. They would return full of snow on them but feeling comfortable, without shivering. They never caught a cold. Adam and Ethan's imagination grew wild, and between the two they would entertain themselves privately competing to see who could come up with the wildest stories. Some involving crashed alien crafts that they found, or the adults got powers or secret rituals in empty caves that made these adults powerful.

Dinner at Woodland Heights became the Saturday evening tradition for Rebecca's vampire family. On some occasions, they would get a text from Veneur saying he was at the internet cafe and they would set up the laptop and skype with Veneur. Veneur got to know Adam and Ethan, and the boys enjoyed talking to another European uncle. They were mesmerized by his bright emerald eyes. When Grandpa Lucan came over for Saturday dinner, it was an even bigger treat for them, especially in the fall when Lucan would bring one of his collections of tents that he used when he was younger and hiking in the deep wilderness in the Rocky Mountains. Lucan would help the boys set it up in the backyard at Woodland Heights. After dinner, everyone would gather around the fire pit. The boys would be wrapped in their sleeping bags. Lucan knew he could never actually bring them out camping, because he couldn't trust the creature not emerging. And Rebecca would never agree to it. The tent was just for the atmosphere.

Lucan would share some of his own experiences of when he travelled through the Rockies, deep into the forest and bush. He told them about the types of grizzly bears and wolves that he saw, strategically leaving out the part about him purposefully hiking through the deep wilderness as a man knowing he could allow his altered state, Lupo, to emerge and run loose in the deep bush. Lucan also left out the part about Lupo attacking, killing, and eating the grizzly bear, and then waking up near the mangled bear corpse, vomiting violently at times.

The boys also enjoyed stories about traditional monsters like vampires, zombies, and werewolves; they took after their mom, interested in monster movies and ghosts. They loved to hear Grandpa Lucan's story about Lupo, the lone werewolf that hunted in the mountains. He used the term werewolf for the boys because he realized lycan was just not as scary to them. The boys were fascinated, asking all kinds of questions. They wanted to know how to become a werewolf and Grandpa Lucan obliged to explain.

"You know, Adam and Ethan, to become a werewolf you have to be scratched by it. You won't survive their bite, because they will grab you in their powerful jaws and start eating you, before you try to even run!" At that point Grandpa Lucan would tickle them, then he would put on his serious low voice and they would-be wide-eyed listening, keeping their sleeping bags tightly wrapped up close to their faces. "But if you are scratched by one, then their lycan blood —I mean werewolf blood, travels into your body, and at the first full moon you become a werewolf." Then he would howl into the air. The boys would get startled at first, because the sound coming through Lucan's throat seemed so authentic; it even startled he vampires, making them nervous. Then Lucan would laugh and slowly the others would laugh too. The vampires listened and enjoyed watching the expressions of pure amazement, wonder, and awe on the boys faces. Even Rebecca couldn't help but treasure these moments, but she knew one day she wanted her boys to know the truth; it was important for her to die with them knowing how much they were loved by not just their human family, but also their family of vampires and lycan. These were not monsters, but loving caring souls. Rebecca felt strongly that she wanted to teach her boys how to open their minds to all kinds of different cultures, customs, and people. But she also needed to make sure to teach them to be wise and careful of those who pretend to be kind but have bad intentions.

Over time, the boys were becoming very cultured, and their minds were expanding. They were very observant and knew when something was not quite right with their mom. At times, they saw their mother's physical appearance change, and this alarmed them. She suddenly became very pale, her voice low and sounding weak, her vibrant eyes fading in color. In those odd moments she would not want them to go near her or hug her. It hurt the boys so much when she gently pushed them away from her. Rebecca's heart broke when she had to do this, but she was always in control of her thirst. The boys were alarmed and they would quickly call out for one of the adults, and in a blink of an eye their aunt Jules would be in the room suddenly, or uncle Sebastien or Adriano, and the boys would not even hear their footsteps, they just *appeared.*

A small commotion would unfold and they could see fear and anxiety on the adult's faces, and an adult would call out to whichever other adult was in the house and they would rush in quickly, leaving bewilderment on Adam and Ethan's faces seeing these adults move at such extraordinary speed. One of them would stay with the boys, usually Juliette, and she would distract them while the other carefully, trying to be nonchalant, rushed Rebecca out into the backyard, saying to Adam and Ethan as they rushed by them in a flash, "Your mommy just needs some fresh air. She'll be fine, not to worry!"

These moments would frazzle Sebastien mostly, because he knew one day he would be in this situation, but he was a bit alarmed and frustrated that Rebecca was moving so much more quickly down this dangerous path. He didn't know if it was just an occasional event happening or if vamprogeria was moving at a rapid alarming pace for her. It was too soon, she hadn't been a vampire that long.

Rebecca was still close to her parents, and would invite them over when she had her sons, but it was just for a coffee; thankfully they were still healthy and had their own social network to keep them busy.

Rebecca quit the university a year after returning to Toronto. It was the right move to make because the commute and daily complexity around her unique health conditions was creating great stress to her and the others.

Adriano believed that he had said goodbye to Paris for good. He never desired to revisit Italy either, or his hometown in Sicily. He just couldn't separate at times the loving memories of his mother, sister Maria, and brother Giacomo, with the abuse from his father Massimo and the horror of Domenico. He struggled to put away and lock up disturbing memories. He carried fragmented remnants of those he loved, and he willed as best as he could those beautiful memories to stay in his heart and remind him that he was human at one time. He missed Giacomo and Maria so much, but somehow without realizing it Juliette found herself becoming at times like an older version of Adriano's little sister Maria.

Friday night to Sunday night life, at Woodland Heights was a different pace. Either all were gathered around in the grand family room watching a movie, or listening to Sebastien play the piano, mostly just relaxing and connecting. Sebastien healed his broken heart and accepted that he would never have a visit from James again. But as hard as it was, at times he would find himself calling out in the dark late at night in his room, when he was alone. Sebastien needed to focus on something important, and through one of Sandra's colleague connections, he got a part-time job in the pathology lab at the Brampton Memorial hospital.

CHAPTER 25

Change

R ebecca opens her sleepy eyes, her mind still waking from its dreamy state. She feels a bit foggy in her thoughts this morning; she stretches and, in a few seconds, more her mind becomes clear of the cobwebs. She slowly makes her way out of her warm bed; she doesn't feel much rested this morning. She had another restless night of tossing and turning in bed and her thoughts are racing about everything and nothing.

She drank enough from the fox she hunted last night before bed, but her thoughts just prevented her from a peaceful sleep. She looks at her side table clock, it reads Saturday October 26, 8:29am. The house seems quiet; she remembers this is her week without her sons, then she hears one of her favorite sounds echoing throughout the house, the treasured grandfather clock that Juliette surprised Rebecca with when they moved in. She had the clock mechanism fixed and she restained the wooden body herself. Rebecca loves this clock; it is a beautiful tall antique piece that is showcased in the hallway on the main floor. When you step foot into the house, the quiet unobtrusive sound of the pendulum moving back and forth welcomes you to Woodland Heights.

Rebecca slowly makes her way to the bathroom, trying to wake up more, and takes her shower and gets dressed for the day. She is aware that her physical state is not doing well. The last couple of years she has noticed more moments or spells of fatigue, especially in the early morning, when she has gone a few hours without drinking. She has also noticed her memory is beginning to change; she has experienced alarming moments where she finds herself in a room in the house and cannot remember why she is there. This frightens her. She remembers Sebastien sharing the symptoms that James experienced in the last few years of his life. She hasn't shared how she is feeling with anyone; she knows that there is enough lingering stress and worry as all the vampires, especially Juliette, wait for the day that Veneur will finally be able to join them. Rebecca tries to be grateful for the years she has had with her vampire family and especially her sons. Life at Woodland Heights has become a daily rhythm of connection, survival, and appreciation between all these vampires.

This is a crisp bright October morning. She leisurely enters the quiet woods and has a successful hunt, returns to the house, and washes up. She walks upstairs to the loft; the room is bright with the large textured glass windows. There is a long sectional couch and coffee table in the center. There is wall to wall bookshelves all over the room. They are filled with Sebastien's new collection of medical and science textbooks, history books, and all kinds of philosophy books. Rebecca too has a bookcase, dedicated to her fictional classics and modern novels, and Adam and Ethan have their own shelves with their books. A section of the large loft has become a library for all the vampires. Sebastien settled on the left-side tower and made that his painting room. Juliette has a spacious room carved out from the large loft and has it set up for her jewelry and painting. Rebecca made the right-side tower her creative room.

She walks into her creative room, sits at her desk, and turns on her desktop. Rebecca hears movements coming from Juliette's room, and then Sebastien's.

Moments later, Sebastien is at her door. "Hey, Hazel Eyes, are you coming?" Sebastien smiles.

"Sorry, I went earlier, just one of those spells."

"Was it that bad?"

"Not what you may be thinking. I feel good now. But you should go. I'll prepare a snack."

"You know if it gets that bad, you should tell me; you shouldn't go out on your own in that condition." Sebastien's voice rising.

"I'm okay, Sebastien. Relax. I was just feeling low energy, nothing that serious, but I know everyone worries and panics. I just want to avoid that, when I can."

"I know. It is not easy for both of us. But this is why you asked me to live with you, remember, we look after each other."

"I know. But I feel my condition has made it hard on you, especially."

"What? Why would you think that?"

"Sebastien, I know you would have preferred to live with Jonathan, and I feel I've stopped you."

"What in the world gave you that idea? Did someone say something to you? Did Adriano say something?"

"No, no. I just noticed that Jonathan doesn't come here as often anymore on weekends. He used to come and stay almost every weekend, and now he only comes maybe once a month, if that?"

"Jonathan and I are dealing with some things. We both understand that his job consumes his time; ever since he became a detective, a lot has changed. He needs to work it out. Right now, his cases fill up his time. I'm enjoying being back in the lab. It was different with James, we both shared this interest, so our work time blended in with leisure. Jonathan sometimes is away on a case for days. I don't hear from him as often. That is because of his job. It has affected us, but I'm sure we'll work it through. As they say, distance helps the heart grow fonder."

Sebastien is feeling fatigued. Rebecca notices as Juliette arrives at the entrance.

"Good morning both of you." Juliette becomes concerned. "Oh Sebastien, I think you need to go."

"Yes, just leaving."

"Do you want company?"

"I'm fine. See you both in a bit. Hazel Eyes, don't worry, okay." Sebastien quickly moves down the two sets of stairs and moves to the back door.

Soon Juliette and Rebecca look through the textured window and see the blurry figure of Sebastien leaping over the fence and vanishing into the woods.

"Is everything okay? I sense tension between you and Sebastien."

"Oh, no, we're okay. If he's calling me Hazel Eyes, I know we are okay." Rebecca grins, but she feels restless this morning, she can't find her creative space right now. "Let's go downstairs, I'll fix us a snack and we can just chill, since it's Saturday."

"I will be down shortly."

Rebecca leaves the loft and calmly descends each set of stairs, always trying to move at human pace; it conserves her energy more. Her eyes glance at the niche carved in the wall, shaped with gothic style arches. Inside the niche is a beautiful delicate glass rose, stained a deep and showcased by the built-in lighting shining down from the top of the niche. She tries every day to be grateful for the life she has now. This home is her sanctuary. She doesn't feel she is missing out on anything. She has no desire to travel out of Ontario anymore. Her health just makes it too complicated. She feels she has experienced enough with the small one- or two-day excursions with the vampires and her sons over the years. But lately she feels uncertain about the future. Her sons are in the middle of their teenage angst years. It has been a challenge, and she worries at times what road they will take.

Rebecca walks into the large family room. The gas fireplace is already on, and Rebecca puts on one of her albums. She goes to the kitchen, opens up the fridge, and pulls out the bowl of mixed berries. She prepares a little snack for herself, Sebastien, and Juliette, and fills three glasses of Pinot Noir. Placing them on a tray, she sets the tray on the large wooden coffee table in the family room and takes a seat at the large sectional couch. Moments later Juliette enters the family room and picks up a glass of wine and some berries. She takes a seat next to Rebecca. Seeing that Rebecca just starting at her wine, she turns to Rebecca.

"You're deep in thought. Is everything okay?"

"I'm just off this morning, you know, one of those days."

"What's troubling you?"

Rebecca takes a sip of wine, getting more comfortable on the couch. "I feel like things are changing—I know they have to, but it can be unsettling."

"What's changing?"

Rebecca doesn't respond right away, she takes a sip of her wine. "Me, I'm changing, I can feel it. It worries me."

Juliette puts her wine glass down on the coffee table and moves in closer to Rebecca, taking her hand. "Rebecca, you know we are all here for you and Sebastien. Talk to me. What are you feeling?"

"I don't know how to describe it. It's like suddenly I'm not me. I look at my reflection in the mirror and I feel like I'm seeing a stranger sometimes. It's like I don't feel comfortable in my own body. I suspect this is a symptom of vamprogeria. I'm worried for my boys, they are so unaware of what lies ahead, I just want them to be prepared for life."

"Hey, your sons will be okay—they're surrounded by people who love them."

"I know, but life is moving fast. I promised myself one day I would tell them my story, I feel it strongly as they are getting older."

Just then they hear Sebastien enter and he quickly moves upstairs to shower. Juliette takes a sip of her wine. "Are you sure this is what you really want to do? Even Veneur has talked about telling his truth. He wants to write a book someday. Why do you both feel this need to reveal who you are to the world? It can be dangerous."

"Juliette, don't you want to live your truth freely outwardly?"

"Not everything needs to be revealed. As long as I accept me and my family does, that is all I need. I don't need to post my personal life out there. I don't see the interest or pleasure in some of these social media platforms. I find they are creating self-centred humans. They want to be noticed for unremarkable things sometimes. I don't know, I don't see the interest in taking hundreds of selfies and posting them. 'Look at me, look at me, eating this hamburger. Look at me at the nightclub'—really, does anyone care?"

Rebecca laughs. "I know, it can be a bit much, that's not us. But to each their own. It's not hurting anyone. Social media does have its advantages if used properly. The world can become smaller in a good way when there is mass mourning. For example, messages of love and peace are sent across the world in times of tragedy. That is beautiful."

"Yes, I understand that, and agree."

"I want my story to be out there for other vampires to know they can choose the right path. It breaks my heart knowing that there are vampires out there who are really alone. You and Veneur have opened my eyes. Especially when Veneur tells us about some of the abandoned vampires he has come across over the years. It's hard to stomach it sometimes. We are so lucky to have a home, a family; a loving one, that is."

"I know."

"Juliette, what if one day you meet someone, fall in love, possibly with a human? You can't keep this secret, it won't work. Adriano tried to hide it from me when we were dating, and it didn't work. Starting off a relationship with secrets is not healthy."

"I feel that is not in my destiny."

"What? Don't say that, you have your whole life ahead of you. You are beautiful and kind and fun, of course you will meet someone."

"Thanks Rebecca. But I'm happy just like this. Life is complicated enough." Juliette takes a sip of wine.

"That it is." Rebecca sips her wine, deep in thought, sighing heavily.

"What else is bothering you? You seem really pulled down today."

"Sorry Juliette, I'm trying not to bring you into these feelings."

"No, it's okay, I can handle it. Don't apologize. I just want to help. Is it the vamprogeria?"

"Not directly, at least I don't think so. I don't know. I just keep wondering if I'm doing the right thing for my sons. Lying to them, it bothers me. I just worry I may never have the opportunity to tell them the truth. I just don't know how long I have. It's just never the right time, it seems. I know they are growing up fast."

"Hey Rebecca, you still have many years ahead. You need to stop thinking about this so much, you are just having a few rough days. It will pass."

"Maybe." Rebecca swirls the wine in her glass, deep in thought. "I need to get out of my head. But Adriano kind of threw me a curve ball a few days ago."

"What do you mean?"

"He is thinking of leaving the university."

"Really? Why?"

"He's got this idea he wants to open up his own theatre company. Make it a family business."

"Wow, that's pretty adventurous."

"I know. I mean, I think it would be great for him, but there is just so much involved with opening up a new company, and a theatre company would take up so much time. I want him to pursue this but I just don't know if this is the right time for such a change. And then I feel guilty for thinking this. Again, I feel like my condition is directing everyone else's life."

"That's not true. Your disease hasn't stopped us from anything. What makes you think it has?"

"Funny you say, that Sebastien said the same thing."

"Well we are telling you the truth. We are a family and you created this family. Sebastien and I would not be here in this home, if it wasn't for you—don't forget that. Your disease did not direct me here. Your friendship, understanding, concern, and love helps me have the life I have now."

Just then Sebastien walks in. The room is silent suddenly.

"Hey, you both look so serious?"

"Look at you, so refreshed—good hunt?" comments Juliette, trying to distract.

"Yup. What are you two up to?"

Rebecca internally shakes her moodiness away. "Not much, just enjoying a leisurely Saturday. Adriano is off to visit Lucan."

"Oh, that's nice. I noticed he hasn't been here in a bit?"

"Adriano? What are you talking about?"

"No, I mean Lucan."

"Yeah, he hasn't been feeling too good lately, so he prefers to be home."

"Oh, when you mean not feeling good—do you mean his condition?"

"Yes, he is struggling a bit with it lately. He knows it is dangerous so he's staying home."

"Wise choice. But I hope he will be okay." Sebastien takes a sip of wine. "Is it safe for Adriano?"

"Yes, Lucan showed Adriano what to do—don't forget Lucan has that secure room."

"True. But I wouldn't want to be at that house if he was changing." Sebastien looks at Rebecca. "Why are you looking at me like that?"

Rebecca grins. "It's nice to know that you care for Adriano."

"Yeah yeah, don't read too much into it—he's still hot-headed sometimes and intense." Sebastien smiles mischievously and takes a sip of wine.

"Oh, come on, admit it, he's grown on you."

"No comment." Sebastien sips his wine, his eyes twinkling playfully.

Rebecca throws a cushion pillow at him.

"Hey, you nut, you almost made me spill the wine!" Sebastien laughs and he puts the wine glass down on the coffee table to pick up some berries, and suddenly two more cushions come at him and both Juliette and Rebecca pounce on him playfully. Sebastien tries to grab a pillow to fight back. The room is filled with warmth and joy once again.

CHAPTER 26

Corpse Blood

everal more years have passed. It is now the beginning of June, and life at Woodland Heights is busy. Adam and Ethan are absorbed in their rhythm and blues band, and receive the exciting news while they are at their father's house that their group is one of the groups chosen to take part in a competition in Paris. Adam is so excited to call his mom and tell her the great news and is happy he reaches her.

"That's fantastic, congratulations to you both. Wait—did you say Paris? Yes, I do think that's really cool, it's just that Paris is—so far. I know this means a lot to both of you—of course I'm excited for both of you! Don't get upset, I just need to think about this—I know you're adults!" Rebecca is struggling to keep her voice level and calm; she feels her blood rushing down to her feet, and she is getting dizzy. "Adam, I do trust you! But neither of you have travelled on your own—that far! Listen, stop yelling. And I worry because—I will always worry about you and Ethan! It's a mother's prerogative! I would feel better if Adriano or one of your uncles could go too—I know you don't need chaperones, but you know I can't travel that far by plane or I would be there. Your dad can't go, so at least if Adriano could join you guys, you would have a family member there to support you, cheer you on! Oh, none of your friends' parents are going either? Umm, well, I would still feel better if you both had someone there. Adam, I'm not treating you like a baby!" Rebecca takes a deep breath and sighs. "Okay, let's calm down, we can discuss this later, okay? We will. I love you—okay, talk later, bye." She sighs heavily again and immediately calls Adriano, leaving a frantic message. "Call me ASAP! It's about the boys— they are going to Paris with their band, and I can't stop them. What lie could I possibly tell them? Oh, please call me back as soon as you get this"

It is Thursday, July sixteenth, six pm. Adriano has just been dropped off to the airport by Rebecca, Juliette, and Sebastien. Adriano is taking his luggage from the trunk. A few minutes later they see Lucan stepping out of a taxi with his cane, and he retrieves his luggage from the trunk of the taxi. Adriano can't risk bringing Sebastien along on this trip, as it would be too complicated to manage his feeding needs, so he asked Lucan if he wouldn't mind coming, just to keep an eye on things.

Both Ethan and Adam finally agreed to this arrangement, however they insisted that they would fly out a day earlier, so they could have a chance to explore Paris on their own for at least a day or two. Rebecca understands that her sons are at the age where they need to experience life and its challenges, to make their own mistakes. Rebecca knows she won't always be there to protect them, that some things are just out of her control. Adriano reassured Rebecca when he booked the tickets that he and Lucan would be on the next flight available after the boys, so at least there isn't too much unguarded time, and that Ethan and Adam didn't need to know this arrangement. Adriano, Rebecca, and Juliette wave to Lucan, who is now approaching to greet his friends. By eight Adriano and Lucan are in the air en route to Paris.

During the plane ride, Adriano learns from Lucan that Nathan has left. "I knew this day was coming, I'm grateful he stayed with me this long. I thought maybe I would hear from him, but maybe it's just as well; better he just moves on with his life, he sacrificed a lot of years dealing with me and *this* condition."

Adriano is surprised to hear about Nathan. He feels so bad for Lucan, and is trying to express his empathy but having to whisper. Since the close proximity of other passengers makes it challenging for him to carry on this important conversation, he chooses his words carefully. "How do you manage *things?*"

"It has taken some adjusting, I admit, but I am doing the best I can." Lucan pauses in thought, then shares a little bit more in a whisper. "I've made some adjustments to the setup at my home so it is even more secure." Lucan looks around to see if anyone is paying attention, then he leans in closer to Adriano, who gets a strong whiff of a wet dog smell, but over the years he has learned to not be strongly averted to it, it just itches his nose a bit now. "I don't know if I ever told you this, but before Nathan came along, I was experimenting already on my own with that room. I was quite curious in the earlier days. I was deep in experimentation but, of course, made some big mistakes." He smirked slightly. "Eventually I discovered which tools and materials would be most suitable to secure the space for *Lupo.*"

Adriano is truly amazed how Lucan is able to separate his own identity into two distinct living things, and he immediately references privately to himself, *Like Dr. Jekyll and Mr. Hyde.* "My God that must have been traumatizing. How did you cope? I mean mentally, emotionally?" His eyes widen with curiosity and bewilderment. Adriano's relationship to Lucan has grown close over the years. At times, Adriano just felt overwhelmed, as if the whole world was on his shoulders. Even though the vampires are very independent and self-sufficient, Adriano feels this responsibility to keep everyone safe.

Lucan continues. "I felt like a scientist at times; I managed to record some sessions, but unfortunately the first few recordings did not survive in the room. I'm sure you can imagine the chaotic scene that unfolded when *he* emerged and discovered he was trapped." He is holding back chuckles. "Now I can laugh about it, but back then, it was so frustrating! There was so much damage in those first few sessions." He leans back in his seat, getting more comfortable, his mind travelling back in time. "I was so naive and inexperienced on how and what to keep in that room. The blanket and clothes left for *me* later were torn to shreds, the piece of meat left for *him,*" obviously eaten, but wasn't satisfying enough, and he must have been frustrated and felt trapped and confused. The walls in that room were severely scratched and damaged, the ceiling light was ripped off its hinges, and there was glass all over the floor. The wall clock was smashed into pieces, too. It was quite troubling to see such destruction. It was very challenging and unsettling." Adriano just sits in his seat listening, observing, admiring Lucan's mental strength, as the lycan carries on. "Then I came up with the idea to record Lupo in his natural state. I have to say that this opened up a whole new insight for me." Lucan again leans in closer to Adriano, whispering deep into Adriano's ear, "Imagine, I could see the transformation that took place from each disturbing, terrifying, and painful stage, every detail all recorded for me to watch over and over and study, and from there I learned how to keep that room and what to keep for him." Lucan speaks calmly, with pride and confidence. "My son, it is devastating, of course; I thought I was in a parallel universe. Oh, it was the most surreal out of body, out of mind experience, watching these recordings. Seeing myself disappear, and *him* emerging, then myself returning again."

"I can't imagine, Lucan; that would be so unbelievably alarming, frightening. I admire how you have handled this all these years."

"Thank you. You can imagine, once Nathan came along and accepted the situation and came on as my assistant, it felt like the first time I could breathe. I wasn't alone in this nightmare. I started to have a new perspective, thanks to Nathan. He really was one of a kind. I was getting spoiled, I became very used to not having to worry as much about certain security features, since he was handling it all." Lucan can't help but sigh heavily suddenly. Leaning back in his seat, he keeps his voice at a whisper. "So now, it's just a matter of programming myself again. I just have to be a lot more alert with my condition, pay more attention to my body, my mind, you know, anything stirring inside."

"I am concerned with you being on your own now that Nathan is gone. How do you manage everyday life, necessities, shopping?"

"Oh, don't worry about me—it's not like I'm an old man. That's years away. I have my groceries ordered in, basically whatever I need, supplies included. I buy it all online. It's quite convenient. I practice yoga and meditation every day; I have cut down my work travels, though. "

"My concern is, I don't want you to be lonely."

"Loneliness and being alone are two different things. I keep myself busy. I still have my private piano lessons; I need music and piano in my life, even if I am more of a teacher than a player." Lucan lifts up his hands that are gloved to keep them warm.

"Well you know you have us. I'm sorry I haven't visited in a while. Rebecca and I have discussed many times the idea that you should move closer to us. Would you consider this? I'm sure we could find a property suitable for you."

"Oh, thank you, but I can't imagine moving. All that stress would inflame the situation further. And don't forget, I would have to have contractors come in again and rebuild that set-up. Too complicated. I was already paying them a bonus just to keep them quiet, their suspicions, you know. No—no, I'm fine where I am. I'm so grateful I have you, and Rebecca and the others, you're my family. Thank you for asking me to come, it is nice to feel needed."

Adriano senses a bit of loneliness in Lucan's tone as much as Lucan was trying to hide it. "Of course, you are needed."

Lucan smiles and returns to his book, but something isn't sitting right with Adriano. He waits a minute to see, then he notices from the corner of his eye that Lucan is pretending to be absorbed in his book, but this isn't the case. Adriano inquires, "Lucan, is something bothering you? I noticed you have been reading the same page for quite a while now."

Lucan doesn't respond immediately; he closes the book and leans back in his seat, fidgeting a little. Adriano sees the worry forming in Lucan's eyes. Lucan turns to Adriano.

"I'm just a little tired lately, some new aches, pains, could be arthritis. Enough about me, this is exhausting to think about. Please, let's change the subject. Oh —I did want to ask you, if you don't mind—is everything okay with Rebecca? She looked a bit frail today."

"We are keeping an eye on this," he whispers. "She is very careful to drink regularly, but sometimes the fatigue gets in the way, making it difficult for her to *go out.*"

"Well, surely, you and the others can help with that?"

"Yes, of course, and they do, we all do. But Rebecca is very independent and stubborn. She is afraid to let go, she wants to stay independent, find her own *food*."

"Tell me Adriano, do you really think Bianca is still a threat? Has Veneur said something to make you feel concerned?"

"No, but Rebecca could not let her sons go to Paris on their own. Bianca is still around. Look how many years have passed, and Veneur still hasn't felt safe enough to leave. Imagine that. I've arranged to meet with him. Maybe I can convince him to leave."

"Oh, are you sure about this? Meeting Veneur could be risky."

"I have to try. This is crazy that he is still here. I wish I could just go to the house and have it out with Enzo and Bianca."

"Oh, that would be very risky. We would need a plan, we can't just knock at the door, and we surely can't sneak up on *them*. How would you even sneak up on a—" Lucan suddenly stops; he caught himself, his eyes aware of the glances of a curious passenger in the seat across from him. Lucan leans over, whispering ever so quietly, choosing his words carefully, "that type of *person*."

"I have one idea that crossed my mind recently, I heard about it actually from Sebastien years ago. We'll talk later." Adriano's eyes gesture that there are too many ears around. "Let's get some rest, I'm actually very tired." Lucan agrees and they both close their eyes. Adriano can't help worrying now about Lucan and his health.

It is Friday July seventeenth in the early morning; both Lucan and Adriano arrive at the hotel and quickly drop off their bags. Adriano texts Rebecca, letting her know they have arrived and that they are just heading out to the woods, he needs a quick thirst quench. They reach deep into the woods, and Lucan remembers about the plan Adriano mentioned earlier.

"By the way, let's talk about that plan you had." Lucan is leaning his back against a tree resting his aching body, holding his cane in front to support part of his weight. Adriano observes carefully and he realizes Lucan has aged further the last two years. Lucan wants to believe he is still young enough, but his body is fighting the reality, even his powerful lycan genes that have kept him from aging at the speed of a human all these years are now failing him.

"Right, so apparently vampires can be subdued with corpse blood— actually, they can die if they drink too much of it."

"What?" Lucan thinks he heard incorrectly.

"Yeah, crazy, corpse blood can kill a vampire."

"You mean blood from a dead body? How do you know this?"

"Sebastien's partner James wrote about it in his journal. Long story, but the main thing is that this might just work. But how do we get corpse blood to begin with, then how do we get Domenico or Bianca or both to drink it?"

"Tell me something, honestly."

"Okay."

"Are you hoping to find them to warn them, subdue them only? Or are you planning to kill them if you find them?" Lucan's tone sounds fatherly.

Adriano doesn't respond immediately, he looks at Lucan with a puzzled expression on his face. "Why the hell would you ask that?" Adriano realizes his outburst and quickly regrets the tone he used.

"They are significant to your life, whether or not you choose to accept this."

"No they aren't! They're nothing to me."

"I don't mean to upset you. But I'm afraid you are wrong, my son, they are significant. Domenico made you and you made Bianca. That is a significant bond that ties you three together, by blood." Lucan still has both hands on his cane while leaning against the tree.

"They are not my blood. I refuse to accept this."

"That's just it. You refuse to accept it, but your mind and heart know what I'm saying is true. I know you don't like it! Adriano, I've been around you a long time now. I know the heart you have. I know you have a good conscious and a loving soul. You struggle internally with the humans you have killed; as bad as they were, you still feel it after."

"No I don't."

"Oh, Adriano my son, you can't fool me. I'm just worried about your conscience, it is one thing to kill strangers and justify it for the cruel evil deeds they inflicted on innocent ones. But, my son, it is another thing to kill blood that binds you."

"Our blood does not blind me to them."

"Okay, I can see this is upsetting you. I'm just going to ask one thing." Lucan walks over to Adriano and sits beside him on the rock. "Are you sure you are prepared to hunt them down and kill them without any present threat to justify the kill? For all you know, Enzo may have changed; even Bianca may have found remorse within. Can you really just kill them without knowing where their hearts are?"

Adriano is struck by the insight Lucan has into Adriano's private feelings. He is touched, but at the same time he feels emotionally exposed. He looks directly into Lucan's warm and caring grey eyes; they are filled with wisdom, and a heavy sigh escapes Adriano. "If they had changed, Veneur would be home at Woodland Heights. Vampires wouldn't have died."

"What?"

Adriano lets out a heavy sigh. "I promised Veneur I wouldn't say anything, especially to Juliette. This stays between me and you."

"Of course, but what is it?"

"A couple of years ago Bianca had Louisa and her vampire son Pietro murdered."

"What? How?"

"Veneur suspects that Bianca made a deal with some nasty vampires, they call them vamps. They apparently swarmed Louisa and Pietro one day when they were returning from shopping in Paris. Veneur didn't want Juliette to know. This would set her back emotionally, and she may have risked calling Veneur. I didn't even tell Rebecca. Now Gabriel is also in danger; he met a human and has fallen in love, and Veneur has been worried that Bianca will have them killed too."

"Oh, this is bad. It sounds like Bianca is taking over from Enzo. Is this right?"

"It seems that way. Veneur couldn't tell me much, but when he heard we were coming to Paris, he was frantic and desperate to meet me. I can't just leave him here now. He is also in danger. I feel so overwhelmed. All these vampires need help, and I can't control any of this. Especially Rebecca. Vamprogeria is becoming more dangerous more often. I just can't pretend that Rebecca is going to live many—many years." Adriano lowers his head. A moment of silence divides them; Lucan knows this truth and he feels helpless on how to comfort Adriano.

"None of us know how long we have. We must live in the present— Rebecca is here, that is all that you have to focus on. And Veneur is still here too, we have to hold on to this."

"I try to. But life is full of so many dangers. At least I know this particular danger with Bianca and Enzo can be dealt with—I can control it. I feel it. Lucan, I'm not asking you to be a part of this, this is my soul's burden with these two monsters."

"How can I not be a part of this? This discussion is already making me a part of this. We may not be blood, but you are important to me, all of you are. I want to help you—I'm sorry if I sounded judgmental a few minutes ago, I didn't mean that. I'm not in any position to judge. Truthfully, I've never told any of you this, but I've wanted to kill Bianca the night I encountered her at the gallery." Adriano looks shocked. "Yes, it's true. I could feel the evil energy around her, I thought her heart was as black as her soulless eyes that were glaring at me. She wanted a fight with me! It is a mistake to purposefully threaten a lycan. If it wasn't for Gabriel keeping her at bay that night, I know in my bones, we would have had a blood bath. Those poor humans would have been slaughtered, and most likely and unfortunately all of you too—by me! That thought has haunted me all these years. I've had nightmares, woken up screaming, believing I had done these horrible things. You know Adriano, your kind would be defenseless against me. You couldn't run fast enough—I would just enjoy the chase more. I would tear you apart, your skin would be shredded, your bones broken. I would eat you—oh God! Knowing I could kill my family in a state of disassociation, that thought frightens me."

"Lucan, calm down! That's not going to happen."

"Promise me, Adriano, if I ever get into that state in your presence and you know you or others are in danger, please I beg you, promise me you will kill me before I turn completely. That is your only chance to escape that creature—kill me before I become Lupo. Promise me!" cries out Lucan in a desperate anguish.

Adriano stands there in silence for a few seconds, shocked and bewildered to hear such fear and violence exploding out of Lucan. And he notices that Lucan keeps referring to himself as doing these evil deeds, not the creature, Lupo. A shadow is cast over Lucan's calm, grounded and positive spirited energy.

Adriano shouts out in reassurance, "I promise. But stop worrying. It will never happen, so put it out of your mind." Adriano isn't sure if he is trying to convince Lucan or himself. He feels a bit unsettled suddenly, knowing that deep down inside, if provoked, this gentle caring man is capable of such horror and violence if the creature comes out. For the first time in Adriano's life as a vampire, he feels apprehensive; he isn't confident that he is always safe with his dear friend Lucan. Adriano's heart sinks with this thought, and Lucan sees Adriano is troubled by what he has confided to Adriano.

Lucan looks at Adriano with his warm grey eyes, genuinely smiling and trying to ease the truth away. "Sorry, I am just tired today, I hope I didn't offend you or worry you." Lucan doesn't want to reveal the fact that his up and down moodiness today is mostly due to the fact that tonight is going to be a full moon. He isn't home in his secure sanctuary, pampering himself, keeping his thoughts clear and calm, keeping the symptoms from stirring. He knows they had enough worry and anxiety on their plates already. He is determined not to feel trapped in his life by who he is. Besides, he can buy the necessary tools if he thinks it is necessary.

Adriano just doesn't know what to make of Lucan's emotions and temperament; he seems to be worried and at odds with something more than just Bianca. "We are both edgy, it's the stress of it all. I need a break, I'm getting thirsty—I will be right back. Rest a little on this rock." Lucan nods his head in agreement. He takes a seat on the rock and watches Adriano, who takes off like a bolt of lightning into the trees. Lucan closes his worried eyes, taking in deep breaths, practicing his mantra, "I am calm, all is right with my body, mind, and soul," as he desperately tries to find that peaceful state within.

Adriano returns to Lucan fifteen minutes later, feeling refreshed and alert again. It is very early in the morning, and they leave the dark woods and head back to the hotel. Lucan wants to sleep a little, then grab a bite to eat somewhere, before they go out to keep an eye on Adam, Ethan, and their friends. Adriano's mind is too restless, thoughts roaming around about different things: he is still thinking about what Lucan told him about his condition, he is worried about the boys being here in Paris, he is worried about Veneur, but mostly his mind goes to Rebecca. His thoughts feels heavy. He showers and changes and decided to list some thoughts and ideas down just in case he was going to confront Enzo and Bianca.

Corpse blood-how?
- *hospital morgue, funeral home: risky, embalming fluid would be detected, need to get to body before procedure done.*
- *stake out funeral home or morgue?*
- *kill predator from Jonathan's files -<u>last resort.</u>*

Tools to extract bld
- *pump, hose. Ask Sebastien*
- *storing bld. Glass vials, 2, 3?*

Where?
- *D's house, or in woods. How to get them in the woods?*
- *vials, drink from good vile, keep 2 bad ones, offer one?*
- *or disguise blood in a bottle of wine?*
- *has to be D's house!*

<u>*other option* </u>*-Lycan -but risky to me and humans -<u>last resort</u>*

Adriano rips the piece of paper with his notes from the notepad and places it in his pocket. He pulls out his cell, then scrolls down to Sandra's contact number.

Sandra wakes to the sound of her cell ringing. She sees Adriano's name on the display, and in a groggy voice she answers, "Hey, what's up? Is everything okay? I was sleeping, do you realize what time it is in Toronto? No, it's okay, I'm up now." She turns her night table lamp on, yawning away her sleepy mind while lying in bed. "A favour, okay, name it—wait, what? Access to the morgue? Why—corpse blood?" She sits up straight and stunned. "What? To subdue a vampire?" She immediately pulls the phone away from her ear in bewilderment, then returns it to her ear. "Yes, I'm here. I see. Through a journal? Fascinating—it would work? He did? You're kidding! Experiments on them—how disgusting. Oh, that is risky. You can't just enter a morgue, there would be security on doors, not to mention cameras. You would need more than just a lab coat; how would you get a mortician's badge? I don't have any contacts in Paris—oh! Wait, yes I do! Francois is a nurse at the hospital. He's a chatterbox, but nice, he mentioned to me a while ago that his cousin works at a hospital in Paris. No, he is an orderly, but maybe you can work your financial charm on him. But even if you got that far, do you even know how to extract the blood? YouTube it? Funny!" She bursts out laughing. "Seriously! Yes, I can walk you through it, but I don't know Adriano, this sounds like a crazy scheme. If you don't mind me saying, but why not just, you know, ask Jonathan to, you know, access the world data file, find you *someone* in Paris? I'm sure he would, he's a detective now, and he has more security access. It would be easier, you could stage the body—I can't believe what I'm saying, what a morbid conversation." She smirks. "Think about it. Or—" She pauses dramatically, "I guess you could also, you know, look around, you know, find someone yourself worthy of this cause. I know, I can't believe hearing me say this—what can I say, my mind has expanded over the years. Okay, I start at two p.m. today, I will see if I can get more information out of Francois, I will call you. But consider the other options, okay? Keep me posted whatever you decide. Alright, yes. Sleep? I don't think I can go back to bed after *this* conversation." She smirks. "You too, be careful. Ciao." Sandra falls back on her pillow, wide awake. "Corpse blood. Unbelievable."

The next call Adriano makes is to Jonathan, to see about accessing the Paris criminal database. Jonathan is with Sebastien, so Adriano doesn't want to elaborate too much further. He doesn't want Sebastien to panic and then stress Rebecca out.

Adriano and Lucan stop at a café across the street from the hotel Adam and his friends are staying at. Adriano is wearing a baseball cap and hoodie. Lucan is wearing dark sunglasses and his Fedora. It is now noon, and Adam, Ethan, and their friends are just leaving the hotel with their instruments; a van taxi is waiting for them. Adriano hears Adam tell the taxi driver to bring them to *Nouveau Cavern*. Adriano takes out his cell, clicks on Google Maps, and finds this small music hall is located in the 10th Arrondissement. Adriano waves down another taxi and gestures to Lucan to enter it. "Okay, you follow them to the *Nouveau Cavern*, keep an eye on things from your end. Call me if anything."

"Wait! Where are you going?"

"To meet Veneur."

"Oh. Be careful."

"Of course. I'll call you later."

Adriano enters the internet café, *Café et Connectez*, and sits at the furthest table in the corner that Veneur has reserved for them. He is a few minutes early. He watches as humans enter and take their seats with their laptops. Adriano pulls the menu to his face. A few more minutes go by. Then the door opens again and he suddenly knows a vampire has entered. He looks up from the menu and is so happy to see Veneur. He signals him and Veneur approaches the table. Adriano stands up to hug him but Veneur refrains and whispers so only Adriano can hear.

"Let's not bring attention to ourselves." He sits down across Adriano and lowers the window shade beside him. Adriano observes Veneur; he looks so thin and pale. Something has happened. His expression shows it.

Adriano whispers in a vampire tone, "Veneur, it is so good to see you. Juliette and everyone send their—"

"We don't have a lot of time. Bianca has been in the city this week."

Adriano is disturbed to see how anxious and nervous Veneur is. After all these years he appears more traumatized. It is difficult for Adriano to stay calm. "Veneur—what's wrong? Something is not right, you don't look good at all."

"I've underestimated her ruthlessness and ambition."

"What's happened?"

"Gabriel—he's gone."

"Gone? Escaped?"

"No." Veneur's eyes show such sorrow.

"How? When?"

Veneur shakes his head, his hands shaking. "A few weeks ago. Bianca discovered that he had a human girl—" Veneur suddenly chokes up; he takes a deep breath. "He was always so careful, but his happiness was showing the more in love he became." Veneur pauses. "Anyways, Bianca must have grown suspicious and followed him. I don't know how she did it, but she convinced Enzo it was time to make some changes. That bastard allowed this! He allowed Gabriel to be killed. Gabe was in this scion for *years.*" Veneur is struggling to compose himself; he wipes his eyes with his hands. He looks around, but thankfully the other patrons are busy on their laptops.

"And the girl?" Adriano is shocked and angry.

"I don't know, I assume she was killed too—Bianca just told me in her wicked venomous bravado about Gabriel. At that point I didn't want to ask further."

"Veneur, we go to get you out of there. I've got a plan."

CHAPTER 27

Fango's

Veneur left the cafe a few hours ago, heading home. He didn't want to create any suspicion. He scales the back of the house to his bedroom window and quietly enters his room. He lays on his bed and closes his eyes. His heart is racing; this plan of Adriano's is risky, but at this point he feels he has nothing left to lose. He lost his brother. He feels so alone and overwhelmed emotionally. This was the first time he told anyone about the trauma he has experienced recently. His emotions are raw, but he has to control them. He can't let Bianca or Enzo see him like this. They would relish in his misery. Veneur takes deep breaths and wipes his eyes.

When he is sure he is composed, he makes his way downstairs so Enzo can see he is home. He soon discovers that Bianca is out for the evening. Enzo commands him to his study, he has some business to discuss with him. He soon learns Bianca wants to bring in some new members of the scion.

"Things will be different now. I know you are not stupid like Gabriel was. Your sister has shown great loyalty to me; I think Bianca will soon be ready to take our scion into the next level of power. I'm disappointed in you. I know you knew about Gabriel's crime—but I'm sure now you won't dare step out of line. This will be a good lesson for you—don't attach to anyone. They are all dispensable to Bianca and I." Enzo laughs wickedly, and Veneur is screaming inside. His eyes remain still. He waits to be dismissed.

Adriano stayed an hour longer at the cafe. He was still processing what Veneur told him. Then he returned to the hotel. His mind racing. He lays down on the bed and his eyes are heavy, his emotions pulling him down. He just needs some time to think before he meets up with Lucan. He can feel his body becoming very fatigued. He hasn't felt this low in energy in a very long time. He needs to rest a little more, then hunt. It's the only way to recuperate from this devastating news he's received.

Adriano returns to the woods to hunt and within two hours he manages to drink from two rabbits. His energy is returning, but his thoughts are still on Veneur. The sun has gone down and he realizes he has left Lucan most of the day alone. He reaches into his pocket and pulls out his cell to dial Lucan, and he sees several texts and missed calls from him. He realizes that he forgot to take the phone off mute. He immediately calls him.

"Adriano! Where the hell have you been!" Lucan is trying to whisper. "I've been trying to reach you—never mind, tell me later. Check your GPS, the boys left their hotel and took a taxi an hour ago, but I couldn't get one in time. Can you see where they went?" Lucan waits patiently on the phone and takes the last gulp of whisky from the glass. "Zango's? What's Zango's? Oh, I see, okay, well they are at that age—what's wrong? Why are you so frantic? Calm down! It's just a nightclub—what? Unbelievable. Anything goes? Drugs, sex? How do you know—never mind that, who knows what trouble they could get into—I'm calm! Just meet me at the café across the street from their hotel, where we were this morning. Hurry!" Lucan accidentally disconnects the call while Adriano is still talking.

Lucan takes a deep breath, signals the waiter, and orders a second glass of whisky. He looks at his watch; it is eight p.m. Lucan's anxiety is growing. The waiter returns with his drink, and he takes it and gulps the whisky down. "Oh, I'm getting too old for this!"

Adriano runs as fast as his vampire lungs and legs can take him, through the woods and back to the main roads, where he hails a taxi and completes the frantic journey to the café. He tells the taxi to wait and rushes inside the café to grab Lucan. Lucan looks Adriano over, he can see the stress and frustration all over him. He has leaves stuck in his disheveled hair, which Lucan points to and Adriano brushes off. They return to the taxi and Adriano gives the taxi directions to the 18th Arrondissement. Adriano instructs the taxi to stop at the corner. Lucan pays the driver, and they exit quickly. Adriano hopes he remembers where the secret entrance is. Lucan can't see any sign of a club, and questions Adriano if they are in the right area. Adriano leads him to a sleazy alley; it looks familiar. They walk through. Adriano is sure this is the right place.

"The club is not visible to anyone passing by."

"And you know this club because?"

"Let's just say I was more reckless in my youth."

"Well, I too had my wild days, ahh youth. If—"

"Lucan! Concentrate, we are looking for a black steel door, it is hidden. You have to feel the walls, there is a latch but it's not easy to find." He slides his hand across the brick and paneling. "Here it is!" Adriano opens the secret door and they enter through a very dark narrow passageway. Up ahead they see red light and they walk towards it. There is no bouncer or anyone to greet you or stop you. If you find this hidden place, you deserve to be there—at your own risk. There are windows covered in black paint, some of which are broken.

Adriano finds another door that leads to a set of winding stairs, which end on another passageway. He finds a second steel door and opens it; they are both confronted with loud music, sounds, and a mixture of so many smells: musk, body sweat, wild incense, weed, and cigars. Music is blaring from the band on stage; strobe lights in various color patterns flash. Adriano can't believe he frequented this hole in his vampire youth.

Adults of all ages track through this place. Lucan observes some of the more intimate activities taking place on scattered couches and chairs. Then he sees two heavy velvet curtains located at the back of the venue, and Adriano turns to him. "Other explicit intimate acts are performed behind those curtains, you have to go through a bouncer and another door."

Lucan is bewildered as he walks around this jungle of wild humans; the music is so loud it is aggravating his ears. "I see what you mean, anything goes at Zango's!" he screams out as he tries to keep up with Adriano, who is moving around trying to find Adam and Ethan. The air is filled with a thick smog of cigar, bong, and pipe smoke. These strong smells are not able to mask another smell for Adriano: his keen vampire sense of smell in overdrive, he can smell vampires in this room. His heart beats faster, and he is starting to sweat, fear and bewilderment rising. Adriano and Lucan move through the crowd, cutting through moving bodies on the dance floor as they continue to scan the room very closely.

Vampires mix with humans on the dancefloor and on the couches. Adriano can smell human blood. *This place sure has evolved, but are these humans accepting these vampires or is this a trap for humans?* he frets privately to himself. Then he sees Ethan and his friend Todd on the dance floor, each with a woman wrapped around their waist. Adriano is relieved that it is humans they are dancing with. He then notices their other friend, Paul, sitting on the couch smoking who knows what with other humans. He feels responsible suddenly for these friends of Adam and Ethan. Then his eyes zoom in very closely and he taps Lucan on the shoulder to get his attention; he signals to follow his eyes and then Lucan gasps. Adriano can only see Adam's profile, but he knows it was him. Adam is sitting at a table in the corner with a drink in front of him. But what suddenly alarms Adriano and Lucan is the vampire sitting beside Adam with her back to the dance floor. To their shock and horror, they recognize it to be Bianca; she is stroking Adam's hair, and he seems to be unresponsive. Adriano feels the blood rushing from his head to his feet. In vampire speed he approaches the table, Lucan following behind with his cane as best as he can, but slower. The strobing lights in the dark make it very hard to see. Adriano grabs Bianca's arm so tight she squeals like an animal in pain. Then she turns around and is shocked to see it is Adriano holding her. Adriano's eyes are glaring, his long razor-sharp canine teeth protruding.

"Adriano! What are you—?"

Horror sinks in for Adriano as he notices the dark substance on Bianca's teeth and to the side of her mouth, which she wipes off with her tongue.

Adriano is overwhelmed with panic. "Bianca! My God! What did you do to him!"

Bianca sees the fear in Adriano's eyes and suddenly wants to squeeze more anxiety and panic out of him. "Don't worry, Adriano, I was just tasting him for now. Young blood is so much more delicious. How life works, imagine this, I was just enjoying my choice of selections here this evening and I see this beautiful handsome young man sitting by himself. I approach and he has the most striking hazel eyes. He was so nervous. I asked him his name and where he was from. He was eager to tell me that he was in a band with his brother. He is so sweet, he was showing off a little trying to impress me—the older woman, you know young men. He went on to tell me that he and his brother and friends were here for a music competition. He was so excited and eager to share some of the songs he and his brother wrote, the lyrics were quite deep. He is quite the philosopher in such a young mind. He then showed me photos of his band, his guitar, and his piano. Very talented young men! Of course, I played along, he looked delicious. As he was scrolling through his photos, what do I see but a family photo including you, Juliette, the other vampire, and *her*! What was her name? Oh right—Rebecca!" There is distaste in her voice.

Adriano tightens his grip on Bianca, hoping she stays distracted while Lucan stays with Adam.

"I couldn't believe my luck, I was in the presence of her son Adam. I couldn't resist the gift in front of me." Her laugh makes Adriano cringe. Adriano's heart sinks as he listens. "Not to worry, I didn't drain him. I had other plans, he would make an obedient vampire pet!" Her cold eyes glint with amusement. She is distracted by her vengeance and all the mixtures and concoctions of smells, and she fails to see Lucan approaching. Adriano can see the panic in Lucan's eyes and he is worried. He tries to distract Bianca so she doesn't see Lucan, but she sees him, and hisses at Adriano speaking venomous threats.

"Release me! I warn you! Or I will threaten your werewolf! You don't want him to come out and play, do you?" She slithers on a wicked smile. "Do you really want to be responsible for all these innocent deaths by me and your wolf pet?" She looks at Lucan; she enjoys watching Adriano suffer, and she thinks she has him now as she continues to anger him more.

"Lucan—don't look at her! Don't react, please. Pay attention to Adam."

"Yes wolf! Keep at bay!" growls Bianca. Adriano looks at Lucan, who is standing still glaring at Bianca.

"Lucan, ignore her, concentrate on Adam!" Adriano keeps his tight grip on Bianca. But he looks at Lucan, and there is fire forming in his eyes; he is livid, and suddenly Adriano is struck with fear. He screams out to Lucan, "Oh God, Lucan, don't lose control—I need you! Please."

Lucan hears the panic in Adriano's voice, and he understands the danger. With every grain of control, he can muster he forces down the wild angry emotions rising. Lucan moves quickly to Adam. His eyes suddenly fill with fear and horror as he looks at Adam's neck and sees the tiny bite mark, with very little blood visible. Lucan turns to Adriano and is ready to lunge for Bianca. Adriano's instincts react quickly.

"Lucan, focus! My God, think of these humans—Adam and Ethan are here! Stay calm. Get these boys out of here back to the hotel."

Lucan is struggling to control the burning rage of anger brewing inside of him; it is powerful, and his fear is evident—that everyone in this place could be in imminent danger if he loses control. He quickly takes hold of Adam and moves through the crowd to finds Ethan, Todd, and Paul; they are shocked to see Lucan with Adam. He tells them they are in grave danger and they see the strange and terrified look in Lucan's eyes. When they see Adam's eyes are closed, they all rush out of the club, helping to carry Adam.

Meanwhile, Adriano's canines are still protruded and Bianca's too, but she underestimates the power Adriano has, especially when threatened. Adriano's vampire testosterone is flowing even more powerfully through him. He waits to see the boys exit first, then with incredible vampire speed he takes the crucifix out from his pocket and slashes Bianca's throat deeply through the muscle. The blood is gushing out, but she still quickly slashes Adriano's face. One of the scratches hits his eyebrow and blood pours out, blinding him temporarily. He is startled and accidentally releases his grip on Bianca. Holding her hand tightly to her open wound, she runs away at vampire speed, knocking down people on the dance floor, and quickly escapes out of the club and down the street. She almost knocks down two humans walking by. They gasp as they see the speed and movement of the woman. Bianca is frantic, she can feel her energy depleting. The loss of blood is extensive. She is struggling now.

Meanwhile Adriano is out of the club running at vampire speed. He is carrying Adam's beer bottle in his hand. He can hear humans gasping in awe and confusion as Bianca runs past them. She is growling and hissing, and the humans back away. Thankfully Adriano is moving so fast in the darkness that humans can't focus on him; some become dizzy and queasy. Adriano can smell Bianca's blood and it drives his anger further to catch up to her. He wipes his eyes of the blood trailing down. Time is of the essence. He knows the deep gash in her throat will slow her down.

Adriano sees Bianca up ahead; she is heading for the Seine River. Bianca feels trapped, she sees her hunter not far behind. She is frantic now and in her panicked state she jumps into the river even though she can't swim. Adriano reaches the riverbank. He sees her; she is gasping, she can't scream, her lungs are filling with water. He knows now that he has her. He moves carefully now, at a normal pace, his eyes always on Bianca. He looks around, and thankfully no humans are nearby. He puts the beer bottle down, takes off his black summer jacket, and jumps in and reaches her. She is going under and he waits patiently. He knows she is suffering great pain in the drowning, but he wants nature to take its course. A few minutes later he sees her limp body floating. He quickly grabs her and swims to the edge, lifting her up and over the bank. He checks to make sure she is dead.

He catches his breath, but he has little time to spare for fear of being noticed. He places his jacket around her, lifting up the high collar to conceal the gash in her throat. He closes the lids of her dead eyes, stands her up, and puts his arm around her. He casually walks away, carrying the beer bottle, and using his theatrical skills to act as if he is drunk. He talks to Bianca as if she too is intoxicated. He makes his way to an alleyway and lays her behind a large trash bin. He looks around and sees an abandoned building, and carries her quickly up the stairs and into a dark room. He drops her corpse on the ground with no care or remorse.

Suddenly Adrian's phone rings; he sees it's Lucan and answers. "Lucan, is everything okay—okay, good, it's better Adam is at our hotel. I will be there as soon as I can—calm down. We need to stay focused—no, as long as he didn't drink her blood we have a chance!" Adriano is trying to reassure Lucan and himself, he hopes this is true, it has to be. "Calm down, Lucan! I need you to focus. Open his mouth and let me know if you see or smell blood on his breath—yes, do it." Adriano's heart is racing. "I'm too old for this too, dammit! Now concentrate, Lucan, just do it please, now." Adriano can hear Adam moaning in the background. "We can't take him to a hospital—you know why. Christ, calm down—did you smell his breath? No smell of blood? Beer is good, check his teeth for any blood stains. Yes, you heard me." Adriano waits anxiously, seconds feel like hours. "Thank God —Ok, he is safe, he hasn't consumed any of her blood, and he hasn't lost enough blood to endanger him. Trust me! Lucan, I need you to focus. I can't worry about Lupo coming out, for Christ's sake. Okay, stay calm. Just stay with him. Adam's body is fighting her powerful venomous saliva, that is why he is weak and in and out of consciousness. Not to mention, he did smoke up too—listen—calm down, Bianca wasn't trying to kill him, she wanted to turn him. We need to flush out her saliva from his bloodstream and cells, or it could make him very ill. —I don't know how long it will take for his immune system to regain strength." Adriano's voice is cracking, he prays his theory is right. "Listen, I'm going to put you on speaker, but keep your voice down."

"Can you hear me?"

"Yes. Adriano, where are you?"

"I'm handling Bianca."

"What? How? Never mind her, Adam needs you."

Adriano takes his crucifix out of his pocket, still stained with Bianca's blood. He slashes Bianca's wrists and squeezes out her blood into the beer bottle.

"Adriano, did you hear me?"

"Yes, just keep watch over Adam. I will be there in half an hour. Grab a damp cloth and keep wiping his forehead, his body needs to stay cool. If you can get him to drink water, do. Let me go, I will be there soon."

"Okay, hurry."

Adriano arrives back at the hotel. They spend the next few hours watching over Adam as he struggles in and out of consciousness. Adriano explains to Lucan that Adam is experiencing similar symptoms to someone who is going through a painful withdrawal. His body is shaking, and he is drenched in sweat. They try to feed him soup they order from room service, and they try to get him to drink water. Adriano knows that Adam's body is fighting the foreign blood, trying to reject it. He knows that the teen's human cells and tissue are confused. Time is crawling at a cruel pace for all of them; Lucan fell asleep a few hours ago, which was a relief for Adriano, he couldn't worry about anyone else but Adam. Ethan had called several times, frantic. He didn't know what hotel Adriano was staying in. Adriano just instructed him to stay in their room. He would be there when he knew Adam was out of danger.

Adriano is so emotionally distraught that his hands and legs are shaking, and he keeps trying to feed the soup and water to Adam. His cell phone rings, and his heart sinks as he sees Rebecca's name. Rebecca is crying unstoppably, screaming and yelling into the phone, and she puts it on speaker. "What happened? Ethan is freaking out." Adriano realizes Ethan had called her. Adriano doesn't know how to console her.

"It's okay. I've dealt with it—but Bianca bit him."

"My God, *no!*"

"Rebecca—Adam will not turn! I promise you. Bianca just took a little blood, not enough to harm him, and Lucan and I both checked—he didn't drink her blood. I promise you. He won't turn. All that is happening right now is his body is healing itself from her saliva. Remember vampires saliva is powerful and hits the immune system, he is very weak—that's all. It's like he has this nasty virus inside of him now that has to be flushed out, but he will be okay. He just needs lots of rest, I promise you. Adam will be okay! We are giving him soup and water, he will be okay." Adriano cries out, "Rebecca, Bianca is dead!"

Ethan arrives; Rebecca has given him the hotel information, and he is not leaving Adam's side. Adriano understands, and Ethan is a great help. But Ethan sees the two bite marks and knows this was not from an animal. His mind refuses to open up the door of truth that he suspected all these years. *It can't be,* he shakes his head, he convinces himself that this is one of those people he's read about, that believe they are vampires, and they drink human blood. His mind accepts this easier, he saw the documentaries of this identify disorder. He is overwhelmed and disgusted that this woman thought she was a vampire and was drinking Adam's blood, but he doesn't let on. He doesn't understand why Adam is not in a hospital, and he is surprised that even his mom feels a hospital couldn't do anything. Again, something inside of him is trying to speak but he shuts it down. There are no such things as vampires. Adriano reassures him that Adam is safer here. They would be waiting for hours in the emergency room, and with his immune system down it could be dangerous for him around other sick people.

Ethan is not convinced, but suddenly Adam slowly opens his eyes; he is gaining consciousness now, and a bit of color is returning to his cheeks. Adriano is relieved. He takes this opportunity to run a couple of quick errands on his mind. Lucan, at this point, is well rested, calm, and can manage with Ethan.

Adriano's first errand involves checking in with the friends. They are fine, but dealing with a massive hangover. He orders them room service and says that when they are up to it, they can take a taxi to his hotel to see Adam. He leaves them money.

Adriano's second errand is to go back to the abandoned building and retrieve the crate with Bianca's corpse. He first stops at a hardware store and buys some heavy rope, a box of garbage bags, and duct tape. He puts Bianca in the garbage bag, duct tapes it closed, then places her back in the crate and seals it tightly with the rope. He carries the crate out and dumps it into the large garbage bin, and set the whole bin on fire before leaving. No one is around, since this alleyway is secluded.

Adriano returns to his hotel; he opens the door and sees Adam's friends around Adam, who is fully awake and sitting up. They spend the morning in Adriano's hotel room, feeding Adam, who now has a healthy appetite. The boys are determined to go on with the competition. Adam too is not going to miss this. He says he will rest; the competition is hours away. He is stubborn and Adriano can see he really is recovering, so he has no choice but to allow them to go.

It is the next day, Sunday, and Adam, Ethan, and their friends are booked on the afternoon flight back to Toronto as instructed by Rebecca. They are still coming down from the excitement that they came in second place in the competition, considering the dramatic ordeal they went through. Adriano wanted Lucan to go back with the boys, but Lucan refused, telling Adriano that he was needed here. Adriano was frustrated; he thought this was too much for Lucan, but Lucan insisted; he has his own personal reason for not accompanying the boys back to Toronto. He knows that he cannot risk being on the plane and feeling the symptoms stirring. All the anger and emotions he had to suppress hours ago are creating a delayed reaction that he is desperately trying to control.

Lucan takes a moment to say goodbye to Adam and Ethan. He gives them a great big hug each. "My dearest ones, I am so proud of you! You were true professionals in that competition. Your mother will be so proud when she sees the video we took. You have a great career ahead of you, believe in yourselves. Keep your passion for music in your heart and turn to it when life brings moments that are difficult. My music is my soul's release, and I feel you both share that same artistic heart. Being considered one of your grandparents is an honor; I will cherish it always."

"Thanks gramps, we'll see you next week," Ethan says, and he and Adam wave goodbye and head to the gate with their friends.

Lucan gives them a warm and loving smile; he has a deep lump in his throat, and he feels very emotional all of a sudden. He holds back the tears forming in his eyes.

CHAPTER 28

Embrace the Light and the Dark

At eight that evening, Adriano and Lucan return to the hotel room. Lucan has had a filling meal and a bourbon at a restaurant; he needed to calm his nerves. Lucan goes to freshen up. Adriano opens the mini fridge and takes out the two small liquor bottles that he filled yesterday with Bianca's corpse blood from the beer bottle. He places both bottles in his blazer pocket. The two men head out, grab a taxi, and instruct the driver to bring them into the 16th Arrondissement. The driver is then instructed to stop at a park. Adriano and Lucan move through the park and Adriano takes the route that Veneur instructed him to take through the woods.

Veneur, in the meantime, left the house, feeling so relieved to know that Bianca is dead. He waits at the internet café with his passport and a small carry-on that holds his laptop, which has his manuscript file saved that he has been secretly working on at the internet café all these years. He can't wait to finally complete his first draft.

It is now nine-thirty p.m., and Enzo Domenico's house is in view a short distance away. Adriano takes Lucan's black knapsack off his shoulder and places it on the ground for Lucan. He observes as Lucan starts pulling out the items he purchased earlier to secure himself for the transformation.

"I'm still not sure I agree with this back-up plan, Lucan. It seems very risky. If I end up having to get Enzo to chase me out into these woods, when he sees Lupo, I don't see how this will be a threat to him, since you will be tied up? Sorry, I mean Lupo will be tied up. So how is this plan supposed to stop Enzo's threats to us? I know you think this is better than killing him, but I disagree. I'm not comfortable with this plan. We didn't even consider the howling—once Enzo hears the howling he will not enter the woods. We need a better back-up plan because we don't know for sure if he drinks the corpse blood how damaging it will be to him. What if it doesn't subdue him? It will just end up being a physical fight between me and him, and I won't wound him, I will just outright do everything in my power to kill him at that point." There was a clear focus coming from Adriano.

"Adriano, my plan will work. Trust me! The howling will attract wolves, he will think they are all wolves howling. I need to be tied up in the beginning, there's no other way to do this. The lycan can't be released once he emerges. God forbid he runs out of the woods and runs miles away and into the public. When Enzo sees the lycan and sees that you are not afraid of it, you can threaten to release him from the chains and ropes if Enzo dares to run. Trust me, Enzo will be putty in your hands, he will have no choice but to listen to anything you have to say. You will have him under your command. I believe this strongly. All we are doing is scaring him. A bully just needs to know you are not afraid of him, and in this case, you will threaten him that you will set this creature loose if he dares to have any of us hunted down."

"I don't think you are being realistic in your expectations. Enzo is evil!"

Suddenly Adriano notices Lucan has started taking off his shoes, and he assumes that Lucan is getting ready to undress. "Oh, wait, I will give you some privacy."

"Privacy? Oh, that won't be necessary, I think this time I want to be fully dressed for the transformation. I just don't feel like being naked; my skin just seems more sensitive to the chains and ropes these days. It's very uncomfortable. It's okay, I packed extra clothes for if these get destroyed."

Adriano is too preoccupied in his own thoughts to really listen to Lucan's reasoning. He just wants to get this over with. Lucan instructs Adriano, and the chains and rope are placed around Lucan. He places his feet and ankles in the shackles.

Adriano doesn't like to see Lucan tied up like this, especially when he just seems a bit more fragile. "Alright, I guess it's time. Are you sure, Lucan? I know transforming is painful, I hate to think of the pain you will go through just to hopefully threaten this vampire."

"We have to do this, Adriano. This vampire needs to be brought down to size. We are dealing with an arrogant, self-centered, and dangerous individual who has done enough psychological damage to our family." He smiles confidently. "Go on, you said this is the most important performance you will ever have done—I wish I could have seen you on stage in your earlier days in theatre. Anyways, remember the lycan will be very agitated and snapping his jaws, you make sure you keep your distance. Go from behind to pretend to untie me," Lucan says, feeling anxious.

"I will, but I'm hoping this will not be necessary." Adriano taps his chest pocket gently. "Are you comfortable? I mean, silly question, but do you need anything?"

"No, I have everything I need." Lucan stares into Adriano's eyes, it's like they are trying to express what Lucan can't.

Adriano starts walking away. "Adriano!" Lucan calls out nervously. Adriano turns around. "Good luck. Or is it break a leg?" He smirks. "I'm proud of you—I mean, for standing up to Domenico. Be careful, my son!" Lucan's voice is tender and his lips are trembling slightly. Adriano looked into Lucan's eyes, and thinks he saw a tear. "Go on! This important stage awaits you."

Adriano nods and quickly vanishes out of sight. Lucan stands there tied up, dressed in his white crisp shirt and black dress pants. He whispers ever so quietly to himself, *This too shall pass.* He takes in several deep breaths and just stands there, looking at the surroundings. He sees the trees filled with birds; a butterfly flutters by, and the warm evening breeze carries a fragrant scent of wild lavender from a bush a few feet away. He breathes it in; it leaves such a sweet and calming aroma in the air on this warm summer night. He closes his eyes.

Meanwhile, Adriano makes his way to the front door and takes a deep breath. He almost feels that nervous twitch he used to get as a theatre actor, just before he went on stage. He purposely knocks. He wants to make sure his presence is known. He opens the door slowly and it squeaks; he calls out, "Master, it's Adriano! Will you let me in?"

A few seconds go by, and Adriano remains at the opening of the door. Suddenly Adriano hears a loud firm voice say, "Enter!"

Adriano cringes, hearing that familiar voice speak to him once again after so many years. He steps in and the floor squeaks under his shoe. He is suddenly confronted by the smell of trapped, musty, moldy air. There is very little light to see by. He walks in further and he hears Enzo call out again, "In here!"

Adriano sees a light coming from an open doorway that has cobwebs dangling. He glances into the room and sees a large shadow cast on the wall; he is bracing himself. He walks further into the room. Adriano sees all the windows are encased with shutters that are all closed. There is a broken skylight, and he can see water stains all over the wooden floor. He feels so bad for the conditions that Veneur has lived in. There is a log burning in the fireplace. Enzo Domenico is sitting in a large wing chair, beside the fire. He is dressed in a long dark green robe that smells dingy. Adriano observes Enzo; he looks frail and much older than Adriano remembered. His face is very thin and gaunt, and his irises are covered in a beige milky hue. One of his eyes looks infected, it is very red. Adriano steps forward and Enzo adjusts his robe then looks directly at Adriano.

"I knew you would come back one day, I have been waiting for you." Enzo's voice sounds powerful and intimidating. "Come in closer, you aren't afraid of me—are you?" He grins, showing his rotting canines. "I would offer you something to drink but I understand animal blood is your choice." His eyes are sharply watching Adriano. Adriano doesn't speak, he has to play this carefully. He slowly steps closer to Enzo, taking on a timid demeanor. Enzo is struck by the sight of his first reborn; he looks older and worn. He remembers how young and frail Adriano was when he turned him all those years ago. "All that animal blood you consume has aged you. You're not the striking young man I remember. Why have you come to waste my time?" growls Enzo, his long-overgrown fingernails tapping on the arm of the chair.

"Enzo, I felt compelled to come, I needed—"

"How dare you," howls Enzo ferociously, his tone threatening. "You will address me as Master if I am to entertain your futile words, is that clear? My patience with your disrespect is thinning—I know all about you. Bianca has told me how you behaved, and I am appalled, disgusted, and ashamed of you. Caring for humans! Protecting them! Drinking animal blood! And the worst of all, associating with those disgusting werewolves."

Adriano panics inside. *What if Lucan's scent is on me, Enzo will smell it.* But Enzo just continues ranting.

"You are an abomination to our kind, you're a pathetic disgrace. You're lucky my sense of smell has severely weakened, for it would be a grave offense to bring the stench of your vampire and human friends into my home!" Enzo shouts out, enjoying lashing out in a cruel offensive manner.

"My deepest apologies my Master, I am ignorant of the proper ways to address a Master! I haven't had your honorable guidance to teach me. I am affected by your presence, I didn't realize how much until I see you now. May I please sit?" Adriano crafts his tone carefully.

"Yes, but don't think I won't reach for your throat and slash you until you bleed out all your miserable blood!" Enzo threatens fiercely, with menace in his tone. "From what I have been told, you are your own Master. Isn't that right?" Enzo hisses. "Speak, you bloody fool!"

Adriano is taken aback by this aggressive presence, and carefully sits on the chair a few feet away from Enzo. It takes everything in him not to lunge at the old vampire. He remains in character, being very cautious and careful to keep his voice steady and unthreatening, keeping his head down. Suddenly it strikes him as odd, he hasn't heard any howling all this time. He is sure it could be heard from inside, but maybe not? "I have spent many years on my own, and I wasn't wise to our ways. I mistakenly believed that I was free to be the vampire I chose to be. I mistakenly believed I should drink animal blood so that humans would respect me and realize I wasn't a threat. In my profound ignorance and shame, I thought if I befriended humans then it would be okay—we could co-exist. I didn't want to admit that I was fighting the killer inside of me, the apex predator that we are. Please, understand, I was a kid, I was rebelling against our kind. I am deeply sorry for bringing such shame to you, Master, all these years." Adriano is mindful not to over-perform; he has to be convincing. He knows he is dealing with a cruel master manipulator who thinks he is the center of all vampires in the world. Adriano has to feed on this insane delusion with careful strategic calm.

"You expect me to believe you?" Enzo's eyes show mistrust and suspicion.

"I realize you have no reason to trust my words, but otherwise I would dare not have risked coming here knowing how powerful and mighty you are. But here I am, your first born, asking to be forgiven. Asking to become a member of your scion. I know I'm not worthy, but I beg you, give me one chance." Adriano's tone appears to express great sincerity.

"You expect to be forgiven for what you have done! You destroyed this scion. You put these foolish and shameful ideas into these vampires' heads—I am the Master! I control what these vampires eat, who they can associate with. Bianca is a great hunter. She took after me for sure. She told me that Gabriel was seeing a human female. Well, that was a fatal mistake for him—he probably got that fatal idea from you." Enzo smirks cruelly, and Adriano freezes; it is like he is on a tight-rope and any slight wrong move could bring him crashing down. Any slight infliction of his voice showing sadness for Gabriel's death, any slight expression of sorrow showing in his eyes, will give him away. He is an actor, and this is the moment to test all his years of crafting and perfecting his theatrical skills.

"Is there nothing I can say or do to change your mind? Please, Master, I have nowhere to go," Adriano pleads.

"Bianca is the only one I can trust. Her loyalty to me is evident. I have a task for her to complete." He leans over to Adriano with scorn and wicked threatening eyes. Adriano doesn't move, and Enzo leans in closer and whispers with such menace in his tone. "You were a fool to come. You are powerless against Bianca and I."

That last threat almost gives him away. He wants to pluck out Enzo's eyes, but suddenly the image of Rebecca comes into Adriano's mind; his rock, his heart's sanctuary. He carefully lifts his head. "Please Master—I have disowned the humans and vampires that I brought into my life. I realized they were holding me back—they demanded too much respect and equality. They were mocking me, but I finally saw through this."

"Why should I believe you?" Enzo's eyes are like lasers scanning Adriano's eyes for falseness.

"I understand your distrust in me. I am not worthy to be here, but I beg you, I have no need for those ingrates. I trust that you had great cause to destroy Gabriel. I curse them all—I hope you destroyed Veneur too." Adriano needs Enzo to believe he is unaware of any happenings in this household. "I want to learn from you, I want to be a version of the apex predator that you are. I know I will never be a Master like you, but I beg you, please give me a chance to prove to you I can change. What must I do to gain your trust? Anything!" Adriano's voice shakes to appear nervous in the presence of this Master. He knows he has to appear submissive and afraid.

Enzo stays silent; he is staring at Adriano with skepticism. Suddenly, he stands up and slowly faces Adriano, who stays very still, controlling his breathing. He doesn't want Enzo too close to him, in case he smells Lucan's scent. Enzo yells out, "Look at me!" Adriano slowly raises his head, his eyes meeting Enzo's. Enzo bends down and whispers, "Kill your family." His putrid breath travels towards Adriano, and the stench almost makes Adriano gag. Enzo's words are razor sharp, and he grins a menacing smile, watching Adriano's eyes to see if he flinches.

"As you wish."

Enzo leans back into his chair, his gnarly fingernails tapping against each other, his voice calm and calculative. "This seems too easy—do you take me for a fool?"

"No, Master. You see, I have no use for them, they destroyed who I really am. I will return to them immediately, and the deed will be done."

"I understand these things can be filmed live. Wonders of technological advancements." He laughs with such evil intent. "Bianca will work out the details. And if you trick me, or if this is a trap, Adriano, there will be nowhere on this Earth you can hide. My associates will find you. There will be no mercy, you will suffer great pain—that is, after you watch us kill your family." Enzo's threatening voice has such an evil calm in it.

"I wouldn't dare try to fool a Master. I want to join your scion. Do as you wish with the others. I've wasted too many years. Thank you for giving me this time in your presence. —I will leave you now. And wait to hear from Bianca." Adriano pauses. "May I rise, Master?"

"Yes."

Adriano stands up slowly and bows. "Master, I forgot, I'm so sorry. I brought you a gift, in my clumsiness I almost forgot to give this to you." Adriano reaches into his breast pocket and pulls out one of the small liquor bottles. He presents it with his head lowered.

"What is this, alcohol?" asks Enzo, irritated.

"It's blood—human blood. I subdued a human before I came here and removed his blood while he lay unconscious. I wanted to give this to you. To show my sincerity in my wish to come back to you. If this is unacceptable I understand—forgive my ignorance." Adriano is trusting himself that he can read Enzo well enough to know he would never resist human blood.

"Blood—in a bottle? My God, bring me a human next time!"

"I'm sorry, I meant no offense, forgive me, I will discard this—so much you can teach me."

"Give it to me!"

Adriano unscrews the cap and, bowing his head in meek obedience, gives the bottle to Enzo. Enzo quickly grabs it and gulps the liquid. Adriano doesn't waste a second of this opportunity, he reaches into his pocket and pulls out the second bottle. "I have one more, but I don't want to overstay your patience." Adriano unscrews the cap, and Enzo immediately grabs the bottle and gulps it down. Adriano stays in a submissive position; with every grain in his body he keeps breathing quietly and slowly to keep his heartbeat steady. He channels all of his years of studying acting and focuses all his energy into this performance, and stays in this weak timid character. This is his greatest performance.

"Leave now, before I lose patience. Be back here tomorrow at sunset— do not be late! And bring me a human alive, I will want to feed and I will want you to feed too! I will know if you are lying to me."

"Yes Master!" Adriano quickly stands up, bows, and walks out of the room. He isn't sure if he took enough blood from Bianca. Enzo seems fine. Adriano walks slowly through the hall, starting to think this plan failed.

His mind is racing in a circle of anxiety and panic. He is screaming in his mind, *it didn't work it didn't work!* Suddenly, there comes a loud crashing sound followed by the sound of a heavy thud. Adriano stops, struggling to control his heart from racing in excitement. "Master?" Adriano calls out timidly from the hallway. Then he hears sounds coming from Enzo, he runs back and to his great delight he sees Enzo on the wooden floor gasping for air trying to speak.

"Whaa-at did-d-d you do-o-o-o to-o-o me-e-e!"

Adriano waits; he needs to be sure how affected Enzo is from the dead blood. "Master? Are you okay?" Adriano disguises his veiled excitement. The only sounds coming out of Enzo now are gasps for air. Adriano stands a few feet away, watching the suffering unfold. Enzo is moving very slowly crawling on the floor towards Adriano, his nails digging into the wood. Adriano steps back. "Master!?" Adriano says in a false tone of alarm.

"Wha-at—have—you-u done—you wretch! You p-poisoned me-e-e! Bianca will—kill-ll you-u-u! —She will rip-p you apart-t! Nowhere for you to hid-de!" Enzo growls ferociously, trying to crawl to Adriano.

Adriano remains in character; he can't take any chances yet, until he knows Enzo cannot get up. Enzo remains on the floor gasping for air; he is starting to convulse. Adriano studies Enzo very closely, and a few minutes go by. Enzo is finally subdued.

Adriano bursts out in a ferocious roar, "You bastard! I loathe you! I will never be under your control. You are a disgrace. And I want you to die knowing that you just drank the dead corpse blood of your precious Bianca. I killed her."

Enzo's eyes widen with immediate shock; he is in such a rage, trying to scream, trying to get up, but his red infected eyes suddenly roll behind his eyelids, his body twitching and shaking violently, out of control. His head bangs on the floor with such powerful force that he cracks his skull. The violent shaking makes him bite his own tongue over and over. Blood gushes out of his mouth, and Adriano can hear gurgling sounds erupting in his throat. Adriano knows he has to finish this here and now.

His rage and hate for Enzo are now unleashed, and Adriano explodes in a desire to end this vampire's existence. He pulls out his lighter and grabs a long candle lying on the shelf. He lights it and bends down. "This is for the mental torture you inflicted on Juliette, the guilt and shame you put Veneur through, forcing him to do you dirty work, and for the death of our friend and ally Gabriel! You evil insane worthless piece of shit!" He growls ferociously, his eyes glaring, and immediately sets Enzo's robe on fire.

Enzo's body is still convulsing, but Adriano is content and satisfied that Enzo heard every word. The flame takes immediately and spreads up and around Enzo's skinny legs and through the silk fabric. Enzo can't even scream, he is barely breathing air, his body still convulsing uncontrollably. Within seconds Enzo's body is in flames, and Adriano just stands there and watches the flames travel to his face, his eyes, and his head. The flames start to spread to the wooden floor, and Adriano quickly takes his jacket off and starts dowsing the flames. He manages to stop the fire from spreading out of control. He is concerned about the smoke escaping through the broken skylight and attracting attention. The stench of the burning body almost makes Adriano sick in this confined suffocating space. The room is shut in, the damp stale air exasperating the stench. Soon after, the body spasms subside, but Adriano isn't leaving until he is satisfied that Enzo is dead, erased from existence.

Within minutes the body is burnt beyond recognition. Adriano kicks the burnt body; his mind just needs final confirmation, and it is hard to believe that Enzo is dead. His mind processes all of it, and seconds later, he picks up the burnt remains and he throws them forcefully into the burning fireplace. The flames rise high and brighter. He feels this sudden sensation of lightness cross over his entire body. The evil darkness of Enzo's presence is gone. He thinks he can see the room becoming bright, a thin trail of moonlight fighting its way through the shutters; he isn't sure if it is his imagination. Adriano feels this sudden hope and elation overwhelm him. Rebecca and the other vampires can finally be free to live without fear.

A few minutes later, Adriano runs out of the house and back into the woods; he is cautious as he approaches near to the tree where Lucan was. He doesn't want to disturb or irritate the werewolf, but finds it odd that he heard no howling or growling as he approached closer. Suddenly a horrible feeling comes over him, and he quickly runs towards the tree. He stops a few feet away and sees Lucan tied up; he is relieved that the werewolf never emerged after all. He runs up to Lucan. "Lucan? I did it! He's dead! Lucan?

It's over. You don't need to transform," Adriano cries out in excitement and joy. He shakes Lucan gently; the lycan's head is bent down. "Lucan! Wake up." Adriano quickly unties Lucan and gently lays him down on the ground. Lucan's eyes are closed. Adriano assumes that Lucan had transformed and is now himself again and in a deep sleep. Adriano knows he is always passed out after the transformation and will be weak and fatigued. But something odd catches Adriano's attention; he notices that Lucan's clothes are torn but not completely. His pants are split in different places, his shirt ripped all over, but all his clothing is still on his body. Adriano thinks this is impossible; the large size of the werewolf should have made the clothes rip off of him once completely transformed. A sudden dread crosses over Adriano and he bends down and listens to Lucan's heart.

He is shocked; there is no beating. He checks his neck, and there is no pulse. He puts his ear to Lucan's nose, and hears no breathing. "Oh No! No! Lucan! *Oh God!*" Adriano screams; he can't process what has happened. His mind is in a frenzy. He suddenly bursts out sobbing, his head and chest leaning on Lucan's dead body. Adriano feels like he is falling into a deep pit, sorrow flooding his mind. He explodes with cries and screams that then change to growls and howls. He cannot control the clash of emotions pouring out of him now, he is wrapped in an emotionally tangled loop of anger, sadness, guilt, shock, love, and despair. Adriano remains hunched over Lucan's body a few minutes more.

Adriano suddenly felt the vibration of his cell in his pocket. It is Rebecca, but he can't talk to her right now, he can't tell her this over the phone. He is heartbroken and he needs to keep his strength up for the difficult task he now has to endure. He packs up the chains, ropes, and shackles and as he is placing them into the bag, his hand feels another bag inside. He pulls it out, and sees a small portable shovel at the bottom of the bag. He is bewildered. *Did Lucan know he was going to die tonight?* He opens the bag and finds extra clothes that Lucan packed and realized he packed a black dress shirt, black suit jacket, black dress pants, and a red silk tie. Adriano realizes Lucan was preparing for his death. Then he finds an envelope and reads the words, "My Son" written on the front in Lucan's handwriting. Adriano's heart sinks. He opens the envelope and finds a letter inside. Opening it, he sees a USB key inside the letter. He looks at the date; this letter was written yesterday. Adriano takes a seat on a rock and starts reading the letter. His hands are shaking,

Saturday, July 18

My Dearest Adriano, and family,

If you are reading this letter, this means that I didn't survive this transformation. I can only hope that you are alive and are reading this. I pray you have succeeded with Enzo Domenico and that he is no longer a threat. I'm deeply sorry that I leave you in shock and sorrow today. It was not my intention, especially if you have succeeded in stopping Enzo; I wanted to be a part of the celebration. I know Rebecca will have a feast for all of you! I had hoped that I had at least a few more years of these transformations. I alluded to you on the plane that I was getting older and my health was suffering. I didn't want to share my real concerns at the time because we had more important matters to deal with, and my focus was on making sure Adam, Ethan, and their friends were safe and that Enzo was dealt with. Please forgive me for leaving you like this. I honestly wasn't sure how many more years or transformations I had left. Well, Adriano, my son, here comes the difficult part, my wishes. I know you can't bring me back to Toronto to be buried. I wouldn't put you through that complicated risky ordeal. Too many questions. My spirit will be with you, it is not my body that matters. All I ask is that you try to find a quiet space somewhere in nature. You will pick the right location, I trust you. I guess deep down something inside of me was preparing me yesterday. I wish to be buried in the extra clothes I packed this morning.

I don't have anything to pass down to you other than my cane. It was a part of me. Please accept it as a keepsake. I also would like you to keep my bag with the tools. It was also a part of me. I know it may sound silly to you but I do have hope that one day humans will accept our truths and it would mean a lot to me if these things were kept within our family.

You will see I enclosed a USB key. On this you will find a recording I made yesterday. Something just told me to do it. I hope this will help you understand why this happened. Also I enclose a storage key; this key belongs to a storage facility located in Guelph, 125 Oakville road, unit #224. I have been carrying this with me for a while now. I was going to talk to you about it when things calmed down. Anyway, when you have time, please collect the recordings I transferred to CD. These are all the available sessions I recorded from as far back as I can remember, including ones that Nathan recorded. These are important to me, please do not destroy them. I hope one day, when the world accepts we exist, these recordings will be an integral part of the scientific study of lycans. You asked me one day how it all began for me, well honestly I don't remember. I have had recurring dreams over the years that place me somewhere in a remote part of British Columbia. I think I was on one of those camping trip tours. I don't know. I think the trauma of it all just blocked out who or what scratched me. To think a scratch could forever impact and change the course of my life.

One last thing, this is a big one. I ask you when the time is right, only you and Rebecca will know this, please tell my truth to Adam and Ethan. I know in my heart they will accept it with understanding and respect. These two young men are truly amazing and open-minded, more than we realize. Trust them with my truth. Don't let them go through their lives with these family secrets. My truth deserves to be known to them. Secrets will destroy. Talk to them, listen to them. Let them decide how they wish to live on with these truths. They have a right to make up their own minds. I want them to see the recordings, this will give them more insight to how I lived. Please trust me, it is the right thing to do.

Thank you for allowing me into your family. Thank you for being like a son to me and trusting me as far as you could. I know it was a huge adjustment to let me in. I am grateful and felt so blessed.

With all my love, your father in all the ways that matter,

Lucan Wylden (Lupo) Forrester

Adriano sits there holding the letter, it feels like time is standing still. He is reading it over and over. *"Tell my truth to Adam and Ethan."*

Adriano dressed Lucan in the extra clothes and carried him deep into the woods. He found a spot under a large birch tree, with wild lavender plants scattered around. He took out the shovel and dug a deep grave. He wanted to make sure that no wild animals could dig him up. He gently placed Lucan in the ground and buried him. He took some rocks and scattered them all around. He stood over the grave, tears streaming down his face.

"I'm so sorry Lucan, I should have seen that you were not in great health! I should have asked more questions. You were an amazing loving, caring man." Adriano is struggling to compose him-self. "You were like another grandfather to Adam and Ethan. They loved you so much. I hope this is a good resting place for you. You will always be in our hearts! Thank you for your love. Thank you for sharing your life with us. I'm going to miss you so much, Lucan," Adriano said, weeping. He put the envelope in his breast pocket, picked up the cane and knapsack, and quickly ran out of the woods and called Veneur.

Adriano was emotionally and physically exhausted. He fell asleep on the plane and didn't wake up until it was time to land. Veneur was still in shock. He couldn't believe he was free. He felt sad for Lucan. They didn't want to call Rebecca until they landed at the airport. Adriano couldn't control his emotions. He was so torn up inside. He lost a father figure but gained a brother.

CHAPTER 29
Vampire Truths

A week has gone by since Adriano returned from Paris with Veneur. The emotional environment at Woodland Heights is as to be expected; a mixture of sorrow, grief, joy, and questions followed the vampires for the deaths of Gabriel and Lucan. Ethan and Adam were grieving in their own ways for their Grandpa Lucan, and they kept Grandpa Lucan's cane in their room.

Adriano had just returned from an errand he ran in Guelph. Rebecca was in the loft painting; she was inspired to paint a picture of Lucan as best as she could. Sebastien was at work, and Veneur and Juliette were out shopping for Veneur. Adriano was carrying a box of CDs. Adam and Ethan were downstairs in their music studio. Adriano hid them away in Rebecca's bedroom closet and went upstairs to see Rebecca, kissing her affectionately on the lips.

"Hi beautiful."

"You're back, did you get them?"

"Yes, they are tucked in the back of your closet for now."

"Sounds good." She observes Adriano. "You okay? You look worn, everything else okay?"

"Yeah, I passed by his house afterward. Just difficult to see his belongings."

"Oh, that must have been difficult." She dips the paint brush into the grey paint. "At least we will keep his house in our family. I'm sure Lucan would have wanted this. It would have been very difficult to explain the room downstairs to agents or buyers. I wouldn't want anyone saying upsetting disturbing things about him."

"Well, thanks to Veneur buying it, we don't have to worry about outsiders. But we should dismantle that room, we just have to find trustworthy contractors who will just keep this as business as usual—never easy."

"So are you ready to watch the video he left for us? It's been a week, maybe it's time? Hopefully it will provide answers to how he died." Rebecca is trying not to choke up with emotion again.

"I know, but I want us all to watch it together, this way we can deal with it."

"Okay, but I want Ethan and Adam to be a part of this too."

"One day, when the time is right, *mon amour*."

"When will the time be right? I read the letter, Adriano, he wished for his truth to come out. There is no right time, they are not kids. I told you years ago I want my sons to know the truth—I think this is the time. I will sit them down first and ease into it, so at least they will be prepared as best as possible."

"Rebecca, this is not like when they were little boys and they discovered the truth about Santa Claus! They may be young adults, but this could be traumatizing to them. And you have to think, how this will affect all of us?" Adriano's voice is getting louder.

"I know. Don't you think I've considered all of this too? But I can't allow my sons to find out one day when I'm gone. They will be left with so many questions that only I can answer for them. I won't do that to them—that would be far worse. If they hate me for this truth, well that is their choice. I will live through it. But whatever their feelings will be, it is their right. I feel like a coward for hiding my truth, just so I protect my relationship with them. I can't do it anymore! I've already damaged our relationship by keeping this secret all these years," she cried out, tears escaping. "You know I'm not getting better!"

Just then they hear footsteps on the stairs, Adam and Ethan are at the entrance. "Mom, what's wrong? We just came up to the kitchen to get a snack, we could hear you yelling upstairs."

"Sorry guys, it's nothing—Adriano and I were just discussing something."

"But you're crying?" Ethan is concerned looking at his mom.

Rebecca wipes away her tears; she puts down the paint brush and gets up from her chair. Suddenly she just blurts out, without thinking, "Adam, Ethan, there is something I need to talk to you about, it is very important, it needs to be discussed."

"Okay, but can it wait until later? We just want to eat then go back down and jam, we have some lyrics we're working with."

Rebecca feels overwrought suddenly—how much longer does she have to hold onto this secret? It is breaking her apart inside. "Actually boys, I need your time, your lyrics will have to wait." The boys are surprised at her stern tone. Adriano is bewildered that she is really stepping towards telling them, now.

"What is it? Is something wrong?" asks Adam seriously.

"Rebecca, we need to discuss things first." Adriano is frustrated, giving Rebecca harsh eyes.

"No, Adriano, there will never be the right time. This has to be done. I'm tired, I'm tired!" she cries out, her voice strained.

Adam and Ethan felt very concerned for their mother, she looked paler than usual. "Tell us!"

Adriano suddenly throws up his hands in complete frustration. "I don't believe this! You haven't thought this through—dammit!" he yells out in anxiety.

"Hey, Adriano, cool off! If our mother has something to tell us, she can tell us! Obviously whatever it is upsetting her!" yells out Adam in a protective tone. Both Rebecca and Adriano are stunned. Adam has never raised his voice to Adriano or any of the vampires, and to hear him speak so abruptly to Adriano sets Adriano back.

"Adam—you don't know what this is about. You're not ready!" Adriano's voice is raised to an alarming level.

"Ready for what? What the hell is going on?!" shouts Adam in defiance.

"More than you can imagine! And don't ever speak to me like that again. We respect in this house," Adriano barked out loudly.

"Okay, let's all calm down. I'm sure whatever it is, we can handle it! Mom—just tell us? You're kind of worrying us." Ethan is trying to keep the waters calm.

"Wait! My God, Rebecca, please think about this, the others, they have to have a say in this," pleads Adriano. He is alarmed, he wasn't ready for this today.

"Others? You mean—this involves our uncles Veneur and Sebastien and Aunt Juliette? Or our other side Uncles Joseph and Marcus? Who? Tell us. What the hell is going on?!" shouts Adam.

"Adam, can't you see Mom is upset, stop yelling!" Ethan shouts, panicking suddenly.

"Boys, please stop! All of us just stop! Adam, Ethan sit down on the couch. Grandpa Lucan left us a video to watch. And I think you are both mature and open-minded enough to watch it with us. It won't be easy for both of you to watch this. There will be confusion, shock, and anger, and it will affect all of us." Her voice is becoming weak. She sees Adriano's eyes are stern, he is not happy that she is doing this. She continues, "There are truths that Grandpa Lucan felt important for you both to know about him, his life."

Adriano can see she is determined to do this, and he doesn't want to fight her anymore; they can't go back now, the boys know something is up, something serious. Maybe Lucan was right, maybe these boys are ready. Adriano sits down on the sofa chair opposite the boys, and Rebecca takes a seat next to her sons. "What I'm about to tell you will sound ridiculous at first, and you might think I'm mocking you or joking, but I swear to both of you it is the truth and you will understand more in time."

"Truth? What truth?" asked Adam, looking confused and worried

"Mom, you're freaking me out—this is—"

"Sshh, Ethan, let Mom talk."

Rebecca takes both her sons' hands and holds them tight in hers. "This is so difficult, and I don't even know where to begin."

"Just say it. You're not making sense." Adam is growing more anxious.

"I know, just let me finish. I want you to watch this video with us tonight, there is an important family history behind it. But that is why we will watch it together so you can ask questions." Rebecca is struggling, she isn't sure if she just created more complexity to this, since she didn't watch the video first; what if Lucan doesn't mention anything in the video?

"This is not making any sense, what is on the video that is so confusing?"

"Like I said, we haven't watched it, but we know it will be important, I'm doing my best to see this through—to prepare you! But there is so much more!"

"Prepare us for what? Tell us!" Adam is losing patience.

"You must watch the video first!" says Rebecca firmly.

"Fine, let's put it on—now!" barks Adam.

"No, we have to wait until the others are here. Uncles Veneur and Sebastien, and Aunt Juliette."

"Oh come on! This is stupid, just put the damn video on! You tell us it is important, truths will be revealed! Now you want us to wait? That's unfair!" shouts Adam

"Adam, don't be disrespectful! Your mom is doing her best, this is not easy for her, can't you see how stressed out and upset she is?" shouts Adriano, irritated

"I'm not been disrespectful! It's just none of this makes any sense. You guys are not making any sense," he cries out in annoyance

"Adam is right, Mom!" Ethan says, confused and nervous, the tension getting to him.

"I'm out of here!" says Adam and he abruptly gets up to leave.

"Adam! I know you're frustrated, and I promise tonight, you will under-stand—I just needed to prepare you before you watch it! I'm sorry, I'm doing this all wrong!" Rebecca emotionally cries out.

"Prepare us for what?" shrieks Adam nervously.

"The truth—all our truths!" says Adriano with a deep controlled tone.

"Whatever that means!" Adam says, and he leaves the room.

"Tonight Mom! This is unfair!!" says Ethan, and he storms down the stairs, catching up to Adam, who is now on the second floor.

Rebecca and Adriano can hear Adam and Ethan whispering very quietly to each other as they descend to the main level.

"I need some weed! I think we're about to hear some explosive stuff later!"

"I think you are right." Ethan swallows nervously, his mind trying to prepare him, "We saw strange things growing up, their strange abilities, you and I both heard it many times, somebody walking on top of the roof. And then there is their diet! I'm not trying to offend any of them, but they're eating raw meat. Drinking in bloody juices too! We got used it, but something is off. You saw it, Adam. Mom would look so deathly pale then go out back and jump over the fence like it was two feet tall, then return refreshed, and her eyes so strangely bright! It's not our imagination, we still see it. How the hell can they do that? It's a ten-foot freaking fence! Mom's not athletic. She looks like death's door sometimes. None of this is normal! It's time we confront them," whispers Ethan. "We're not kids anymore."

"I hear you man, you're right, it's time we ask questions, get to the truth about many things," They look at each other, deep down they both know a truth that is so impossible to comprehend is closer to been revealed. Their minds desperately wanting another explanation to all they have witnessed over the years. They both go to their secret stash of weed in the basement and head to the garage. Not a word spoken between them. They just needed to escape from their minds, from the truth they suppressed all these years.

Rebecca and Adriano just sit there, Rebecca's face buried in her hands. "Lucan was right, they have been observing us all these years. I know you think I made a mistake, but it is my decision, they are my sons!" whispers Rebecca so only Adriano can hear.

Adriano sits beside Rebecca and puts his arm around her. "It wasn't a mistake, and I realize this now. I just hope we are prepared for the consequences once they learn that for twelve years their mother has lived a secret life, including me and the others. You can't put this back into the box and shut it. This will change everything," frets Adriano with a heavy sigh of dread and concern.

Evening comes, and Adam and Ethan are still downstairs in their music room. They stayed downstairs the whole rest of the day. Adriano, Rebecca, and the other vampires had a heated discussion in the woods, but then Rebecca revealed to them that she is sicker than she has led on. She told them that the vamprogeria is changing. She is noticing she is starting to forget things, she is losing muscle strength. She can feel a shift in her mood swings and is doing her best to control these. Adriano and Sebastien already knew what was happening. Sebastien saw the same symptoms creeping up in James. Adriano remembered what Sebastien had revealed to them years ago. He just couldn't believe this was happening to his Rebecca!

The vampires were all concerned for her. Rebecca said she needed to do this before she was not able to be there for them, to process all of it. "I need to be able to prepare them for my own decline in health, they won't understand and will question why I'm not seeing doctors. I can't lie to them. I'm sorry for forcing this decision, but I can't wait! Please try to understand!"

The vampires did understand and empathize with Rebecca's reasoning. Juliette was nervous and anxious, because she could feel all the emotions from the other vampires.

Now, they all come back into the house and settle in the family room. Rebecca calls down to Adam and Ethan, and they don't respond, she goes down to get them. They have their earphones on at the computer. They say they will be up in a few minutes. They come up and both go to the garage. Everyone knows why.

"It's okay, they just need to calm their anxieties, they haven't been doing it as often," says Sebastien, he can see the worry in Rebecca's eyes.

Meanwhile Adriano hooks up the laptop to the TV. The boys come back into the house, the smell of marijuana in the air. They take a seat on the couch. Veneur is sitting on the chair, Juliette on the other couch with Adriano and Sebastien. Rebecca sits between her sons. Adriano presses play and the video starts. As Lucan's face appears on screen suddenly some tears were flowing and sniffles could be heard coming from some of the vampires. Suddenly everyone heard Lucan's voice coming from the TV.

"Hi my dear family, it is June eighteenth, I'm sitting in my den. Okay, I'm stalling a bit. I admit it. There's something I've been meaning to share with all of you. I just wasn't sure when would be the right time. Just got the exciting news that Adam and Ethan are in a music competition! I was so touched that you asked me to come along, Adriano, to watch over Adam and Ethan in Paris. I couldn't say no to this. I am just as worried about

Bianca, and in some ways, I wish the lycan would come out just for her! Sorry, just had to get that out!

"Anyways, if you're watching this, it means that most likely I am not around anymore. I'm sorry for any pain this will cause, and confusion to Ethan and Adam. You probably don't understand what happened, why I'm gone. You see, I've noticed in the last few years, some changes in my body. I don't feel as steady on my feet. My legs don't seem to have the same strength. I realize with old age comes aches and pains, and it could be signs of arthritis, however these particular aches and pains in my muscles and joints are more acute. Jolts of pain come on suddenly, so strong my body starts to shake, and then I get this ache in my chest. I'm just a little concerned, not sure how many more of these transformations my body can handle without causing severe permanent damage. As you know our kind cannot go to a doctor for any ailments, we can't risk been examined, questioned, then experimented on! I'm not trying to worry any of you. I feel fine, really, I do. It's just difficult at times to manage the pain after I have become me again. I get more tired after the change.

"When I was younger, in my late twenties and thirties, my body needed to become lycan at least once a month to slow down the instinctive urge for him to come out unpredictably. I had incredible energy, and felt strong and healthy, so it wasn't that big of a deal. Of course, the pain was excruciating during the change, but after, once I was me again, I was fine within hours. I never got colds, flus, I was in the best of health. My mood swings on full moons were barely noticeable. By me forcing the transformation each month, regardless of it was a full moon, I had more control of the lycan emerging. That is why I have managed this condition so effectively all these years, and wasn't worried about depression or anxiety creeping in during the full moon cycle.

"But in the last few years, I noticed I was feeling less energetic. My mood swings were growing in frequency, I had more depressed days, I had trouble sleeping. It was very difficult on Nathan too. So Nathan and I experimented to see if we could find the right balance between me allowing him to emerge. I tried to force him to come out and stay out more than the few hours that we were used to. We had him in that state for twelve hours. We thought this would satisfy his needs and he wouldn't need to emerge every month. This strategy seemed to work for a little while. I went three for four months, sometimes six months, without changing. Nathan was actually quite relieved, too. But then I noticed I was starting to get more angry, moody, and just not nice to be around. Nathan did his best to deal with my extreme mood swings and aggressive verbal outbursts. But then I started getting these symptoms without any warning at all, and it was a race for Nathan and I to get me back home if we were out, back to that secure room.

"This was a wakeup call to both of us that I cannot stop the change intentionally. I had to let the lycan emerge frequently again. So then I tried to go back to once a month and stay longer in that state. I increased it to twice a month, and still we didn't feel safe. So I had to increase the transformations to three times a month, and finally over a year I was feeling in control again. I then reduced it back to once a month later on, and that is where I'm at. However, there was internal damage to my muscles and joints and possibly my lungs. I feel out of breath at times, I feel I have aged quicker as a result within my body. Now, even though I am alert to symptoms when they come, I sometimes have to transform twice a month or as needed, that is, when I can feel symptoms starting to rise. It makes it difficult to plan outings or travel long distances.

"One important thing, before I forget. This is serious, I've thought a lot about this. So I hope you respect my wishes. I want Ethan and Adam to one day see this video. It is important to me that they know my truth! I trust them with my secret. They are mature beyond their years. I could see how curious and inquisitive they have always been. They probably know more than we assume. This is my wish, tell them my truth.

"Adam and Ethan, if you are listening, please forgive all of us for keeping this hidden as long as we did. Everything we did was to protect you, and to protect us too! Adam and Ethan, if you learn of my truth, I hope you can understand me. I have recorded sessions going back many years, I hope you will one day watch them. Don't be alarmed by what you see. There are many mysteries and wonders in this vast universe and world yet to be discovered and revealed. I trust you will guard our truths until the world is ready to realize our kind exist! Lycans and vampires!

"Well, this is a lot, I don't mean to overwhelm you further. I've said all that I needed to say. I hope you understand why I had to do this in a video. It would be too difficult emotionally in person. I have to reserve my strength and I think its best this way. I love you all, be good to each other. Adriano, Rebecca, I am grateful you let me in to this amazing, warm and close-knit family. I will treasure it always.

"Adam and Ethan, you are surrounded by so many of us who love you, human and other, and that is all that really matters. Try to remember that when you feel in a dark space as our secrets are unfolded to you. Love to all of you, bye."

The TV screen goes dark. The room is so eerily quiet that all the vampires can hear the rapid beating of Adam and Ethan's hearts increase at a concerning rate. Then Adriano is tearing up; it is difficult to see Lucan, but also he is finally accepting that Rebecca is going to die. Sebastien too is sniffling; he can't imagine going through the horror of watching another person he loves fall victim to the mental and physical decay this disease brings. He is crying inside, bracing himself for Rebecca's last disturbing stage of this disease. All he can think of is how to give Rebecca a peaceful, pain-free death. He has to find his own way, he is a scientist, and there must be something he can do. Juliette can feel the intensity of their emotions, and it is overpowering; she braces herself for a powerful explosion of anxiety and more. She holds on tight to Veneur's hand. He knows she is suffering in panic.

"What the hell was that?!" cries out Adam, his voice shaking; he is laughing nervously, feeling very uncomfortable and uneasy.

"That isn't real! Why did Grandpa Lucan make such a crazy video?" smirks Ethan nervously, too, feeling that they have been tricked. Rebecca and the other vampires just sit still, not speaking a word for a few minutes. They know it is about to get very tense and uncomfortable in this room.

"Adam, Ethan, I know this is shocking, difficult to process—" Rebecca says in a gentle soft voice.

"What? This isn't real! What's going on? I'm so fu—" shouts Ethan tensely

"Ethan! Please watch the language—talk to us! We are here for you both!" Rebecca says, trying to keep her voice calm and steady

"Talk to you? What is going on? Is it real?" asks Ethan frantically. The effects of the weed are already gone.

"That's eff'n crazy, Ethan, don't be stupid."

Rebecca sighs heavily. "I know this is a lot, just let's calm down and talk it through."

"Are you for real? What the f—"

"Adam! Language!" cries Rebecca. "I know you're upset, but let's be respectful."

Adam is in disbelief and he abruptly stands up and walks away from the couch; in shock, he begins pacing up and down the family room. "This isn't real, no no!"

Ethan gets up too, he starts screaming, "What the hell is going on! You people and your secrets! Tell us!"

Adriano stands up, but Rebecca quickly holds him back, and Juliette can't take the negative emotional intensity; she excuses herself and runs to her room. Veneur remains with Sebastien.

"It's true, Adam and Ethan. It's all true what Grandpa Lucan said. We are vampires. We are vampires! He was a werewolf!" Rebecca breaks down in sobbing tears. "'I'm so sorry I hid this truth from you all these years. I thought it was best. I thought telling you now that you are older, you would understand! Please talk to me. Talk to us!" Rebecca cries out in sobs.

Adam and Ethan are trembling with emotion, disillusion, and anger. They see the truth revealed in their mother's eyes and they look to their uncles and Adriano; they too have such truth in their facial expressions. Adam and Ethan feel their hearts are going to explode, their beats increase. Ethan is suddenly having trouble breathing, a panic attack coming on rapidly, and he has tears flowing down his face.

They both just need to get out, and they storm out of the house, slamming the front door. They run down the front of the long driveway. Adriano signals to Veneur and Sebastien to go after them, while Adriano stays behind with Rebecca, doing his best to console her as she falls into his arms, weeping uncontrollably.

"I thought this was the right time! What if I destroyed my sons? I had no choice. My time is ending."

Adriano just rocks her in his warm and loving arms, his voice tender, soft and caring. "Sshhh…don't say that, it's okay *belle âme*—this too shall pass, this too shall pass." He kisses her head. Struggling to console her and fighting back his tears, he is confronted with the harsh painful reality he keeps putting away; but now he knows he must face this head on. He will lose his Rebecca soon.

Rebecca is grateful to Veneur and Sebastien, who spend the rest of that evening talking and listening to Adam and Ethan's fears, worries, anger, and hurt. The boys feel betrayed by all of the vampires. They are also angry at Lucan, and are frustrated that they cannot express this to him. The warmth, love, and family connection at Woodland Heights is shadowed that week by all the tension and confusion being felt by Adam and Ethan. Veneur and Sebastien manage, after many hours of listening, to convince the boys not to leave and go stay with their father. They at least need to stay at Woodland Heights and talk to Rebecca, tell her how they feel. It takes a few months for Adam and Ethan to feel they are home and safe amongst the vampires. They are torn between their anger and hurt, and the fear that their mom was declining in health as they learn and began to understand the disease known as vamprogeria.

They spend hours with their uncle Sebastien and Adriano, learning about the disease that their mother has. It is very difficult for them to process everything they learn about their vampire family, including their lycan Grandpa Lucan. They watch the recordings of the sessions that Lucan left for them, over and over, pausing at certain frames, studying each step in the transformation. The shock and disturbing feelings of what they are watching eventually wears off.

CHAPTER 30
Allure Sensuelle

I t is Halloween, and several months have passed since the truths of Rebecca and her vampires were revealed to Adam and Ethan. Adam and Ethan both feel this incredible responsibility with this new powerful secret and truth. Their whole belief system about the world, humans, and humanity has shifted. It takes them a few months to feel grounded in their own minds, to feel they can handle this truth.

The vampires keep a close careful watch on Adam and Ethan to make sure they are handling all of this and not falling into a deep depression. Any time they have a question there is someone there to answer them. Now Adam and Ethan have gained a new perspective about the truths they have learned. They still watch the recorded sessions over and over, hoping to learn more each time. It is frustrating for both of them, because they are so skilled and intelligent when it comes to researching things they want to learn about, but they can't find anything factual relating to shapeshifting and vampires, even on the dark web.

All they came across in their exhaustive research were mythical creatures, archetypes, literary characters, and people with disorders who believe they are vampires or can shapeshift, or believe their ancestors were wolves or cat creatures. They are sponges now, eager to learn as much as they can about this particular family history. They conduct individual family interviews, and all of the vampires agreed to tell them as best as they can about their experiences, even if it brings back difficult and traumatic memories. All they care about is the mental wellbeing of Adam and Ethan. Many nights are spent with Adam and Ethan, writing and recording all the notes they've taken, including anecdotes that were shared. Without realizing it themselves, everyone is healing in their own way through this therapeutic process they are subconsciously undergoing.

It is now November, and Sebastien approaches Adriano quietly one evening while they both are out hunting, just the two of them. Sebastien explains that there might be a way to help Rebecca to die in dignity.

"It has to work, it will be different then Enzo's experience with the dead blood—we will not just give Rebecca the corpse blood, we will mix it in with a small amount of healthy human blood. This way the effects of corpse blood will not rapidly destroy her insides. It will be a gradual, painless death." Sebastien is trying to stay emotionally composed.

"But how can we be sure? I saw what Enzo went through. The suffocating, the violent convulsions. I cannot allow Rebecca to go through a torturous death. I can't!" Adriano's voice filled with anxiety.

"Of course not. I know that any barbital we tr, will not work. It didn't work for James. No human medicine can kill a vampire—I don't want her to die like James did either—she will not be able to digest any blood soon, her body will starve her. No matter how much blood we give her, her body will absorb it so quickly, she will starve while she lives. Adriano, I have to believe my method will work. We both know that soon the Rebecca we all love will not be the one with us in that house!" Sebastien is overwrought with emotion, his mind propelling him back immediately to James and the creature he became in the end.

"My God. What do we do?" Adriano's voice becomes low and despairing. Sebastien's heart is heavy with sadness, and gently he puts his hand on Adriano's shoulder. He feels now is the time to bring up something else.

"Adriano, I know my time will come up one day too." Adriano looks sad for Sebastien, this is all too much. "There is something I need to tell you—it's a cross I've had to carry and I feel I need to tell you because I feel I did wrong to you for years."

Adriano looks at Sebastien, puzzled. "Sebastien, whatever it is, it can't be as important as Rebecca's situation."

"It is important. Please—I owe you this truth."

"Truth?"

Sebastien's eyes stare directly into Adriano's with genuine honesty. "I did once kill a human." Sebastien's eyes lower to the ground, his face red with shame.

Adriano just stands still as a statue, processing what he just heard.

"Jacques brother—I killed him after I turned. I didn't know yet how to control my cravings. I know I gravely sinned, and anything I've done for Jacques and his family still leaves a stain in my soul."

Adriano remains silent. Then after a few seconds, in a calm and steady voice, he says, "Let's go talk to Rebecca, she needs to know about the corpse blood."

"Adriano? I—"

"Thank you, Sebastien. Carry your cross with less weight now. Time is precious, and remorse is powerful for the soul."

Sebastien reaches in and hugs Adriano and then he releases, clearing his throat and composing himself. They walk on together silently back to the house.

That night they sit Rebecca down and explain their theory. Rebecca listens, trusting in Sebastien's scientific mind. Sebastien takes her hand in his. "Hazel Eyes—we just don't see any other option. Unfortunately, pentobarbital or anything else will not affect you. I know you are afraid, so are we. But we don't want you to suffer the way James did, and I know in my gut my method will give you a peaceful end. We don't expect you to answer us tonight." Sebastien holds a caring smile for Rebecca, but he is crying inside his heart. Rebecca puts her frail hand over Sebastien's and squeezes it tight; she is too tired to speak, but she nods in trust and agreement.

It is now December fifteenth, and Woodland Heights is busy with festivities shadowed by the reality that Rebecca is failing in health unpredictably. All the vampires, and Adam and Ethan, do their best to make the home feel festive for Rebecca. Her spirits are low, and she is more tired. Adam and Ethan have learned not to be afraid when Rebecca's condition sent her in a fit of desperate thirst. They trust the vampires will take over, and they do. They rush Rebecca into the woods, and now they don't have to worry about who stays behind with Adam and Ethan. The boys have adapted quickly, and found their own private way to deal with the reality of their vampire family. They go to the music room in the basement and play out their worry and fear through their music.

Their mother is dying, and all they have now are a few more precious moments with her to cherish. Her undying love for them carries them through the dark moments when her spirit is unrecognizable due to the disease. Rebecca is determined to hold on until New Year's Eve. She wants her family to at least have one last Christmas with her and start the new year with new hopes and dreams. She feels that it is a blessing that her parents have already passed away a few years ago from illnesses. She can't imagine the heartbreak they would have experienced, watching their daughter die. But it is a challenge with her siblings and their families. Of course, they want to visit and help as best as they can, but that is just not possible for the vampires. It is a trying time for everyone just trying to keep up appearances in the company of Rebecca's human family.

They have to come up with a plan to pretend Rebecca is getting hospital care. They set up an in-home palliative care room using Sebastien's study. Sebastien and Sandra manage to get hold of an old hospital bed that was put in storage. They also collect older models of IV stands, and blood pressure and heart rate machines. With the technical help from Veneur and Adam and Ethan, they create the illusion that a palliative nurse is coming every day. And with guidance from Sandra's nursing skills, they create a false schedule chart for daily and hourly medicines, and have it displayed beside Rebecca's hospital bed. When Rebecca's human family comes to visit, they see Rebecca hooked up to the IV and machines. The visits are kept short, and a vampire or Adam and Ethan always stay in the room, just in case they have to quickly rush the visitors out, saying Rebecca is exhausted.

This stage of vamprogeria is unpredictable, and only Rebecca can detect when the dangerous symptoms are rising. Rebecca is so proud of her sons for taking charge in a lot of the strategic technical aspects. The vampires and Adam and Ethan are overwhelmed with the strategic measures they have to put in place just to keep anyone from questioning anything.

It is now New Year's Eve, at nine p.m. Rebecca is lying on her bed in her own bedroom. The snow is falling, and she suddenly sits up, just staring out her window watching the snowflakes fall. She is grateful she had one last special intimate Christmas with her Woodland Heights family and sons. She feels grateful that she didn't have too many more disturbing episodes during the holidays that forced her to be tied to her bed, and Adam and Ethan restricted from visiting her. They only had two such incidents, and both times Juliette was right there to swiftly move them out of any possible danger and bring them out of the house to distract them.

Veneur and Juliette just left the room minutes earlier; they knew deep inside this was the last time they would see Rebecca. Juliette knew she couldn't be in the room when Rebecca took her final drink. The room is filled with the pleasant calming aroma of lavender from the flowers placed in the vase beside Rebecca's bed. Rebecca asked Veneur and Juliette to stay with the boys. "Please, just make sure they are not alone tonight." Her voice was frail and heartbroken.

Now, Sebastien is at the entrance of her door, and he steps in. "Hazel Eyes, can I come in?" Rebecca smiles, and gestures for Sebastien to sit beside her on her bed.

"Adriano called earlier, he said they found someone for me?"

Sebastien lowers his eyes, holding back tears. "Yes, they connected with an intern in the morgue. At least we have a chance to pay it forward; the intern will have the next year of residency costs covered." Sebastien is struggling with what to say.

"Do you know anything about my donor?"

"Yes, but let's not talk about this." He tucks in the blankets close to Rebecca.

"I want to know." Rebecca is keeping her voice calm.

"Alright—apparently your blood donor just passed two hours ago. A woman, age forty, but I don't know the details of her death."

Rebecca closes her eyes; she is struggling to keep down the growing pains of thirst rising again.

Sebastien realizes and holds her hand tightly. "Feeling it again?"

Rebecca nods her head, her facial expression revealing it all; she is in pain. She opens her eyes again and takes Sebastien's warm hand. "Sebastien, I want to say thank you for everything you have done for me."

"Oh, Hazel Eyes, you —"

"Shh…let me finish. I 'm so proud of our friendship. I have always treasured it. You brought so much joy to my life. I almost gave up on real lasting friendships until you came along. You made me believe in best friends again." A tear pushes through and falls down Sebastien's cheek, and he sniffles and clears his throat. Rebecca continues, voice steady, she needs to get through this. "You made me laugh. Thank you for trusting me with your personal life—I'm glad you and Jonathan found your way back to each other. I hope one day you will venture out and explore with him. The world is yours to discover." Rebecca pauses, her warm hazel eyes still present. "I love you."

Sebastien can't contain himself, he breaks down. "Oh, Hazel Eyes—you are the one that I should be thanking! Your relentless persistence all those years ago to make me come to Toronto was the best move I ever made. You are precious, you are my blood link—you are my best friend. There will never be anyone like you. I will miss you=." Sebastien reaches out, tears flowing, and hugs Rebecca tightly.

"It's okay, I need you to be strong for Adriano and my sons. Promise me you will take care of each other. All of you."

Sebastien wipes his eyes, composing himself again.

"Sebastien, please bring me Adam and Ethan. It's okay, I'm not feeling those symptoms, I'm still me." Her voice trails off in weakness. Sebastien can't say no; he leaves the room and minutes later Adam and Ethan step in. They see their mother sitting up in bed. Her eyes are normal, but they notice how frail and pale she looks. Rebecca manages to give them a warm loving smile.

"Adam, Ethan, come sit down beside me." Rebecca's voice is weak but she reaches inside of her and pulls out all her strength to carry her in these precious moments with her sons. The boys each lie beside Rebecca, she has her arms around them, kissing the top of their heads. "Oh God, I can't believe how handsome you both are." She smiles tenderly. "I still remember the day each of you were born. Starting with you, Adam, it was the most amazing and frightening experience for someone like me who was not used to being around babies, kids in general. Suddenly I was responsible for my own tiny baby. I will never forget how at two years old you snuck down the stairs as your father and I watched Jurassic Park. Suddenly we heard you gasp and I ran to see and instead of you crying you were fascinated, eager to understand these giant creatures. Well after that, we could not get you away from that movie. We had to replay the video for you over and over again, and it was amazing to watch your expressions. Thank you for being the inquisitive intelligent critical thinking person that you are. I've learned so much from your perspective in many things in life. How you both handled our truths is remarkable." She turns to face Ethan.

"Ethan, the moment you were born you already had this determined energy and mindset, that what you wanted you were going to get! You too amazed me with how you took difficult personal challenges and struggles, and found a way to walk through them with amazing emotional growth. I'm so impressed by both of you for how you have handled life at such a young age. I'm so amazed at the talent you both have musically. Please promise me you will both always keep music in your life. It will help you stay grounded when life hits back, as it is now. I will always be there in spirit to watch over you, know this! I know you need evidence, Adam, but I believe life will show you that in time. Love doesn't die."

Rebecca's voice is gentle and soft, her lips doing their best not to quiver. Adam and Ethan just sit quietly, sniffling, tears running down their faces. Rebecca gave them a big tight hug. "I love you both so much. I know you will be okay, you have a large family of love surrounding you, both human and vampire." She can feel her energy depleting. "Do me a favor, play your music compositions, I want to hear your music travel through this beautiful home." Rebecca smiles, warm and loving. The boys hug her tightly and kiss her on the cheek. Rebecca just looks at her boys, taking in the miracle of each of them. "I love you more than life or words could ever measure or express. Go on, and please send Adriano in, I heard him come in earlier." Her lips are trembling, but she has to stay strong for her sons. They don't want to leave, they know this is their last moments with their mom.

Adam looks back at her, then Ethan, both struggling. "Mom—I—"

"It's okay, I know, I love you both so much." Both Adam and Ethan hug her again so tightly they can't hold back the sobs. Rebecca lets them express their emotions, soothing them. After their crying subsides, Rebecca speaks in a soothing voice, "Please let me hear your music—play for me." Both Adam and Ethan recover and compose themselves; they kiss her on the cheek and leave her bedroom, taking one last look at their mom. Then they disappear.

A few minutes later, Adriano walks into the room. Rebecca is sitting up just admiring her sexy incredibly loving vampire. "I can't believe sometimes when I see you approaching me that you are mine. You are the most sexy and desirable man. Come sit beside me."

Adriano smiles and lays beside her on the bed. Rebecca curls into his chest, and Adriano can hear her heart beating, steady enough, considering.

"I have so much I want to say to you, Adriano, I'm overwhelmed with emotion. Let me say this—I can't thank you enough for giving me a life that only happens in fairy tales, as far as I'm concerned. The love you have shown me, my parents, my brothers, their families, the other vampires, and especially my sons, I will never ever forget." Rebeca puts her soft finger on Adriano's lips. "Please let me finish—promise me that you will always be there for my sons. They are not living normal lives; their world is going to get a lot more complicated when they find someone to love and want to bring into the family." Adriano just stays quiet. "We did good, you and I, we have always made a great team. We gave other vampires a chance at happiness. How amazing is that? We brought deep love and connection to each other and we made this beautiful home a sanctuary for us. Thank you, my love, for your presence in my life all these years. Thank you for showing up for me and everyone we care deeply for. Adriano, promise me you will open up your theatre company. Live out your dream, for me." Rebecca can't help but weep as she speaks now, her tears flowing with Adriano's.

"Rebecca, I can't —"

"Promise me."

"I promise, *mon amour*."

Rebecca manages a smile, but her voice is failing, her strength dwindling rapidly. "It's time, I can feel the change coming. This is the right thing to do. Each day it's getting harder to hold onto me, who I am."

Adriano hugs her tightly. "You will always be my beautiful Rebecca. I will carry the spirit of you in my heart and memory forever, *mon amour*." Adriano is choking up, the lump of sadness in his throat making it hard for him to speak. "Thank you so much for coming into my life thirteen years ago. You showed me what it means to love deeply, to trust and forgive. I am the man standing here because of you, *mon amour*. I don't want to let you go, beautiful soul." He kisses her lips tenderly, trembling.

Rebecca holds him, no words spoken. A few minutes go by.

"It's time, my love, don't be afraid. I need you to be strong for my sons. I will always be with you." Adriano looks into Rebecca's hazel eyes and sees her loving smile. He rises from the bed and slowly he leaves the room, returning a few minutes later with Sebastien.

Rebecca suddenly hears the beautiful sound of music coming from the living room. Adam is playing the piano, and then she hears the electric guitar played by Ethan. She smiles. "Listen to that magical sound, what beautiful music my sons are playing, their own masterpiece—I'm so blessed. I love all of you so much, never forget that." Sebastien can't speak, he is afraid he will burst out crying again. He focuses his attention on the task at hand; he takes out the bag of corpse blood and pours it into the champagne glass, and then carefully and meticulously pours in some of the healthy human blood from the bag that Sandra gave Adriano from the blood clinic.

Sebastien gently mixes the bloods together, death and life intertwined. Rebecca takes the glass and just holds it, looking at Sebastien and Adriano one last time, capturing all her love for them and everyone in her circle of life in that moment into her mind, her heart and her soul flooded with peace. She closes her eyes and drinks the mixture. The warmth of the liquid moves down her sore dry throat and it begins to soothe the pain. Rebecca lies back down in her bed, just listening to the music.

Sebastien leans in and kisses her on the forehead. "Sleep well Hazel Eyes, I love you." Then he brings the chair closer to the bed holding her hand still.

Adriano takes Rebecca's other hand and holds it tightly; he lays down beside her, his head resting on her chest. He needs to hear her heart beating, but it is evident, it is slowing down.

Suddenly Adriano and Sebastien both hear a small little growl coming from Rebecca; they both pay attention, and she is now moaning a little. Adriano gently lifts himself from her chest. "Rebecca, Rebecca, are you okay?"

Rebecca doesn't respond; her eyes remain closed, and he listens to her heartbeat. The beats are slowing down, then slower, slower, and then he lets out a heavy sigh of sorrow. Adriano looks at Sebastien, and Sebastien knows; he buries his face in his hands. Adriano gently kisses Rebecca lovingly on her lips one last time.

"Rest in peace Rebecca, my beautiful soul." Adriano's lips quiver, his eyes filling with tears, and he lays again on her chest. The harmonic sound of Adam and Ethan playing their own music composition for their mom travels through Woodland Heights.

It is a week before Thanksgiving, 2021. One of Rebecca's candles is burning on the kitchen counter. Adam and Ethan are determined to continue the tradition of lighting candles just like their mom used to. Juliette and the boys are at the kitchen table. The boys are browsing through their mom's treasured recipe collections. Their aunt Juliette is beside them, deep in the manuscript *A Life Beyond Human*, written by Veneur Monet. Moments later, Adriano, Veneur, and Sebastien walk in, holding a glass of wine each. They are in the middle of discussing the next steps to opening up the theatre company. They want to call it Performing Arts Theatre for Beautiful Souls.

Suddenly, Ethan cries out in excitement. "Holy crap! I found it!"

Adam quickly takes the binder from Ethan. "Mom's secret famous pumpkin pie recipe! We have to make this—Aunt Jules, will you help us?"

All of a sudden, a gust of wind from outside gently rattles the kitchen windows, but it doesn't stir much reaction; the wind has been blowing on and off throughout the day. Moments later a light pleasant fragrance travels through the air. "Do you smell that?" Ethan is looking at Adam, his nose sniffing into the air. Adriano too is struck suddenly by this familiar fragrance.

"Yeah, I do. But how can that be? It's Mom's favorite perfume—she always wore it, Allure Sensuelle." Adam is stunned. He looks around, not knowing exactly what he is looking for, his skills in critical thinking working full speed coming up with possible theories in his mind.

"What? No. That's not possible." Ethan looks at Adam nervously, then to Juliette, who is now focused on the increased flicker of the flame on the candle. Sebastien and Veneur too are concentrating on the candle. Adriano is quiet and far away in his mind; the scent of her perfume travels his body, and he is deep in thought in his own world of memories filled with Rebecca.

At that moment, Juliette feels this light, positive, and warm energy surround everyone, and it feels like a loving hug. Juliette smiles so tenderly at Adam and Ethan; she knows Rebecca will always be a part of Woodland Heights.

THE END

CPSIA information can be obtained
at www.ICGtesting.com
Printed in the USA
LVHW041632011120
670390LV00023B/538